It
STARTED
in
FLORENCE

PRAISE FOR 2020 and 2021 PUBLICATIONS OF
GALWAY GONE AND **COLORING ON THE WALL**
BY GABRIELLE NEORD

". . . .To conclude my thoughts on this exceptional story, I would say if you have been bored of late of the same old books that do not captivate you, then take a chance with this one because it is an all-consuming assault of brilliance that will keep you entertained and moved from beginning to end. Coloring on the Wall gets five stars from me!"

___**Red Headed Book Lover**___

"Coloring on the Wall by Gabrielle Neord is a fascinating novel with a touch of crime, romance, and suspense. Violence, spousal abuse, loyalty, selfishness, courage, and wit were some themes explored in this book. I loved the storyline and development, as they were realistic and relatable. It shocked me to realize that many people who champion the fight against abuse are actual victims themselves. We cannot change adults, so catch them young. Parents who fail to raise their kids right will go down with them. Gabrielle told a beautiful and emotional story, wrapping it around Skylar's vulnerable yet formidable character. However, Shiloh was my best girl! Thank you for an outstanding book, Gabrielle. We're the architects of our own lives."

___**Reader's Favorite** ___

"I am in love with Galway Gone and think it is a captivating and poignant novel with a moving and memorable plot, I have no choice but to award it a dazzling five stars because it deserves this!"

"Author Gabrielle S. Neord spins a beautifully woven tale of emotive and entertaining fiction to deliver chick lit which has real issues and realistic characters at its heart."-Five Stars

5.0 out of 5 stars **A great love story!**

"This novel is a fantastic read! I couldn't put it down! The story involves love, betrayal, forgiveness, and finding inner strength. The perfect mix of romance novel and fantasy! A must-read!!"

5.0 out of 5 stars **Epic tale of love and family**

"Ms. Neord takes the reader on a journey from life on an American ranch to behind the scenes in the life of a rock star, wrapped around an incredible love story. The author blends music + art + friends + family to create a passionate and sincere story. Highly recommended."

TO READ COMPLETE REVIEWS AND EXCERPTS VISIT:

www.gabrielleneord.com
Email: thegabrielleneord@gmail.com

It STARTED *in* FLORENCE

A NOVEL

Gabrielle Neord

It Started in Florence is a work of fiction. Names, characters, places, and incidents are the products of the author's imagination or are used fictitiously. Any resemblance to actual events, locals, or persons, living or dead, is entirely coincidental.

Print ISBN: 978-1-66784-053-6

eBook ISBN: 978-1-66784-054-3

Printed in the United States of America on SFI Certified paper
First Edition

Cover design and images by Judy Arntson Howard

Dedicated to Professor Sharon Park for her wonderful suggestions, hours of reading, and encouragement when I was struggling with the plot of this book. A friendship that I treasure and has made my life richer.

and

For my father, George Klanecky, who nurtured my love for Nebraska and my family, who live there still.

RIP Dad.

PROLOGUE

I've been walking the dark, anonymous streets of downtown Chicago for hours. I didn't care if it might not have been the safest thing to do in a city where street crime runs rampant, especially at night. Should someone make me their target, my worries would be over, taking the easy way out. I was in a state of disbelief when I left the doctor's office this afternoon. Things like this didn't happen to people like me.

I have always taken good care of myself, eating right, exercising, having regular medical checkups, and living a safe lifestyle for a single woman in her 40s. I never smoked or over-indulged in alcohol, yet here I was, feeling drained of energy, yearning to crawl in bed and sleep for a week. The only other time I felt this way was when my husband, Marco, was killed over ten years ago. Anemia plagued me for months. I knew something was going on with me, but afraid to see the doctor. It seems since I hit that milestone 40th birthday, my body has been functioning differently. I feared what I might find out.

After being goaded by my best friends, Betsy and Michele, I made an appointment with my doctor. Dr. Roberts had been our family physician for years, and I knew he would give any news, good or bad, to me straight. After listing my issues with him, he ran a panel of tests on my blood and urine. I waited for a half-hour when Dr. Roberts called me into his office.

The typical stoic expression he usually had on his face was missing, replaced with a look of concern as he looked at me. "You're not dying, Brenna, at least not for many more years. There is an issue we need to address," Doctor Roberts said.

Here it was; he was going to tell me something serious was happening with me. I clutched the purse sitting in my lap as if it offered a lifeline, and my body was trembling. After the first couple of words, all I heard was "wah-wah-wah" in Charlie Brown's adult speak. My head was spinning, and I tried to focus on his words, ". . . . you have some decisions to make. Take a couple of days, Brenna. Let me know how we should proceed with treating you. Don't wait too long; call me by the end of the week."

I know I must have thanked him before leaving the office, but that's about all I remember clearly. After my appointment, I didn't go back to work but just started walking. My cell phone was chirping every couple of minutes, but I ignored it. I wasn't even paying attention to where I was going. Instead, my thoughts were whirling in a thousand different directions.

⋆   ⋆   ⋆

Chicago in the fall was beautiful as the trees turn from various shades of green to the brilliant colors of cranberry red, golden yellow, and vibrant orange. The burning bushes were turning red, and fallen leaves danced along the sidewalks. The early evening breeze had a crispness to it, but I didn't notice a thing during my favorite season of the year. I soon found myself outside my condo on a bench in the small green space in front of the building.

I thought of my boys, twins, Gage and Chase, a world away in Japan and China. What do I say to them? Or do I keep this news to myself? I don't want them to worry about me. I didn't know how they would feel. Their independent lives were just starting at twenty years old. They followed in their father's footsteps, majoring in Economics and Finance at Columbia University in New York and now in immersion programs in Asia. My husband, Marco, had been an Equities Trader for the New York Stock Exchange-Chicago.

The evening was closing in as I entered my building and took the elevator to my condo on the 14th floor. I didn't bother turning on the lights as I undressed and fell into bed. I called in sick to work for the following two days. My phone was beeping with messages until my voicemail was full.

I woke to my door buzzer being pushed non-stop on my second day of self-imposed house arrest. It was time to face the music. Michele and Betsy were on my doorstep. After buzzing them into the building, they rushed in the door. Betsy unloaded on me, "We have been so worried about you. Why didn't you call us back? What did the doctor have to say?"

Michele was a little calmer. "Whatever it is you're dealing with, you don't have to do it alone. We're here to support you in every way we can. Tell us, what did the doctor say?"

"I'm sorry I didn't call you back. There were things I had to think through on my own," I said.

"You haven't been eating either, have you? You look so drawn and tired," said Michele.

"Let me get us some tea, and we'll sit down. I'll tell you what's happening. My doctor gave me some news I hadn't prepared myself to hear." I walked into the kitchen and brewed three cups of tea. We sat down at the kitchen table. I took a deep breath. "I haven't been feeling very well since shortly after I returned from my Italy assignment."

"I knew it. You picked up a bug while you were in Europe. Is it serious? Can your doctor treat it?" asked Betsy.

"He's given me some options, but I have to figure out how to deal with it and what's best for everyone."

"Please tell us what's wrong so we can help you. We have always been the three musketeers and it will not stop now. We can't stand the thought of losing our best friend," said Betsy.

I looked at my dear friends with tears in my eyes, "It Started in Florence . . . . ."

CHAPTER ONE

TEN MONTHS BEFORE

"SURPRISE! Happy Birthday to you, Happy Birthday to you, Happy Big 4-0 dear Brenna, Happy Birthday to you. YEA!" as the sounds of laughter and whistles filled the office.

"You guys, you shouldn't have, and I mean you SHOULDN'T have," said Brenna as she looked at her fellow workmates in the President's Office at the School of Art and Architecture of Chicago. Twenty grinning people gathered around a big chocolate cake and a large gift-wrapped box with a big pink bow, waiting to cheer on their beloved Brenna on her momentous 40th birthday.

"Come on, Brenna, open your present. Betsy and I spent a lot of time picking out just the right thing," said Michele. Brenna's two friends sat Brenna in a chair and handed her the box wrapped in paper covered with pictures of horses.

"This isn't anything embarrassing from Victoria's Secret, is it? I'm a little scared to open it, knowing you pranksters as I do. But remember, I know where you two live!" Brenna slowly peeled off the paper and opened the box to find a box of Polident tablets, a tube of Ben Gay ointment, a package of bladder leak underwear, a giant jar of wrinkle cream, a tube of hemorrhoid cream, and a subscription card for Senior Citizen Monthly magazine. With a face blushing crimson red, Brenna was choking with laughter. "Thank you? Everyone—for raiding your medicine cabinets to share your bounty with me. Now let's have some cake."

"Don't worry, Brenna, I baked all the calories out of the cake, not that you have to worry about it with that little size four figure of yours," said Michele as people laughed at Brenna's comeback and enjoyed a comfortable camaraderie. Even President Michaels joined his office staff in the celebration.

It was Friday night as people started drifting out of the office on a chocolate high as Michele and Betsy prepared to take Brenna out to dinner at Eddie V's Seafood and Steaks on Rush Street and give her the real birthday gift they had for her. After flagging down a cab, the three close friends enjoyed spending time together away from the office. They were a support system for each other.

The three women banded together to comfort and counsel each other over the last ten years they had worked together. A night of comradery without husbands and children was a real treat. It didn't happen very often. The women lived in the downtown metropolitan area of Chicago but came from very diverse backgrounds.

Michele had three children and a husband battling Multiple Sclerosis for the last four years. Her children were grown and spread out all over the country, pursuing their interests, and didn't come home nearly enough by their mother's calculation. In addition, Michele was dealing with her husband's declining health while keeping lines of communication open between herself and her children.

Youngest of the trio, Betsy, had four children at home and a workaholic husband. She lived her entire life in Chicago, born into a large family; Betsy was the youngest of seven children. All her siblings married early, had large families, so whenever her family got together, vying to be heard in a free-for-all with a crowd of over sixty adults and children, was trying.

Brenna had been a widow for over ten years, raising twin sons on her own. Brenna was two years old, an only child when her father died. She lived most of her early life in Nebraska in the care of her widowed grandmother.

Even with the diversity of their backgrounds, the three women developed a close friendship more than merely workplace friends. Holidays were spent together, and they celebrated birthdays as special events. They relied on each other for comfort and solace and could talk about anything, sharing the most intimate and sometimes darkest feelings without censure.

Dinner out was terrific, with the three friends eating whatever they wanted, not worrying about calories or hangovers. Soft warm lighting and classical music played in the background as they reviewed plans for Christmas in two weeks. The college would be closed starting Christmas Eve through New Year's Day, giving everyone time to relax after the hectic pace of the holidays.

"I almost forgot," said Betsy. "What are you doing tomorrow, Brenna?"

"The usual; laundry, bill paying, a little Christmas shopping. Why?"

"Forget the 'Doris the Drudge' stuff. This is what you're doing tomorrow. You are having a day of beauty at Elizabeth Arden's Red Door Spa on Michigan Ave. for a facial, massage, mani/pedi, and hair. Be there at 9:00 am. Happy Birthday from Michele and me," said Betsy.

"You guys. That's way too generous. Thank you so much." As Brenna hugged her friends, "I can really use it. I have a deadline for the college budget due next Friday, and stress has been my middle name for the last couple of weeks. What an incredibly wonderful and generous gift. I can't thank you enough."

"Our pleasure. You deserve it. You never take enough time for yourself. Perhaps you'll feel confident enough to date again—finally," said Michele.

"That's not in the cards for me. Have you seen what's out there? Pickings are pretty slim. I told you the story of my one foray into internet dating. After about ten dates for coffee, I gave up. If the man was a widower, it elevated the dearly departed wife to sainthood. Or if divorced, they were still angry and continually spewed vitriolic rhetoric. Wonder who was at fault in that marriage after listening to non-stop complaints?"

"I'm glad that I'm not out in the dating pool," said Betsy.

"I waded in the sallow end and didn't feel it was worth it to take a deeper dive," I said.

"There's a lot of pee in that pool," said Betsy.

"Oh, ick, that's a thought I can live without," said Michele.

"And what's with the facial hair?" I asked. "I have nothing against a well-groomed goatee or mustache. But if I have to see what they had for lunch nesting in their facial hair, that's so wrong. The 'Duck Dynasty' look doesn't do it for me. I would rather stay home with a good book."

"You can't live the rest of your life vicariously through the latest Sandra Brown sexcapade novel. Marco's been gone for over ten years.

You're still alive. You're a beautiful woman with a lot of living to do, that's all I'm going to say on that subject," said Betsy.

"I appreciate what you're saying, and I've thought of it myself. If it's in the cards for me, it'll find me, and I'm tired of looking for someone who might not exist. I want to get through the holiday, enjoy my sons, my friends, and get on with work."

"Just saying," added Betsy. "If you don't use it, you lose it. The statute of limitations on abstinence from sex is seven years, and then you're a certified virgin again."

I had to laugh. "Certified by who? The Cooter Cops? Only you would think of that, Betsy. So, on that note, let's get a cab, and I'll drop you guys off, and I'll go home and crawl into bed and read about all the sex I'm missing."

CHAPTER TWO

Home. It seems so empty with the boys off at college. They love New York, and I have a feeling that Chicago will no longer be their home. Once they graduate and get jobs, the action they crave won't be here. I guess that's what most parents go through when the nest is finally empty. Parents nurture and prepare their children to fly on their own with confidence. I wish I were just as confident about my future.

When the children were younger, life had always been so busy. Marco was entrenched in building his career. My beautiful Italian husband, gone ten years. Sometimes it seems so fresh, like it happened yesterday, and at other times it feels it was a lifetime ago.

* * *

Marco and I met at Northwestern University. I was nineteen years old on scholarship, and Marco was twenty-six working on his Master's Degree in Economics. To me, he was so sophisticated, handsome, and romantic. He was from Siena, Italy, and seemed so cosmopolitan. I was a farm girl from Nebraska, and his charm bowled me over. We dated for six months when I found myself pregnant with the twins and a mother by twenty. We married right away as soon as we realized a baby was on the way. I quit school, and Marco finished his degree program and started work to support our new family of four.

Marco was a rising star in the world of finance right from the beginning. Chicago became our home. Before the building construction ended, we purchased our condo at a bargain price on a four thousand square foot space. I spent my time raising our children and designing and furnishing the interior of our home. We spent a month every year in Siena visiting his parents, who didn't speak English. Soon, the boys and I were fluent in Italian and looked forward to seeing Nonno and Nonna Herrera every year. Their grandsons were magnificent in their eyes, and I grew to love my in-laws. I took the boys to my grandmother's farm in Hartsuff, Nebraska, for a couple of weeks in the summer and the week between Christmas and New Year's.

I missed my Nebraska home and my kith and kin. There was more Nebraska in me than there was Chicago. Sometimes I yearned for that slower pace of life than the big city's hustle, bustle, and competitiveness. The advantages of the city were immense; the waterfront, theater, museums, major league sports, and incredible shopping. My sons had every advantage for sports, cultural events, and excellent schools.

The boys and I regularly visited The Field Museum, Museum of Science and Industry, the Shedd Aquarium, and our favorite, The Art Institute of Chicago. While I was comfortable with the vast advantages of living in a large city, I still yearned for the wide-open spaces, the rolling hills, and the starry skies of my childhood. Our urban lives were busy. It seems every minute of the day was a frenzy of activity until the day came when time stood still.

CHAPTER THREE

The twins were nine years old when I returned to school to complete my accounting degree. The three of us were sitting at the kitchen table doing homework after supper, waiting for daddy to come home.

Marco had gone out to dinner with some new clients downtown. After their meeting, street thugs held Marco and his companions up at gunpoint while exiting the upscale restaurant. One man refused the demand for their wallets. My husband and the man who resisted were shot and killed. The other two men were wounded.

· I assumed that my husband's dinner meeting was running late when he wasn't home before the boy's bedtime. So, I ushered Gage and Chase to bed and told them that dad would be in to kiss them goodnight when he got home. An hour later, the Chicago Police were at the door to deliver the devastating news of Marco's death.

After the officers left, I sat down in shock and in a state of ambiguity about what to do. How would I tell our sons that dad wasn't coming home and my in-laws had lost their youngest child? What could I say to them? Their son, half a world away, was dead. I had to be strong for the boys as I moved by rote. I called my grandmother to deliver the news. She would be in Chicago the following day to comfort the boys and me. She and my cousin Maggie would drive to Omaha and catch a plane to Chicago.

Grandma never flew on a plane before. She did this for me, knowing how much I needed her, and her fear of flying would not stop her from being at my side. She offered me the comfort and courage she had always provided me my entire life.

When it was a reasonable time in Italy, I called Nonna and Nonno's priest to be at their house when I called to tell them the news that would devastate their lives. It broke my heart all over again to hear their grief. There was nothing I could do to console them. I promised to let them know the funeral details, acknowledging that they could not make the trip to Chicago because of their health issues and advanced age. I sat on the sofa for the rest of the night, waiting for dawn when the boys would be awake.

The hardest thing I have ever faced was to tell my sons that dad was dead. We cried for what seemed like hours. I reassured them they were safe and we would get through this together. Finally, Grandma and my cousin Maggie arrived at noon. That's when I fell apart, and reality hit me with full force. One morning, like any other, we get up, have breakfast and go off to our own pursuits, not knowing that life was about to deliver a punch in the gut that would change our lives forever.

Grandma held me as I cried to the depths of my soul for the wonderful man that had been my husband for ten years. She knew exactly what I was going through, having buried her husband and only child, my father. How does anyone get over having your heart ripped out of your chest? "How do you go on?" I asked her.

"When I lost your grandfather, I knew I had to go on for my son. He was the same age as your sons are now. Your father gave me the strength I needed to get through another day. You will have your boys to give you that strength. You put one foot in front of the other and do the things you know you have to do. First one day and then another until you accept your new circumstances. Your life will never be the same, it will be different.

"You have the boys to care for, and you will make it as easy as possible for them to survive and thrive, and you will too. You may not think it now, but life will get better. Give yourself time to adjust. Don't make any hasty decisions. Let life simmer down until you can think clearly. Slowly the hard edges of grief will not be with you waking in the morning and the last thing at night. It softens with time. The wonderful memories will always be there, but the sharp pain of today will diminish. I promise, my darling girl, life for you and the boys will go on. You will smile again and laugh and be able to talk about Marco without tears. You'll appreciate and treasure the time and memories you made together. Marco will never be gone. You will see him in Chase and Gage every time you look into their eyes."

Grandma was my rock as the flurry of the funeral consumed the days ahead. First, I had my husband's remains cremated immediately after the police released Marco's body. Then, I phoned Nonno and Nonna, letting them know that the boys and I would return Marco's ashes to Siena for a memorial service and burial in the family plot in Italy when the boys were out of school for the summer in two months.

Grandma and Maggie returned to Nebraska one week after the Chicago funeral. After that, life continued on for us. Sports and other extracurricular activities sheltered my sons from their pain, and I threw myself into supporting them. We made the pilgrimage to Italy for Marco's memorial service and spent a month with Marco's parents. We then spent the rest of the summer in Nebraska in my childhood home with Grandma. My return to Nebraska renewed my spirit through the love of the people who surrounded me since I was three years old.

* * *

Grandmother Vernie took custody of me when my mother dropped me off at the farm for the summer. My father had died the year before from a farm accident, then my mother took me to California after my father's death. Life with my mother was very unsettled. I may have been only three years old, but I can still hear her words and see the ugliness in her face. Not understanding, but repeated frequently. "You're nothing but the biggest burden on my back. I can't wait to get rid of you." And rid herself of me she did when dropping me off for a visit with Grandma.

Grandma told me years later that the three-year-old that came to visit was in pretty sad shape. I didn't talk for the first two weeks at the farm and would tremble if anyone tried to touch me. I wet my bed every night and if my great uncles came over and voices grew loud, grandma would find me under the bed or hiding in the closet. Bruised and underweight, I hoarded food on the sly. It took weeks before I would let grandma hold me. With patience and love, Grandma changed my life and became my salvation. Any mention of my mother coming to pick me up sent me into hysterics.

When the summer was over, I waited with trepidation for my mother's return. That never happened. Grandma petitioned the court for permanent custody. We never heard from my birth mother again. As I got older, I had no desire to find her. There were no memories to savor, no yearning for a physical connection or curiosity. My birth mother failed to exist for me. I had all the answers I needed.

Grandma told me repeatedly, "You're my little girl now, and I love you with all my heart. You are my gift from God, and I am so blessed to have you."

Our life was simple, but comfortable. Great uncles and aunts and multitudes of cousins surrounded me. Birth or marriage related almost everyone in the county, it seems. Grandma's farmhouse was about ten miles from the nearest town, Hartsuff. The school bus was my mode of transportation for the trip to town.

I excelled in my classes, extracurricular activities, and graduated as valedictorian of my senior class of eighty-four, acing my SATs. I applied for every scholarship available and decided on Northwestern University in Chicago. The direction of my life changed when I met Marco.

CHAPTER FOUR

How fast the next few years slipped by. I was a mother of twins, going back to school and enjoying life with my family. When the twins were six years old, Marco and I decided we wanted another baby, a little girl. We tried unsuccessfully for three years until Marco's death. Severe endometriosis left me unable to conceive in the usual manner. We were about to avail ourselves of medical intervention when Marco died. The expansion of our family became an unfulfilled fantasy.

I knew I had to live life again after Marco's death, and on my graduation, I got a part-time job in the President's Office of The School of Art and Architecture of Chicago. With my accounting background, I worked on the college budget and became adept at curriculum development. In addition, my part-time employment allowed me to take the boys to Siena to spend a month with their grandparents. It followed with a couple of weeks to Nebraska with my grandmother in the summer.

Time moved on, and my sons thrived, graduating from their private school with honors. They applied and were accepted for entrance to Columbia University in New York for the International Economics Program. Gage studied Japanese, and Chase was into the Chinese Mandarin language, customs, and economics program. They were becoming multi-lingual, fluent in English, Italian, Mandarin, and Japanese.

I enjoyed my job at the college and friendships with Betsy and Michele, my workmates in the President's Office. We became very close friends, relying on each other when times get tough. My beloved grandmother passed away just before the boys left for college. With her passing and my sons off in New York, I felt deserted. My life was changing again.

Grandma left the family farm to me with all her possessions. I took a month off from work and returned home to Nebraska, planning with my Great Uncle John to monitor the house and take care of the three horses. Uncle John was long retired and lived a short distance down the road from grandma's farm. I disposed of all the other livestock: a cow, some pigs, and the chickens. Marco left me well off financially with investments, life insurance, and savings. Still, it gave me added security that my childhood home would be there for me whenever I needed comfort and escape.

* * *

A few weeks before my 40th birthday, I was anxiously awaiting Thanksgiving when Gage and Chase came home for the holiday during their sophomore year of college. I planned for weeks baking all their favorite goodies and prepared to cook a festive holiday meal. They were so excited to come back to Chicago and see their friends during school break. After our Thanksgiving dinner, the boys said they had something they wanted to discuss with me. Oh God, I hope no one is pregnant or getting married. They were too young, much as I was at their age. My early marriage worked out, but most marriages for those that young did not survive. So, before leaving for the airport to return to school, we sat down for our talk.

They were both invited to apply for a yearlong Immersion Studies Program, Gage in Japan and Chase in China. The program would start in May on completion of their sophomore year. The Immersion Program would count as their junior year of college. They were incredibly excited about the program and wanted to know my thoughts about the possibility of their yearlong absence. They had concerns about me being alone in Chicago when they were halfway around the world.

I was dumbstruck. Grown up, my babies didn't need me anymore. I had to put my selfishness aside and think about their happiness and the incredible opportunity they had been given. I knew in my heart there was reason to believe that their acceptance into the program was a lock. They were excellent scholars, handsome and personable like their father. This foreign study experience would become a valuable asset in their future careers. How could I not let them go?

I swallowed my uncertainties and tried to show enthusiasm for their adventure. If accepted, they would find out by Christmas and leave for their foreign studies immediately after finals at the end of April, not even coming home. I made them promise to spend spring break with me in Chicago. When they were notified, the boys said they would let me know the decision. I took them to the airport for their flight back to school in New York. They would be home again in less than a month for Christmas.

After dropping my sons at the terminal for their flight, I returned to my condo and cried buckets of tears. I called Betsy and Michele to tell them the news. They hurried over with a couple of bottles of wine, and we sat down as I poured out my feelings.

"Honey, you knew this time was coming. Your accomplished young men are confident, self-sufficient, and independent. You've done a wonderful job as a single parent since Marco died. Now it's your turn to live life again. You're still young, beautiful, educated, and a good person," said Michele.

"I'm turning forty in a couple of weeks; it seems life is turning to shit all at once. My husband is gone, and my children soon will be. What am I going to do with myself? This birthday is the mid-point of my life, with nothing to look forward to."

"You're going to make a life for yourself. Marco left you financially secure, and you can do anything you want. You can visit your sons in Japan, China or take a cruise around the world. You can 'Eat, Pray, Love' yourself into a coma or you can go home to Nebraska for a long visit and relax. The last ten years have been hard, and now you can concentrate on YOU. You're beautiful and still young. Forty is the new thirty, so cut loose and have some fun without worrying about everyone else," said Michele.

CHAPTER FIVE

After my 40th birthday party at the office and dinner with Michele and Betsy, I returned to my apartment. Gage and Chase called to wish me a Happy Birthday, telling them about the party at work and the gifts from the staff. They got a kick out of it. My sons reminded me they would be home for Christmas in a couple of weeks. They were still waiting for the news about their foreign studies applications.

I took a cab to my appointments at Elizabeth Arden's the following day. I have never felt so pampered. It lifted my spirits considerably. I called Michele and Betsy when I got home to thank them again for the marvelous birthday gift. I had the weekend to rest and accept the changes in my life.

The office before the holiday was a whirlwind of activity. I had to complete the budget items I was working on and finish a couple of new classes I was developing. My escape from my thoughts was to bury myself at work. I did some shopping for Christmas gifts for the office, my friends, and tried to find unique gifts for Gage and Chase to carry to their foreign assignments. I knew they were going to qualify.

I purchased new luggage, voltage converters, and new phones equipped with great cameras with international call plans. Next, I would have to learn about health insurance and sending money to them in different countries.

I made Christmas cookies and all the boys' yuletide favorites, hauled out the holiday decorations from storage, and ordered a Christmas tree to be delivered. I wrapped the gifts but waited to decorate the tree until Chase and Gage got home. Christmas cards were ready for the mail. All that was missing were my sons. I sent out invitations for the Christmas Eve party to my boss, Betsy, her family, and Michele and her husband. Gage and Chase would probably have a parade of friends stopping in throughout the holidays. How I will miss all this flurry of holiday togetherness. But, of course, if the boys are in Asia, they wouldn't be home next year. If that should be the case, maybe I'll go home to Hartsuff and surround myself with my extended family.

My sons arrived three days before Christmas. As soon as they hit the door, I had to ask, "Well?"

"Well, what, mom?" They asked, with big grins.

"You know what. Don't keep me in suspense. Did you get into the Immersion Program?" With big smiles on their faces, they both nodded in the affirmative. "I'm so proud of you. How do you feel about it?"

Chase answered with a giddiness so unlike him. "I can't wait. This program will be the first time on our own, me in Beijing and Gage in Tokyo. I know it'll be hard on you, mom, but we'll be able to FaceTime and call. We can set up a Zoom meeting so the three of us can talk together. Of course, we'll have to keep in mind the time difference. I'll be thirteen hours ahead of you, and Gage will be fourteen hours ahead. We need to check our passports to make sure they don't expire before we come home."

"This will be hard on all of us. This program is the first time it will separate you two since you were born," I said.

"I thought about that too. It had to happen sometime. Chase and I will only be a short four-hour flight from each other," said Gage. "You can make a trip over to see us. We'll have to find out what our schedules look like when we get there."

"I'm happy for your both. Your dad would be so proud of you," as I teared up.

"Don't cry, mom. You've spent half your life taking care of us, and now it's your turn to kick up your heels and have some fun without worrying about what we are up to. So, let's turn the tables, and we'll worry about what you're up to," laughed Chase.

"Yeah, you have a wild and crazy mom; I might stay up past midnight and watch X-rated movies." I laughed along with my sons. "Let's enjoy our time together now before you two handsome men become international sensations."

Gage and Chase put their duffle bags in their rooms, and were off to do their Christmas shopping and meet up with friends. How did my babies grow up so fast? I have to accept that my children are now grown men preparing to live their own separate lives. I didn't know it would be so hard to let go.

Chase and Gage were so full of holiday joy, it was hard not to join in with their merriment. We decorated the Christmas tree, and I filled the house with the smells of holiday baking. I had one more day of work before everyone separated for a week's vacation between the holidays.

I can't say we accomplished any work the day before Christmas Eve in our office. No one was in the mood to get anything done. We all brought a dish to pass and had lunch together as we modeled our outrageously ugly Christmas sweaters. We had a great time opening up our Secret Santa gifts. I had drawn my boss's name, gifting him with a rubber stamp that said "Bull Shit" and a small whip. I thought he would have a coronary; he laughed so hard. I received a big bag of Unicorn Farts-fluffy pastel balls of cotton candy. Someone passed around Mike's Hard Lemonade, pretending they didn't know it had alcohol in it. By the time the workday was over, we were all in the holiday mood.

I got home to a house full of my son's friends. It was loud, crowded, and wonderful. They were all hungry. No surprise there. I ordered ten pizzas for delivery and had to watch that no one was sneaking in any alcohol since the kids were under twenty-one. The party broke up about midnight as a blizzard piled up the snow.

On Christmas Eve day, we prepared for our small party for close friends. It would be low key with thirteen people if everyone could make it in the snow. I baked a honey ham and all the accouterments with a yule log for dessert. Everyone had a relaxing time. Dr. Michaels had a long discussion with the twins about their foreign study opportunity. He seemed to be interested in all the details delving into the structure of the program.

Betsy's kids were hugely excited that Santa was coming that night, and Michele and her husband were trying to enjoy a little Christmas cheer without their children close. After our casual evening, I saw everyone to the door together with bottles of aged six-year-old bourbon and cookie baskets for the children as their Christmas gifts. I couldn't help but question what next Christmas would be like with my sons gone.

We slept in late on Christmas morning. I fixed our traditional breakfast of chocolate chip pancakes and sausage. We opened our gifts; Gage and Chase shrieked with excitement, viewing their new traveling items, and the phones were a tremendous hit. They promised to have all the programs loaded to keep in communication on their travels. Crowding together on the couch, we spent the rest of the day watching football, movies and quietly enjoying being together. We nibbled on the leftovers from last night, played cards, and remembered dad and grandma with funny stories. I placed a call to Nonno and Nonna, wishing them a joyous holiday. Then, the boys were off to visit friends while I cleaned up the kitchen and headed to bed early.

The rest of the week was for relaxing and doing a little shopping for things the boys needed in Asia. Too soon, I was taking them back to O'Hare Airport for their return flight to New York. They wanted to be in Times Square for the big ball drop on New Year's Eve.

After talking with Michele and Betsy, wishing them a Happy New Year, I spent my evening with an early night in bed with a good book. So much for the holidays. Oh, Marco and Grandma, how I miss you both so much.

*   *   *

I was eager to get back to the office and put my mind to work on something other than my empty home and missing children. The new semester started with the chaos of returning students and beginning classes. There were always complaints to deal with, unhappy parents with their student's grades, students failing because of absenteeism, and instructors unhappy with their teaching assignments and hours.

When Dr. Michaels called me into his office in mid-February, everything was settling down, or so I thought. Oh shit. What did I do or didn't do? Did I make a big mistake on the budget projections, or did the curriculum I developed suck? Before the meeting, I stopped in the restroom to relieve my nervous bladder then strolled to the President's office.

I knocked hesitantly on Dr. Michaels' door, preparing myself for a flogging. I waited for his signal to enter. He was sitting at his desk with a smile spreading over his face. Good sign; he would probably not fire me today unless Dr. Michaels was a closet sadist.

"Come in, Brenna, and take a seat. How are the new classes going?"

"Fully enrolled, Dr. Michaels," I answered.

"I wanted to tell you how much I enjoyed talking to your sons over the holidays. It got me thinking about something our college needs to research and, if feasible, incorporate into our programs. It's a growing trend in higher education, and I believe you are the person best suited to work up a budget and design the curriculum. We need to stay competitive in our market to offer our students an in-depth cultural experience outside their comfort zone. As I recall, you speak fluent Italian, don't you?"

"Si signore, lo Voglio. That's yes, sir, I do. My husband, as you know, was Italian, and we spent a month in Italy with his parents in Siena each summer. They were not bilingual. We continued speaking Italian at home until the boys and I were fluent. During my summers off work, I resumed the trips with the boys after my husband died so that my in-laws could know their grandsons. It made traveling back to Italy a lot more fun and comfortable for Nonno and Nonna knowing their language."

"Are you familiar with Florence?"

"Like the back of my hand. Florence, or Firenze, as the natives call it, is about 48 miles from Siena, and my family spent a lot of time there. It's the center of the Renaissance period and home to Michelangelo. It's a beautiful city. There's much to see and do in Florence."

"What about Rome? Your thoughts."

"When my husband was alive, we met many of his business associates there acting as tour guides and translators. Rome is an incredible place for art, architecture, history, and great food. Anyone traveling to Europe has to see this city to take in the culture and history. It's something we don't have here in the United States. It's a can't miss destination."

"My wife and I visited several years ago when our children were young. It was the highlight of our vacation."

"Venice, Milan, and Pisa also hold their special magic, along with all the picturesque small villages and towns scattered throughout the country. There's history at every turn, and the Italian people are warm and welcoming."

"I knew you were the right person for this assignment. Let me outline what I want to do and you mull it over, so hear me out before you say anything. I want to set up a program for foreign study in Italy lasting about a month. To start a small group of ten carefully screened, serious students to tour Florence and Rome. A smaller group would be manageable at least for the first couple of offerings so that we can shake any kinks out of the program.

"I will assign an instructor to lecture, give out reading assignments and quizzes generating a grade, and the students will receive academic credit. The program needs someone on the ground to put it together. I want a point person to contact the appropriate people for accommodations, museums, and tours.

"We need to research the requirements for foreign study and what our liabilities are when overseeing a group of students. I want to limit the student applications for such a program to juniors and seniors with top academic standing, parental approval, and independent funds to cover those costs not included in the college program.

"We also need information on health coverage while our students are out of the country and what to do if they get into trouble with the law. So, covering every aspect of what could happen while the students are in our custody, a 'What To Do' handbook per se for student travel outside the United States.

"I think you are the perfect person for this overseas assignment. You know the country, are fluent in the language, a big plus. You're mature, level-headed, and detail-oriented. There isn't anyone else I would trust to do this assignment in the most professional manner. Please think about it. Talk it over with your sons, and let me know by the end of February.

"The college will cover all your expenses, and you will receive your salary plus a bonus for a foreign assignment. I'm thinking two months or possibly longer to compile a complete plan starting the first of May. I don't want to hear your answer now. Consider it carefully. I know your sons will be off on their immersion programs, so you are free of obligations here. Let's get together in two weeks. Thank you for hearing me out."

Dr. Michaels rose from his desk, dismissing me. I walked out of the President's office in a state of astonishment and conflict when Betsy and Michele almost tackled me.

"We heard Dr. M. called you on the carpet. What happened? Did you make a mistake on the budget or slap the hell out of one of the instructors?" asked Betsy.

"Nothing like that. What are you guys doing after dinner tonight? If you can get away, let's meet for drinks, and I'll give you all the details."

"The heck with drinks. Let's do dinner. It's my husband's bowling night," said Michele.

"My husband can feed and get the kids to bed. He owes me for our Valentine's orgy," laughed Betsy.

"It's almost quitting time. Meet you at Leo's in a half-hour," as I dashed off to finish a couple of items on my desk before leaving for the evening.

We ventured to our favorite neighborhood, "greasy spoon", for some deep-fried carbohydrates and ice-cold beer. Over hamburgers and onion rings, I gave a capsulated version of the assignment Dr. Michaels wanted me to take on.

"OMG, what an incredible opportunity. You're going to do it, aren't you?" asked Betsy with glee.

"I have to think this through. I'll be away for two or more months. What if the boys need me? What if I'm not capable of delivering what Dr. M wants? I've never been on my own before for that length of time. I don't know if I can do this," I questioned.

"Of course you can. You're the best curriculum developer the college ever had and anal about details. You cannot NOT do this. The boys will be in China and Japan, and now you can have an exciting adventure in a place you are not only familiar with but love. I would trade my husband and kids for an opportunity like this," said Betsy.

"It's not like you'll be in Siberia. With modern methods of communications, you'll be a keystroke away. Your boys are adults, and now it's your time. It will thrill Chase and Gage to know that you'll be doing something that you love. You have friends there and your in-laws close by. What's to think about? It's like a paid vacation in romantic Florence. You'll be free to do what you want when you want. Just tell me, what's the downside?" asked Michele.

"This is an enormous responsibility and commitment of time. Who's going to do my work at the office? I don't want to let anyone down."

"Stop looking like someone stole the toy from your Happy Meal. If you don't grab this opportunity with both hands, the only one you would let down is you. Michele and I will be green with envy and miss you while you're gone. But knowing that you are having the time of your life, doing what you love to do more than makes up for having you away. What are you going to miss here? Your empty condo? The weekdays going back and forth to work? Your lonely nights and weekends? You take every summer off, so you could even stay through the summer if you meet someone interesting," said Betsy.

"Have you kept in touch with that gorgeous Giorgio? Doesn't he have a B & B that you like to stay at when you're in Italy?" asked Michele.

"I've kept in touch with him and his partner, Carlo. They still have their converted palazzo on the via dei Macci. It would be a convenient place to stay in Florence, and their mini-apartments would be all I need IF I decide to do this."

"There ya' go. You're financially secure, and your condo, free and clear. You could even get a reliable short-term renter while you're gone and make a little extra money," said Michele.

"We will support you in whatever your decision is, but we will be very disappointed for YOU if you don't do this," said Betsy, with Michele nodding in agreement.

"Let me think this through and run it by the boys. Dr. M wants my answer by the end of the month. Now let's table this and order a decadent dessert to top off the calories we will regret by tomorrow."

"Ya' like you have to worry, you booger," moaned Betsy. "The carb police have never had you on their radar."

*　*　*

When I got home, I called Gage and Chase, going through the details of the offered assignment. They were no less than ecstatic about the opportunity that landed unexpectedly in my lap.

"Mom, that's fantastic. Gage and I won't worry about you being alone for so long while we are away. You have given us your everything since dad died; you deserve this. Think of yourself for once and GO FOR IT! We know how much you love Italy, and you'll be able to check in with Nonno and Nonna. They will love having you so close. We'll have to have a big 'Bon voyage' party when we get home for spring break."

"Sounds like a plan, but first, I have to decide if I can do this."

"Of course you can. You can do it with your eyes closed. Sleep on it, and I will talk to you in a couple of days. Love you," said Gage.

"Love you both, too. Good night." A thought just occurred to me. I ran into the home office and looked in the file cabinet for our passports. Just as I thought, my passport was going to expire in two months. I had to get a rush renewal whether or not I accepted this assignment. The boys were good for another five years. A doctor's appointment was in order to make sure our vaccinations are up-to-date, and inoculations needed specifically for Asia. I had better start making a list of things to accomplish, just in case. The boys should also have a physical and dental appointment when they're home for spring break. Our surprise opportunities were getting more complicated by the minute.

I tossed and turned most of the night. My thoughts were whirling around in a continuous loop. Should I or shouldn't I? Can I do this? I tried to list all the pros and cons in my mind. The following week, I moved through the motions of completing my open projects and avoiding the questioning looks from Betsy and Michele. I made list after list of things to consider if I took the assignment. Then, during my lunch hour, I walked over to a local Walgreens store and had a new passport picture taken. I downloaded a copy of a passport renewal form, filled it out, and dropped the paperwork at the Chicago Passport Agency downtown.

I made appointments at the doctor and dentist for my sons and myself for pre-travel checkups while they were home on spring break. Then, I called a realtor friend to estimate how much I could rent my condo for if I traveled out of the country, making it clear it would be short term. Shirley, Chicago realtor extraordinaire, would work up some numbers for me, and I promised to let her know when I decided what my plans were.

I can't go through another week of this uncertainty. I had to decide. No equivocating, no wavering, and no vacillating. So, Brenna Maureen Souchek-Herrera, what do YOU want to do? Good question. I slept on it another night. By morning, I had my answer.

I emailed Dr. M as soon as I got to my office, requesting a couple of minutes of his time. He emailed me back immediately. He will be available at 10 AM. I girded my loins and confidently walked to the President's office, and softly knocked on the door at the appointed time. After a cheerful greeting, I took a seat.

"I hope you have some good news for me," said Dr. Michaels.

"I have given it a lot of thought, weighing all the pros and cons, consulted my sons, and have decided. Thank you for having the confidence in me to offer such a wonderful opportunity. At this time I must. . ." I could see the smile on his face fall. "accept this assignment and hope I can deliver on all your expectations." I had to laugh at his expression.

"You almost gave me a heart attack, Brenna. You had me going for a minute. I'm pleased that you will take this on for the college. I have confidence that you will do a great job like you do everything else. Let's meet again in two days. Compile a list of questions for me, and I will outline what we are attempting to build. Do you have questions right now?"

"I'm going to meet with our IT person about loading the software for Zoom meetings with you and anyone else that needs to be privy to this project. I will need a ballpark figure for budget and solidify the dates for the assignment. Thank you again, Dr. Michaels, for this terrific opportunity."

"My pleasure, Brenna. This addition to our curriculum will raise our profile as one of the best educational institutions for the arts and architecture, not only in the state but the country."

I left Dr. M's office with a smile on my face, pep in my step, and a great sense of relief. I was happy with my decision, and now that I made it, it was full steam ahead. Betsy and Michele were waiting to hear what answer I had given Dr. M. They had given me the space to mull over my thoughts without haranguing me about my decision.

"Well?" they asked.

"I'm going to do it," I said as Betsy and Michele squealed with delight. They grabbed me in a three-way hug, dancing around in a circle to the amazement of the others in our office in what was usually a quiet and dignified atmosphere.

"This is so exciting. I'm so happy for you," said Betsy. "Knowing you, you have probably made a dozen to-do lists of everything you need to accomplish before you go."

"How d'ya' guess?" I asked.

"You have Post-it notes stuck to the sleeves of your dress," said Michele with a chuckle.

CHAPTER SIX

When I got home, I called Gage and Chase to tell them my decision. They were ecstatic, knowing they wouldn't have to worry about me home alone through the summer. I was happy they would have a complete sense of freedom to enjoy their well-earned adventure. I reminded them to make an appointment with their college health clinic and go over the CDC vaccination requirements for travel to China and Japan. They needed a lot more in vaccinations than I would require for Italy. We sounded like such globetrotters.

Next, I called Shirley, my realtor friend, to give her the go-ahead for renting the condo from May through July. If I didn't stay in Italy during my summer off work, I would go to my house in Nebraska to reconnect with my extended family and decompress.

To my surprise, Shirley was sure she could rent my furnished home for four thousand dollars per month, plus the maintenance fees and utilities. Also required would be a four-thousand-dollar security deposit. Shirley agreed to act as the contact person in my absence, aka rent collector. However, I was adamant that she had to find a mature renter, clean freak, non-partier, and respectful tenant to the neighbors.

I left a phone message for my insurance agent regarding the need to have health coverage for international travel for myself and my sons. At a rapid rate, I was checking off items on my lists. I felt a great sense of control, knowing that I was taking care of everything that needed my attention.

Now I could relax for the week. Gage and Chase would be home for spring break, and I could enjoy them. Well, maybe not enjoy the mountain of dirty clothes, toxic smelling gym bags, and finding my kitchen dishes under their beds encrusted with dry food, but having them home for what will be more than a year of separation was precious.

This first long absence would prepare me for our future, easing me into the empty nest feeling that would become a permanent feature of my middle-aged life. I will try my best to be upbeat during their stay at home. I didn't want to dilute their confidence and excitement for their adventure since I had a venture of my own to look forward to.

We spent our treasured time together cooking their favorite meals and selecting more clothing to pack. Then, going to the bank, I purchased a quantity of Japanese yen, Beijing dollars and euros for myself. I arranged ATM cards for each of my sons loaded with enough money for at least six months. If more was necessary, I could direct my bank to load more funds onto the cards. I knew my sons weren't frivolous spenders and would use their funds wisely.

I had purchased a new cellphone with all the bells and whistles for myself, hoping I could learn how to use it. Chase was my IT tech at home and ensured I had all the programs I would need while in Italy. He also updated my iPad and laptop. As a result, it drenched me in new technology that boggled my old school mind.

My sons must have felt like pin cushions after their doctor's checkup inoculated for Hep A & B, Rabies, Yellow Fever, Typhoid, and Japanese Encephalitis between the school health clinic and their family doctor. More peace of mind for this anal-retentive fussbudget that always painstakingly investigated the dark clouds before looking for the silver lining.

Too soon. Time to take Chase and Gage to the airport for their return to New York. As we walked to the security gate, I made it my mission to be strong. This parting was the hardest thing I have ever had to endure since their father died. With many kisses, hugs, and "I love yous," they were off. I sat in my car in short-term parking and cried for a half-hour. Our family dynamics were changing. My boys were men now, discovering the world on their own, flying off, and living their dreams.

In my youth I was never a crier or a whiner, but now with every change in my life, the waterworks took hold of me. If I don't watch it, I will be stuffing tissues up the sleeves of my shirts or a handkerchief nestled in my soon to be sagging cleavage. I hated change in my normally well-ordered life. I guess I will blame it all on perimenopause or some other delightful sign of growing older. *Someone needs an attitude adjustment—grab those big girl panties and get with the program, Brenna!*

* * *

I filled the following five weeks with completing my office assignments and packing for my journey. Shirley found the perfect tenant for my condo. A single, retired Professor Emeritus from Northwestern University needing a quiet place to write a book on the history of Chicago architecture. Shirley assured me that Dr. Lloyd Moseby is a very private person and a friend of Dr. M's and would respect my property during his stay, eliminating any of my concerns on that front.

I was leaving for Italy the fourth week in April. I would stay at Giorgio and Carlo's B & B in Florence for my entire stay. As a bonus, Giorgio knew everyone in town, giving me an advantage with introductions to people I needed to contact. I was eager to see my Italian friends again. I called my in-laws and let them know they would see a lot of me during my project in Italy.

On my last day in the Chicago office, the staff arranged a little going away party. There were no tears this time; I was over-the-moon itching to be on my way as I hugged everyone goodbye and told them not to get comfortable in my office. "I'll be back," I said, using my best Arnold Schwarzenegger impression.

Betsy, Michele, and I proceeded to dinner. In a festive mood, they presented me with a bon voyage gift. I opened the gaily wrapped box and peeling the tissue paper away, I uncovered the sexiest black lace demi bra, matching thong panties, garter belt, and silk stockings. Speechless didn't cover my reaction.

"We decided to jazz up your underwear. We know that you have a drawer full of white cotton granny panties and white cotton bras, standard issue for all female army recruits. You're not just a mommy, but you're a woman foremost. You have a great body; flaunt it. At least if you get a chance to get laid, you'll have something sexy to wear," said Betsy. "If you're going to be bad, be really good at it!"

"You know, guys, you're right," I said.

"We are?" questioned Betsy, mystified at my 180-degree about-face.

"Yes. Since Marco died, I have been hiding away, telling myself that my sex life was over. I opted for the comfortable and practical instead of va-va-voom. I dated little, nor was I interested in doing more. I'm going to try my best to get out there again and change. It's my time now that the boys are adults. I can't promise I'll change overnight, but I'll try my best," I said.

"That's what we have been waiting to hear. Here's to more va and a lot of voom. You're a beautiful woman in her prime. You don't look a day over thirty. Don't forget sex is good for a cold nose and a shiny coat," laughed Michele.

We parted with kisses and hugs as we took off in different directions. I pulled all my plain jane white underwear out of my suitcase when I got home. My flight tomorrow, an overnighter, and I didn't have to be at the airport until 3 PM. So I had time to take a cab downtown in the morning to La Perla, the mecca of intimate female apparel, on Oak Street and update my boring, no-frills geriatric lingerie.

I dropped a bundle of money outfitting myself with five sexy bra and panty combinations, sleepwear, and a new figure-flattering swimsuit. Michele and Betsy were right. My femininity had laid dominant. Arriving home for the last time, I packed my new undies in my luggage, emptied the trash, made a quick look around, and left my condo for O'Hare Airport.

At the check-in desk for my non-stop flight to Rome, I paid the difference to upgrade my seat to first-class from the business class ticket that the college had provided. I had two suitcases to struggle with: my briefcase, laptop, and purse. Certainly, traveling alone had its downside without the extra helping hands to do the heavy lifting.

My 6 PM Emirates Airline flight would take ten hours, and with the seven-hour time difference, I would arrive in Rome at approximately 11 AM local time. My connecting flight to Florence departing at 2 PM arrives at 3:30 PM. I hope I would sleep, or I would feel like a zombie when I finally arrived at the B & B in time for dinner.

I had never flown Emirates Airlines before. I was so glad that I paid the difference for first-class. As soon as I boarded and directed to my seat, I had a glass of Dom Perignon champagne and wild caviar on toast points set in front of me. The first-class section of the plane had a lounge and bar. I would be entirely crocked by the time dinner arrived if I didn't watch myself. All the seats looked like spacious Lazy Boy style lounge chairs with walls separating each spacious seating area. After my sumptuous dinner of lobster and steak, my flight attendant gave me a set of moisturizing pajamas and a Bulgari amenity kit.

While in the restroom, the cabin crew converted my chair into a full-size twin bed with lavender-scented sheets, blankets, and pillows. Doors enclosed me in my private haven equipped with a television, computer outlets, fancy bottled water and a fruit basket. There were on-board showers I could use at my convenience. WOW. This must be the way the other half traveled. I had a late evening snack and turned off the lights. This flight was so freaking fantastic I could hardly believe what I was experiencing.

I slept for seven hours, took a shower, dressed, and had another incredible meal. The luxury was insane on this airline—I kept the pajamas! I had to take a video of this sumptuousness with my phone, or no one would believe me. I never felt so indulged. The flight crew fulfilled every wish at my command. The rich and famous must travel like this all the time.

On arrival in Rome, I felt fresh as a daisy. Emirates Airlines ground courtesy staff drove me and my luggage to the Alitalia terminal for my flight to Florence after I cleared customs. I had a couple of hours to send emails letting Dr. M, my sons, Betsy and Michele, know that I had arrived in Rome. Unfortunately, it was way too early in the morning for them to respond, so I made myself comfortable until my flight to Florence boarded.

Arriving in Florence, I engaged a cab to take me to the B & B. Giorgio and Carlo met me at the door, smothering me in hugs and kisses. We chatted in Italian, and the language was rapidly coming back to me as if I had been nowhere else. Then, sitting down with a glass of vino, we caught up on each other's lives.

Giorgio and Carlo made dinner in their apartment, serving my favorites. Pasta and chicken with a delicate parmesan sauce, antipasto salad, fresh bread, and a bottle of outstanding white wine. It was a relaxing evening with old friends that filled me in on all the local news. I outlined my assignment for the college, and my friends were a treasure trove of information regarding the best student hostels for me to check out. Giorgio supplied me with the names of the contact people and each location. Tomorrow after some rest, I was going to hit the ground running.

Carlo and Giorgio owned one side of a converted palazzo facing the street. The building formed a large square with open-air, light well garden space in the interior center. From the street door, a stairway reached up fifteen feet to the entrance of the B & B. Since the Arno River poured over its banks in 1966, flooding Florence, residents took everything of value to higher floors. Most residential first floors now remained empty or used for temporary storage. The flood waters permanently destroyed or severely damaged many of the city's magnificent art pieces, with ongoing restoration still being performed decades later. Over one hundred people lost their lives when the river surged. The floodwaters reached just short of the second floor of the palazzo, now Giorgio and Carlo's home.

The B & B housed six tourist apartments; they saved the largest and the best guest accommodation for my stay. Spacious and facing the street, the twenty-foot ceiling displayed the colorful original fresco art with gods, cherubs, and clouds. It had a roomy living room with a workspace, a full bath, and a small kitchen that I hoped never to use except for coffee. A narrow metal spiral staircase led to a generous sleeping loft with a queen-size bed. I could see where the stairs would be a dicey if I should be the least bit tipsy.

I slept like the dead on my first night in Florence, followed by a breakfast of a hard roll with prosciutto, fresh fruit, and a caffe latte with Giorgio and Carlo in the communal dining room in their apartment. I had to laugh. In the background, Giorgio's much-beloved Italian soap operas played on a large flat-screen television. The television was always on, with Giorgio taking peeks frequently, hopelessly addicted. I felt like I was home again.

In the Italian style, I dressed for the day in a short navy-blue pencil skirt, white silk blouse, gold jewelry, and knee-high leather boots with a three-inch heel. I hoped I hadn't lost my ability to walk on the cobbled or brick streets with spiked heels. Wrapped in a light jacket and a cap on my head to ward off the chill of early morning, it was such a pleasure to once again walk the familiar narrow cobblestone streets toward the Piazza del Duomo. All the shops and houses along the way were sand-hued, constructed of Tuscan limestone with pots of flowers adding touches of color. Doors facing the street displayed colors of bright red, forest green, or blue, looking like a picture postcard.

Once I left the deep shadows of the narrow medieval streets, I burst onto the open Piazza del Duomo with its centerpiece, the Cathedral di Santa Maria del Fiore. In 1436 Filippo Brunelleschi, the father of Renaissance architecture, designed the dome that dominates the skyline over the incredible cathedral's exterior. The walls of the church are sheathed with white, green, and salmon-colored marble, luminous in the sun. The piazza was already crowded with groups of tourists, citizenry, and beggars so early in the morning. I sat down at a sidewalk bar facing the cathedral, ordered an espresso, pulled out my notebook, and worked on a list of student hostels to inspect across the Arno River. Sitting back to savor the atmosphere, I enjoyed the leisurely pace of the Florentine populace.

After a couple of minutes people watching, I noticed that there were multiple groups of three to four people with a guide and what seemed to be bodyguards, shepherding the groups around the massive Cathedral and Baptistery structures.

They were better dressed than the typical tourists on the street. As I watched, I noticed that younger individuals ran up to the groups with paper, pens, and cell phones. I asked the server if he knew what was going on. He told me a movie was being filmed across the river, and the actors and crew were taking a tour of the cathedral grounds. Well, that put a hitch in my plans on the other side of the bridge if the filming was blocking off streets and buildings. So, I switched my plans to a visit to the Uffizi Gallery and the Basilica Santa Croce, staying on this side of the river, avoiding the chaos of egotistical actors and slobbering fans until I could pinpoint where the filming was taking place.

I walked the two blocks to Piazza Santa Croce, one of my favorite places in Florence. The Basilica, the guardian of Florence's glorious history of art and religious fervor, was a smaller version of the cathedral. The building housed the memorial vaults of Dante, Galileo Galilei, Machiavelli, and Michelangelo, among others. I met with the overseer of the Basilica di Santa Croce, Father Francisco.

I explained my mission, and we made arrangements for in-depth private tours for our somewhat knowledgeable students. I got his contact information and told him I would be in touch when plans were completed. I spent an hour enjoying the magnificence of the sculptured memorials, the incredible wall art, stained glass windows, and the stunning altarpiece. Chills overtook me mire feet away from the mortal remains of some of the most celebrated people in history. The beauty of the towering vaults was breathtaking, magnificent works of art capturing the incredible skill of master sculptors.

When I left the Basilica, I headed across the piazza down another block toward the river to the Uffizi, one of the most heralded art galleries in Europe. I was steps away from the entrance when a man behind me grabbed the hat off my head and pulling it on his own. He hauled me into his arms, backing up into a doorway with my back to the street, slumping down, and placing his hands around my waist, under my jacket. This stranger locked his lips to mine as a group of girls ran screaming by. Once the street was moderately quiet again, he let me go.

I hauled off and slapped his face while unleashing the most vicious epithets, mostly questioning his parentage as lesser than homo sapiens, with every nasty word I could remember in Italian. I continued my tirade for a full five minutes, shaking with indignation as he stood in front of me with a big grin on his face. My country girl was coming out. If I had a good-sized rock, this David would have lobbed a shot at Goliath right where it hurt the most, wiping the grin off his smug face.

He took off my hat and offered it back to me. I flipped my hand in an Italian gesture of disgust. I turned my back to him and walked away when I heard him call out in halting Italian for my name.

"Come . . . si. . . . chiama?"

I looked over my shoulder, "Si, Jane."

"Cognome-last name?"

"Doe!" I shouted as I heard him laugh as I hurried away from his line of sight.

What nerve. I don't know what this stranger was hiding from. It pissed me off to be used as a barricade. What an asshole. I would not let this incident ruin my day or delay my mission. After finding the street clear, I proceeded to the gallery. I met with the Uffizi curator, Roberto Martino, and made the same arrangements with him as I did with Father Francisco. He introduced me to the instructional director and took his leave. Roberto gave me free rein to walk around the gallery as long as I wanted. I took advantage of his generous offer and headed to my favorite room that displayed the stunning painting The Birth of Venus by Sandro Botticelli.

I sat down on the padded bench facing the colossal painting, taking in its beauty. It must be wonderful to live among all the priceless art and iconic architecture Italy possesses. As I gazed at the beauty before me, it gave me a renewed sense of well-being, and happy for the opportunity to reinvigorate my love for Italy, its people, and art.

Later, after stopping to thank the instructional director of the gallery for her help, out of the corner of my eye, I thought I saw the "phantom kisser." I turned my back and concluded our conversation, leaving the gallery and walking back toward the B & B. It was late afternoon, and the temperature hovered around 70 degrees. I stopped at a refreshment stand and indulged in a double scoop of mango gelato while walking around, refreshing my memory for the different shops and buildings of interest. Someone tapped me on the shoulder as I was almost back at my apartment. It was the "Tonsil Assessor".

"I know you probably don't understand me, but I want to apologize for my behavior earlier today." He searched for a word, "amiche?—friends?" As he held out his hand.

I looked at his face, then at the offered appendage, and overturned my cup of gelato, dumping it in his outstretched hand. While he was wiping the cold contents off his fingers and clothes, I ran down the street, unlocked the door, and escaped into my building. Climbing upstairs, I let myself into the B & B and ran to my apartment, cautiously looking out my window facing the street. "Mr. Smooch" was standing in front of the door with a grin on his face. Oh crap. Now he knows where I'm staying. I have to tell Giorgio and Carlo about the lunatic that seemed to be stalking me. Not the way I wanted to start my assignment in Florence, fighting the advances of an amorous stranger.

At breakfast the following day, I told the guys about the man who followed me the previous day. I asked them if he should come to the door, not to acknowledge my existence. Concerned for my safety, Giorgio and Carlo wanted me to have the Pathfinder app. on my phone, so they could find me if the mysterious letch continued to give me trouble. We programmed our phones so that Carlo and Giorgio would know where I was at all times, and I could send a distress signal to them if I needed help.

In my room, I constructed a spreadsheet for the information I had collected so far. I looked out my window; the coast was clear. After leaving my apartment, I walked back to the Piazza del Duomo, stopping at a sidewalk bar for a lunch of antipasto, pasta, and vino. I planned to cross the Ponte Vecchio, the old bridge, over the Arno River to check out all the hostels Giorgio recommended. If I had time,

I wanted to stop at the Pitti Palace and Boboli Gardens on that side of the river. I kept my eyes peeled for the movie people filming somewhere in the area. I was thankful that I didn't see any commotion. It pleased me to visit all the hostels on my list, inspecting the cleanliness and amenities such as nearby laundry facilities and small, inexpensive eateries. I collected all the information I needed and a clear picture of the premises available for student lodging.

While the accommodations were not luxurious, they were adequate for the students on a limited budget. Each room would sleep two people on cots, room to stow one suitcase under the bed, and space to dress. Most hostels had communal bathrooms with hot water rationed for two brief showers per week, per student. The girls with hair concerns would have to learn to shampoo and rinse swiftly. Certainly not the Ritz, but adequate with cleanliness and safety in mind. The hostels were situated just across the Arno, walking distance from the Ponte Vecchio and the heart of old Florence.

By the time I finished with accommodations, it was getting too late for anything else. I window shopped while walking back over the two-story Ponte Vecchio. The bridge held store after store of jewelry shops on both sides of the walkway. It was far removed from the original butchers and tanner shops that once lined the bridge. Built in 1345, it was the only bridge in Florence to survive World War II.

I knew I would come back and do severe damage to my credit cards when I had time to shop leisurely. I stopped at a ristorante to pick up a panini and a small bottle of wine to take back to the apartment for dinner. While back in my room, I added the new information to my spreadsheet. I emailed my friends and sons and then ate my dinner. Finally, I was ready for a shower and bed after an exhausting second day with my feet howling in pain from the miles I covered in uncomfortable footwear. Travel survival rule number one: Wear well broken-in shoes.

The following day at breakfast, Giorgio and Carlo were giddy with exciting news. My stalker had stopped by the B & B for a visit yesterday. "You didn't tell him I was here, did you?" I asked.

"We played dumb, the Italian way, pretending not to understand English," said Carlo. "But there's more. Your stalked is Ben Langford. THE Ben Langford, the film star."

"WHAT?" Horrified, I wanted nothing to do with a Hollywood glamor boy and People magazine's latest Sexiest Man Alive.

"He is one hot guy, and he seemed to be a delightful man," Carlo grinned as Giorgio frowned at him. "Don't worry, Giorgio, he isn't interested in us. What do you think, darling? Is he worth another look?"

"Unequivocally no. I have no interest in someone who probably is so self-centered with an attitude of entitlement that comes with fame. Mr. Movie Star acted like an all-around dumb ass with me. He runs in the fast lane, and that's not me, nor do I want it to be. Remember, he's an actor adopting any role suitable for the situation. I won't trust his 'nice guy' impression, and the brief interaction I have had with him doesn't say 'Mr. Nice Guy' to me. Non vale la pena." It's not worth the trouble.

Carlo continued, "I do not know how long the film crew is going to be here. There's nothing in the newspaper about an end date. There always seems to be filming going on in our city. It's not uncommon to see famous people walking around. No one but tourists pay that much attention to them.

"The famous are usually irritations more than anything else. They're demanding, often rude, and cause our area business owners to deal with havoc if they come into their establishments. I can't understand the contempt these famous people have for their admirers when they come up to ask for a signature or photo. These are the people who made them popular, paying money to watch their films."

"I'm completely in agreement. I don't want to be anyone's fling or quick lay. I believe in everlasting love and commitment. That's not what Hollywood types portray. These high-profile people don't have lasting relationships, just brief encounters." I said.

"What are your plans for today?" asked Giorgio.

"I have a reservation at the Galleria dell'Accademia with the director this morning. Then I thought I would wander around checking out cheap, inexpensive places for students to eat this side of the river."

"See you later, cara. Keep your mobile with you."

With double cheek kisses from my friends, I was off. I walked to the Galleria dell' Accademia a few blocks from my apartment, housing Michelangelo's celebrated statue of David.

I met with Piero Rossi, the director, and his assistant/gallery guide, Antonia Bianchi, going into what was becoming my standard spiel for setting up guided tours for students. They were very accommodating and happy to ensure that our students would have reservations and a guide on any visit we requested. I gathered the contact information, noted admittance prices and hours. Mr. Rossi excused himself, leaving Antonia and me to wander around the gallery. We shared a spirited conversation only Italians can have with hands and arms flying, emphasizing our speech with enthusiasm. I liked her a lot, and we made plans to meet for a glass of wine the following evening. I gave her my mobile phone number. Antonia was so energetic and charming I could see us becoming friends.

After another hour, we parted. Visiting the smaller display rooms and the avenue of unfinished Michelangelo's sculptures, I walked back to the rotunda to where David dominated the space. I sat down on a bench at the rear of the seventeen-foot-tall statue, and I literally mean rear, David's spectacularly sculpted gluteus maximus. While making some notes in my portfolio notepad, someone sat down next to me. I looked up, and there was Mr. Hollywood, watching me. Closing my notebook, I looked back at him with a stone-cold stare, not saying a word.

"You probably won't understand what I'm saying, but since I saw you, you haven't left my mind. What a beautiful woman you are with the deepest emerald green eyes and dark red hair that can only be described as blazing fire when the sun hits it. Will you have a glass of wine with me? Vino?" as he pantomimed lifting a glass, drinking and pointing at me and then himself.

I looked at him for the longest time, not changing my expression. I got up and turned to him. In English, I spoke succinctly. "I understand you perfectly, better than you think. Really? That's quite a line. Have you road tested it a lot? . . .Oh, of course you have." I raised my voice addressing the room, "Hey everyone; it's Ben Langford, the movie star."

The shocked look on his face was priceless as hordes of gallery visitors rushed to surround him, leaving him unable to move as I walked out of the gallery. I sped back to my apartment. I felt guilty that I left the gallery guards with a near-riot on their hands. Well, okay, maybe not terribly guilty, but with a feeling verging on glee.

I stayed in my apartment for the afternoon, making more notes and adding information to my spreadsheet. With a scheduled Zoom meeting at 4 PM with Dr. M; I wanted to be ready to show my progress.

I took a shower and traded in my dress slacks and jacket for jeans and a knit top.

The meeting progressed well with Dr. M. I emailed him a copy of the spreadsheet, and it impressed him with all the contacts I could nail down. He told me I was working too many hours and to take the next three days off and let myself adjust to the jetlag. I told him I would try my best to dial back.

I emailed Chase and Gage. They had arrived in their respective countries and were beyond tired. It took almost twenty-two hours of travel time to get to their destinations. They were both happy with their student housing and would email or phone after they got some rest. After many I love yous, I sat back to contemplate how our lives had changed in a manner of months. They had grown up while I was growing down, letting loose and feeling young again.

I no longer focused on preparing family meals, keeping tabs on my son's activities, checking homework, or scheduling medical and dental care as the responsible adult. I had married so young, not that I regret having my babies, but I had never had very many youthful experiences. Now I felt free to discover the real ME. Not Mrs. Herrera, not mom, but the real Brenna Maureen Souchek-Herrera.

CHAPTER SEVEN

I walked down to the piazza by the Duomo, sitting down at a ristorante to dine al fresco. I ordered an excellent sweet white wine and an antipasto plate at the waiter's suggestion. After opening my portfolio notebook, I scrutinized my notes when a shadow fell over the table. I looked up.

"May I join you? You owe me at least that after the stunt you pulled on me today," said Ben Langford.

"I guess I do, but you deserved it," as I pointed to the seat across from me.

"You know who I am, but I highly doubt that your real name is Jane Doe."

"It's Brenna."

"Just Brenna?" he asked.

"Just Brenna." The waiter hurried over to the table, trying to hide his excitement.

"I'll have a glass of merlot, please." Ben turned his attention back to me. "You're American, aren't you?"

"Yes, I am. What gave me away?" I asked.

"Your command of English and the accent. I'm very impressed with your Italian language skills. Every time our paths crossed, you spoke like a native. You convinced me at first that you were Florentine. Do you live here?"

"Temporarily. What about you?" I asked as a smirk spread across my face.

"I know you're yanking my chain. I'm just a guy from Hutchinson, Kansas, in movies. We're filming on the other side of the bridge."

"I heard that. Why are you stalking me?" I would not let his killer dark good looks, abundant charm, and sparkling smile eradicate my abhorrence for his despicable behavior from the previous day.

"Not really; you happened to be at the same places I was; however, kissing you was an added and enjoyable bonus."

"About that. What gives you the right to accost women on the street? I don't give a damn who you think you are. If the polizia had been around, I would have had you arrested," I said.

"I apologize for that, but it was necessary, not necessarily the kiss part, but to use you as a shield. A gang of girls chased me down the street, and it gets dangerous when several people are involved. Last year I had my shoulder dislocated because a couple of enthusiastic fans were pulling my arms while others were ripping my clothes to shreds. I didn't want a repeat of the shoulder injury and didn't want to run down the street naked. Being well known is not all it's cracked up to be," Ben said.

"I guess I have to forgive you, somewhat, in that case, for using me as a safeguard, but not the kissing. If you had asked for help instead of manhandling me, I would have been happy to show you an escape route. Don't you people travel with a posse or a coterie of handlers? Does this happen often?"

"More often than you might think, but going around with body-guards or a bunch of hangers-on draws more attention. It gets old fast. I appreciate people like what I do, but I'm tired of it after twenty years in this business. As for asking you anything, I didn't realize you spoke English. My Italian is very sketchy. I'll try to be more polite if it happens again."

"It must be like living in a fishbowl. I don't envy your life. Not having a moment of peace when outside your door, or not being able to enjoy the simpler things in life, like going to a museum."

"That was quite resourceful of you. I can laugh about it now, but it was a little unpredictable and disturbing. I meant what I said to you at the Accademia. Ever since I saw you by the Uffizi, your image lingered in my mind. You're a beautiful woman, and I would like to know you better. Would you consider having dinner with me? A normal conversation with someone who isn't after me would be great. I will even replace your gelato if you promise not to dump it on me. I have one question before we consider dinner. Are you married?"

"I'm not married, and according to a People Magazine I read in my dentist's office, you're not either. Yes, I would like to go to dinner. To take a modified line from a Tom Cruise movie, 'you had me at gelato.'"

We continued to chat, becoming more comfortable with each other. I called Giorgio and let him know I was with Ben, looking for a ristorante that would offer good food and privacy. I wasn't dressed for anything fancy. Giorgio gave me the name of a place a couple of blocks away. He offered to call the proprietor, a good friend, and have him save a table in a secluded corner. I thanked him for his help. He was laughing when he said he would see me tomorrow.

We found the ristorante off the main tourist streets that seemed to be frequented by the locals. The lighting was dim; the proprietor seated us away from the main dining room in a quiet alcove surrounded by greenery. As we caught up on our conversation, I felt my angst easing. We talked about our families and growing up in rural mid-America. Ben had parents and three siblings still in Kansas.

While he spoke of his early childhood, I took in his physical perfection—black hair, long-lashed intense brown eyes, square jaw, and a smile that lit up the room. Ben had enough scruff on his face to be sexy, short of the unkempt look. At six foot four inches and a body best described as Chippendale flawless, he towered over my mire five foot six inches. What surprised me was that Ben didn't seem to put a lot of importance on his looks. He said his three brothers were better looking than he was. We talked about our marriages.

"I was nineteen when I met Marco, married and a mother by twenty. We were happy for ten years until my husband passed away. Since then, I have been both mother and father to Gage and Chase. They are off on their own in Japan and China for the next year in a foreign study program."

"That must make you around forty years old. My official publicity bio says that I'm thirty-seven, but in reality, I'm forty-two. As for my marriages, the first lasted one year and the second six months."

"If you don't mind me asking, what went wrong?"

"I wanted children. Both Simone and Courtney said they did too, until they got the rings on their fingers. Before the ink was dry on our marriage licenses, all they wanted from me was 'Could I get them in this movie or that movie? Could I help them get an audition for this or that?' I concluded they didn't love me as a person but as a vehicle to boost their careers. As I think back, I probably didn't love them either. I wanted a family, a more normal life.

"Sure, the glitz and glamor of acting were exhilarating, and I lived the lifestyle. After a while, I knew it wasn't the real me. The people I associated with were plastic and fake. I was living in a superficial world with no substance, only self-aggrandizement. I love acting and seeing a great story come to life, but I don't love the lack of a private life or the lies printed about me. While I can live with the gossip, my parents, brothers, and their families get upset and have difficulty dealing with the more salacious stories.

"Most of what people see in the gossip rags are less than half-truths, with no way of fighting it without creating more drama. Now enough about me. How about you? Do you love what you're doing?"

"I enjoy what I'm doing, especially this assignment, researching a foreign study program for the college. The people I work with are wonderful and supportive and were there for me through the rough times. I was busy raising the boys and ensuring they felt secure and loved, but I never felt that Chicago was my home. I inherited my grandmother's house after her death in Hartsuff and have been giving more thought to returning to my roots when my sons are secure in their careers. Meanwhile, I can't see myself continuing to live in a big city away from my large extended family. I miss the smell of the earth at home, the sight of the rolling sandhills, the glowing sunsets, the big starry skies, and a simpler way of life. I'm surrounded by the people I have known all my life. Sometimes I feel like I'm going through the motions of living since Marco's death."

"No boyfriend or thoughts of marrying again?" Ben asked.

"I dated, but I couldn't work up the enthusiasm for a relationship. Perhaps a person has only one great love in their life, and I had mine for a short ten years. Let's change the subject; this is too depressing."

"How did you become so familiar with Italy? I am so impressed with your fluent Italian language skills?"

"My husband was born and raised in Siena, a small town about fifty miles south of Florence. Every year, we traveled back to Italy since the boys were born to visit his parents. Over the years, Marco spoke only Italian at home so we could perfect our skills.

"It has been an absolute delight to talk to my in-laws and keep them up-to-date with their grandsons. I have always thought it was a real benefit for any child to be bilingual. Now Gage is fluent in Japanese and Chase in Chinese as well as Italian. Their language skills will be a big boon as they develop their careers in International Finance."

"You must be very proud. It must be hard enough to raise children with two parents, more than doubly hard with only one, especially with the stresses in today's world."

"It's had its moments, to be sure. Chase and Gage did their best to push the limits of my tolerance, but we all came through. I am very proud of the men they have become."

"Do you think I'm too old to be a father? I want children, and someday I will find the right woman for me—My One Great Love."

"I hope you do, and you're not too old. Many men didn't have children until later in life. I have no doubt you would be a good father. But you have to stop kissing random women, not a great way to find your true love. Ben, do you realize we have been here three hours? I need to get back to my apartment and do some work. You must have something to get back to."

"We're shooting late tonight and tomorrow night. We won't start until 2 AM. I'll grab some shuteye for a couple of hours before I have to be ready. Let me walk you back to your apartment, so I know you're safe. You never know if there are people around stalking beautiful women waiting for an opportunity to take advantage," Ben said with a wink.

"That seems to work as your modus operandi. Well used and moderately successful, is it?" When Ben did not comment, I was sure there was some merit to my statement.

We left the restaurant after Ben discreetly paid the bill. Then, walking back to my apartment, I gave Ben a brief history of Florence and the surrounding towns and villages with some tips for the must-sees. I suggested he visit the Tuscan Hills, the Wine Country, the many Medici palaces, the Duomo Skywalk, and the Leonardo da Vinci Museum. And if adventurous, a Tuscany Vespa tour would give him a genuine feel for the history and culture of Florence and the Italian people.

"Are you cold?" he asked as I tried to stifle a shiver. Lost to the night, the sun dipped, and the temperature cooled as we walked through the dark, narrow streets. Ben put his arm around my shoulders; neither of us had a jacket. We stopped in front of my building.

"This sure looks familiar," he said.

"About that, I asked Giorgio and his partner Carlo not to tell anyone that I was staying here. And they both speak fairly good English. You amused them when you were pantomiming what you were trying to say in your limited Italian."

"Gee, thanks. Now I feel totally foolish."

"Don't be; they only played stupid for me, so blame me, not them."

"I'll only forgive you if you let me hang out with you tomorrow afternoon."

"Won't you be exhausted after your night shoot?"

"I can sleep in the morning and take a nap before I'm needed at work. What do you have on the agenda for tomorrow?"

"I was going to wander around and find places the students might be interested in visiting for recreation, fast-food places, clubs, and anything else younger people might be interested in. My boss told me to take the next three days off since I have accomplished so much already. I want to go over to Siena and visit my in-laws. I have a date for a drink in the early evening with Antonia from the Accademia. Won't it be uncomfortable for you to be out in public?"

"I'll think of something. Getting to know you was fun. I haven't felt this comfortable with anyone for a long time. If you would rather not have me along, I'll understand."

"That's not it. I had a good time with you, too. I don't want to see you get mauled or carried off by a bunch of crazed fans. How are you going to get back to your hotel unmolested?"

"What's the address here? I'll call one of the crew to come pick me up." Ben made his call. "Someone will be here in five minutes."

He asked for my cell number. I felt it was safe enough to give it to him.

"If you see the name 'Bob Smith' come up on the caller ID, that's me. I promise I won't make a pest of myself." A compact car drove down the street as we stood in front of the door. "That's my ride. Again, I had a great evening. Thank you."

He leaned over and kissed me on the forehead. I waved goodbye and slipped my key into the lock, and ran up the stairs. Unfortunately, I didn't get to my apartment before Giorgio and Carlo waylaid me.

"Well? What happened? Is he as nice as he seemed?" Giorgio asked.

"I found him a decent man and good company. So unless he's doing a real number on me, I wouldn't mind having him as a friend."

"Only a friend, cara? You are single; he is single. This is Italy where the national pastime is making love, no problem."

"I can't do that, Giorgio. If I make love with someone, I have to be IN love. It wouldn't be casual to me. There's no likely future with Ben. He's a well-known film star with a lifestyle that I don't want any part of. We're too different in what we want for the future."

"I know the kind of woman you are. Promise to enjoy what's in front of you for the time you have with each other."

"I will, Giorgio. Good night." I entered my apartment and collapsed on the sofa. I didn't feel like doing any work tonight. After checking my email, I found some messages from my sons, Betsy, Michele, and my cousin Maggie, in Nebraska. I took a shower, washed my hair, and then tackled my college email, answering everyone back with the highlights of my fact-finding. Not mentioning meeting Ben in my responses, I kept that tidbit to myself. I didn't want to answer questions or appease their curiosity about him. Our association was an acquaintance and over soon, nothing more. Betsy and Michele said the office was running smoothly, and Dr. M was happy with my reports. My sons seemed to be doing well, enjoying their studies and familiarizing themselves with their exotic locations.

With Maggie, I was more open. I described meeting someone and having a good time, then asked her for a favor. I wanted to find a contractor to look at grandma's front wrap-around porch and see if we could save it. The last time I was home, it was deteriorating, and I wanted it preserved before it fell completely apart. I didn't think it could withstand another prairie winter. Also, I wanted to replace all the windows and add insulation to the walls and attic. I wanted to do that for Grandma while she was alive, but I didn't want to embarrass her with the offer. She was a proud, independent woman with limited income, and I didn't want to hurt her feelings.

After finishing all my emails and drying my hair, I climbed the spiral stairway to the sleeping loft. I tried to read a book, but my mind kept wandering. I couldn't deny that I was very drawn to Ben. Not the movie star, but the man. I was feeling long, dormant twinges of physical attraction. I had to get a grip. Nothing good could come from having a brief affair with Ben, a man I didn't really know. I would only get hurt and kick myself later for being so foolish.

I gave up any attempt to read and was about to turn off the light when my phone beeped with an incoming text message. It was from 'Bob Smith'. I opened the message: *I like you very much. Sleep well.* That did it. I knew I would spend the night tossing and turning.

CHAPTER EIGHT

At a relaxing breakfast the following day, the B & B had four new guests at the table. Carlo offered my help for recommendations on sightseeing locations. I gave the two couples a history of the area and a list of the must-sees. Then, with cameras ready, they headed out the door.

Giorgio asked what my plans were for the day. I mentioned I planned to spend a couple of hours with Nonna and Nonno, do some afternoon wandering, and then meet Antonia for drinks. The three of us avoided mentioning Ben, but that topic was foremost in everyone's mind.

On my return to Florence from Siena by bus after visiting with my in-laws, I took a leisurely walk to the Piazza di Duomo and sat at what was becoming my usual spot to have a cup of espresso. I read the regional newspaper, La Nazione, to see if I could glean information on things to do and find anything that would hold the interest of the college crowd.

While sitting outside, people watching, I got a text from "Bob", asking if I wanted company and where to meet. A fleeting thought was to ignore the message. I could nip whatever this thing was, in the bud—no harm, no foul. I could go on my merry way, not risking my emotions. But, is that what I wanted? I thought about it for a couple of minutes, staring down at my phone. I knew I wanted to see him again, and I recognized I would probably regret it if I didn't.

I texted him back. *Yes. Piazza di Duomo.* I sat down on one of the benches by the Cathedral, closing my eyes with my face to the sun. I felt someone sitting down next to me. As I pried one eye open, I squinted at an older man next to me. I closed my eye again when I heard a familiar voice.

"Brenna."

I looked around, not seeing Ben, when I heard a chuckle coming from the older man with gray hair and a goatee. I took a closer look; to my astonishment, it was Ben. I burst out laughing. "How did you do that?"

"We have a very talented makeup department."

"Do you want a cup of coffee or do some sightseeing?"

"Let's do the sightseeing before this getup gets too hot. I have to get back to the shoot later this afternoon for some car chase scenes. I'll need time to get this camouflage off."

"Aren't chase scenes dangerous?"

"Not for me. My stunt double does all the driving. I have to be in a stationary car and look like I'm driving. Would you like to come to the set and watch the filming?"

"I'd like that if I wouldn't be in the way."

"Not at all. We have guests on set all the time."

"Would it be too much to include Giorgio and Carlo?"

"No problem. Have your friends meet us here at 4 PM, and we can go over to the set together."

I called Giorgio and extended Ben's invitation. It was as if he had won the SuperEnalotto, the Italian lottery. They would meet us at the appointed time. Ben and I strolled over to the Cathedral. We walked in and took in the beauty of the centerpiece of Florence, the Cattedrale di Santa Maria del Fiore, or the Cathedral of Saint Mary of the Flowers. It's one of the most beautiful churches I have ever seen, and I've seen many. I told Ben about Brunelleschi's dome for the church and what an incomparable architectural triumph it was for its time. We slowly walked through, looking at the details and examining the fresco art. There weren't any adequate words to describe our feelings amid the beauty before us. Finally, we left the church and walked over to the Baptistery just steps away.

Reproduction doors of Lorenzo Ghiberti's Gates of Paradise stood at the threshold with doors composed of ten rectangular bronze panels displayed in two lines depicting scenes of the Old Testament. The original doors were at a small museum behind the cathedral under restoration. We entered the building, the oldest religious monument in Florence, with an octagonal shape and lantern with a cupola. The interior was more breathtaking than the cathedral. It was like being encased in a golden snow globe, but instead of snow, it was gilt. We wandered around in awe, trying to take everything in. Then it was time to leave. Ben had to get back to work.

"You are so knowledgeable. How did you come by all this scholarly information?" Ben asked.

"When my sons were old enough, I researched the history so that I could give them the details of what they were seeing. It fascinated me. The more I dug, the more I wanted to know about everything in Florence and Siena."

"I hate to stop, but we have to go. Do you see your friends?"

I spotted Giorgio and Carlo waiting for us in the piazza. Ben called a crew member to pick us up. We arrived where the film crew worked that day. We "civilians" found a place to watch all the action. It was interesting to see how the stunts were rehearsed before they filmed the scene. There were a lot of stops and waiting while they set different scenes. Ben had shed his tourist makeup and was too busy to talk with us. After a couple of hours, everyone broke for a meal. We ate at tables next to a catering truck.

After dining, work continued, and I watched Ben go through several takes. I thought we, or me specifically, were a distraction. I signaled to Ben that Giorgio, Carlo, and I were going to leave. Ben nodded as we walked a couple of blocks and got a cab for our return to the real world on the other side of the Arno River.

Carlo and Giorgio were chattering in supersonic Italian like howler monkeys. The guys left for home, and I walked to meet Antonia for a glass of wine. I remained quiet while Antonia told me all the details of a near-riot yesterday at the Accademia caused by Ben Langford. It took almost an hour to restore calm. Once I got her off the subject of Ben, she supplied me with some helpful information on places for recreation for students; soccer fields, running tracks, and cinemas. We chatted for a couple of hours and had a bite to eat. I thanked her for meeting me, and we departed for the evening.

I walked back to my apartment and enclosed myself in solitude. After seeing Ben at work, it gave me concrete evidence of how very different our lives are. We live in two separate worlds. As much as I liked Ben, there was no sense in furthering our acquaintance. I sent him a text thanking him for allowing me to watch him at work, finishing my message with an ambiguous: *See you around.*

I let Giorgio know I was spending the weekend in Siena with my in-laws at breakfast the following day. He asked me to tell his godmother, Nonna, hello. I asked him not to tell anyone where I was. He gave me a questioning look; I turned away without further elaboration.

Giorgio let me use his car, a Fiat Spider, to drive the fifty miles to Siena. It was a lovely day, and driving through the beautiful, vibrant green of the countryside worked to clear my head. The scenery was gorgeous, with patchwork fields, olive groves, and terraced vineyards dotting the landscape.

I took my iPad with me so that I could contact my sons and they could talk with Nonno and Nonna. After arriving at their little stone house, I was happy to see my in-laws looking relaxed. They embraced me, welcoming me back with enthusiastic kisses and hugs.

I could tell the years were catching up with them, and losing their son didn't help. Nonna ushered me into their home and insisted I stay with them for the night. She called her other son and daughter, which precipitated a big family dinner with the grandchildren. I got out my iPad and connected with Chase in China. He was six hours ahead, so the timing worked out for him. Grandpa and Grandma Herrera chirped like magpies for a half-hour. Then it was Gage's turn in Japan.

It thrilled Nonno and Nonna at the technology that allowed them to keep in touch with Marco's sons. Our sons looked so much like their father. I spent the day in the kitchen helping to make bread and fresh pasta. The families arrived, and we ate and drank on the terrace until the wee hours. I was so relaxed reconnecting with my big Italian family, but missing Marco more than ever. The specter of his presence was everywhere in his childhood home. The family gathering felt so incomplete without my husband and our sons.

Marco's sister took me aside and asked me if I had found someone to love again. I told her that no one could ever take her brother's place. She reminded me I was too young to spend my life alone. I wouldn't be replacing Marco, but moving on was something I had to do to find happiness again. Marco would want that. I thanked her for her kind thoughts.

I lay in bed that night, going over her words. This was the middle point of my life. I didn't want to spend the rest of it alone. My sons would be independent soon. What did I have to look forward to? Another twenty-five years at the college? More years alone in a city I didn't feel was home? A kernel of thought was germinating in my brain, but I put all thoughts of my future on the back burner for now. I was trying to live in the moment, a foreign concept for me. I was a full-fledged member of Worrywarts Anonymous.

I drove to church in the morning with my in-laws, and after a mid-day meal, I started my drive back to Florence. Giorgio and Carlo were waiting for me when I came through the door. Ben had been by yesterday morning asking for me. They assured me they didn't tell him where I was, just out of the city for the weekend. I thanked them for their discretion and let myself into my apartment. I knew it must puzzle them as to my disinterest in furthering my acquaintance with Ben.

I turned on my phone, the first time in two days. Ben had texted me a half dozen times and left a voice mail. I shut off my phone again, then worked on my spreadsheet. I wanted to keep everything up-to-date and make a list of what I hope to accomplish the following week.

It had been a tiring first week, and I felt exhausted. I took a long bath in my skinny little European tub and soaked for an hour. I hand-washed my fancy underwear and set it on the towel warming bars to dry. After emailing the boys, I dragged myself up the stairs to bed. The only relationship I was interested in furthering was with Morpheus, the god of sleep.

CHAPTER NINE

Breakfast was late for me the following day. I had slept so soundly that I didn't hear my phone alarm. After the eight guests staying at the B & B left for the day, Giorgio turned to me.

"Did something happen between you and Ben?"

"Why do you ask?"

"Cara, I can see with my own two eyes how smitten you are with each other, and you are both miserable. Have you talked to him?"

"It's useless, Giorgio. I'm very attracted to him, but I don't know him. His life is very public, and I am not. I don't want my heart broken or to be another conquest for him. It can't lead anywhere, so why go any further? He has a parade of women chasing him all the time. I will not be one of them."

"Have you ever considered that he might be just as lonely in a crowd?"

"I can't be a temporary diversion for his loneliness. For a long time, I have been a single parent. I'm tired. I can't take care of another person until I can take care of myself."

"Oh my cara, if only I were straight, I would be on you like a warm fuzzy blanket on a cold winter night."

"I love you, Giorgio. You'd be in deep trouble if you were straight," I laughed.

I spent the next three weeks making more connections for the college students, interviewing licensed tour guides and bus drivers. Hospitals, health clinics, and van rental businesses were visited. I found the perfect mode of transportation for out-of-the-city trips: a Mercedes-Benz fifteen-passenger van with handicapped accessibility at a local dealership. I entered all the contact information into my growing spreadsheet. My boss seemed to be happy with my progress when I held weekly Zoom meetings with him.

"I knew you were the right woman for the job," Dr. M commented.

"I'm planning on researching Rome my last two weeks and scoping out all the points of interest for a three to five-day tour. We might want to consider trips to Venice, 167 miles from Florence, for a two-day trip and Pisa only 60 miles away for a one-day tour. Anyone visiting Italy might feel cheated missing these close cities, which have architectural value for our students. How else would our students be able to send the goofy pictures of holding up the Leaning Tower with their hands home to their parents and friends?"

"That's perfect. Keep me up-to-date and take some time to enjoy."

My last weeks in Florence, I visited all the other points of interest; the many Medici Palaces, including the Pitti Palace across the river and the Ponte Vecchio for some serious shopping. I stopped on the bridge and got some gold earrings for Michele, Betsy, and Maggie, adding cufflinks for my sons. The piazza Santa Croce offered a vast array of leather goods, and I purchased a leather notebook for Dr. M.

I did a slow tour of every location of interest mixed in with my shopping. I had time to enjoy the details and talk at length with the curators. After making brief trips to Venice and Pisa, collecting contact information adding more information to my spreadsheet, I spent a whole day in my apartment writing thank-you notes for all the contacts I made in Italy, including my contact information. I had delved into every nook and cranny in Florence, Pisa, and Venice that I thought had value for our students. I nailed down all the information needed to make this academic offering a success.

Before I left for Rome, I had two more days in Florence. I returned to the Uffizi Gallery and sat on a bench in front of my favorite painting, The Birth of Venus. Tourists were coming in and out of the room until I felt a lingering presence behind me.

"She looks like you, you know," said a voice I was all too familiar with.

I turned and looked behind me; it was Ben. We looked at each other without saying a word. He walked around the bench and sat down beside me.

"Why didn't you return my calls? Did I do or say something to offend you?"

"This might sound kind of trite; it wasn't you. It's me."

"How so?" Ben asked.

"You can't be part of my life, and I can't be part of yours. I'm very attracted to you. That hasn't happened to me in a very long time. I was afraid I would get hurt. You lead a very public life in the fast lane. I'm a country girl at heart waiting to decide where I belong."

As he looked at the painting, Ben murmured, "Do you think Venus was afraid to step out of her shell and find out what life had in store for her? You are her, a goddess of love, beauty, and desire. Can you see giving me a chance? Can we be friends?"

"I don't know if that's possible," I said.

"Will you go out to dinner with me? We need to talk."

"It won't change anything, but yes, I would like to have dinner."

We left the gallery and found a quiet restaurant nearby. No one noticed Ben with his gray hair, even with the missing goatee. Ben took my hand in his over glasses of wine after the waiter took our order.

"I missed you. I've been in Rome for two weeks and will be there for two more, finishing up the set work at the Cinecittà Film Studios. It's been hard to keep my mind on my work, thinking about what might have happened for you to shut me out as you did. I wanted to think we had become friends. I have people around me all day, but I can't say they were friends. I enjoyed your company so much and appreciated getting to know you."

"I enjoyed spending time with you, too. Maybe too much. You did nothing wrong. What you do for a living was overwhelming, a world I couldn't relate to."

"What I do for a living is smoke and mirrors. It's not real, and I know that. I have two short failed marriages and a few staunch friends that I can count on one hand. I'm forty-two years old, and could walk away from it all tomorrow. My career is not the real me, but what I do."

"Do you think you could ever be happy doing something else?" I asked.

"For a while, I have been thinking of getting behind the camera instead of in front of it. I have an interest in directing and producing. Many film people live normal lives outside Hollywood; Ron Howard, Tom Hanks, and even George Clooney. I want a family to come home to."

"I want to see more of you as friends. I will be in Rome for two weeks. I am leaving here in two days. Perhaps we can get together when you're not working. Friends?" I asked.

"Friends."

We had a wonderful dinner, and Ben walked me back to the B & B. He was flying back to Rome that night. When I got to the city, I promised to call him. I spent my last two days doing my laundry, saying goodbye to my in-laws, and spending time with Giorgio and Carlo, telling them about my dinner with Ben and how we agreed to be friends.

"I wish you well, cara. Don't look for obstacles that aren't there. Life is to be lived, and you haven't lived since Marco's death. The next time you visit Florence, I want to see you happy."

After kisses, hugs, and a few tears, I packed my bags and caught a cab for my trip to the Florence airport. It was a short flight, just under two hours. I had made a reservation for my two-week stay at the moderately priced Condotti Boutique Hotel in central Rome. First, I texted Ben, letting him know I had arrived. Then, I set up my laptop and emailed my sons, Dr. M, Betsy, and Michele.

I received an email from my cousin Maggie with the estimate for the restoration and improvements for grandma's house in Hartsuff that I had requested. She contacted my old high school boyfriend, Sam, now in the construction/remodeling business. Great Uncle John had taken him through the house. The estimate sounded reasonable, so I emailed Sam directly and told him to start the porch restoration and order the windows. I directed my banker to transfer the money to his bank. Then I would make a trip to the house on my return from Italy to discuss the rest of the renovations. I made enough money from the rental of the condo to pay for the repairs and improvements.

With that taken care of, I started making my lists for the sights of Rome that would fit into a three to five-day student trip. Ben called and invited me out to dinner. I was too tired to think about finding a place to dine on my own, so I said yes. He would pick me up at 7 PM, leaving me a couple of hours to unpack, bathe, and take a catnap.

I was ready when Ben texted he was downstairs. After taking the elevator to the ground floor, I saw Ben with a huge smile on his face. With my hand in his, we got into his car for a nerve-racking drive to a restaurant that he was fond of, for the incredible food and privacy. We arrived after a harrowing journey through crazy Roman traffic without mishap to a beautiful restaurant across from the Coliseum. A table in a private, quiet corner sheltered us as we looked out over the ancient ruins. After ordering some wine and our entrees, we slipped into easy conversation. He inquired what my schedule looked like for my two weeks in Rome.

"More of the same as what I did in Florence, except for a shorter schedule. I'll have to whittle down what we can tour in a reasonable time frame."

"Don't you tire of running around planning and not seeing the sights at leisure?"

"I've been here before with my husband and children several times, so I had the chance to take my time. I know the highlights, so I have to make some contacts and pick the places that make the most sense for a brief tour. What does your schedule look like?"

"It's not as frantic as a location schedule. The filming is short takes, and all indoors, we don't have to deal with unpredictable weather. I'm not on the shooting schedule for a couple of days this week. Another camera crew is busy shooting exterior shots that don't involve me. Mind if I tag along with you when you go out? If you go to St Peter's in Vatican City on one of those days, that would be great. I have never taken the time to see it."

"I'll arrange to go there when you're free. Just let me know the dates."

"Have I told you how beautiful you are? You have the most wonderful hair; it looks dark red until the sun hits it. Not red and not blond, but a combination of the two. I love looking at you."

"Thank you, Ben. That's very sweet of you."

"Just wanted to tell a friend what I think."

I smiled as our antipasto salads arrived with a discreet waiter who looked Ben over but didn't say a word. That was refreshing, since he wasn't wearing a disguise. The wine was excellent, and I had a second glass, which I rarely did. It loosened my tongue enough when Ben asked about my early life in Nebraska. I held nothing back.

"My father died when I was two years old. My mother took me to California with her. She had always hated country life, so she escaped with me in tow after my father's death. Even at a young age, I remember that life wasn't easy, and I feared her.

"She had a temper and would often slap me. I didn't know why. It became normal after a while. When I was three, my mother took me to see Grandma and dropped me off for the summer. She never came back, and I never heard from her again. Grandma formally adopted me and raised me as her own. I would like to think that the only thing inherited from my birth mother was my Irish coloring and name. Everything I am today is because of my grandmother.

"Our life in the country was simple yet wonderful. I knew love for the first time. We had a cow, chickens, and my Great Uncle John kept some pigs in one of our pens. I lived with Grandma until I attended college at Northwestern on a scholarship. Nothing out of the ordinary, just the love of a large extended family and a beautiful, wholesome place to grow up. What's your family in Kansas like?"

"My parents are Will and Vickie or Victoria, when my dad gets mad. I have three brothers still in the area around Hutchinson. They are all married and produced a pack of grandchildren, numbering twelve at last count. I'm the oldest and a disappointment to my mother for not providing any offspring to add to the grandbaby scorecard. Other than that, they seem to be proud of my success. Unfortunately, I don't get home to see them enough. After high school graduation, I attended the California Institute of the Arts in Santa Clarita for film school. Somehow, I ended up an actor instead of a filmmaker. As the saying goes, the rest is history."

Our entrees came with a different wine. My mushroom risotto was excellent, and Ben's chicken alfredo was equally delicious. We traded plates when we had eaten half finishing our dinner with a small glass of aged Italian brandy called Grappa, a digestif with the intense flavor of plums and a twist of honey. We continued talking about our lives. Our early years were very similar, and we had many common interests. Before I knew it, three hours had gone by.

After dinner, we took a walk around the Coliseum hand-in-hand. I needed the fresh air. I was a little tipsy. "You can almost hear the echoes of the thousands of spectators, the cries of the animals as they are slaughtered, and the clash of the gladiators as they fought to the death. All in the name of entertainment for the blood-thirsty ego of an emperor," I said.

Traffic calmed a little by 11 PM, and Ben drove me back to my hotel. He parked and escorted me to the door of my room. I thanked Ben for a delightful evening and reminded him to let me know when he had a free day. He took my face in his hands and kissed me on both cheeks, as is customary in Europe. I unlocked my door. The echo of his footfalls faded as he disappeared down the hallway.

The first four days of my Rome assignment were searching out accommodations for the students in the Eternal City. There was a lot of student housing available, and I made the connections for future tours, again checking for cleanliness and security. I had to condense what the students would see in a limited stay, highlighting the most important sights.

The Coliseum has to rank as number one, followed by The Victor Emanuel Monument, The Pantheon, The Roman Forum, and The Palatine Hill for the first two days. I would reserve the third day for St. Peter's Basilica in Vatican City. I would devote another day to the Trevi Fountain, and a city bus tour with free time for group shopping on the last day. There was so much available for so little time. There was a regular commuter schedule of pre-dawn flights to Rome and post-midnight flights back to Florence. It would be a whirlwind of activity. I hoped that the student advisors/instructors acting as chaperones could keep up with such a frantic pace. In the city, mass transit systems were reliable for moving from one place to another. This portion of the program would not be for the faint of heart.

Ben had a day off from shooting to join me for an in-depth tour of St. Peter's. I suggested he make use of his "Grandpa" hairpiece. St. Peter's Basilica was highly populated with tourists every day of the week, and his presence would certainly be noticed if not in disguise.

I made a reservation for the earliest entry time to avoid standing in line at the Basilica. Ben met me at my hotel with time for a cup of espresso before taking a taxi to Vatican City. The crowds were already assembling at an early hour, but we sailed right through the church entrance with our reservation.

Ben's mouth dropped open in awe as he surveyed the magnificent interior for the first time. I enjoyed seeing his reaction. Since we were not on a guided tour, we were free to wander the glorious splendor at our own pace. Raised as a Catholic, for Ben, this mecca of faith meant a lot to him. We spent the entire day going from the chapel to chapel from Michelangelo's Pieta right inside the basilica door on the right to the Sistine Chapel and the Vatican gardens. St. Peter's Basilica is an overwhelming experience for a first-time tourist. There is so much to take in and vast in scope—almost more than what the mind can absorb in one visit.

I met a few minutes with Monsignor Father Franco, director of the Basilica museums, introducing myself and my mission. We exchanged contact information for a future tour. Ben bought a dozen Pope blessed rosaries for his family in Kansas at the Basilica gift shop. I had to chuckle when the gift store attendant read the name on Ben's credit card and looked at him with awe. Ben took his purchases and gave the shocked young lady a wink. We left the shop before she could spread the word of his presence.

Ben and I walked hand-in-hand along the cobbled streets at a leisurely pace, enjoying the atmosphere. We stopped at a ristorante for some dinner and a glass of wine. Falling into a comfortable companionship, and we felt at ease with each other, not talking about careers or pressures but our families' interests. We took a taxi over to the Trevi Fountain as night set in.

Packed tightly together, the tourists inched their way up to the base of the fountain to toss coins and make wishes. We pushed our way forward, and Ben handed me three coins to throw. I noticed he had three as well. I think he was aware of the significance—one coin for a return to Rome, a second coin to find love, and the third coin for marriage. We turned our backs, closed our eyes, and let the coins fly. As we slowly made our way out of the crowd, Ben's hairpiece slipped, and someone shouted out his name. People turned and approached with their cell phones pointed our way. To avoid being accosted, we ran for a taxi and sped away.

"I'm sorry that happened. Are you okay?" Ben asked.

"I'm fine. How about you?"

"I still have my clothes on, so that's a plus. But unfortunately, it's almost an expected occurrence."

"It must be a pain to deal with not being able to come and go as you please and experience the simple pleasures the rest of us take for granted. Don't you ever tire of it?"

"I'm thankful for the fans that like what I do, but sometimes it gets out of hand and downright scary. One incident stands out in my mind. I was in a restaurant and ventured into the restroom when some guy started taking pictures of me peeing. Regrettably, there have been many other ridiculous instances of invasion of privacy. I know how fortunate I am to have achieved my dreams, and I appreciate that, but sometimes I want to be a normal human being."

The taxi stopped in front of my hotel. We walked into the hotel bar and sat down at a table in the corner. Ben ordered some wine, and we continued our conversation. I was getting a real insight into his day-to-day life.

Ben continued, "I want to compartmentalize my life, separating the personal from the professional. That's why I think I want to try my hand at directing, removing myself from journalistic and public interest. I purchased the film options of a new book not too long ago that I thought would make a great movie. I contracted an award-winning writer to transform the book into a rough screenplay and now I'm waiting to see how it comes out."

"From what I have seen, I wouldn't trade my life for yours. I may not have drooling fans, but I live a quiet and satisfying life, raising my sons to be great adults. I have a job I enjoy and am good at, but I come and go as I please, having the freedom that you don't. It's sad that you have to miss out on the simple pleasures."

"At times, I would trade my life for yours. You are the kindest and bravest person I know. You have had to go through some very tough times, and you have come through it whole. I admire you and your strength. You are a beautiful woman with so much love to give, and you deserve to be loved just as much in return. Before I get all maudlin, I better walk you up to your room and get myself back to my hotel for some sleep. I have a couple of very heavy days coming up."

We walked to the elevator, holding hands in silence. Ben looked into my eyes at the door of my room, took my face in his hands, and lightly kissed my lips. "Thank you so much for giving me this incredible day." He hugged me tight and then stepped back, turning, and walked away.

I sat down in my room and thought about that kiss, thinking about my deep feelings for Ben. The possibility of more than friendship was fighting a war within my mind. I was yearning for a physical relationship again. That kiss told me I hadn't died with Marco but felt the healthy physical desires that a normal woman would feel with a man she loved.

Yes, I am in love with Ben. I tried to fight those feelings, but I had been a widow for a decade. I was too young never to love again. No one could ever take Marco's place, the father of my children, but I could add another chapter in this life and be happy again. But I didn't know if it was worth the risk with someone like Ben. Falling in love with him had disaster and heartache written all over it; warning myself wasn't working. I was sticking my head in the sand.

*   *   *

By late in the second week of my Roman stay, my last visit was to the U.S. Embassy to check on documentation required to enter the country with a group of students. I spent the next couple of days compiling all the data, making entries into the spreadsheet, and preparing sample itineraries with cost projections. I constructed sample permission documents for the student's parents or guardians, lists of readiness to travel duties, CDC immunization requirements, medical treatment releases, and an affidavit for proper student behavior. In addition, I prepared what I thought should be a checklist of the elements for acceptance as a student for a foreign study class. Did I mentioned that the legal age to order a drink in a bar or restaurant in Italy is sixteen? -yikes! I sent everything off to Dr. M. A couple of hours later; I received a return email from the President's Office:

> *Congratulations Brenna, I have never seen a more complete program developed by anyone. You did an incredible job, and I am very pleased. Now take the rest of your summer*

off and relax; you earned it. I look forward to seeing you in September.

Sincerely, Dr. Robert R. Michaels Ph.D.

President of the School of Art and Architecture of Chicago.

* * *

With my mission complete, the heavy weight of responsibility lifted off my shoulders. I had three more days until my scheduled return flight back to Chicago. I emailed my sons, checking in to see how everything was going for them and touching base with Betsy and Michele to tell them I had completed my assignment and would soon be back in the United States. How I missed having them as a sounding board for what I was feeling. I hadn't mentioned to them I was seeing anyone. That news could wait when I got home to Chicago.

The repairs on my Nebraska home were going well. Sam emailed me pictures of the progress on the porch project. He was restoring it to the original design to meld with the style of the house. I asked him to check the wiring to see if I needed to upgrade anything for an internet connection and satellite television. Grandma was not into modern technology. She was content as long as she had a working landline and television to watch her afternoon soap operas. I planned to visit the farm sometime soon to check on other improvements I wanted to make.

Ben texted me to see what I was up to. I returned his text saying I had completed my obligation and now I was a free woman for the next three days. Ben called and asked me if I was free for dinner. I told him I didn't know yet. I was waiting to hear from George Clooney. He responded that if a date with George fell through, would he be an acceptable substitute? I answered I would make the sacrifice and put George off until another time. Ben texted back to be ready at 7 PM and dress up. He would be by to pick me up.

I had only one dressy outfit with me. I pulled the black lace illusion dress out of my suitcase. It was so wrinkled it looked like a shar-pei puppy. I called the front desk and asked if the housekeeping staff could steam out the wrinkles. They would send someone up to my room immediately to collect the dress and have it back to me in short order.

It sounded like dinner tonight would be a special occasion, so I washed my hair, shaved my legs, and moisturized. I applied a careful makeup application and dug out my high-heeled shoes. The hotel staff returned my dress, ready to wear with the lacy black underwear that Michele and Betsy had given me as a bon voyage/get laid gift. Ben was in the lobby when I was ready to go.

The elevator took me to the first floor. I got the reaction I was hoping for. I could see in his face that I hit the mark on my fashion choice. Ben took my hand and led me out to a limousine. Settling ourselves in the back of the roomy car, I was curious about where we were going. "Is this a special occasion that I'm not aware of?" I asked.

"It is. I hope you'll think of it as a pleasant surprise. By the way, you look incredibly beautiful, stunning, in fact."

"Thank you. You cleaned up pretty well yourself, but I was growing fond of the gray hair and goatee." Ben was outfitted in a black Armani tux that fit him to perfection. I was getting a little nervous, not knowing what was in store for the night, and Ben wasn't giving out any hints. This evening would not be a regular dinner date. We made the short drive back to his hotel and walked into a private dining room.

The room was swarming with people I recognized from the film set dressed to the max. It was their wrap party. Glasses of champagne were soon in our hands, and Ben took my elbow and introduced me to his costars and crew. I thought I would be nervous, so far out of my element, but I wasn't with Ben by my side. I enjoyed meeting everyone and dancing in Ben's arms. We filled plates with finger foods and partook of the generous offers of champagne. I enjoyed myself, and the crew members were so friendly and complimentary with their comments about Ben. He was a favorite with the crew for being down-to-earth and not full of himself like others they had worked with.

We partied until about 1 AM when Ben asked if I would like to go up to his suite so we could have some private time. There was something he wanted to ask me. I was relaxed but not drunk, and I wanted this alone time with him, too. We held hands after leaving the party and walked to his suite. We sat down on the sofa in the living room. Ben took my hand, kissing my palm. He looked deeply into my eyes.

"I can no longer only be your friend, my darling Brenna. I'm in love with you. I want to be your best friend and your lover. I want to make love with you."

We stood up, and he took me in his arms and kissed me with all the passion he had been holding back. I kissed him back, matching his desire, wanting him to touch me as my tongue searched out the depths of his mouth. He molded his body to mine, and I could feel his hardness against my cleft, eager for entry. My breasts flattened against his chest. I was reaching a height of desire I had never felt before. Ben stepped back and took my hand as he led me to the bedroom.

"Are you sure, Brenna?" he asked.

"I want you, Ben. I want to make love with you."

We stood together, looking at each other, communicating without words. Ben reached behind my back and dragged the zipper of my dress down until it stopped. His fingers slipped the shoulders of my dress to the side of my arms as the material glided down my body and puddled with a whisper at my feet. Ben circled my waist with his hands and lifted me free of the silky black fabric. I stood before him, watching his eyes as he surveyed the length of my body.

"You are so beautiful, darling Brenna. I want to touch and taste every inch of you."

I whispered back, "You have too many clothes on. Let me make you more comfortable."

I slipped off his tuxedo jacket and dropped it on the floor, joining my dress. I pulled the ends of his tie and drew it slowly from his neck as our eyes remained locked on each other. My fingers worked their way down the placket of his shirt, removing the studs, revealing his muscled chest matted with black, curling hair. I peeled the shirt slowly off his shoulders, pulling it gently from the confines of his pants and dropping it to the floor. My hands lay flat on his chest as I moved them toward his nipples. I left a trail of soft kisses from his chest up to his neck. His scent invaded my senses and filled me with a need to taste his smooth, warm skin as my fingers surveyed the contours of his strong, well-muscled upper arms. The texture of his skin was so fluid, yet masculine at the same time. I wanted to explore every inch of his chest and arms, feeling every curve, every tendon kissing every inch that my fingers had touched.

Ben's need to touch and taste was as strong as mine. He lifted his arms and unhooked my bra, allowing it to fall off my body. He cupped my breasts, running his thumbs over my nipples. The peaks hardened as his mouth took command. His tongue laved the tips as he drew more of my breast into his mouth, with his teeth nipping gently at the tightening bud. My back arched with this exquisite pleasure that sent stabs of need down the length of my body. I dug my fingers into his shoulders as a moan escaped from my lips as I held on, wanting more, needing more as my breasts seemed to swell with my demand to consummate our coupling. My hands moved to his waistband as I lifted the belt free, and the button at the top of his trousers lost its hold. His zipper slowly lowered as my hand caressed his stiffness.

"Not yet, darling, I've just started," as Ben picked me up and laid me on the bed. He unhooked my garter belt and released the black silk stockings, rolling them slowly down my legs. He lifted the shoes off my feet. His lips kissed my ankles and slowly trailed up my calves, behind my knees, to my inner thighs. His warm mouth found the black scrap of lace covering my femininity, drawing the fabric to his lips. Ben moved to my side as his fingers found my thong and pulled it from my body. My fingers searched for his pants and underwear as I pushed them down his long legs. His thick, exposed sex found its way to the throbbing bud of my core.

Ben placed his fingers in the folds of my feminine flesh. He whispered, "You're wet and ready for me." As the tip of his penis found my moist opening. "You're so tight, darling; I don't want to hurt you."

My body stretched to accommodate his length, searching for my inner warmth. Then, as he slowly slid into me, we moved together in the timeless dance of bodies, seeking total fulfillment, meeting need for need. My legs circled his body as he moved inside me with accelerating speed, touching my inner bud as I fell over the edge as he came with his release.

I held him tight inside me as our breathing slowly returned to normal. Ben lay on top of me with his hands cupping my bottom, bringing me closer, burying himself as deep as he could while my fingertips traveled down the furrow of his spine. After a few minutes, we separated as Ben rolled to his side and encircled me in his arms.

Without words, we held each other as our bodies relaxed. I drew the sheet over us.

"Are you cold, darling?" he asked.

"A little. I already miss your warmth on me."

"Stay with me tonight?"

"I'm not going anywhere," I said.

We made love throughout the night, never seeming to get enough of our newborn intimacy. As the gray of early dawn slipped through the window, I got up and walked into the bathroom. I looked into the mirror and saw the face of a well-loved woman. My lips were swollen, and I was a little sore. Whisker burn painted patterns over my chest as my hand feathered over the slight abrasions. I used the toilet and then took a warm washcloth and wiped some of Ben's semen off me. After taking the two hotel bathrobes off the handers on the back of the bathroom door, I brought them to the bed. I crawled back under the sheet and pressed my body next to Ben's. I fell back to sleep with my arm across Ben's chest and my body molded to his side. A couple of hours later, I woke to Ben kissing my face and his hand cupping my breast.

"Good morning, my darling Brenna."

"Umm, yesssss, it is a good morning."

"Are you still planning on leaving in a couple of days?" Ben asked.

"That's the plan. Why?"

"Do you have to get back for any specific reason?"

"I finished my assignment. But, unfortunately, the boys aren't there, so I guess I have nothing to go back for immediately."

"Since my film wrapped, a friend of mine is lending me his house on one of the Greek Islands for a month. Would you consider coming with me?"

"I might. I don't want you to think I'm easy," I murmured, half-asleep.

"I know better than that. You're a beautiful lady that I happen to be in love with, and I can't bear letting you go."

"Tell me about this house?" I asked.

"It's secluded, and we won't be bothered. I've stayed there before when I needed to rest. There's a discreet staff to cook, shop, and clean. All we have to do is relax and enjoy each other. The house is on the island of Santorini."

"Have you brought other women there? I refuse to be one of the many or the flavor of the month in the knowing eyes of the staff."

"I have never brought any women to this house. It has only been me alone, and I have never even wanted to bring anyone else until I met you."

"I think you can talk me into it."

"Good. I'll make the arrangements for the flight, and we can pick up your things at your hotel later today."

"That sounds good, but can we have breakfast first? I'm hungry."

"Yes, we can. What would you like?"

"You." We headed for the shower a couple of hours later before we ordered breakfast.

*   *   *

I was a little embarrassed leaving the hotel wearing the same clothing from last night, with my silk stockings and garter belt in my purse, relieved that I didn't run into anyone we knew at Ben's hotel or mine. When I got back to my hotel room, I emailed my sons to tell them I was staying in Europe for another month. I would still be in communication should they need me. While glancing through the received emails, I saw a message from Shirley, my condo rental agent.

She wanted to know what my plans were and what the date of my return might be. I let her know I was staying in Europe for another month and then going to my house in Nebraska. I will be back in Chicago on September 1st. She got back to me within ten minutes. My renter would like to stay for the entire time I was away and vacate by my expected return in September. I confirmed with Shirley that works for me and continue collecting the rent and monitoring the place. I contacted the airlines to change my return flight ticket to open-ended with an additional fee that I was happy to pay. My path was clear to enjoy Ben without guilt and appreciate the beauty of a Greek island.

All the stars seemed to align, allowing me to take this time with Ben. I would not think about what would follow when the month was over. I'll cross that bridge yada, yada, yada. For once, I wanted to live in the moment, be carefree and enjoy the complete abandonment of my structured existence. There were no lists or thoughts of the future. This summer is my time, and I was going to enjoy it as long as it lasts.

I placed a call to my hotel's front desk and notified them I would check out in a couple of hours. Ben had given me a generous amount of time to refresh myself, pack everything, and be ready to go to the airport. Ben picked me up, and we headed for my next unexpected adventure.

CHAPTER TEN

The taxi took us to a terminal building some distance away from the major airline boarding areas. Instead of a scheduled commercial flight, we would fly on a private jet to the island. I felt overwhelmed again with this show of opulence that far exceeded anything I experienced or felt comfortable with. I didn't know how to act; this was so far above my social knowledge. The flight would be less than two hours.

We boarded after we stowed our luggage. I was a little happier to see that the plane was small, seating ten and not a flying pleasure palace. Ben and I were the only passengers. Two flight attendants were on board to see to our needs. First came the champagne, followed by some fancy club sandwiches and coffee served on fine china, with crystal stemware, linen tablecloth and napkins, and silverware that Tiffany would be proud of. The seats were large, comfy, butter-soft taupe leather with deep carpeting at our feet. Ben and I faced each other with a small table between us and windows at our side.

I had to ask, "Do you do this often?"

"What? Eat? I try three times a day. These sandwiches are delicious."

I gave Ben a "cut-the-crap" look. "You know what I mean. Do you travel like this often?"

"Not my usual way of getting around. It's not something I do frequently, but I take advantage of the extras when offered."

"Good to know. If you're looking for normal, this isn't it," I said.

"I know. Sometimes I get embarrassed with the toadying. My parents keep me grounded in reality if they think I'm getting too big for my britches. I confess I enjoy the perks, but I don't take them for granted. My business is very mercurial. Could be here today, gone tomorrow. A couple of poor performances or rumors, true or not, could sink my career and make me box office poison."

As we got closer to the island with the plane descending, the incomparable sight of Santorini, the mystical site of Atlantis, as some legends expound, was mesmerizing. It took my breath away. Primarily white cube-shaped buildings clung to the rocky cliffs, some with startling blue domes. The domed churches paid homage to the sky and the sparkling blue-green Aegean Sea. It is postcard-worthy and a perfect painting scape.

Our plane landed at a small inland airstrip. A car with a driver was waiting for us after the island customs officer passed us through. We slowly drove up the rugged and zig/zag roads on the cliff sides to the top on the island's west coast to a spectacular modern-looking white βίλα or villa in Greek.

Once in the house, I met Thea and Demitris, a husband and wife couple who were the caretakers of the villa. Thea would be chief cook and bottle washer, with Demitris as our driver.

Thea showed me around the incredible house. All the rooms had windows looking out over the volcano and the caldera; this side of the island is known for the fantastic sunsets. The terrace off the master bedroom had a sunken hot tub and a small infinity lap pool overlooking craggy volcanic rocky peaks down to the sea. The caretakers lived in a separate house about fifty yards down the cliff road.

It was scorching hot, the sunlight intense, radiating off the rocky cliffs. I would have to take special care with plenty of sunscreen on my fair skin, or I would look like a disgruntled Elmo by the time the month was over.

"Is this okay?" Ben asked.

"Okay? Are you kidding? This is heaven. I love it. I feel the ancient history of the Minoan culture all around. The house on this beautiful island is better than any image I could come up with in my wildest imagination."

"Yeah, it's pretty fantastic, and Thea is a wonderful cook."

We unpacked and napped on the king-size bed that faced sliding glass doors looking out to the sea. We made slow, exquisite love before we fell asleep. I felt like Cinderella, sans the gown, glass slippers, and trading in the pumpkin coach for a private jet.

I wandered around the house after waking. Thea had dinner in a warming oven with a chilled bottle of the renowned local wine. The couple would only be at the house from 10AM to 5PM. Demitris would be on call to drive us down the cliff whenever we needed him. I was happy that an experienced driver was available for the really scary twisting and turning rocky roads.

Ben and I took our dinner out to the terrace. The sea breeze kept the heat of the late afternoon tolerable. When I looked out at sea, I saw a three-masted wooden schooner at anchor in the bay. Tourist ships cruised along the coastline, docking and carrying hundreds of day-trippers. I had to grab my phone and take dozens of pictures and videos. After our leisurely dinner, I refilled our wineglasses.

"Let's get in the hot tub. Are you game?" I asked Ben.

"Beat you in." He shucked his clothes on the terrace and stepped in the swirling water.

I stood in place with my mouth open. I had never been at ease walking around in the nude, even in my home. But, of course, Ben had seen me without my clothes. Even so, I was a little uncomfortable and couldn't make myself follow his lead.

Ben was chuckling, "I'm sorry. I didn't mean to shock you."

I grabbed one of the large fluffy towels stacked next to the hot tub. I walked into the bedroom and disrobed, wrapping myself in the towel. I walked back out to the terrace, slipped into the water, and tossed the towel over a chair. "It's the modest mother in me, cautious about not wanting to send my sons into early therapy with any display of motherly flesh," I laughed.

I drifted over to Ben, and he put his arm around my shoulders as we sat leaning against the wall of the tub with the jets massaging our backs. As the swirling waters soothed our tired bodies, we sipped our glasses of wine and started talking, asking questions about the minor details of our lives.

"Did you ever want more children after you had the twins? You were so young when they were born."

"It was rough dealing with twin babies. Marco was gone during the day and some evenings with clients. Sleep was at a premium; if one baby was sleeping, the other was crying. One would be hungry and the other one with a dirty diaper. I actually walked into a wall one time and apologized to the wall. I was so tired. Half the time, I didn't know who I fed and who I didn't. Things eased up a lot when they got to be about three months old, sleeping through the night. After that, I was afraid to have another baby for a while, fearing another set of twins.

"When the boys turned six, Marco and I tried for three years to conceive, with no success. I had medical issues that prevented me from getting pregnant. I wanted a little girl so badly. We were about to start medical intervention when Marco was killed. That was the end of that dream. I made peace with the fact that I would have only two children but so blessed and thankful they were healthy and happy."

"You are so small. I can't imagine you carrying a baby, much less two."

"At the end of my pregnancy, I was quite a sight. I probably was as wide as I was tall."

"You must have been beautiful even if you were a little porky," Ben laughed.

I playfully socked him in the shoulder. We talked about our early years of growing up in rural mid-America. Our backgrounds had some similarities, 4-H projects, school plays, proms and pushing parents to the limits with teenage hijinks—drinking beer, staying out after curfew and chopping down wild marijuana in the pastures, drying it out in the oven, and trying to smoke it.

"Tell me about your town," Ben asked.

"Hartsuff is in the middle of the state in the sandhills, built around an old Army Fort. The town is half-deserted. It still has wooden planks for sidewalks and hitching posts. It has the requisite cowboy bar, a deserted bank, a convenience store/gas station, and a cold storage locker. Most family farms have disappeared and were absorbed into the huge corporate ranches in the area. I attended the high school in the larger town of Sanders, about twenty miles away.

"I love the smell of the fresh clear air, the lumpy sandhills, and the mostly treeless plains. The star-filled skies after sunset and the complete blackness of the night with the occasional howl of a coyote, the only sounds. No artificial lights for miles, it says home to me. I've been in a debate with myself about making a permanent move back to the country and my extended family." A tear ran down my cheek. "I didn't mean to make this a boohoo moment."

"Didn't cry, baby," said Ben as he kissed the tear away. He wrapped his arms around me as I smiled up at him with my watery eyes. We stayed in the hot tub as the sun set over the island. Ribbons of gold, vermilion, violet, and pink streaked across the sky like a living Impressionist seascape painting. Lights started coming on at the buildings down below the villa. It looked like a fairyland. We could hear the faint strains of music from the village clubs drifting up to the terrace through the warm night air.

"Tomorrow, what do you say about going down into town and see what's there?" Ben asked.

"Didn't you ever explore when you stayed here before?"

"I didn't have any interest in wondering around by myself. After filming a physically challenging movie, I was exhausted and banged up. I spent my time eating, sleeping and laying in the sun. About the only thing I did was work out in the home gym and read. I really needed the downtime."

"I might have to do some shopping. Unfortunately, I didn't bring many hot weather casual clothes with me. Do you think you can walk around without a hassle?" I asked.

"If I wear a fisherman's cap and sunglasses, I think we'll be okay."

I handed Ben a towel as he got out of the hot tub. He started laughing again. "There might be someone with a powerful set of binoculars on one of those boats out there in the bay. I don't want to see either of us on YouTube naked," I said.

"You have a point."

CHAPTER ELEVEN

Showering off after spending so much time in the hot tub made my skin feel parched. I came out of the bathroom wrapped in a towel with a bottle of moisturizer, ready to slather myself with lotion. Ben took the bottle out of my hand.

"Let me give you a massage," said Ben.

He had me sit down on the bed. Ben started with my arms, gently smoothing the lotion into my skin. Next, Ben turned to my legs, starting with my feet. He took his time as he worked up my legs to my thighs, reaching every inch of skin. I got a very different sensation than dry skin. Ben had me lie down on my stomach, removing the towel, exposing me in my entirety to his questing eyes. His firm but gentle hands massaged the backs of my legs, my butt, and then my back and shoulders. I was all but whimpering with mindless lethargy. My body felt completely limp, with my mind devoid of the ability to put two thoughts together.

Ben turned me over and smoothed the lotion on my neck, then moved to my chest. His touch was doing magical things to my breasts and nipples, trailing down to my stomach. His fingers discovered every point of pleasure on my body. Soon, the massaging stopped to be replaced with the movement of his lips over my skin. Ben drew a nipple into his mouth. He softly bit the tip and worked it with his tongue while fanning his fingers over the other nipple. He molded my breasts with his hands. I could feel my breasts swelling, and my nipples were tight, super sensitive beads. My body was arching off the bed, and my legs spread apart with a throbbing need concentrated in my feminine center.

Ben's mouth moved down my stomach to my womanhood. I loved the feel of his emerging whiskers feathering over my body. He nuzzled the curls at the apex of my thighs. Ben moved to the end of the bed, positioning himself between my spread legs. He looped my legs over his shoulders, Ben lifted my bottom with his hands, and feasted. His tongue invaded my intimate folds. He sucked the tiny nub of tissue that shattered my senses. After experiencing the most explosive orgasm of my life, I begged to have his hard shaft slide into me. I pulled at his hair, bringing him up to cover me with his body. I looked into his glazed eyes as he reached the pinnacle of pleasure while trapped inside my body. I climaxed a second time. Ben thrust himself even deeper inside me until he was solidly embedded, his arousal still hard and throbbing. We moved together in the age-old dance of physical pleasure while staring into each other's eyes. I felt his second climax was near as I heard his inarticulate groan, and I let myself go over the edge to mind-numbing oblivion.

We lay together, savoring the calm and quiet aftermath, holding on to each other with Ben kissing the top of my head and running his hands up and down my arms. This man knew his way around a woman's body, giving incredible pleasure before satisfying his own.

"Are you okay, my darling?" asked Ben.

"More than okay. That lotion is incredible. I'll have to buy a gallon," I whispered. He chuckled as he wrapped me in his arms as we fell asleep for the night as one.

* * *

I woke up early the following day, leaving the bed with Ben sound asleep. I slipped on my robe and gathered the dirty dishes from last night's meal on the terrace to take back to the kitchen. Thea was already at work. She had a big pot of coffee ready that smelled like heaven. Thea had a basic command of English, certainly better than my Greek, which was nonexistent.

She looked at me holding the tray of dishes, "No. No. No. I get—you rest."

I wasn't used to people waiting on me, having grown up with entrenched guilt for not cleaning up after myself or making the bed every morning. Not wanting to insult her by taking over her job, I restrained my natural impulses.

Thea fixed a tray with two mugs of coffee, a bowl of sugar, and a pitcher of cream. I hadn't paid attention to how Ben took his coffee. But then I realized I didn't know the basics of Ben's life. I didn't even know his full name, nor did he mine. Usually, people know a little something about each other like birthdays, ethnic heritage, or mother's maiden name before jumping in the sack. I suppose I could Google him, but who knows what the truth was and what was not? Thea asked about breakfast, and I said I would let her know.

The smell of fresh coffee seemed to stir Ben from sleep. I took the tray out to the terrace. Climbing vines were full of dark pink bougainvillea blossoms growing over the door and around the terrace walls, sending their fragrance through the air. The smell of coffee called and Ben soon followed, wrapped in his robe. The sun was blinding. I hurried back into the room for a hat and our sunglasses.

"Good morning, darling. How about breakfast?" He asked.

"Thea asked about that when I got the coffee. What would you like?"

"I don't care, whatever she wants to fix. I'm not fussy."

"I'll go tell her. Want to eat out here?"

"Can't think of a better place."

I slipped into the kitchen, asking for breakfast on the terrace, whatever she wanted to serve. I returned with a carafe of coffee.

"A woman after my heart. I have to warn you, I can be a little grumpy before my morning coffee." As Ben took a big gulp of the coffee he continued, "I'm glad Thea remembered to make coffee Americano. Normally Greek coffee is so strong it's guaranteed to put hair on your chest regardless if you're a man or a woman."

"Good to know." I watched as he fixed his second cup of coffee—a drop of milk, no sugar. Thea arrived with our breakfast; a basket of bread, pastries, buns, a bowl of yogurt, fresh fruit, olives, a cheese pie, and wheat cereal. "This looks wonderful. Thank you, Thea." I filled a bowl with cereal and topped it with fruit and yogurt. I nibbled on the local olives that were a Greek staple at every meal. Ben tried the cheese pie with the fresh fruit and bread. After our leisurely breakfast, we watched some big passenger ships coming in to dock.

"Are you done, sweetheart?" asked Ben. I nodded. "I'll take the tray back to the kitchen. If I have Demitris ready with the car to take us into town in an hour, will that give you enough time to get ready?"

"That's more than enough time for me. Of course, you might take longer," I said with a grin.

"No way. A quick shower and a shave, throw on some clothes, and I'm ready to roll."

"We'll see," as I ran into the bathroom for a shower. I was putting on my makeup when Ben came into the bathroom, stepping into the shower. I finished with what I had to do and left him with some privacy. Finding some shorts, a light knit top, and sandals for our late morning foray into the village completed my preparations.

I was a little uneasy with the familiarity of Ben walking into the bathroom while I was still in there. It had been so long since I shared that kind of intimacy with a man. Ben seemed to be pretty comfortable with it. It got me thinking that this was a very common situation in his life. I know he had to have had many lovers and had married twice, and this was no big deal for him, but it was for me. What if I had been using the toilet? Next time—lock the door.

Demitris was ready with the car when we emerged from the villa. We let Thea know that we would have lunch in town, and Ben noted Demitris's mobile phone number so he could call for a pickup when we were ready to return. We went down the cliff to Fira Town, the island's capital.

I picked up a couple of brochures as we walked along the rough, sun bleached stone streets. The town was very cosmopolitan, with a plethora of bars, restaurants, and nightclubs. Shopping ran from touristy to upscale. I couldn't wait to investigate all the museums the island offered. I was also interested in a tour of the volcano.

Ben had his fishermen's hat on, and with his dark glasses, no one gave us a second look. I enjoyed walking hand-in-hand with him on the twisting, narrow, sun-drenched paths clinging to the cliffs and the volcanic rock-paved streets, pretending that we were like everyone else. I did some shopping, picked up a couple of shorts, tank tops in various colors, and a white sundress. Ben moved to pay the bill, but I insisted that this was my purchase. I wasn't a woman that expected a man to pay my way. The trip to this island was more than enough of a contribution from him. However, I was feeling guilty with his generosity. I didn't want to feel like a paid escort. We needed to talk about setting some boundaries.

We stopped at a waterside restaurant for lunch. I tried a Greek salad made with tomatoes, cucumbers, onion, olives, and green bell peppers with an olive oil dressing and a meat kabob, while Ben tried moussaka, a Greek eggplant lasagna. Again, we tasted each other's selections. I can't say I'm a big fan of feta cheese. My salad had an enormous slab on the top, but I liked his lunch choice. After satisfying our hunger, we breathed in the tangy, salty sea air, walking along the waterfront retaining wall. I peeked over the side into the water and saw a fascinating sight.

Clustered together were about a dozen jellyfish undulating in the crystal clear sea. They were so beautiful to watch, performing a delicate aquatic ballet with their translucent umbrella-shaped bells and trailing tentacles. As we continued our walk, I could see an elderly fisherman mending nets as he sat at the foot of the waterline on an overturned boat. His gnarled hands moved with speed, shifting the wooden shuttles of twine in and out of the netting, probably in the same way as many generations before him.

It was getting to be late afternoon, and the extreme heat was leaving us enervated. Ben called for the car as we walked to the pick up point. We got back to the villa and slipped into the lap pool to cool off. I put on a swimsuit this time, and Ben did the same. After a little pool time, we sat under an umbrella on the terrace with a chilled glass of wine. We looked over the brochures I collected to decide what we wanted to see. Ben reminded me we had almost an entire month to take on as many activities as we wanted. That brought up an issue that was on my mind.

"I won't go on any of these excursions unless you let me pay for half of what we do."

"Honey, I can more than afford to pay for us both, and you're my guest."

"I don't know how to word this. I don't want it to appear like I'm taking advantage. I'm grateful to have this invitation to stay at this beautiful villa with you, but I don't want to feel like a woman out to get as much as she can from a man. It makes me feel cheap. I'm here because I'm in love with you and not for what I can get out of you. Please understand what I'm trying to say."

"I think I recognize what you're feeling. I guess the women I have been with in the past were all too interested in taking everything I had to give, have conditioned me. You're so different from anyone before you. You have integrity and are unselfish. Please let me know if I do something that makes you feel uncomfortable."

"I've only been with two men intimately in my life, and you're one of them. I'm not very sophisticated like the women you're used to being with. At heart, I'm still a small-town girl with the traditional small-town values I grew up with," I said.

"That's what I love about you. Somewhere along the way, I've lost my value system in the atmosphere of La La Land narcissism. That's not the man I want to be or how I grew up. You're the best thing that has ever come into my life. I don't want to lose you. You're real and take me back to the values that my family instilled in me growing up."

"Thank you for hearing me out," as I looked up at him with tears clouding my vision.

Ben stood up. "Come here, sweetheart." He took me in his arms and held me tight.

In the following two weeks, we established a routine. We breakfasted on the terrace, dressed for the day, drove to the town, and investigated every museum available, marveling over the ancient pottery, sculptured figures, and fresco wall art. We took the Volcano Tour and some day trips out to sea, island hopping. No one recognized Ben, or if they did, they didn't act on it. Ben asked if I wanted to go to one of the nightclubs.

"Do you?" I asked.

"If you want to go, I will," Ben offered.

"Not really. I have never been a clubber or into alcohol-fortified merriment. But if you want to check it out, I'm game," I said.

"I did a lot of clubbing in my youth as my career took off. It wears thin fast, the same music, the same people looking to get laid or there to make a drug score. I've grown past it. I would rather spend a quiet night with you," he said.

Our nightly lovemaking developed added dimension as well. There was a new tenderness making sure we gave pleasure to the other before meeting our own needs—gentle caressing, soft words of love, and reaching for each other through the night. We still had our frenzied need and immediate want, but a new softness and emotional commitment grew between us. I would frequently find Ben staring at me with the gentlest smile on his face. My heart melts when I look at him. Not the high-profile personality, but the man I knew him to be. I love him.

At the beginning of our third week in paradise, Ben received a special delivery, the film treatment, and the rough screenplay he had commissioned.

"Can I ask you for a favor?" he said.

"Of course."

"Could you read this book and let me know what you think?"

"I'd love to." I looked at the book he held in his hand, *Galway Gone*. After dinner, we sat on the terrace while I read, and he scrutinized the script busily making notes. By 11 PM, I hadn't moved a muscle other than turning the pages. It enthralled me. Ben called my name as I looked up with tears running down my face. I was halfway through my reading, and I knew this story had to be told on the big screen. Not only did the book make me cry, but it also made me care.

We had to take a break for the night. Heading down to the kitchen, we foraged for a snack. To my delight, there was an entire tray of homemade baklava, a layered dessert made of filo pastry, filled with chopped nuts, and sweetened with syrup or honey. It is so good we should consider it a mortal sin, as in so sinfully rich and delicious, it was to die for. God bless Thea. Ben and I cut enormous pieces, topping them with vanilla ice cream. Then, opening a bottle of wine, we carried our late-night bounty back out to the terrace. Under the starry sky, we gobbled up the pastry treat and the wine of the Gods. Then, with only the dim lights in the hot tub on, we shed our clothes and slipped into the warm, bubbling water.

I moved into Ben's arms and kissed him with a feverish passion and a desperate need to have him inside me. I didn't want soft and gentle, but a ferocious and frantic, mind numbing, uninhibited physical sensory invasion. With my fingernails digging into his shoulders, my need was frantic, filled with whirling urgency. My tongue ravaged his mouth, biting his lips and grinding my hips against his, wanting him rock hard and inside me. He pulled me out of the water and laid me on the apron of the tub. He entered me, meeting my needs with an uncompromising need of his own. We grabbed with abandon, tearing at each other, wanting more. More touching, more taking as our breath mixed, our bodies became one and our minds stopped functioning until we reached an explosive "le petit mort", the little death. We lie under the stars in an exhaustive silence, regaining consciousness.

"If whatever that was, was from the baklava or the book, I'm going to make sure that you have plenty of both," murmured Ben.

*   *   *

I finished the book the following day, a perfect story for Ben's directorial debut. I told him how much I loved the deeply romantic tale of love, loss, and renewal. He slowly analyzed the treatment and script and let me read it when he finished.

"I value your opinion. I can see location shoots in Ireland, London, the Midwest, California, and the studio, and I want you to be part of it."

"Let me think about it," I said with some reservation.

"Did I mention that I have to go back to Rome for a couple of days to shoot voice overs and B-shots and check on the editing? Will you come with me for a couple of days before you go home?"

"Yes." There was no mention if our romance would go on from there unless with the casual comment to become part of his first directorial project. So this was it, the end. We had been together for two months, living together for one. I love Ben with everything in me, but I could see that his thoughts were returning to his career with an indefinable feeling of remoteness, and a tenuous disconnect creeping into our intimacy.

Ben had many romantic attachments before me, but never seemed to have made a permanent emotional commitment to anyone. I wasn't so naïve to believe that we would walk off hand-in-hand into the sunset and have a mutually compatible life together. Our odyssey was a delicious slice of life that I enjoyed and would cherish in the recesses of my memory forever. Hidden from all but me to savor quietly in my later years, bringing a secret smile to my face.

Moving to California or traveling around on location shoots like a groupie was not for me. I wanted stability instead, a partner to come home to, wanting to go to bed with the same man every night, grow old together, taking joy in our togetherness, and celebrate family. I will try my best to keep up a brave face as our idyllic days came to an end, not wanting to make it any more complicated when the time came to say goodbye.

We finished out our last week at the lovely villa in Santorini, packed our suitcases, and bid Thea and Demitris a fond goodbye at the airstrip, thanking them for a wonderful stay. After the short flight to Rome, we checked into a suite at the Anantara Palazzo Naiadi, one of the most impressive hotels I had ever seen. A crescent-shaped palazzo fronting the Piazza della Repubblica suspended over the ruins of the Baths of Diocletian. I felt like an imposter walking into this incredible bastion of luxury, offering a big helping of narcissistic indulgence. I kept my feelings to myself while Ben seemed to accept all the attention as his due.

The hotel had prepared for his arrival with all his preferences on hand, from his favorite champagne, chocolates and flowers in the suite to how he liked his bed turned down and his morning coffee prepared. Staff were assigned just to fulfill his needs. I turned down the valet and maid, who wanted to unpack for us. Enough already.

*　*　*

Ben had two to three days of promotional work, and then he thought we could take a couple of days for ourselves. He invited me to the studio to watch the short little stints being filmed. Ben gave me the treatment and the proposed script to reread with his notes, trusting my opinion.

Standing in the living room of his studio trailer, after reading the entire script, I had to express my excitement for such a remarkable story. "Ben, you have to do this. The story is heartfelt, with multifaceted evocative imagery, compassionate and dramatic. It has a relatable human quality that everyone can respond to."

"That's what I thought. Do you think I can direct something like this and give it the justice it deserves?"

"Of course you can. You've been in this business for over twenty years and have worked with the best in the movie industry, knowing what it takes to make a brilliant film. You can make this a story for the ages with style and feeling. I have every confidence in you," as we smiled at each other. A loud and insistent banging on the trailer door interrupted our conversation. I looked up as the door swung open and Deborah McIntyre, Ben's most recent celebrity playmate, glided into the room.

"Hello, darling. Surprise!" Deborah threw her impressive breasts and attached body into Ben's arms. Ben looked at me with confusion as I stared into his eyes, waiting for his response.

"Deborah, what brings you here?" he asked.

"What do you mean? We love each other, and I missed you, so I got on a plane after my film wrapped so we could spend some time together," as her plumped-up lips traveled over his face with wet, smacking kisses. She looked over her shoulder at me with a self-satisfied smirk. "Dear, could you take care of this for me? My arms are full," as she hurled her designer jacket in my direction. "And could you get me a glass of water with a teeny, tiny little slice of lemon? Long flights leave my skin so dry."

My heart was pounding as the reality of the situation seeped into my brain. I thought I was going to vomit. I opened my mouth to say something, but words wouldn't come forth.

"Deborah, this isn't a good time. We need to talk," said Ben.

"I know darling, that's why I'm here—our engagement," as Deborah rubbed her voluptuous body up and down Ben's. "We need to talk about announcing our commitment and my ring." With Ben looking back at me, a shocking paralysis took hold of my body; I was unable to move. Deborah continued, turning to me, unaware of the awkward vibes filling the room. "I love your hair, dear. Who's your colorist?"

"Genetics," I choked out.

"Is that in Beverly Hills?" she asked. MENSA wouldn't be knocking on her door any time soon.

I was gob smacked as I looked at Ben. He stood there, not saying a word, looking like a kid caught with his hand in the cookie jar.

"You can go now sweetie, Ben is going to be very busy," Deborah giggled as she gave me a sly look.

"It's not what you think, Brenna," Ben said, looking at me with his expressive eyes, asking for understanding.

I finally found the strength to push my words out. "Wrong, Ben. It's precisely what I think." I held up her jacket hooked on my middle finger, dropping it on the floor.

"Ben, you need to fire her. She's incompetent and rude. Look what she did to my new five-thousand-dollar Armani jacket," said Deborah with a well-practiced pout on her surgically enhanced face.

"Consider it done," I said as my brain freeze morphed into a raging inferno. "Get your own damn water with your teeny, tiny little lemon slice." I turned and moved toward the door. "Better watch those projections, Ben. Someone could lose an eye," As I gave her chest a less than admiring look. "Take this in its purist context. Goodbye, Ben."

CHAPTER TWELVE

Running out of the studio, as if the devil himself was nipping at my heels, I grabbed a taxi and sped to the hotel. I called the Emirates Airline counter and found a flight to Chicago scheduled to depart in two and a half hours. I had just enough time to make it. I secured a seat with my open-ended ticket. Calling down to the hotel desk, I requested a bellman to come to get my luggage, that I had not even unpacked and summon a taxi.

Racing to the airport terminal, checking in, I cleared customs and security just in time to board. My cell phone was exploding with message after message from Ben. I deleted every one without listening. Finally, I blocked his cell number. Once seated, I got out my laptop and emailed my sons that I was heading back to the States.

Chase and Gage were having a great time at their schools, assuring me they were fine and enjoying their experience. Next, contacting Michele and Betsy, I let them know I was on my way to Nebraska for the rest of the summer until I was due back in the office on September 1st. Next, I contacted Sam, my contractor in Hartsuff, informing him I would arrive at Grandma's house sometime the next day to meet with him and go over the renovations. Last, I emailed my cousin Maggie, my most trusted confidant, letting her know I was on my way home to the farm. With all my correspondence handled, I blocked Ben from my email and Facebook accounts.

I took my first deep breath since I left the film studio. My body was running on pure adrenalin and was now about to crash. I accepted a glass of champagne from the cabin attendant and ordered my dinner. The meal was a gourmet repast, but I could only choke down a couple of bites. Concerned, the flight attendant retrieved my dinner tray uneaten. I told her I wasn't feeling well, and I just wanted to get into my pajamas and call it a day. I enclosed myself in my little private cubicle and crawled into bed, crying myself to sleep.

*   *   *

I slept for eight hours, dressed, and ordered breakfast. I moved to the restroom, splashing cold water onto my blotchy face with eyes that were puffy and red. Oh great, I had done the big ugly cry. I looked like shit, but I was entitled. After I returned to my seat, I booted up my laptop and searched for a connecting flight to Omaha. The soonest flight I could find was in two hours after I arrived at O'Hare. After I got through customs, getting to the correct terminal would be close time-wise. I booked it and requested a rental car to be ready on my arrival in Nebraska. I asked the flight attendant to contact airport transport to pick me up and whisk me to the United Terminal for my domestic flight. With the time change, I would drive the four hours home in the dark of night, exactly matching my state of mind.

I got to the gate of my Omaha flight as the door was about to close, hoping my luggage had made it on board. My guardian angel must have been sitting on my shoulder when I landed. I grabbed all my luggage, carted it to the car-rental desk, and was on the road by 2 AM local time. With any luck, I would be home for breakfast.

*   *   *

HARTSUFF. The only place I wanted to be to lick my wounds. I was angry and hurt, blaming myself for being so trusting and gullible. Passion came at too high of a price and his love for me was an illusion. The scars would run deep and raw for a very long time. I had to forget this monumental lapse of judgment and take it for what it was—incredible sex, a handsome but unattainable lover and a vacation from reality. I knew deep down in my heart that this disaster would happen, with only myself to blame. Thank goodness I hadn't told my sons or friends any details about my absence of common sense.

I rolled into my driveway at 6:30 AM and walked into my home. Maggie must have been here. There were fresh flowers in a vase on the dining room table. The refrigerator was on and filled with enough food and beer to last a couple of days. I checked that someone had turned the water heater up before I collapsed on my freshly made bed. Bless you, Maggie. Somehow, she knew exactly what I needed.I woke after a couple of hours to an insistent knocking. I shuffled to the back door, half-awake to find Sam, my contractor.

"Good morning, Sam. It's been a long time." We hugged and told each other a bunch of lies about how we hadn't aged a day since high school.

"I wanted to touch base with you. Have you seen your new porch?" He asked.

"I haven't had a chance. I got in very early this morning. Let's look now."

We walked to the front of the house. I stepped out onto a magnificent new entryway. I walked down the five steps and looked at the front facade. "It's perfect, Sam. The gingerbread matches the rest of the house perfectly. The porch looks exactly like I remember. I can't wait to get some rocking chairs and a porch swing out here."

"It'll be a wonderful view once you get the brush and some scrub trees cleaned out and clear the growth over the driveway to the front. I didn't paint it yet, waiting for the new windows to go in first," said Sam.

"Let's go in the house. How about some coffee? I want to talk about some other improvements I've been thinking about." We sat down at the kitchen table, and Sam got out his notebook. "Let's do this by priorities. Priority one: new windows, insulation for the walls, and attic and wood-look vinyl siding to stay with the Folk Victorian style of the house. If you could get me some color samples compatible with the era of the house, that'd be great. Have you looked at the roof?" I asked.

"Your Granny Vernie had the roof redone about eight years ago. It should be good for another ten to fifteen years, but I'll look again to make sure."

"Priority two; there are four small bedrooms with minuscule closets upstairs. I want an estimate to make the four bedrooms into two with more spacious closets and a bathroom. Part two; downstairs, I want to take the front left twin parlor that Grandma was using as her bedroom, merge it with the old butler's pantry and storage area behind it and make it into a master suite with a sitting room, full bath, and walk-in closet.

"Priority three; I noticed that the detached garage is still leaning about fifteen degrees to the right." It has looked that way since I was a little girl. "I want to demolish it and put up a two-car garage. What do you think?"

"I hope you don't want this all done by tomorrow, Brenna. The Property Brothers are not my close personal friends. I have a great crew, and we can do the job and do it right. I can get together an estimate by next week. We can concentrate on the interior as soon as we can get the outside buttoned up while the weather holds. I checked the electrical. Vernie did an update when she had the roof done. It should hold you unless you want to put in more electrical appliances. I have a question. Are you thinking of moving back?"

"Someday, I want to retire back here, so I might as well get it done while I have someone I can trust to do the work."

"What about the outbuildings?"

"They stay as-is for now. I have a sentimental attachment to the washhouse, chicken coop, barn, and even the outhouse. I can still picture grandma going from one building to another. My memories are precious, and I wanted her spirit to have her familiar surroundings and know that I'm home with her."

"Be prepared to be stunned when you get the estimate for the siding. This big, ol' Victorian may need some underlayment repair. We'll see what's, what when we do the insulation and get the windows in."

"Thanks, Sam. I appreciate all your hard work. I'll be here until the end of the month. See you soon." I walked Sam to the door, then got my luggage out of the car. Grandma had an internet connection installed so that my sons could keep in touch with their friends when we came out to visit.

I got out my laptop to see what's been going on in the real world. After shifting through the daily dose of new spam messages about penis enlargement, Viagra sales, or a date with a hot, horny man, I looked at the messages from Michele and Betsy.

Both women had received multiple phone messages at work from a "Bob Smith" asking for me. Who was Bob Smith? They asked. I wrote back that he was a stalker I had trouble with in Italy and asked them if he should call again, that they should say they never heard of me.

Maggie called and wanted to come out to the house the next day for a long overdue chat. I was ready to spill my guts to my faux sister, my best childhood friend. Instead of dwelling on the recent past, I would throw myself into the house renovation to forget my brief moment of insanity with Ben. I tried to tell myself that it wasn't love I felt but a craving for a physical release that had built up for ten years. If I said it enough, I might believe it.

I spent the rest of the day looking over the house for any interior problems, removing dust covers from the furniture, and powering down. A beer and a sandwich for dinner filled my stomach while I watched the news and then crawled in bed—back to my bucolic life. I was trying my best to block the disastrous ending to the last couple of months from my memory—any success was minimal.

Maggie was at the door at 10 AM the following morning with a bottle of wine and ready to hear what was on my mind.

"Promise me that nothing I tell you will ever leave this room," I asked.

"I have divulged nothing you have ever told me or did, even the time you threw a skunk stink bomb into the outhouse, blocking the door while the boys we had over were using it. Since we were three years old, you've been my best friend — the sister from another mister, as the saying goes. So anything you say is safe with me."

"I met a man, Mags, and I fell head-over-heels in love."

"You met a man in Italy? Is he Italian?" she asked.

"No, he's American over there on business. We saw each other several times in Italy, and then I spent the last month living with him in Santorini."

"Wicked! You finally got laid. What's his name? Do you have a picture?"

I got out my phone and scrolled through images until I found one taken on the island. I held my phone up for Maggie to see.

"WOW, but that's. . . . . that's . . . that's," Maggie stuttered. "You VAMP."

"Vamp? Have you been watching Sonny and Cher reruns again? But yes, it's Ben Langford."

"Holy shit, Brenna. He's one sexy bolt of man material. So you guys swapped bodily fluids?"

"Yup, big time. We met in Florence and got to know each other there. After his film shoot was over, Ben invited me to stay with him at a private home on the island for a month. We spent every minute together in and out of bed. We fell in love; at least he told me he loved me. After our month together, we returned to Rome for a couple of days to film some promo work for his new movie, then in walks 'Hilda Hooters' aka Deborah McIntyre, his fiancé. I told him goodbye and jumped on the next plane home. End of relationship. End of story."

"Have you heard from him since you left?"

"He's been sending emails and text messages, but I deleted all without reading them. He's even called my office at the college. I've blocked him on my phone, email and told the people at work to tell him they didn't know who I was. I don't want to hear from him ever again."

"How do you feel about that?" she asked.

"I loved him, Maggie. I fell so deeply in love, or at least I thought I did. Something that I thought would never happen to me again. I knew we didn't have a future together, but it still broke my heart. I'll never forgive him for playing me for a fool, a cheap diversion for him while he had someone else in a serious relationship waiting. He humiliated me in the worst possible way. I will never forgive and hope to forget he ever existed."

"Do the boys know?" Maggie asked.

"No. Thank God I mentioned nothing to them. They didn't need to get mixed up in my departure from reality. They need to live their own lives without worrying about me. You're the only one I've told."

"So, what are your plans for life after the prickmister?"

"I'll go back to work and pretend it never happened. Ben will tire of trying to contact me after a while. I'm probably the only woman in his life that ever walked away, or in my case—ran. That has to be a blow to his inflated ego, but I'm sure he has many others waiting in the wings to salve his bruised self-esteem, including his over siliconed and liposuction'd fiancé."

"That sucks, Brenna. I am so sorry that happened to you. Are you turning your anger and frustration into manual labor? You're doing a lot on the house. Are you thinking of coming back here to live?"

"I will eventually. I don't know where I'll end up. The boys will probably never live at home in Chicago again. After college, they will want to be on their own, probably in New York or some other financial capital in the world. They've grown up. I rattle around in a huge condo by myself, going to a job I like, but don't love." As I burst into tears, I said, "I miss Hartsuff. I miss my family." I cried and cried as

Maggie held me close as I lost the tight hold on the emotions I had been trying to control since I left Italy.

"You'll get through this, Brenna. You're a strong woman, and you've done tough before. Come home where you belong."

"I've been seriously thinking about it. I need to go back to work for a while and see how I feel after a couple of months. At least I have options. My Chicago realtor tells me that the condo is worth five times what Marco and I paid for it. Along with his investments, I would be financially independent and could live a comfortable life. The boys could stay here when they want to visit or to live. The best part is I would have you, Maggie." We both burst into tears, and that's how Sam found us. Inviting him in, I excused myself to blow my nose and wash my face. I got back to the table, and Sam had that "deer in the headlights" look, trying to ignore that Maggie and I were a sniveling mass of fragile feminine emotion.

"I brought some siding samples for you to look at," said Sam, looking like he wanted to be anyplace but here.

"Great. How about a beer or some wine?" I asked. Both hands raised up for the beer while I popped the wine cork for myself. After much deliberation on house colors, we narrowed it down to two—light blue and sand.

I selected the sand color siding with white trim and forest green accents. The siding looked like it was brush-painted, keeping more historically correct for the era of my house. I asked Sam to preserve all the woodwork inside the house when we got to the interior spaces. With decisions made, Sam was off. I think he couldn't wait to escape two emotionally unstable women.

Maggie and I planned on meeting in town the following day. I had to go grocery shopping and wanted to stop in and see some of my great aunts and uncles. It did me a lot of good to be home with family. I was getting excited about the house renovations and trying to keep my mind off Ben, my temporary aberration from lucidity. It would have been so much better for Ben and me if we could have ended our relationship with a gentle leave-taking, kind words, and appreciation for the wonderful time we could spend together. Not the in-your-face slap of reality delivered by the chemically enhanced science project, Deborah McIntyre.

*   *   *

The weeks flew by, and it was time to get back to Chicago. Sam had a key to the house, and we would be in touch. He had given me an estimate for the siding, and after my choking attack was over, I agreed to have him start the process. I reminded him jokingly that I knew his mother, father, brothers, sisters, and grandparents. If the crew did not do the job right, they would hear about it. Sam only laughed.

Leaving the farm, I drove the rental car back to the Omaha airport and boarded my plane for Chicago. Michele was going to pick me up. I ran to Michele on deplaning, seeing her smiling face as a beacon of calmness and normalcy.

"Oh, how I've missed you," I cried as I hugged her with all my might. "Let's get my stuff and we can get out of here."

Stuffing my luggage into her SUV, we battled the airport traffic and headed downtown to my condo. I checked with her to see how her husband was doing. He was still on the decline, but staying hopeful and upbeat.

"I have gifts for you and Betsy. When I find them as I unpack, I'll get them to you." I talked about my travels and the research I did for the college. Michele indicated that Dr. M was so impressed with the package I put together that I might find myself with more foreign assignments.

Michele dropped me off at my building, and the doorman got a dolly to take my luggage upstairs. I had three days until I had to go back to work. I had the oddest feeling that I didn't belong here anymore. I had changed in more ways than one. Everything seemed so foreign, as if a part of another life. I had been gone so long that I had to walk around and touch the once so familiar pieces of my life. The days would erase the ambiguity and I would resettle back into the familiar surroundings and to life as I left it in Chicago.

My home was immaculate; the tenant left everything in pristine condition. I unpacked and turned on the television while I sorted through my things. *Entertainment Tonight* was airing when I heard the host mention Ben's name. I stopped what I was doing and sank down on the bed. There he was in full living color, announcing that he would direct his first film taken from the book *Galway Gone*. It was currently being cast and would be in production soon. BLAH, BLAH, BLAH. I gave the television the bird. That's all I needed swirling in my brain before bedtime.

CHAPTER THIRTEEN

I returned to work as if my four-month absence never happened. Dr. M welcomed me back with a list of new projects to consider. In addition, plans for student travel in Italy were being planned for a year from next June. I tried to work up some enthusiasm for my job, but I wasn't feeling well by mid-September. My stomach somersaulted frequently. I had dizzy spells and slept for ten hours every night. Michele and Betsy became concerned when I almost passed out at work. Finally, after being goaded by my friends, I made an appointment with my doctor. I called in sick to work for the following two days after my doctor visit. My phone was beeping with messages until my voicemail was full. I woke to my door buzzer shrieking non-stop. It was time to face the music. Michele and Betsy were on my doorstep.

After we had a cup of tea and a chastising from my friends, I worked up my nerve and told them the details I had been withholding. "There's something I didn't tell you when I got back from Italy. It started in Florence . . . and I fell in love."

"You what? Why didn't you tell us? Who is he? Is he Italian? Are you going to see him again?" asked Michele.

"It's over. He's American, and there was no future for us. I did, however, pick up a little bug . . . . . . I'm . . . pregnant."

After their initial uproar, "HOLY F-ING HELL!" choked out Michele.

"Exactly."

"What are you going to do?" asked Betsy.

"My doctor has given me some options, but I can't see having an abortion. I still care for the father of my baby, but he will never know about this child. I concluded that we have no future. Our lives are too diverse. It wouldn't work out for us. I have to face the fact that I will be a single mother again. At least I have experience with that."

Betsy continued, "You know Michele and I are here for you. We have noticed how unhappy you have been since you returned to work. Are you sure it wouldn't work out with this man? He's not married, is he?"

"No, he's not married. He's just history. I'm going to take the rest of the month to decide if I'm going to stay in Chicago or go home to Nebraska," I said.

"I wish there was some way we could help you. We will support you in any decision you make. We will certainly miss you if you decide to return home, but your happiness is our utmost concern. Is there anything we can do for you now?"

"You two are the most wonderful friends I have ever had. If you could keep this news to yourself, I would appreciate it," I implored them.

"You got it, honey. Let us know if there is anything you need. Now we are going to let you get some sleep. Take the weekend and relax, if you need us-call," said Betsy.

I showed Michele and Betsy to the door, thanking them for their concern. Then I slipped into bed, having made at least one decision. I was having this baby. I called my doctor's office the following morning to inform him I was going forward with my pregnancy. He had several prescriptions to phone into my pharmacy for morning sickness and vitamins, and I immediately started on the medication. I was to come into the office for an ultrasound to determine the fetal age and schedule an amniocentesis, since my age classifies me with advanced maternal risk. Oh great. I can see it now; "Hey kid, is that your grandma?" or "Mommy, can you play with me?"

"No, kiddo, I have to find my walker and take my arthritis pills."

I called Shirley, my realtor, to research the market value of my condo. I hadn't decided if I was selling, but I wanted to arm myself with the information should circumstance change.

Back to work on Monday, I was going through the motions with Betsy and Michele, keeping a close eye on me. I knew I wasn't producing the high caliber of work I was capable of. Dr. M was aware I wasn't my usual self but mentioned nothing, and I felt guilty letting him down.

I took a cab to my doctor's appointment for my first ultrasound. With measurements taken, and the date of my last period, I had a due date of April 1st. What more is there to say? April Fools? The doctor scheduled my amnio for the sixteenth week of pregnancy, before Thanksgiving. Once I saw this new little being on the screen in the doctor's office, I was in love, and it thrilled me to know that there was only one. I wanted this baby, the product of the love I once felt for Ben. Not wanting to know the sex of the baby before birth, boy or girl, I didn't care, only that the baby was healthy. I wanted to be surprised.

September turned to October and then to November. In October, my contractor in Hartsuff had finished with the new siding, window installation, and insulation. I gave him the go-ahead to start on the master bedroom suite. Sam wanted to plumb both the master suite and the new bathroom upstairs to save me some money; that was a go from me. Sam talked our mutual Great Uncle John into coming over and cutting the brush and wack down some trees in my front yard so that the house was visible from the road. My house was on a corner section of the property so that I would have two driveways, one for guests coming to the front door and another on the side for farm traffic in the back of the house.

*　*　*

I was through the difficult pregnancy period when miscarriage was most likely to occur. I had my amnio test and would have the results by mid-November. My breasts were growing at an astounding rate. After twenty years between pregnancies, I had forgotten about the changes I was again experiencing.

I got the results of my amnio, and everything was perfect. That sealed the deal. I was going home. I called Shirley and told her to put my condo on the market. She indicated that an offering for 1.5 million dollars for a 4bed/4 bath 4000 sq. foot home in metropolitan Chicago reflected fair market value. We would start at that figure and negotiate from there. I was astounded. The housing market in Chicago was hot, and I could expect a bidding war and a quick sale which would increase the ultimate selling price over list.

I prepared my resignation letter for Dr. M, effective with two weeks' notice. I would be done by December 1st. But letting Betsy and Michele know of my decision was the hardest thing to tell them. I would miss these loyal friends in my new life, hoping they could come to see me at home in Hartsuff. We had been there for each other through the good times and the bad, and I hoped while distance may separate us, our love for each other will endure.

I scheduled a meeting with Dr. M to give him the news. He ushered me into his office, pointing to a chair. Then, before I could even say anything, he started the conversation.

"You're leaving, aren't you?"

"Thank you, Dr. Michaels, for all the opportunities and responsibilities you entrusted me with. I have enjoyed your friendship and my tenure at the school, but it's time to move home. So, yes, I'll be leaving by December 1st."

"Is there anything I can say to change your mind?" he asked.

"No, I'm afraid not. I'm pregnant, and I want to have my baby back home."

"Congratulations, Brenna. That's a surprise. I wish you the very best, and if you ever want to come back, you will always have a job here. Please keep in touch. My wife and I think of you as a dear friend. You will be missed."

After a hug, I walked out of Dr. M's office with my eyes flooding with tears. It was official. My duties are over by the end of the month. Meanwhile, I would complete all my open projects by the time I left. I didn't want to leave my position in a mess.

Soon the news of my leaving made it through the office, and people I had worked with for years stopped by my desk to say a few words. These last two weeks were going to be rough on my emotions. I was closing this chapter of my life and opening a new one with a new baby, a different home, and complete contentment with my decisions, still trying to erase Ben from my thoughts.

I had run the plan by my sons a couple of weeks ago, without the baby news, and they were both good with it. They worried about me rambling around an empty condo and for my physical safety in a city that took their father's life. So I enlightened them on my renovations for the house in Nebraska, letting them know that they would have bedrooms waiting for them there.

I inventoried my home furnishings tagged those items that will make the move with me and the rest to be sold. I boxed up all the boy's mementos left in their rooms. My realtor had five serious offers on my condo right after Thanksgiving. I mulled them over and chose the highest one over asking, closing on December 6th and occupancy requested by January 1st.

Betsy and Michele came over and worked like whirlwinds to get everything packed up and ready for the movers. Shirley knew of a firm that would come over, inspect and make an offer on the furniture I wasn't taking with me.

On my last day at work, my office mates had a small goodbye luncheon for me. I was in tears by the time I walked out of the office for the last time. Betsy and Michele took me out to dinner, and we all watered up several times. I knew it would be hard to leave them; I didn't realize it would be this hard.

I got through the closing on the condo, and with a check in hand, I had one less obligation to worry about. I sold all the furniture I wasn't taking with me for a reasonable price and movers took it away within two days. I made arrangements with a moving company to come over and load the remaining furniture on the 21st of December, with the expected delivery in Hartsuff on January 15th. That will give me time to move Grandma's furniture to the barn. Most of it was in pretty rough shape, but I wanted my Nebraska family to take anything they could use or if something held special memories.

I had my last checkup with Dr. Roberts. I got copies of the medical records for the family to take home with me. He wished me well and let me know I could still call him if I had any concerns.

Flying out of Chicago on the 21st after the movers loaded the furniture, I had a flight booked to Omaha, where I would stay overnight and purchase a new SUV to drive home. I kept the boys informed on the tidal wave of events that consumed my life. They sent their love and were sorry that they weren't home to help.

The day finally arrived. The condo was empty when I turned over the keys to Shirley. I left the yearly tips for all the doormen with a bonus. They all wished me well. I had lived in the building for twenty years, filled with a lot of memories, mostly good, as the door closed after me for the last time.

CHAPTER FOURTEEN

I was almost six months pregnant and just starting to show, flying to a new life. Arriving in Omaha, I purchased a new Ford Expedition in a pretty blue color, easy to spot in a snowy Nebraska winter. After staying overnight, taking delivery of my new car, I headed home to Hartsuff. Five hours later, I rolled in the driveway, delayed only slightly with the blowing snow.

Sam and his crew were busy working on the master suite when I entered the house. The new bathroom needed the fixtures for completion; the suite opened to the master bedroom and a sitting room waiting for paint. Sam greeted me with a hug and a funny look.

I answered his unspoken question. "Yes, I'm pregnant."

"Well, now, that's a surprise. I didn't know you got married."

"I didn't and don't plan to." Sam didn't know what to say. So I brought in my one suitcase and told him of my plans to replace some of the furniture with my stuff that was arriving in January. When I decided what was to go, he and his crew would move the discards to the barn for me.

All the work on the outside of the house looked beautiful. The old tired Folk Victorian now looked like a well-dressed, dignified lady again. I could immediately tell that the new insulation and windows kept the house so much warmer, eliminating the drafts. I had always been so cold when I lived with Grandma, bundled up like an Eskimo, even indoors when the cold winter winds blew.

The following morning I dressed, then wandered around, wanting to let the house know I was home to stay. I climbed the stairs to the second floor, searching for a particular piece of furniture I remembered from my early childhood. I found it under piles of quilts and other long-forgotten items, an antique Jenny Lind crib. My father had slept in it, and so did I, and now I would prepare it for my new baby.

The work crew arrived, and Sam had some pictures of the hardware for the new bathrooms. I picked out what I thought would be in the house's style. He would place an order, and I would have a completed master bath by the end of the week. In the next couple of days, I would drive into town, pick up some groceries and painting supplies for my new bedroom and bath. I wanted to do the painting myself, placing my stamp on the house and keeping my mind off any thoughts of Ben. Every time I felt my baby move, it reminded me of how much Ben said he wanted children and how much he was missing through his duplicitous behavior. His loss, my deliverance.

I called Maggie and let her know I was back in Hartsuff, this time to stay. It thrilled her I had come home. She immediately invited me to spend Christmas at her home. The family would gather, making it a perfect time for a welcome home celebration.

Another major holiday without them. I missed my sons on the other side of the world. I have yet to decide how I would tell them about their new sibling. For a couple more months, I could put that off. I was more than a little apprehensive about their reaction.

Sam and the crew left for the day as Maggie pulled into the driveway with a pizza and six-pack of beer. I hadn't told her about the baby yet, so sharing a beer would remain a distant memory.

Maggie looked up at the new exterior as she juggled the beer and pizza. I took the pizza box out of her hands as she looked around. It was then she took a good look at me.

"Oh, my God. Why didn't you tell me? Is it . . . his?" I nodded my head. "Have you talked to him since you left Rome?"

"No, I severed all communication."

"So, you are going to go it alone?"

"I have no choice—he gave me no choice. He's involved with someone else. He lives a lifestyle in a place that I can't accept. I can take good care of the baby myself and will always love Ben for the time we spent together. I've made peace with it; having done something foolish that left me with what will prove one of the greatest joys of my life."

"'at a girl. Surprise pregnancies don't bother anyone anymore. It happens. I'm proud of you for holding your head up high and moving on. Now let's have our pizza, a beer for me, and milk for you."

We talked about all manner of town gossip, family news, and my further plans for the house. I showed her the crib I found upstairs. It finally sunk into my prego brain that I have nothing else for the baby. So, Maggie and I made plans to drive to Grand Island for a baby shopping spree after Christmas. I'm going to make the sitting room of the master suite into a nursery.

After Maggie left, I watched a little television, avoiding any show biz talk shows, and jumped into bed. Something about being home corseted within the safe walls of my childhood, I felt safe, secure, and content. Maybe by the time Antarctica grows palm trees, I'll believe it.

Christmas Eve morning dawned with Sam and his crew working a half-day. I drove into town and did some grocery shopping. It took me three hours to get home between seeing many familiar faces and talking for a few minutes and the slick country roads. Sam was the only one of the crew left at the house. He was busy doing a final clean-up of the master suite, ready for paint after the holiday. He helped me drag all my grocery bags into the house, and we sat down in the kitchen for a coffee break.

Sam, it seems, had divorced with no children during my years in Chicago. He wasn't seeing anyone and was putting all his energies into his business. We reminisced about our school days when we were high school sweethearts. I had many fond memories of those carefree days of adolescent love. Sam had moved on to trade school when I left for college at Northwestern. Our undying love soon faded like many adolescent romances, and our worlds separated.

Sam married a couple of years later. We lost touch completely. On our family tree, we were fifth half cousins. We made plans to get back to work the day after Christmas to go over the upstairs improvements. There were a ton of things to go through that grandma stacked away in one of the bedrooms.

"Are you going to be okay here by yourself, in your condition?" Sam shyly inquired.

"Thanks for asking, Sam. I'll be fine. The baby isn't due until April 1st. No jokes, please," I grinned. We hugged goodbye and wished each other a Merry Christmas. It was almost 6 PM, and I wanted to Zoom chat with the boys on their Christmas Day, so many time zones away.

The Christian holiday would be pretty low key in their countries, where the major religions were Shinto and Buddhism. I let them know

I sent a monetary gift to their accounts instead of going through the nightmare of posting a package for international delivery. We chatted a few more minutes about the sights they were seeing.

Chase trekked a portion of the Great Wall of China and inspected the Terracotta Soldiers now housed in Beijing. Gage ventured to the Hiroshima Memorial, climbed Mount Fuji, and toured many temples and islands in Japan. The boys made plans to visit each other in their Asian countries and trade experiences. Gage and Chase arranged to meet up and celebrate the new year in Macau, a territory occupying two small islands off the southern coast of China.

Macau, while part of China, is the only place in that country where gambling is legal. The islands are filled with magnificent, futuristic looking buildings, many of which are luxury hotels and casinos. Chase said it was known as "Las Vegas on Steroids". I was so happy that they were enjoying their adventure. They wished me a Merry Christmas sending their love across the world.

Except for dinner at Maggie's tomorrow, Christmas this year was just another day on the calendar. I thought about my boys and our Christmases past, the decorations, and the parties. Then I promised myself that next year would be different, and we would enjoy a real country Christmas together.

I called Michele and Betsy, wishing them a Merry Christmas with their families. I let them know I was doing well and feeling okay. We promised to get in touch for a long chat after the holidays.

I turned on the television, showing several holiday movies while I walked around the house, tagging the pieces of furniture I wanted to move to the barn. I ran upstairs to the bedroom used as storage to see if there was anything else I could use for the baby. There was a mountain of odds and ends that grandma had accumulated over fifty years. I would have to go through all this before the renovation could start. I could toss most of it except for a treasure trove of pictures. It would be fun to go through them with the older family members to learn their stories.

I pondered how Ben was spending his holiday. Was he home in Kansas with his family or out on the town with "Torpedo Tits"? I wonder if he ever gave me another thought or if I became another conquest joining the many other meaningless relationships populating his past?

I slept in late on Christmas morning and then dressed and drove to Maggie's for dinner. Again, no one seemed overly concerned about my condition. Instead, they offered congratulations and talked about having a baby shower for me in March. I felt so loved by my family. They voiced no criticism or condemnation, knowing they would defend me from anyone in town who might think differently.

The following day, I drove into Sanders to the paint store. I loaded my cart with paint rollers, brushes, painter's tape, and paint pans, selecting a soothing blue-gray color for my bedroom and sitting room. My house had beautiful oak trim, doors, stair rails, posts, and two magnificent pocket doors, one set leading to my new master bedroom. I wanted to preserve the wood by not painting it. The floors were in good shape and would revive with a good cleaning and polishing. I couldn't wait to get my Chicago furniture in my room and get the nursery set up, satisfying my powerful urge to nest. I wanted to have as much as possible done in the house before I delivered, knowing my energies would be needed elsewhere, taking care of my newborn baby.

Sam and the crew arrived for work. They grabbed everything from my car and took it in to the house while Sam chastised me.

"You shouldn't be lifting this heavy stuff in your condition. I'm not equipped to deliver a baby."

"Sam, I'm pregnant, not incapacitated," I said.

"I know that. Let the crew handle the heavy lifting, and you direct. Is this for the master?"

"Yes, I was going to paint as soon as I moved the furniture to the barn."

"We'll get the furniture out, and then we will paint the walls, and you can boss us around. Those ceilings are ten feet high. There's no way you are getting on a ladder."

In no time, the furniture was out, tarps covered the floor, and the painting began. They did the rooms in under three hours, and they looked beautiful. The crew resumed moving the rest of the tagged furniture to the barn, and I went upstairs to the storage bedroom and started going through the debris of generations. Sam brought up some boxes for items to be stored and had the crew bag up the stuff I didn't want for disposal. The room was bare by quitting time. The crew left, and I invited Sam to stay for supper.

I cooked some hamburgers, fried some potatoes and made a salad. Sam had a couple of beers while he scarfed down the food like a hungry bear. It was nice to have someone to eat with. During our conversation, I wondered aloud if it was possible to fit a dishwasher into the kitchen's cabinetry and if new appliances would overtax the electrical circuitry. The appliances hadn't been updated for forty years.

Previous owners had added a building addition in the back of the original 1895 home when indoor plumbing became available. The additional space included an enlarged country kitchen and a mudroom housing the washer, dryer, and chest freezer.

Sam replied that the electrical system could handle the updates and be more energy-efficient. We could drive into Sanders sometime this week and shop for replacements if I was up for it. I asked him to do one more thing before he left for the night to measure the height of the windows in the new master bedroom suite, so I could do some Amazon shopping. We made plans to shop for appliances the next work day after giving the crew their orders. He gave me the requested window measurements, and I bid him goodnight.

After getting the kitchen back in order, I sat down at my laptop and let my fingers do the shopping. I may have gotten a little carried away. Call in the troops and a semi-truck for my humongous order. I bought four pairs of long white draperies with a soft sheen, matching valances, and sheers for the windows in the master bedroom and the sitting room/nursery. Also, double drapery rods and new blackout window shades finished the window treatments. I added to my internet cart a new duvet cover with hand-painted wildflowers on a white background, matching pillow covers, two large square euro pillows in white, a plain white dust ruffle, and blue and white area rugs. I found some bedside lamps with an antique look and new wall artwork, Claude Monet's painting of the Garden at Giverny in an antique-looking frame. With everything coming together, it offered the perfect effect of restfulness and peace for my personal space. I delighted in the amount of work accomplished today. Grandma would have been happy with my changes.

I wandered into the mudroom to check the condition of the washer and dryer. Grandma's milk pail was sitting by the back door as it had always been and would remain as long as I lived in the house. I found small ways to have grandma's spirit visible in my home as a reminder that she was still there with me. I didn't feel that I was erasing her presence in the house but bringing her home back as she would have done if she had been able.

I slept on the sofa that night since we had moved all the beds to the barn, not the most comfortable mattress, but it would do until my furniture arrived. When the crew arrived in the morning, I was up and dressed. Sam took the squad upstairs and gave the instructions for demoing the walls separating the four bedrooms, making them into two, reminding his men to keep the door at the head of the staircase closed so that the dust wouldn't migrate as much downstairs.

Once the noise started, Sam and I drove into Sanders for appliance shopping; he had all the measurements for the spaces. I picked out matte finished stainless steel matching French door refrigerator, dishwasher, propane-fired six-burner stove with double ovens, and a microwave. Sam ordered everything with his contractor discount, after checking the measurements, to be delivered in a week. Next, he picked up the master bath fixtures that had come in at the hardware store. Finally, I picked up some more paint chips and wallpaper samples for the upstairs bedrooms and new bath.

On our drive back home Sam asked, "I'm surprised that you didn't want a wine frig for the kitchen."

"I have grandma's root cellar/tornado shelter for that. It's the perfect temperature, year-round."

"That's another thing I should make sure is stable and critter free."

Sam also suggested I get a professional wood restorer to moisturize and polish the woodwork when all the dirty construction ended on our drive back to the house. He gave me the name of a man that was qualified to do the work. Sam's recommendation was good enough for me. I asked him to contact the man and have him come out and look at the job. The coffered ceiling, built-in bookcases, and the fireplace mantel in the right parlor/living room needed some care. This company could also give me a price to buff and polish the wood floors and trim throughout the house before the furniture arrived.

Sam voiced some concern with the amount of money I was spending, hoping I wasn't digging myself into a financial hole. I assured him I had gotten a princely sum for my condo in Chicago, and I was financially secure. I didn't tell him how well off I was monetarily, but that he could put those worries to rest.

As soon as we were back at the farm, Sam checked on the progress of the demolition. It filled the air with dust. The old walls were plaster and lath, not drywall, so deconstruction was messy. The final clean-up could begin after the new framing for the closets and bath were up and drywall and sheetrock hung.

I set out a sandwich and potato chip lunch for the crew. They worked like demons to get the work done before the movers arrived.

Sam looked around and asked, "Where did you sleep last night? We took all the beds to the barn."

"I slept on the sofa. It'll do until the Chicago movers get here."

"You slept on that?" as he pointed to the sofa in the living room. "That sofa is older than I am. It's older than Methuselah. Let me bring you a rollaway bed. It has to be better than that thing. Also, would you allow me to take the crib and refinish it as a gift to the baby? It needs to be checked for lead paint."

"I hadn't thought about that. Thank you so much. I would love to accept your kind offer to refinish it for my baby. That will make it even more special," I said as my eyes watered up, and I leaned over and kissed his cheek.

With a red face, Sam asked, "Should I do it up in blue or pink?"

"I don't know what I am having better make it white."

The day ended, and I was exhausted. I made my bed up on the sofa and fell into a deep sleep. The following day, the crew returned with lumber and drywall for the upstairs. Sam arrived with a rollaway bed, taking it into the living room. Sam came downstairs after an hour and kind of hemmed and hawed for a couple of minutes.

"What's on your mind, Sam?"

"New Year's Eve is tomorrow. Would you like to go out to dinner?"

"I'm not dating Sam; it would be a little awkward considering my condition."

"It's not a date, simply dinner between two friends. I'm not dating anyone, and I don't do parties; a nice dinner sounds relaxing after a long week of work."

"Now you made me feel guilty, working you so hard. Let's do it. I could use a change in scenery."

We enjoyed dinner at a pleasant restaurant in Sanders and celebrated the beginning of a new year. Then, as the month aged by the end of January, all the pieces fell into place. Sam installed the new appliances, the woodwork cleaned, moisturized, and polished, the bedrooms upstairs completed, and the furniture arrived and placed. It took quite a hit to my bank account, but it was well worth it. My home looked incredible. I had put my stamp on it, but it still felt like grandma's arms were holding me close.

In February, Maggie and I drove to Grand Island, and I filled my car with a vast assortment of baby needs. I had to start at ground zero with clothes, bedding, diapers, and toys. Maggie was in an inquiring mode while driving back to Hartsuff with a jam-packed car.

"What's going on with you and Sam?" she asked.

"What do you mean? He's my contractor."

"I think Sam might think it could be something more."

"Where is that coming from?" I asked.

"People in town have seen you together often, and you know what small towns are like."

"Sam and I are just friends. He did a great job on the house, and that's as far as it can ever go."

"You might want to relay that to Sam," said Maggie. "Now, let's talk about the baby shower. How does the first of March sound?"

"You don't think it will be a little uncomfortable?"

"You'll be among family and close friends, everyone that supports you."

* * *

The baby shower was so much fun, and my family was beyond generous with gifts of gender-neutral baby clothes, a car seat, and the most beautiful bassinet with a silk organza and lace-trimmed white floor-length skirting. Maggie helped me set everything up in the nursery. I had one month to go and was feeling so cumbersome. My doctor's appointments were now every week, and everything seemed on schedule.

Sam brought the Jenny Lind crib back. He had restored it, and it was perfect. He took it into the nursery for me and stood there, taking everything in. Sam turned to me and took my hand.

"Brenna, we have known each other for most of our lives. Would you consider marrying me and giving your baby a father? I would love your baby as my own, and we could make a family together. What do you think?"

"Sam, that's the most wonderful and generous offer . . . . but I can't. It wouldn't be fair to you. You don't love me in that way, and I don't love you as a wife should. I treasure our friendship and don't want to lose you. I still love the man that fathered my child and probably always will. You deserve better than that. Thank you for asking. I hope we will always be the best of friends."

"We'll always be friends, Brenna. I wish you all the happiness possible." Sam kissed me on the cheek and left me in a puddle of tears.

CHAPTER FIFTEEN

My next hurdle was on me; I had to tell Chase and Gage about the baby. Time was running out, and I had put it off as long as possible. My due date was three weeks away. I emailed Chase to arrange a time for a video chat. I sat down at my laptop as we connected.

"Hi, sweetheart. How is life in Beijing? Everything going well?"

"It's been great, mom. I've learned so much, and I can speak almost as well as the natives, but I am getting a little homesick. I wondered if I could spend the summer at the farm before going back to Columbia for my senior year. Good ol' home cooking has been a dream of mine. No one cooks like you, mom."

"Of course you can. With the house renovated, bedrooms are waiting for you and Gage. So you will always have a home with me. But there's another thing I have been putting off telling you."

"What is it, mom? Are you okay?"

"I'm fine. Let me get this out before you say anything . . . . when I traveled to Italy last year . . . . . I met a man, and I fell in love. We spent two months together. Since your father, he's the first man I have ever had a deep interest in. I loved this man with all my heart, but I knew it would not work out for us in the end. Without going into the details, we come from two different worlds, and I couldn't become part of his, and he couldn't be part of mine.

"When I got back home, I found out. . . . . .I was pregnant and having a baby the first of April." I looked at his face on the screen with tears falling from my eyes.

"WOW, mom. That's a lot to take in. Are you okay, feeling alright?"

"I'm feeling good, just fat. I hope you're not disappointed in me."

"Mom, I love you, and I will love my new brother or sister as well. I could never be disappointed in you. I figured out a long time ago that you're not only a super mom, but you're human, like everyone else. Since dad died, you have been so alone and unhappy, and I prayed you would find someone to love again. Are you sure that it won't work out with this man? Does he live in Italy?"

"He's American, originally from Kansas. I'm sure that what we had has ended. He doesn't know about the baby, and I plan to keep it that way. I was so scared to tell you and lose your love and respect. Thank you for understanding."

"Mom, I love you; that will never change. I wish I could come home and help you now, but I can't leave until mid-May. Will you be okay until then?"

"I have lots of family here, and they have been very supportive. I can't wait to see you. Finish your studies, and I will be here when you get home. Do you need anything? Have enough money?"

"You don't have to worry about me. Let me worry about you. Am I having a brother or a sister?"

"Don't know. I wanted to be surprised."

"Whatever it is, it'll be great. Have you told Gage yet?"

"No, you're the first one I called. Do you think Gage will be as understanding as you have been?"

"I honestly don't know. He can be a little judgmental sometimes, but Gage loves you as much as I do, and we only want you to be happy again."

"I'm going to call him next. I hope he will be as accepting as you have been. Thank you for understanding, Chase. I love you and will talk to you soon."

"Bye, mom. Good luck and take care of yourself." I took a couple of minutes to get myself together before I placed the call to Gage.

"Hi Gage, how is everything going? I hope all is well with you." Gage filled me in on all his activities and studies. He was full of enthusiasm for Tokyo, loving the culture and the people. He thought he might stay through the summer before returning to Columbia. I let him go on with his chatter, adding my support to his excitement. Then it was my turn. I repeated the same dialog I had with his brother and was met with silence. His eyes turned from loving warmth to stone-cold disgust.

"WHAT! Are you telling me you got knocked up by some random guy in Italy? Did you turn into a slut suddenly, or has this been going on under my nose since dad died?"

"That's not fair, Gage. I told you I fell in love with this man, and I still love him, hoping you would understand, but I can see that you don't want to, nor do I deserve your unkindness. I love you and wish you could deal with it."

"Don't expect me to accept your bastard. I never expected this kind of behavior from you, Saint Brenna, preaching to me about safe sex when you're out whoring around. Have your kid, mom. Good luck."

Gage severed our connection, leaving me devastated. I knew this was going to be hard, but I didn't think that I would lose one child while awaiting the birth of another.

I cried the entire night, which brought on contractions. I had to calm down and not go into labor; it was too early. My phone was receiving calls by morning, but I didn't make any effort to answer. I couldn't deal with talking to anyone. Finally, an hour later, Maggie was at my door. I let her in, and she knew right away that something drastic had happened, telling her about my conversations with my sons and their reactions. I couldn't stop crying. Everything was my fault, and I would never forgive myself for destroying the unity of my family.

"Get ahold of yourself, Brenna. IT IS NOT YOUR FAULT. If Gage can't accept that you're human, then screw him. You allowed yourself to love again; that's a gift. You have always been a wonderful, loving mother to your sons, raising them alone after Marco died. The fault lies with Gage if he is so self-righteous that he can't see past it; that's on him, not you. I'm sure he will come around in time, but until then, don't let him rob you of the joy of a new life soon to come into the world."

Maggie held on to me as I cried myself out. My contractions had stopped, and I knew I had to move past this for the sake of my baby. Maggie stayed with me through the afternoon until I calmed down and could eat something. Chase called. He had talked with Gage after I had talked to him. He tried to reassure me that Gage would get over it and make amends.

Not so sure it would be soon. I had to live with that. I moved through the next few days trying to renew my excitement for the upcoming birth. Sam called and wanted to come out and talk about starting the new garage since the weather was breaking toward spring.

As soon as he saw me, he could tell that something was wrong, and I poured my heart out to him about Gage's reaction. He took my hand, and we walked out to the garage. As we looked it over, Sam could see that nothing was salvageable. The only reason it hadn't fallen was that it was leaning against the enormous tree next to it. We walked back to the house. He continued to pat my hand and tell me that everything would be okay. Sometimes, guys thought of their mothers as not women with the exact needs as men.

I okayed the go ahead with the garage demo and construction before the baby came, so that the sound of hammering and sawing would be over when there was a new baby in the house. Sam would be back tomorrow with a crew.

I drove to my doctor's appointments and stayed pretty close to home. The nursery was ready, and I was fielding calls from my friends in Chicago, those in town, and Chase. Betsy let me know they received a few more calls from Bob Smith. They finally informed him I no longer worked at the college. He asked where he could find me, but they didn't give out any information.

Every time I was in the grocery store, I would glance at the tabloid papers while in line at the checkout. There would be pictures on the covers of Ben and Deborah. Deborah was spouting her imminent engagement plans while stories of Ben centered on his directorial debut. I didn't stoop so low as to purchase any of the "rags" on display; why bother?

One afternoon, I was reading a book while Sam and crew were outside working on the new garage when Grandma's house phone rang. I had just found it and plugged it in the week before. I looked at the caller ID. It was Bob Smith; I let it ring. Was he going to haunt me here, too?

I reached the end of March. I was very uncomfortable, sleep was impossible, and heartburn was my constant companion. The doctor said it could be any day now. I packed my hospital bag for my delivery at the Sanders hospital; it was now down to a waiting game.

The first couple of days of April were sunny and warm as I strolled around the farmyard. I made mental lists of the repairs that needed to be attended to as soon as I was back on my feet. I couldn't wait to hang my bed linens on the clothesline, loving the fresh smell of sheets that had been hanging outdoors in the sunshine. I wanted to get Grandma's vegetable garden going again and plant oodles of flowers around the house. Spring was going to be busy.

Sam was sitting with me in the house having a beer after another hard workday on the garage. The crew poured the slab, and after curing, framing could begin. As we chatted away, I felt a small pop, and water ran down my legs; mild, erratic contractions were right on its heels.

Sam looked at me quizzically.

"I think I'm in labor, Sam."

He had a look of horror on his face. "Should I call someone for you? Do you want to lie down? Should I boil some water?" he asked.

"Only if you want a cup of tea. Hand me my phone," I called my doctor. She said to come to the hospital. This was it. The baby was overdue, and she said it was time for the baby to join the family. I looked at Sam. "Can you drive me to the hospital?"

Sam looked terrified. "I can. Just don't have the baby in my truck."

I handed Sam my bag, and he hurried outside to declutter the cab of his truck. I wiped up the floor and changed my clothes. We locked the house, and Sam held me around the waist and hefted me on to the truck seat. He shot down the road like he was on fire.

"Slow down, Sam. We have plenty of time," I said. I groaned as the contractions continued in earnest. In record time, we were at the hospital. As I was wheeled away, thanking Sam for getting me here, I texted Maggie that I was in labor at the hospital. I also texted Chase with the same information.

After an examination, I measured at five centimeters dilation. Staff called my doctor; this was no false alarm. Labor advanced at a fierce rate, transporting me to the delivery room by 10 PM. My baby was born seventeen minutes later.

Dr. Krason held up the baby. "Brenna, you have a beautiful baby girl."

I cried copious tears as they placed my daughter in my arms. She was so perfect with dark hair and eyes. While I was in recovery, Maggie and Sam came to the door to see the baby.

"Sam, you're still here. Thank you for getting me here and staying. Oh, Maggie, she's so beautiful."

"Yes, she is," as Maggie cried too. "Do you have a name for her?"

"This is Alexandra Victoria Herrera." Sam kissed me on the cheek, held the baby for a minute and then took his leave. The poor man was a nervous wreck.

"She looks like her father, doesn't she?" asked Maggie.

"Yes, I think she does," I murmured. A nurse took the baby, and they moved me to a private room. Maggie congratulated me again, gave me a hug and a kiss, and said she would be back tomorrow after I got some rest. I texted Chase, Betsy, and Michele—*It's a GIRL!*

My phone started beeping with texts of congratulations, wanting to know the name, weight, and length. I sent a group text: *Alexandra Victoria Herrera was born in Sanders, Nebraska, at 10:17 PM weighing in at 7 pounds and 8 ounces, 21 inches long and perfect. Easy delivery.*

I fell asleep with a mixture of great joy for the safe delivery of my beautiful daughter and tears of sadness that she would be without a father. Ben should have been here to see his child being born. Instead, he would never know the miracle of her birth. This was my baby, the little girl I had always dreamed of having.

Maggie drove us home from the hospital two days later, along with the flowers sent by Sam and my family members. Finally, I was feeling pretty good. I nursed my daughter every couple of hours and slept when I could. Maggie came out to help. She had a husband and two teenagers at home to take care of with a busy schedule, but still had time to help me. Blessed with the best sister and friend, I couldn't have asked for more.

The crew was hard at work on the garage. Sam knocked on the door and wanted to see the baby. I handed Alexandra to him. He held her as if she was the most delicate thing he had ever seen. It was a perfect picture of contrasts—big, rough workman's hands holding a tiny newborn baby as if she was made of delicate spun glass.

"She's so light," he said.

"Her weight is about average for a newborn. She's beautiful, isn't she?"

"Yes, she is. You did a good job, Brenna. I never had children of my own, so I would like to be her 'Uncle' if you don't mind. Of course, that marriage proposal is still open if you change your mind."

"Thank you, Sam, but no, I won't do that to you."

"Well, I better get back to work. Will it be okay to come and check on you both while I'm around?"

"Of course, you're family and a good, good friend."

* * *

Loads of little pink outfits arrived by mail from my friends in Chicago. Chase sent a big pink teddy bear via Amazon. No word from Gage. I sent pictures to my closest friends and Chase. He would be home in five weeks, and I couldn't wait to see him. If someone had told me how my life would change in a year, I never would have believed it possible.

It took some getting used to being on call as the "chuck wagon", but the quiet times I spent with my daughter as she nursed were priceless. Finally, we got into a routine, and after a month, she was sleeping longer between feedings.

Spring was in full bloom, and I potted colorful geraniums and hanging baskets for the front porch. I planted annuals around the house's base and tried to revive Grandma's rose bushes. In another week, I wanted to plant the vegetable garden. I would take Alex out in her carrier as I tilled a spot for the garden. The new garage was complete; I could get my car out of the scorching sun and dust, our way of life in the summer.

One day, I investigated the contents of the old washhouse. Before there was indoor plumbing, these long-gone hardy people took infrequent baths in this building. The old footed cast iron tub was still there with a wood-fired stove to heat the water. Once the tub was full of water, the cleanest person in the family bathed first, followed by increasing degrees of dirtiness, all sharing the same water. There was no leisurely bathing here; it was in and out before the water got cold. Also in the washhouse were the hand crank wringer washer, washtubs, and washboards. I can't imagine how tough it was in the old days, especially for women with babies in diapers. It made me exhausted thinking about it.

Working in the garden and nursing Alexandra, my figure was coming back. I had another ten pounds to go. I had let my hair grow over the last year, and it was now down to the middle of my back. Our life on the farm was quiet and relaxed. Alexandra seemed to grow and change every day. She was filling out, and no longer looked like a squished-up puppy. Her hair is still dark, as are her eyes. It doesn't look like they're going to change. She has Ben's coloring and inherited his demand for attention.

I tried not to think about Ben; it was almost a year since that first kiss in the doorway in Florence. I had heard nothing further about his attempting to contact me, probably married to the "Brain Trust" by now, working toward his third divorce.

I filled my days by stocking the freezer with fresh baked goodies. Friends and family stopped by frequently to see the baby, and it was nice to have something to offer them. Sam stopped by periodically to see how we were doing. We grew into a comfortable relationship as friends.

Alexandra reached the six-week mark and was sleeping for most of the night. I was getting things ready for Chase's visit. His room upstairs was ready and waiting. I had Sam look at the old corral fencing and the small horse shed. I was thinking about having Great Uncle

John bring my three horses back home. But first, I had to get hay, feed, and straw and check the tack and water troughs. I knew Chase would enjoy riding again, something we all did a lot on our visits to Grandma when my sons were children.

Sam came out, fixed up the corral, and put a fresh coat of paint on the horse shed. I cleaned the tack and ordered the feed and bedding for the horses. I bought a new steel trough, replacing the old wooden one that had been in the corral since I was a child and leaked like a sieve. When Chase gets home, I'll have the horses moved back to the farm.

Great Uncle John's, or Guncle John as I called him, grandson planted our fields that I continued to lease to him, the same arrangement he had with Grandma. I loved the smell of the newly plowed earth, with the faint smell of the grazing animals perfuming the warm spring air. Everything dormant during the cold winter was coming back to life again. Trees had leafed out, and I could open the windows in the house, letting in the fresh sun-warmed air. Sheets and blankets were on the clothesline, flapping in the wind, soaking in the fresh outdoor smell.

A life on the farm was where Alex and I belonged. Sure, farmers worked hard, long hours, and people sometimes got hurt and weather was turbulent at times and unpredictable, but I chose this life for my daughter and me. There is a tight sense of community where we look out for each other and pitch in to help those in need. Unlike the city where I hardly knew my neighbors and eye contact was absent while walking on the street. Instead, a nodding acknowledgment was all anyone could expect.

Alexandra was down for her afternoon nap, and I emptied the dishwasher and was doing laundry when someone knocked on the back door. I looked to see who drove in for a visit, and my heart stopped. The most handsome man stood there with a big smile as I cried out, and we threw our arms around each other. Chase was home.

Over a year away had changed him. He was an adult, looking more mature—no longer a child but a grown man. We kissed and hugged each other, rocking back and forth as I repeated how much I missed and loved him.

"I missed you too, mom. Let me look at you." He held me at arm's length. "You don't look like a woman who had a baby six weeks ago. You are more beautiful than ever, and you're happy; I can see it in your eyes."

"I am happy more so now that you're here."

"Where's my sister? I want to see her."

We walked to the nursery in my bedroom and tiptoed to her bassinet. Chase looked down and fell in love. "She's beautiful, mom. Are you feeling okay? Everything progressed well when she was born?"

"I'm fine. Alexandra was eager to come into the world. She is beautiful and a perfect baby." Alexandra was waking up and stretched her arms in the air. She opened her eyes and burped.

"That's my sister, alright," Chase laughed. "Can I pick her up?"

"Sure you can; she's been waiting to meet her big brother."

Chase picked Alexandra up, cradling her in his arms; he smiled from ear to ear. Alex looked into her brother's eyes, and she knew instinctively this person would love her. She gifted him with the slightest beginnings of a smile. Chase put a finger to Alex's tiny hand, and she wrapped her fist around it.

"Let me get to know her, mom, and you can go do whatever you have to finish in the kitchen."

I left them together in the nursery as I walked away with tears running down my face. I put the rest of the clean clothes away and did other chores while my son bonded with his sister.

Chase walked into the kitchen. "Mom, I think she needs a diaper change. Will you teach me how to do it?"

Back in the nursery, I showed him how to clean Alexandra up, replace the diaper, and dress her in a stretchy pink playsuit. I handed her back to him, and we moved to the kitchen so I could start supper. It was hamburger night, and I had made some potato salad earlier and had some fresh fruit. I got a cake out of the freezer for dessert.

Alexandra fussed. "Chase, can you watch the burgers? Alex needs to be fed, and that's something you're not equipped for."

He blushed with understanding, "Sure, mom. I'll set the table and finish the burgers. Whenever you're ready."

I took Alex into the nursery, and we sat down in the rocking chair as I unbuttoned my blouse and settled her at my breast. She nursed lustily; my girl was hungry. Then, switching her to the other breast, she continued her gluttony. Once satisfied and burped, we returned to the kitchen. I placed her in her bouncy seat so that Chase and I could have our supper. Alexandra was content as we took the time to talk about his year in China.

He loved it, but thought living for an extended period in China wasn't something he was interested in pursuing. There was an adjustment period for dining and some of the exotic foods the Chinese loved, but Chase couldn't bring himself to try; pig blood, chicken testicles, and pig brains. In addition, Chase stood out as quite an anomaly. He was much taller than the average Chinese man, and it was hard to find long enough clothes. All-in-all it was a great learning experience, and his language skills improved dramatically, but it wasn't home.

I ventured to ask, "Have you talked to your brother lately?"

"No, I haven't. Gage told me what he said to you, and I told him he was a sanctimonious ass. So until he apologizes to you, I'm not talking to him. He had no right to say the things he did, and until he comes around, I don't need to listen to him piss and moan."

"I'm sorry that happened. I hope you two can make amends. As for me, I will have to live with it."

"Until he falls off his high horse, I don't want to hear from him. That's enough about him. The house looks beautiful, mom. How do you do it all? Fix up the house, have a baby, and still be a great mom?"

"I did what I had to do, and I had a lot of help with the house. I love it here; this is where I am meant to be. I love my family and hope that we can all be together again; my love for each of you will never change. I know I am truly blessed, and Alexandra made it perfect."

"I am here now to help you until late August. Just tell me what you need me to do. The farm will be a great place for me to recharge for school in the fall."

"I know how much you love the horses. The shed is ready, the tack is clean, and I have feed and supplies. Guncle John will bring over the horses when we are ready. If you would like to take care of them, that would be great."

"Love to mom as long as I get to help take care of my sister too."

"Deal. I'll get the dishes in the dishwasher and then a lesson on bathing a baby."

Chase took to caring for his sister like a duck to water. He would do everything but feed her. Alex was beginning to notice different people; she would gurgle and wave her arms when she saw her brother. Chase would play with Alex so that I could get things done in the yard. I got my garden in with tomatoes, potatoes, onions, green beans, lettuce, cabbage, cucumbers, peppers, and carrots. We planted a couple of rows of honey and cream sweet corn in the back of the garden, staggering the planting so we would have fresh corn throughout the season. There's nothing like fresh produce right out of the garden and on the table within minutes. I had an apple tree and chokecherry bushes to make great pies, jelly, and syrup.

Guncle John planned with Chase to get our three horses back to my farm. Chase loved the country life. The only fly in the ointment was Gage, with complete radio silence.

Maggie and Sam would drive out for visits, or Alex and I would go into town on grocery day and have lunch with them. The girls in town and surrounding farms were all atwitter and would make random drives past our home, hoping to glimpse Chase.

With all his work with the horses and the chores that accompanied them, he was tan and developing farm muscles. Not only was he drop-dead handsome, but a good, kind man. I was so proud of him. How I will miss his daily presence when he goes back to college in the fall.

By early June, the garden was growing well, crops were in, and I was going through the stuff I had moved to the barn when I moved in. Maggie's truck came roaring into the driveway. After checking at the house, she ran to the barn and, out of breath, spilled the latest news in town that was going to turn my comfortable and restorative country life upside down.

CHAPTER SIXTEEN

O ur cousin Gary was on the Sanders Town Council, and at last night's meeting, he announced a movie crew would arrive soon to film on the massive Nelson Cattle Ranch, eight miles from my farm. People were excited to be extras in a new film produced by Robert Merrill and directed by the one and only Ben Langford.

My heart dropped to my feet. I thought I was going to be sick. I looked at Maggie, and she looked at me as we realized the complications this would present. What was I going to do? The crew and actors would film off and on for six weeks. Ben knew damn well this was where I came to get away. What were the Nelson's thinking? The commotion of filming a movie would disrupt the lives of everyone for miles around.

Massive numbers of trailers and trucks were on their way, along with generators, food trucks, and everything needed to set up for a location shoot. It may be good for the local economy but devastating for me. I couldn't leave my farm or take my baby and hide. I sat down and cried. Why couldn't he leave me alone? We were over. He had Deborah now, and he was welcome to her with her plastic body and empty head. I would have to hide out on the farm, sending Chase into town for groceries or supplies while Ben was in the vicinity. I had to protect my baby and myself.

The following week, over thirty trailers rolled out to the Nelson Ranch. Setting up would take another week, and then the cast would arrive, and filming would begin. So I drove into town before all the actors assembled and bought all the groceries I would need for the next two months. I would not leave my bastion of safety until the film people left town.

It mystified Chase that I wasn't showing any enthusiasm for our Hollywood visitors. Instead, it intrigued him as well as everyone else in town. I told him I had seen the chaos of filming a movie while I was in Italy, and I didn't need to get involved with a sequel.

By the middle of June, filming had begun. I sequestered myself on the farm, never leaving the confines of my property. Chase noticed the change in my once happy and content behavior. He often asked if everything was okay. I assured him I was fine, but he knew something was bothering me. After that, I barely left the house, only to water the garden or hang the bedsheets on the clothesline.

Maggie came out to the farm to fill me in on what was happening. "At the grocery I was standing in line at the checkout. Patti Sepchek was the checker, and you know how flighty she is when the man ahead of me got to the register. Patti just about had an incontinence issue, recognizing the man ahead of me. It was Ben, Brenna. Patti gushed and gushed, asking for an autograph and babbling endlessly. Ben asked her if she knew where you lived. I waved my hands around behind his back and shook my head, trying to let her know not to say anything. Finally, she got it and said she didn't know for sure. He turned around and looked at me, and I pasted a look of angelic innocence on my face.

"I have to say he is one gorgeous male specimen, and he was very nice to Patti. He didn't act like a stuck-up snob, but a regular guy. Brenna, he's going to find out from someone where you live. Be prepared. He will not let this go."

"That's what I'm afraid of. Maggie, what am I going to do? I don't want to see him. What if he finds out about Alex? I can't let that happen."

"You still love him, don't you?"

"I still care about him. He gave me Alex, but he's moved on with Deborah. His lifestyle is something I don't want my daughter exposed to. He deceived both me and Deborah. I was a piece on the side of no importance to him, just a diversion. Our breakup wasn't pretty. He was engaged to another woman all the while we were together. He betrayed my trust, and I can't forgive that."

"I'm coming out tomorrow morning early. You need to get out of the house and clear your head. Let's go for a ride."

"Sounds good. I'll get the horses saddled, say about 8 AM, and we can kick up some dust."

"It's a date. See you then." Maggie took off back to her home in town. I did a little more sorting in the barn, and then it was time to feed Alex and get her down for an afternoon nap. Chase was playing with her when I got into the house.

"Mom, what's going on with you? You've been so nervous for the last couple of weeks. What's changed?"

"Just all the craziness in town with the film people. They're driving everyone nuts, including me."

"Okay, mom, if you say so." Chase walked out the door to feed the horses and do the daily grooming.

I fixed lunch, nursed Alex, and put her down for a nap. I paced back and forth in the kitchen. For Chase's sake, I had to calm down.

He wasn't swallowing my impotent explanations, but didn't challenge their validity. I wasn't fooling Chase, only fooling myself. I wish I could throw down a beer or two; it might help.

After supper, I gave Alex her bath and nursed her before bedtime. My little angel was sleeping through the night, and I hit the sheets soon after Chase drove into town for a beer with his cousins. I heard him come home in the wee hours and go upstairs to bed. Again, there was that sense a mother has with an ear tuned to the movements of her chicks, not able to fall deeply asleep until the last one is back in the nest. I turned over and fell into an exhaustive sleep.

I was out of bed as the sun was rising with the promise of a blazing hot day. Alex was still sleeping, so I stepped out and saddled two of the horses and tied them to the corral fence. Next, I got breakfast ready for Chase and started a big pot of coffee. Both Chase and Alex emerged shortly after. While Chase sat at the kitchen table downing cups of caffeine, I changed Alex, fed her, and got her ready for the day. Soon, Maggie arrived, and Chase took charge of his sister.

"Go out and have a good ride, mom. Try to relax. I'll keep the home fires burning."

Maggie and I saddled up and rode over the fields until we came to open pasture. A soft breeze stirred the prairie grasses, undulating like the waves in the ocean. We rode around the ravines, washouts, and loped over the sandhills. I felt my spirits rise. I filled my lungs with the essence of my prairie home. Then we indulged in an impromptu race to a prominent ridge in the distance, filling the air with our laughter. As we pulled up on the reins, bringing our horses to a halt, I looked over the other side of the ridge, where, unfortunately; I found the film crew at work.

I heard "cut" shouted out as the assembled company turned and looked up in our direction. The director rose out of his chair, and our eyes met even at a distance. I turned my horse around and headed back toward my farm at a gallop. After a couple of miles, I slowed to a walk. Maggie caught up with me.

"It's the first time I've seen him in almost a year," I said.

"Are you doing okay? Can you handle seeing him again?" Maggie asked.

"I don't know, Mags. To build a new life with Alex, I tried to forget him and leave him in my past. I don't want to feel the things I'm feeling. Just a glance is bringing everything back, the good and the bad. How do I fight this?"

"It's no accident that he's here. He could have picked any number of locations to shoot his film, but he came here knowing that you would be nearby. He can't let go any more than you can. You should talk to him; it might help excise him from your mind."

"I'm afraid if I talk to him, all my anger and hurt will come billowing out. I can't take the chance that he will find out about Alex," I said.

We galloped back toward the farm, then cooled down the horses in a walk as the barn came into view. Finally, I unsaddled the horses and put them in the pasture. Maggie came into the house for a cup of coffee and chatted a couple of minutes with Chase before heading back to town.

"Mom, I have something to tell you. I was in the bar last night with Troy and Travis when a couple of people from the film company came in with Ben Langford. He came up to the bar where we were sitting, waiting for the bartender, and started talking to us.

"He introduced himself, like we didn't know who he was, and shaking hands, we did the same. When he heard my last name, he asked me if I was your son. When I confirmed I was, he told me about meeting you in Florence a year ago. He seemed to know a lot about you, mom. Is he? . . Alex's father?"

I took a couple of seconds to get my thoughts together. I had never lied to Chase, maybe evaded answering some questions, but never lied, and I would not start now. "Yes, he is. I fell deeply in love with him, and I thought he was in love with me. We spent a lot of time together in Italy and spent a month in Santorini before I came home."

"What happened?" asked Chase.

"Deborah McIntyre happened. She came to visit him and complete their engagement plans. I turned tail and ran back home as fast as I could. I couldn't deal with the fact a Hollywood playboy had duped me. When I found out I was carrying Alex, I made it my mission to come back home, have my baby, and live as far away from his reach as possible. He broke my heart, Chase. I don't want to talk to him or see him or have anything further to do with him."

"Of all the ranch land in this country, I don't think it was an accident that he's here. He hasn't let you go any more than you have left him in the rearview mirror. He knows where we live. I'm so sorry, mom."

"Not your fault, Chase. This is a situation that I made myself. He's either still engaged or married to Deborah by now, and I don't want him to know about Alex. His lifestyle and wife would never be a good influence on Alex. So I have to protect her; I don't want him to know about her existence."

"Do you think that's fair to him?"

"Fair or not, I was a passing fancy among a parade of women in his life. Alex deserves a life of security and love. But, unfortunately, I don't think he's capable of either."

"I don't know him, but I think he might feel for you more than you think. He's here for a reason, not just because of the movie he's directing. Now I'm going to get to work, and I think my sister is waking from her morning nap and is hungry. See you later; I love you, mom."

I got Alex up, changed her diaper, and fed her. She has grown and changed so much over three months and was smiling, gurgling, and almost ready to turn over when I laid her on her blanket on the floor. She's so beautiful with her dark hair and eyes, just like Ben's.

I fixed lunch, took all the sheets off the beds, and ran them through the washer. I wanted to get them on the clothesline. We would have rain tonight. I could smell it in the air. The storm was a while off, so I would have to get the sheets on the clothesline fast.

Alex was down for her afternoon nap; Chase was emailing friends and listening for his sister in the house. The sheets were dry as I took them down from the clothesline and folded them. I heard a car drive into the driveway. Without turning around, I knew who it was. I was dreading this moment, and I wasn't sure if I was ready to face him. I could hear him walking toward me with his boots crunching on the sandy driveway with every step.

"Brenna."

"Ben."

"Will you turn around and look at me?"

"I don't think that's necessary. I don't want to see you. When I left Rome, I thought that was clear. Please go; we have nothing to talk about and no reason to see each other. It's over; move on and leave me in peace." I continued to fold the sheets and fill the laundry basket as the wind picked up. The clouds had darkened; we were going to get a soaking. "You better get back to town before the storm breaks. Our kind of rain can make it hard to drive. Goodbye, don't come back." I walked past him and marched into the house, closed and locked the door. As the rain pelted the thirsty ground, Ben got in his car and left. The rain came down in buckets as I fried chicken in the kitchen. Chase came in to put his arm around my shoulder.

"I saw him drive in and talk to you. Are you doing okay?"

I looked at Chase with tears clouding my eyes. "About as well as expected."

"I heard, mom, the window was open."

"I couldn't even look at him," I said.

"Doesn't that tell you something? You're not over him, and he is certainly not over you. I saw how he looked at you."

"I'll always be grateful to him for giving me Alex, but gratitude isn't enough for a relationship. He travels around the world, flying in private jets, staying in the most luxurious accommodations with people to satisfy his every whim. Then he goes back to L.A. or his Malibu beach house in the glow of his fame and mixing with the other members of the glamorazzi with all their excesses. That kind of life is not for me. I'm home, and that's where I'm staying."

CHAPTER SEVENTEEN

The 4th of July was coming up, and the town fathers decided that Sanders and Hartsuff would jointly host a party for the filmmakers. Sanders would have their traditional parade and then a barbeque in the city park, inviting everyone in the surrounding area. The production company donated fireworks to follow. Although I wasn't planning on going to town for the celebration, I could glimpse the fireworks from my open field. I encouraged Chase to get his morning chores done, take the rest of the day off, and have some fun with his friends. He took a few minutes to play with his sister while I busied myself out in the vegetable garden with some much needed weeding.

A car drove in the driveway; I kept weeding and fertilizing the tomatoes.

"Nice garden, Brenna."

"Thanks, a lot of work, but well worth it by August."

"Can we talk?"

"I don't think there is anything to talk about."

"I think there is. Why did you leave Rome before we could talk?" Ben asked.

"Don't you think that three's a crowd when you're talking about your engagement and wedding with your fiancé?" I stood up and finally faced him with the garden fork in my hand.

"I never asked Deborah to marry me."

"Well, she sure thought so, and I didn't see you fighting her off while she stuck her tongue down your throat and her hand in your pants."

"You didn't give me a chance to explain. That was all a publicity stunt on her part."

"You both played your parts very well. After all, you are actors; every supermarket magazine had your pictures splashed all over the covers—The engagement. The ring. The wedding plans. You denied nothing. Meanwhile, I have moved on."

Chase came out of the house. "Mom, Alex needs you."

"I'll be right there," handing the garden fork to Ben. "Now get the 'fork' out of here." I hurried to the house while Chase walked over to Ben, as I mumbled, "eat shit and die asshole". Isn't it ridiculous that one man can turn a mature woman like me into a teenage potty mouth?

*　*　*

"Make yourself useful until Mom comes back. Help me feed and brush the horses," said Chase as they walked toward the horse shed.

Chased handed Ben a brush, "You groom Curlie, and I'll get Moe and Larry."

Ben laughed, "Are you kidding? Larry, Moe, and Curlie?"

"Mom named them years ago." The grooming progressed in an uncomfortable silence. Chase filled the feed buckets and made sure the trough was full. Then, leaning against the fence with his chin resting on his crossed arms on the top rail, looking at Ben, he said, "If you hurt my mother again, I WILL come after you."

"I don't want to hurt her. I love her. Who is this, Alex? Are they living together? Does she love him?" asked Ben.

"Yes, Ben. She loves Alex with all her heart, and they have been living together for three months. I love Alex too, you could say, like a brother."

"What does this Alex do for a living? Does he love her in return? Are they happy?"

"Why don't you go in the house and find out, Ben? Go through the kitchen door, turn right, then left past the dining room down the hallway and left through the pocket doors. Tell Mom I'm going to town."

Chase got in his car and pulled out of the driveway as Ben walked slowly to Brenna's house. Ben let himself in the door quietly. He followed Chase's directions and found Brenna coming out of a room, closing the pocket doors and re-buttoning her blouse.

"Did I catch you after a little afternoon delight? Who is Alex? Did you wear him out?"

"That is none of your business. This is my house, and I decide who stays and who goes and that would be you. Please leave, Ben. I'm not discussing this. I'm accountable only to myself and certainly not to you."

"Stand aside, Brenna. I can either break down this door, or you can open it. Your choice, but either way, I'm going in."

I stood still as Ben shoved me out of the way and opened the doors to my bedroom.

"Interesting choice of music." Ben followed the sound of Alex's mobile and stood staring at the sleeping baby in the crib. Then, turning, "Whose baby is this?"

I looked at him with a mix of anger and fear. "It's my baby."

"With all the pink, I assume it's a girl. How old is she, Brenna?"

"She's three months old today," as I watched him do a quick calculation in his head.

With rising anger, he asked, "Is she my daughter? AM I HER FATHER? ANSWER ME." Ben looked at me with fury in his eyes.

"Ssssssss, keep your voice down. If you wake her, she'll be cranky for the rest of the day."

Ben grabbed my arm and yanked me out of the nursery. "Let me repeat, is she my daughter?"

"Take your hands off me, you ass. She's MY daughter. The place for the father's name on her birth certificate lists, *Father Unknown.*"

"Damn it, Brenna. Is she my daughter? I want an honest answer."

"You want an honest answer? Do you know what honesty is? Yes, you fathered her, but she's my daughter."

"What did you name her, Brenna?"

"I named her Alexandra."

"What's her full name?"

"Alexandra Victoria Herrera. Satisfied? NOW GET OUT."

"I'm not going anywhere until we come to an understanding. Why didn't you tell me you were pregnant with my baby?"

"When was I supposed to do that, Ben? At your engagement party? Or your wedding reception? I won't see my daughter's picture splashed all over the tabloids, 'See Ben Langford's Love Child—Read All About It'. She doesn't deserve that, and neither do I."

"If I have to go to court and fight you for custody, I will."

With tears running down my face, I looked at Ben and quietly asked, "Would you really do that to me, Ben? Do you hate me that much?"

The anger fell away from Ben's face and voice, "I wouldn't do that to you, Brenna. I don't hate you. I love you."

I sat down on the sofa in the living room and put my hands on my face, and burst into a violent siege of crying. Pain speared through my body as if my heart was rupturing. An agony so deep that I thought it would swallow me as I beat my fists on his chest. Ben wrapped his arms around me, holding me as I cried for what we lost.

"Please don't cry, darling. I'm so very sorry I said what I did. I would never try to take the baby from you. Deborah robbed us both of sharing in the birth of our child. You had to do this yourself, and I am sorry I wasn't at your side. I've missed so much. Will you let me see her? I want to be part of her life and yours, if you'll let me."

I was so limp that I couldn't distance myself from his hold on me, but uttered my deepest fears. "I don't want her birth announced; this is between us. I want her to have a normal, secure life. So I won't keep you apart, but I won't let her become part of your celebrity lifestyle and the excesses that go with it. I will fight you every inch of the way to protect her," I said with inevitable resignation. "I hear her now. I'll go get her and introduce you."

We returned to the nursery. Alexandra kicked her feet in the air and waved her arms around as she gurgled in her unique language. I picked her up to change her diaper, dress her in a clean outfit, and then handed Alex to Ben. She got a funny look on her face, as if trying to decide if she recognized this person holding her or not. Finally, she broke into a big smile as Ben kissed her forehead.

"She's beautiful, Brenna. Is her middle name for my mother?"

"I've always liked the name, and it crossed my mind that it was your mother's name, too."

"Will you tell me some of what I missed? Where was she born? How much did she weigh? Was it hard for you to give birth?"

"Alex was born at the Sanders Hospital," and I told him the vitals. "Labor and delivery were no walk in the park, but it was fast, less than five hours."

"It must have been a surprise when you found out you were pregnant."

"I didn't think it was possible. When I started not feeling well, I thought I had a serious disease. I think I was in shock. I didn't know what to do, but I knew that abortion was out of the question for me. I loved this baby from the moment I knew she was on the way. That's when I decided I was leaving Chicago for a better life for her and me. I have family and friends here, and I knew I could give her a good life in the country. Chase fell in love with Alex at first sight. He plays with her, bathes her, and changes diapers."

"How about your other son?" Ben inquired.

"It didn't go well when I told Gage I was pregnant. He called me some very unpleasant names, and I haven't heard from him since. It breaks my heart that he can't seem to accept Alex and me as we are. Where's Chase, by the way?"

"Chase left for town a couple of hours ago. He's the one who told me to go into the house and find out who Alex is. I thought you had a lover stashed away. I am sorry that I caused the fracture in your family. I hope Gage can come to realize and what he is missing not knowing his sister."

"I'm going to have to feed Alex soon. If you're hungry, there's some cold chicken leftover from last night and some potato salad in the refrigerator."

"I'm starved. I didn't stay in town and eat at the barbeque before I drove out here."

"Hold on to Alex, and I'll put something on the table for you." I got out the chicken and the salad, and he sat down to eat. Ben had a beer, and I had a glass of milk. My appetite had evaporated. He gave me a quizzical look when I didn't join him with wine or beer.

I asked him how the filming was going and where they were off to after the shooting here finished, trying my best to form a new relationship with Ben with a fragile truce, since he would be in Alex's life in the future. I didn't want to appear the embittered ex-lover to Alex, with her feeling she was a mistake or a burden to me. I owed it to her to let her know her father and develop a bond with him. The question—was Ben serious and capable of establishing a lasting relationship with his daughter? Or would she become a momentary curiosity like so many others in his world? Ben did not have a long attention span and the novelty of fatherhood would lose its appeal, leaving a broken-hearted child in his wake.

"The filming so going okay. The weather has caused some delays, but it looks like we will finish by the end of the month. I want to get some footage of the rodeo before we go. Then it's off to Ireland for two weeks of fast shooting and then London for a week. After that, I can shoot the rest of the scenes in the studio in California. We should wrap by mid-September or thereabout."

"Glad it's going well. It's a fantastic story."

"Your house is incredible. Will you give me a tour later?"

"It turned out well, but it took months to get it renovated. I sold my condo in Chicago, packed and shipped some furniture here, and sold the rest. At the end of the year, I quit my job and moved. I knew this is where I belong, where I have always belonged."

"You did that all while you were pregnant? That couldn't have been easy for you. I hope you had a lot of help."

"My friends in Chicago helped me pack, and the condo sold right away. Everything fell into place." I cleared the table and cleaned up the kitchen. It was time for Alex to have her bath. In the master bathroom, I filled her plastic bathtub, undressed her, and placed her in her baby bath. Ben watched every move and chuckled when Alex kicked her feet and slashed water all over herself. I washed her hair, something she hates, and washed her body with her baby soap. Out of the tub, I took Alex over to the changing table, diapered her, and massaged her little body with lotion. Dressed in nightwear, I put Alex on her tummy with a blanket on the floor in the living room with her toys. Ben and I sat and watched her, trying to get to her toys and grasp her target. She was raising her head and trying to figure out how to roll over. Not there yet, but it wouldn't be long before she would master this new move.

Alex screwed up her face and cried. She was hungry. I left Ben in the living room and moved to the nursery to breastfeed her. We were in the rocking chair when Ben walked in.

"You've never been more beautiful, Brenna, feeding my daughter. I never thought I would ever have a child, and you made it possible. Thank you for our daughter and the chance to get to know her. I know I don't deserve it, but thank you for the chance, anyway."

"She looks like you, doesn't she?"

"I think she does. But how am I ever going to have the strength to leave you and her behind?" Ben asked.

"You'll do what you have to do and know where we are. I can't do anything better than that. So you'll come back when it suits, and I'll send pictures and let you know how Alex is."

"I never wanted to be a part-time father if I ever had the good fortune of having a child. My stupidity created this. I have only myself to blame."

"I won't argue with you on that point," I said.

Alex was full and fell asleep in my arms. I wrapped her in her light summer sleeper and tucked her in bed. Ben bent over and kissed her goodnight, passing his hand over the silky soft hair on her head. I turned on her night light and left my angel to sleep. We sat in the living room, and I showed pictures of the house renovations, the before and after.

"The house is beautiful, and I'm happy that you have your grandmother's house. I know how special it is for you."

"It's the place where I found a home and was privileged to have Grandma to love me as her own. I could live nowhere else."

"I better go. We have another early morning shoot tomorrow, and you need your rest."

"I promise not to disturb your set again," I said.

"When the sunbeams hit your hair, I knew it was you. I wanted to see you so badly, and there you were, like a dream come to life. Can I kiss you goodnight?"

Ben took me in his arms, and I melted against him. Our bodies fit together just as I remembered, perfectly. I felt his lips feather over mine as I felt a hunger for his touch. My lips consumed what he offered, and his tongue slipped between my lips. I welcomed his invasion and returned it with growing zeal. But then, I had to step away. I couldn't go through the loving and leaving again. The woman on Santorini was no longer naïve. I had come out of the ether with a whole new perspective for my life.

"I love you, Brenna. I never stopped," as he turned and left the house and drove away.

"I love you, Ben. I never stopped," I whispered as the taillights of his car vanished in a swirl of dust.

CHAPTER EIGHTEEN

The filming continued through July, with Ben spending his down time with Alex and me. Ben attempted to get to know Chase, and every indication was that they were becoming more comfortable with a resigned acceptance of each other. When we had time together, we did a lot of talking. We kissed and hugged frequently, but I won't let myself go any further. I didn't want to cross that bridge to physical intimacy again and then find the bridge collapsing around me. I made peace with the situation knowing that Ben would soon be on his way to Ireland, and I would resume my life after shoving him out of my thoughts—again.

The rodeo was the last film footage that the movie company was shooting at the end of the month. The rodeo was always a big event, and I enjoyed going to the performances. I attended once with Maggie and her family while Chase took care of Alex. Then, returning home, I told Chase to have fun with his friends. He worked so hard this summer, and he needed to be young, single, and experience more of life than staying home, babysitting, and helping me with the farm.

The movie trailers had moved out, and the county was getting back to normal. The day had finally come when Ben would be leaving. Chase said his goodbyes to Ben and left the farm to meet friends, giving us time alone with our daughter. I tried to create tactile memories taking in his scent and the way he felt as my hand moved over his skin. The life he lived made it unreasonable that he would or could be faithful to one woman. If I was to give myself physically again, I needed commitment and devotion. I kissed Ben goodbye, promising to send pictures of Alexandra to his phone. I bathed and put my daughter to bed after feeding her. Chase came home, and we sat down to a cup of tea.

"How are you handling it, Mom?"

I didn't need any clarification; Chase was concerned that I would fall apart after another leave-taking with Ben. "I'm fine; I knew this day was coming, and I prepared myself for it. I have accepted the circumstances, whether or not I like it. Ben will be in and out of Alexandra's life, and I have to make the best of it for her sake. I won't rob her of the chance to know her father."

"Mom, I hate to leave you and go back to school in a couple of weeks."

"I know you do, but it would break my heart if you didn't follow your path and pursue your dreams. I won't be alone; Alex is here and my family and friends near. There is nothing more important than for you to enjoy your life and soar, doing what you want to do. Your father would be so proud of you. I have a new project that will keep me busy this fall and through the winter. I'm going to renovate the chicken coop. It would make a great playhouse for Alex when she gets older."

"Are you thinking about keeping chickens again, like Grandma?"

"Unquestionably no. I think it traumatized me when I was a child. When grandma wanted to fry chicken for supper, she would grab one, chop the head off, and the chicken body would run around in circles, and the head flop around on the ground. I prefer my chicken plucked, cut up, and wrapped in plastic. I'll have the horses to take care of, so I will be busy and content."

The next three weeks flew by. Alex and I took Chase to the airport in Omaha for his flight to New York. We hugged and kissed as tears clouded our eyes. Chase hugged his sister with so much love and tenderness. They had formed a special bond after their months together.

"I hope she doesn't forget me until I can get home for Christmas."

"Not a chance. We'll have FaceTime, and I'll put your picture in her room so she can see your face every day."

"Thanks, Mom. I love you. Be happy." Chase turned and moved through security and was gone.

While we were in the big city, I did some shopping during the late summer sales. I bought summer clothes for Alex, a couple of sizes bigger that she could grow into, and some fall and winter clothes for the next season. I nursed Alex in the car before we started the drive home. She acted a little cranky; I could tell she wasn't feeling well. By the time we arrived back at the farm, Alex was feverish. I checked her mouth, and her lower gums were swollen; she was teething. I had a bottle of teething medication ready for the occasion. After a soothing bath, Tylenol, and the gum medicine, she slept with some relief.

For the following two days, Alex was drooling and chewing on anything she could get her hands around. Finally, two little white teeth popped out of her lower gums on the third day, and I knew it was time to wean her from breastfeeding. My baby was almost five months old, sitting up by herself and rolling over on the floor. It wouldn't be long before she was crawling. I shared these milestones with Ben via FaceTime. Alex would smile into the laptop camera, proudly showing off her new chops to her daddy, and Chase took almost as much joy as I did when Alex did something new.

My heart ached that there was no word from Gage. Chase had talked to him at college, but he didn't share their conversations with me. I had paid both of their tuition for the senior year and put money in their accounts for living expenses.

By September, my garden was full of fresh produce. Maggie and I spent days making salsa, enough to supply a medium-sized Mexican restaurant for a year. We made applesauce and apple butter from my tree and chokecherry jelly by the quarts. Fresh right from the garden, salads were served twice a day. Alex ate some solid foods since weaned and drank from a sippy cup. She loved sitting in her highchair and sampling whatever I was cooking or baking. I made a lot of the vegetables into baby food; carrots, squash, and corn.

Alex was an excellent sleeper after a meal of baby cereal before bed. She would sleep a solid nine hours. It gave me whole evenings alone with my thoughts. I tried to analyze, chastise and conceptualize where my actions had landed me and what I needed for my future to remain healthy physically and attain emotional stability. Easier said than done.

* * *

Ben called to say he finished with the shooting in Ireland and London. He had four days off and wanted to spend them with us. The film producer was flying from New York to California on his private plane and could drop Ben off at the Evelyn Sharp airstrip in Sanders. The airstrip was long enough to accommodate small private planes that frequently arrived for horse sales at the nearby Pfizer Horse Breeding Ranch.

Why do some people seem to have an umbrella over their head and a golden fleece sheltering them from discomfort? *Want to go to Nebraska? No problem. Oh, cherished one, let me drop you off in my plane with no more fuss than going across town, parachute included and curbside pick up available.* God, I sound like a sour, resentful shrew. Guilty as charged.

* * *

I told Ben I would be okay with a visit. He gave me the arrival time, and Alex and I drove into Sanders to pick him up. I dressed Alex in a little pink dress, white tights with ruffles and lace on her bottom, and black Mary Jane shoes. She was quite the fashion plate. Her hair wasn't long enough for a ponytail, but I put an elastic band with a pink flower on her head.

Ben and his producer descended from the plane. I shook hands with Robert Merrill, and Ben introduced Alexandra as his daughter. The man was a little shocked while offering his congratulations. I'd give anything to be a mind reader right now. Then, after some general conversation, Mr. Merrill re-boarded and was soon off, winging his way to California.

Ben took Alex out of my arms, holding her high. "She has grown so much since the end of July." Alex smiled and chattered in her baby jargon. Ben kissed me. "You are more beautiful every time I see you."

"Thank you. Are you ready to go to the farm?"

"More than ready. I have to admit, with the time change, I'm whipped."

"You can get your beauty rest while Alex takes an afternoon nap and I get some chores done."

We stowed Ben's two suitcases in the back of my SUV, strapped Alex in her car seat, and hit the road. We were halfway to the farm when rounding a curve; a steer was standing in the middle of the road. Thankfully, I wasn't going too fast to stop to avoid hitting 1,400 pounds of beef on the hoof. He finally moved enough to get by after blowing the horn and inching the car close to the steer. I will have to call the Warchekski's and let them know they had an escapee on the road with some fencing down. An animal that size can do a lot of damage to a vehicle. We reached the farm, Ben got his luggage, and I carried Alex inside the house.

"Where should I put these?" asked Ben, with questions written all over his face.

"You can put the luggage down in the hallway next to the staircase." I thought this might be a decision I had to make when Ben came to visit. But I didn't want to set a pattern for his visits or be a booty call between New York and California. I would not be the willing and ready participant for his sexual convenience whenever he worked me in to his itinerary. "I'll get Alex ready for her nap; if you want to sack out on my bed, that's fine for now. Alex can be your alarm clock."

While Alex and Ben were sleeping, I walked out to the garden and cut some fresh lettuce, cucumbers, and tomatoes for a salad. There was enough late sweet corn left for one or two more dinners, and I dug up some potatoes. Next, I raided my supply of homemade bread in the freezer and got out some chicken to fry and a chokecherry pie. Finally, I filled my afternoon with laundry and checking on the horses. When I returned to the house, Ben had gotten Alex up, changed her diaper, and dressed her in a playsuit.

"Feel better?" I asked.

"Very much. With the time difference and a busy schedule, I was bushed."

"How did the filming go?"

"It went well. Ireland is a beautiful country. I would like to spend some more time there. It's magical, but before I tell you about Ireland, I want to give you a proper hello." Ben took me in his arms, kissing me with a passion I remembered from our days in Santorini. "Brenna, my Brenna. How I've missed you, I can't get you out of my mind. You occupy my every thought, every minute of the day, and haunt my nights. I can't live my life without you. I love you to the depths of my soul."

I looked at him with tears cascading down my face. I took his beautiful face in my hands. My fingers traveled over each feature, followed by my lips. "I love you, Ben, but. . ." then Alex cried. "I have to get the baby." I got her out of her bouncy chair and put her in the highchair. I filled her sippy cup with milk and gave her a graham cracker.

"But? . . . continue," he asked.

"I can't right now, later. I'm going to start dinner." Turning my back, I got out the black iron skillet. "Would you peel the potatoes for me?"

"Sure, my darling."

I got out pans and the peeler for him. I put on a big pot of water to heat the corn and prepped the chicken for frying. Soon, the potatoes were ready to boil while Ben set the table in the kitchen. I fried the chicken, mashed the potatoes, and made gravy; I took out the chilled fresh garden salad and home-baked bread. Finally, I got everything to the table and poured a lovely Prosecco.

"This looks wonderful, darling. It reminds me of Sunday dinner with my parents."

"Everything but the chicken and the wine is homemade or home-grown. My garden did well this first year," I said.

"I see you have wine tonight. Is that good for the baby?"

"I stopped nursing when Alex got her teeth. She's a big girl now, drinking from a sippy cup and eating some table food."

"Was that hard to give up nursing?"

"I miss it, it was our bonding time together, but it doesn't go on forever. It was time. Oh. I almost forgot. Sam, my contractor, is coming over after supper to look at the chicken coop."

"What are your plans for that?" Ben asked.

"I want him to check and see if the building is stable; if it is, I want to turn it into a crafting area/potting shed. It could eventually be Alex's playhouse. It'll take some work, but I think it will be well worth it. If you're done, I better get this cleaned up."

"Thank you for a wonderful dinner. We'll have to save the pie for later. I can't eat another bite. Let me help you."

"Why don't you clean up our daughter? She's covered in mashed potatoes."

"I'll give her a bath and ready for bed while you're doing your thing. Let me know when your contractor gets here. I'd like to meet him."

"Deal." The dishwasher was powering up when Sam knocked on the back door. "How are you? I haven't seen you in ages," I asked.

"I know. This is our busiest season, and I have been running three crews all summer long. Where's my niece? She probably doesn't remember me," said Sam.

"My friend, Ben, is giving her a bath and ready for bed. They'll be out any minute."

"Ben, who? I didn't know you were dating."

"I'm not. It's complicated, Sam."

I had to take a minute to laugh; there was Ben with a shirt soaked through holding Alex, who was smiling and giggling. "Let me take her so you can change your shirt." I introduced the two men. I could feel the animosity stirring between Sam and Ben immediately.

"Be back in a minute. Don't start without me," said Ben as he headed to the hallway where his suitcases were sitting.

Sam had a question in his eyes, which I ignored.

"Let me see that little girl," said Sam as he held Alex to his chest. "You probably don't remember me, your Uncle Sam. You've grown so big since I last saw you."

"Let me go grab a blanket for her before we go outside. Ben, are you ready?" I called out.

"In a minute."

We walked over to the long-abandoned chicken hotel. "This is what I want to do, Sam. If the building is still solid, I want to turn it into a year-round space for crafts and potting. I'll need insulation, a wall unit for heating and cooling, new windows, and up-to-date wiring for plant growing lights. We should side it to match the house and garage with a little touch of Victorian to mesh with the other buildings. Possibly a water source, a small sink. What do you think?" I asked.

"Let's look at the building first. At a glance, it doesn't look in terrible shape," said Sam. We walked around the building as Sam inspected, poked, testing several areas. Then, going inside, he jumped up and down on the floor and poked into the corners. Ben got a ladder out, and Sam climbed up on the roof to see if there were any visual issues.

"While you're making a few notes, Sam, Alex needs a diaper change. So let me run into the house for a couple of minutes, and then I'll be back for the verdict," I said.

Sam and Ben seemed to square off with each other, all but hissing like tomcats ready to pounce, protecting their territory.

"Langford, isn't it? You seem pretty comfortable with Brenna and Alexandra."

"Brenna and I met in Italy last year," said Ben.

"Alexandra is your daughter, isn't she?" asked Sam.

"Yes, she is."

"Let me fill you in on a couple of things. First, I'm the man who drove Brenna to the hospital to have the baby. Second, I'm the man who paced the waiting room floor while she labored. Third, I'm the man that held that newborn baby in my arms. So where the fuck were you, Mr. Movie Star?"

"I didn't know there was a baby until July, or I would have been here," said Ben.

"And why is it you didn't know?" asked Sam.

"Brenna wouldn't talk to me. We didn't have an amicable parting."

"I asked Brenna to marry me not once but twice to give the baby a name and a father. Brenna turned me down both times; you want to know why?" questioned Sam; not waiting for an answer, he continued, "she told me it wouldn't be fair to me because she still loved the father of her child. So fair warning, you better not take advantage or mistreat her, or you'll have to answer to a lot of people around here, me being at the front of the line."

"Chase told me the same thing. I love Brenna and have since we met, knowing what a wonderful, loving woman she is. I never wanted to see her hurt, and I love my baby. We have things to work out. Maybe they will or maybe they won't, but I will never hurt her intentionally."

"See that you don't." Brenna and Alex soon rejoined the men, sensing an undercurrent of unease between them.

"Let's go in the house. It's getting a little chilly out here for Alex," I said. "Want a beer, Sam?"

"Sure, I could use one."

The coop was on a concrete slab, which was a plus. The structure was reasonably sound. Everything that I envisioned was possible. Since the coop was next to the windmill pump, a water line could run off the pump with a small on-demand water heater for the sink. Sam would put an estimate together and have it to me next week.

After a couple of beers for Sam and Ben with a glass of wine for me, I bid Sam goodnight. I fixed some baby cereal for Alex, fed her, and got her to bed. I had a question for Ben. "I felt a weird vibe between you and Sam. Is there a problem?"

"Not for me. Is Alex down for the night?"

"She's good for the next eight to nine hours. I finally can get a good night's sleep. Let's take our wine and sit in the living room."

We sat down and finally had some quiet time to talk. "It must have been very hard for you in the early months," Ben said.

"It was rough, but every new mother goes through it."

"But other new mothers usually have help from their mother or spouse, and you did it alone. I regret I wasn't here for you and Alex."

"Fortunately, I had Maggie, but that's water under the bridge now. I dealt with it. It's history, so let's not rehash it. It stirs up a lot of uncomfortable memories for me I would rather not revisit."

"I love you, Brenna. You're a great mom, not only to Alex, but to your sons as well. Chase is a wonderful young man. Have you heard from Gage?" Ben asked.

"Not a word, and I have to accept it. I miss him, but that's his decision. There's nothing I can do, nor will I apologize for having Alexandra to appease him."

"I'm so sorry about his reaction. He doesn't know what he's missing. There are some people who can't wait to meet you and Alex—my parents. I told them about the baby and you. I had to hold them back from jumping in the car and driving up to your door."

"What did they say about you fathering a child without being married?" I asked.

"It pleased them that the baby wasn't mothered by what my father refers to as the 'bimbo wives'. I told them about you and how we met. My mother ripped me a new one, and my father was very disappointed in me. I hate to upset them. They brought me up better than having babies out of wedlock."

"This is a new age, and children don't carry that stigma around with them anymore. Alex will be fine with it."

"I want her better than fine with it. I want to marry you and make us a real family."

"That's not possible. We have too many differences. I can't see any way to reach a compromise that we are both happy with. The thing I started to talk about before supper, the man I pledge my life to, gets my fidelity, loyalty, and trust, needing the same in return. I want to know that the man I sleep with will be true to me with his body and soul. I can't live with anything less. That trust is missing from our relationship."

"I'm not an angel and don't pretend to be. I've had more than my share of women and certainly married two of the worst connivers in Hollywood. You may not believe me, but I haven't had sex with anyone else since I found you again in June. The opportunity was there, but I lost interest when I looked at them and thought about you. You're the woman I want, the woman I need, and the woman I want by my side for the rest of my life."

"I love you, Ben. What we had was special for a short time. You gave me Alexandra. But I have to know that trust between us is solid before I can commit to anything beyond my life today. We really don't know each other. Our time together wasn't real life, but idyllic circumstances and surroundings. I won't take a ride on the merry-go-round that is your life."

"I want to earn your trust. I don't have to work out of L.A.; The coop would make a great office for me. I would have to travel a bit, but I would always come home to you. What do you think?"

"Let me think about it. I don't know if I can take the coming and going. It breaks something in me when you say goodbye. It's an emotional upheaval every time, and I can't nor won't do it."

"I know, darling. For me too."

"Brenna, I want to make love to you."

I held my breath. I thought of a thousand reasons I shouldn't let Ben back into my heart. The foundation I tried to build for my new life without him crumbled beneath me. I threw caution to the wind and surrendered to my wants and my needs. "Ben . . . . take me to bed."

CHAPTER NINETEEN

I was very apprehensive about Ben seeing my body so soon after childbirth. My weight was back to pre-pregnancy numbers, but my stomach was a little loose, and after nursing for over four months, my breasts would never be mistaken for perky. I am forty-one years old and rolling up to another mile marker in December. Hardbody, never again. I couldn't compete with those inhabiting the land of plastic surgery and personal trainers of the Hollywood elite.

How long would it take for Ben to tire of me and the farm life and seek younger, more cosmopolitan companionship? When I look in the mirror in the morning, would I see the face of a fool? What's that saying? "Fool me once; shame on you. Fool me twice; shame on me."

Would I ever have a minute of peace when Ben was away pursuing the profession he loves, surrounded by women eager to catch his eye and would do anything to advance their careers? A high level of trust was missing in my relationship with Ben. If I was to consider marriage, I had to have complete confidence in my partner, and Ben didn't have a sterling reputation in that area.

We walked to the bedroom and after checking on Alex, I turned the lights down low—very low. Ben walked up to me, laying light butterfly kisses all over my face. I put my arms around him, drawing him close. Our bodies fit together like two pieces of a puzzle. Our lips sought each other with a burning desire like our times before. Ben unbuttoned my shirt slowly as he stared into my eyes. Our passion was too intense, our need too frantic to take our time for foreplay. My jeans slide down my legs. I kicked off my boots and socks and stepped out of the clothes that separated me from Ben. I took his shirt in the hands and ripped the pearl-covered snaps apart, releasing their hold. Unbuckling his belt, the sound from the rasp of the zipper as it lowered was the only sound to be heard. I pushed the jeans down his long, hair-dusted legs. His boots and socks soon joined the puddle of clothing on the floor. I placed my hand over his hard, swelling, passion-filled manhood. Ben relieved me of my bra and panties, and his underwear disappeared. We fell on the bed, clinging to each other. Ben slid into my waiting body, and our reunion came fast.

"I'm sorry, darling, but I couldn't wait any longer. Next time I'll be able to take my time giving you pleasure," Ben murmured in my ear.

"I was as anxious as you. It's been so long; I needed you."

Ben held me in his arms, running his hands up and down my body, re-familiarizing himself with the curves and hollows. "My darling Brenna, I was so lost until I found you again, and then I found myself. I love you so very much; I never stopped looking for you."

I pulled the sheet over us as we lie together.

"Are you cold?" Ben asked.

"I'm not really cold. My body has changed since we were together the last time. My skin had more elasticity twenty years ago. I'm not the same anymore."

"We made love to each other, and our loving made our baby. Your body carried my baby for nine months as she grew and developed. Then you fed my baby with your body. I love this body. It gives me the greatest pleasure, and it gave me the greatest joy of my life, our daughter."

We stayed in each other's arms through the night, reaching out and making love repeatedly. I treasured every moment, every touch; this man had never left my mind or my heart as much as I tried to make it otherwise. He had broken that heart, but it was slowly mending, becoming stronger.

Alex was stirring, and before she cried, I left our bed, changed the baby, and got her ready for the day. I pulled on some clothes quickly to not disturb Ben, still sound asleep. I took a couple of minutes to look at him. He was so handsome with his black hair, the slight scruff of beard covering his cheeks and chin. His body, just as I remembered, was muscular and fit. His sculptured, muscled chest, sinewy toned abs and pecs made my mouth water.

Ben was almost forty-four years old and still looked like every woman's dream. Nature's cruel trick. When they get older, men are as handsome, desirable, and sexy with age as Cary Grant and George Clooney. Unfortunately, aging for women isn't the same. We seem to get old, feel old, act old, and look old. How long would Ben want me— five years or ten—before he traded me in for a newer model? I didn't want to think about the after when we were in the midst of the now.

Alex was in her highchair hungrily, taking spoon after spoon of rice cereal and a smashed-up banana. I started a pot of coffee for myself when Maggie pulled into the driveway. She came in the door and poured herself a cup, sitting down at the kitchen table. We discussed my plans to renovate the coop when Maggie stopped talking, and her mouth dropped open. My back was to the hallway door, but I knew without looking what had caught her attention. Ben came strolling into the kitchen with his jeans unbuttoned, shirtless, and yawning.

Ben paused. "Good morning, ladies. I hope I'm not interrupting. Let me get a cup of coffee, and I'll get out of your way."

Maggie recovered quickly. "You don't need to leave. Sit down. I'm Maggie, Brenna's cousin," as she held out her hand. They shook hands, and Ben joined us at the table after putting on a shirt.

"Very nice to meet you, Maggie. Brenna has told me so much about you, considering you more like a sister than a cousin."

"We grew up together since we were three years old. Granny Vernie was the greatest, never too tired to take us into town for a soda or shopping. She would have that little twinkle of devilment in her eye and not beyond playing a prank on one of her siblings. She was always ready for a cold beer or a shot of whiskey, never turning down a get-together with family. I still miss her every day. She was the cornerstone of our family, and as a family we would do anything to protect each other," Maggie said, as if in warning.

"We practically ran the legs off our horses, and Grandma was there with us. I miss her too more than you can imagine," I fondly recalled, trying to soften Maggie's veiled warning. "Maggie, are you and Ted busy tonight, free for dinner?"

"We have nothing going on; the kids will be out with their friends, so 'Pops' and I will have another exciting night of Wheel of Fortune followed by Jeopardy on television. Why?"

"If you're free for dinner, why don't you and the other half come over, and I'll throw some steaks on the grill, or better yet, how about a cream can supper? It'll give me a chance to talk to Ted and get his opinion on the coop reno."

"Sounds like a plan, but only if you let me bring the dessert," said Maggie.

"You're on, 6 PM, okay? And another thing, if you could let no one know that I have a houseguest, I would appreciate it."

"Perfect, that'll give Ted time to shower the office off. See you then, and my lips are sealed. Nice meeting you, Ben," as Maggie stood up and hurried out the door.

"Do you mind a little company? I think you'll like Maggie's husband. He's a real laid-back, down-to-earth good guy, an estate and real estate attorney, and an amateur electrician. I wanted to pick his brain about wiring for the internet in the coop and to see if I have enough power to support plant lights and other equipment that's necessary."

"I would love to meet more of your family; it's your house. Invite anyone you want. Does this electrical inquiry have anything to do about setting up an office?"

"Just trying to cover all my bases. It'll be a multi-purpose area. Can you finish feeding Alex while I get breakfast ready?"

"What the heck is a cream can supper?" Ben asked.

"You're in for a treat." I got out the cylindrical stainless-steel cream can that Grandma used, holding it out for Ben to see. "After milking, grandma would set the milk aside until the cream floated to the top of the milk pail. Then Grandma would skim the cream off and save it in the cream can until she had enough to make butter. Now I use the can for a quick dinner of vegetables from the garden. First, I stand up fresh, dehusked ears of sweet corn ringing the inside of the can. Next, I add layers of potatoes, cabbage, carrots, and onions in the middle with kielbasa or some other meat on the top of the veggie layers. Next, I add some butter, pour two cans of beer over the meat, and put a whole potato on the top. Finally, I seal the cream can and set it on the grill over a low fire. It takes about 45 minutes or when the potato on the top appears fully cooked. It's fast, easy, and delicious." I winced as I turned back to the cupboard.

"I can't wait to try it, but I have to ask—are you okay, darling? Are you hurting from last night? You had a funny look on your face."

"I'm wonderful, sweetheart. My period is due in a couple of days, and I always get cramps just before."

"No chance I got you pregnant again last night, is there?"

"You're safe. My doctor told me it was a fluke that I got pregnant with Alex and not likely it would happen again with my extensive female reproductive issues."

"That's too bad. If you were pregnant again, then maybe you'd marry me before the clock ran out."

"Alex will probably be your only child by me, I'm afraid."

"I'll only have children with you. I'll only make love with you if you'll have me."

Not making another comment, I got some bacon frying and asked how many eggs he wanted. I remembered how he liked his eggs cooked from our time in Santorini. There wasn't much I forgot about our time on the island—or unfortunately, our time in Rome that followed.

After breakfast, we cleaned Alex up and strolled over to the coop. There was still debris left over from Grandma's chickens long gone. The coop would have to be cleaned out, sanitized, and sterilized if necessary. I wanted to save the multi-tier wooden nesting boxes if possible.

"Wouldn't they make great cubbies for crayons, markers, and other art supplies, along with my gardening things?" I asked.

"That or office supplies, files, and electronic equipment?"

"What are you trying to say?"

"To put in the current vernacular, duh. It kills me to be separated from you. I can work, mostly, anywhere. An office here would allow us to have more time together, and I can have a bigger part in bringing up our daughter."

"I'll think about it. We only met sixteen months ago and spent less than two months together. Our time has been under extraordinary circumstances. We don't know each other that well not enough time to build a future on. This is moving too fast. It's too soon.

"Sure, our sex life is everything I could ask for and more, but I don't know that much about everyday life. Will you get bored out here on the farm? Will you eventually miss the glitz and allure of Hollywood? Yearn for more excitement than a farm in Nebraska out on the prairie? What if you wake up one morning and realize this isn't for you? The farm will always be my home. My roots are here deep in the soil of the sandhills. Abandoned as a child, I won't go through it again."

"I understand. Let's work on our relationship, get to know each other, and see where it takes us. I will be going back to California in a couple of days for some last-minute studio shoots and then seeing to the editing process. If you allow me, I would like to come back here when I get time off," Ben said.

"Promise me you will be honest if you feel this isn't going to work or drag anything out, and I'll do the same," I said.

"I promise. Now it looks like the horses need some attention. So I'm going to muck out the shed. Are all the brushes, hoof picks, and curry combs in the shed?"

"Chase has a cabinet in there with everything you'll need, but better get his rubber boots on, or I'll have to hose you down later."

Ben was off to do his chores with a grin, and Alex and I stepped into the house. It was nap time for my daughter, and I had baby laundry to do. My garden needed some work before the first freeze overtook the growing season. I took some bread out of the freezer and retrieved the fresh vegetables from the garden for our supper. The Nebraska air carries a lot of dust, so I want to ensure my housekeeping was up to snuff before the company came over.

I got the lawnmower out in the yard and prepared to start it when Alex woke from her nap. The grass looked a little overgrown, and the flowers needed watering. There always seems that something needs attention on a farm.

Ben was walking back to the house, having completed his chores, when he stopped dead in his tracks at a sight that was beyond his immediate comprehension. He walked up to the chain-link fence surrounding the yard. Ben couldn't help but burst into a body-shaking belly laugh.

With head down, concentrating on the grass, Brenna was mowing the lawn after she strapped Alex to her back in a baby backpack with baby-sized noise-canceling headphones and safety glasses over her eyes. Alex was having a great time giggling and tapping her hands on Brenna's shoulders as if on a carnival ride. After a few minutes of unbridled hilarity, Ben waved his arms, catching Brenna's attention, shutting down the mower and walking over to the fence.

"Let me finish that for you," Ben said.

"I'm not too proud to let you. I'll go in and make lunch after I water the flowers while you finish up here. As Brenna watered, Ben was finishing up the lawn when he was hit full on the chest with a blast of ice-cold well water from the outdoor hand pump.

Not waiting for retaliation, Alex and I ran into the house. Ben finished the lawn, washed the mower down, and put it back in the garage. I was busy at the stove and Alex in her highchair, chewing on a teething cookie, when Ben came up behind me and folded his arms around my waist. Turning around, I was expecting a kiss to find Ben stark naked in the kitchen. "Yikes, put some clothes on; someone might come to the door." I laughed.

"It's your fault. I couldn't walk into the house with wet, smelly clothes. Don't worry, I shucked them in the back porch mudroom and not in the yard. Sometime when you least expect it, it'll be payback time. I'm going to take a shower."

I made sandwiches and soup for lunch. Ben returned to the kitchen, and we sat down for a simple meal and relaxation.

"Brenna, I'm afraid that the horse shed will not make it another winter. The roof leaks. The boards are so warped that I can see a lot of light. If the wind blows, the walls shake. Is there any room in the barn for the horses this winter?"

"That's my project for October while you're gone. The barn is relatively new, relative, meaning twenty-five years old. I have all grandma's furniture that I didn't use and a ton of castoffs stored in there. The family can take whatever they want. I'll donate what is decent and trash the rest.

"Once that stuff is gone, we should have plenty of room for horses. I'll have Sam build some stalls, a tack room, and install some electricity. The hay, straw, and feed can be stored there, handy for the horses. Finally, I can have Sam demolish the shed and get the scrap out of here."

"Woman, you amaze me, always thinking, excellent solution. What's that little building next to the outhouse on the other side of the yard by your garden?"

"It used to be a brooder house for baby chicks, but Grandma didn't use it. When I was a child, I played in it. It was my private sanctuary for reading and girl talk with Maggie. I suppose since it's so close to the garden, I should use it as a tool shed."

"Brenna, seriously, are you ever afraid to be out here alone?"

"Not really. I have a gun, and I know how to use it—keep that in mind," I said with a laugh. "Between Guncle John's house and mine, we know about everyone that comes down the road. So if a stranger rolls through, Guncle calls me, or I call them, and we watch out for each other."

"Have you thought about installing a security system?"

"Yes, I have. A dog. A big ass tearing dog, a German Shepherd on steroids. Shepherds are also good herding dogs for horses."

"If you change your mind about something more, let me know. If it should become known that I am here, there might be people who wouldn't think twice about trespassing. I want you and Alex safe, and I won't worry so much."

"I hate to think that my sanctuary, my safe place, would have to become an armed fortress. Let's hope that it won't become well known when you are here."

"That might be wishful thinking when I fly in on a private plane to the strip in Sanders."

"Many big ranchers use that strip, so activity is not unusual. Just keep a low profile as much as possible."

Maggie and Ted arrived for dinner. The men got on like a house-on-fire. They were just two guys talking and arguing about sports. Maggie helped me in the kitchen while the cream can was heating. I set the table in the dining room. While our dinner was steaming, I gave Alex her bath and put her in jammies so that the four of us could have some adult time later.

With dinner ready, we all sat down for a relaxing supper. Ben couldn't get enough of the cream can meal while he and Ted talked like they had known each other forever. Maggie had made one of her famous cheesecakes for dessert.

"I can't believe I ate so much," said Ben while patting his stomach. "That's the best meal I have ever had, and the cheesecake was spectacular. Thank you, ladies."

I fed Alex her cereal, and she drank her milk and was ready to hit the sack. The four of us moved out on the front porch to the rocking chairs and swing I had put out there for mild nights like this. Fortified with plenty of beer and wine, Ted asked how we had met. Ben took the lead and relayed the story of my covering him with gelato in Italy, and then I told them of the incident in the museum when I announced his presence to a swarm of tourists that all but tackled him while I ran out of the building. Maggie laughed so hard tears were running down her face.

After the laughter died down, I filled them in on plans for the coop and now the barn. Maggie made me promise to let her go through the barn before the family scavengers got called in. Ted shook his head, saying they needed no more useless crap sitting around collecting dust.

"Not crap dear, treasures," said Maggie.

It was such a wonderful evening; I hated to see it end. Maggie and Ted headed back to town, and Ben and I headed to bed. Our lovemaking was gentle and soft. We took time to touch and taste and nibble, enjoying each other. Unfortunately, Ben would leave in two days back to California, not exactly knowing when he could return. The saving grace was that we could talk and see each other over FaceTime or Zoom, and at other times I would listen to sad Adele songs. We decided that tomorrow, we would do chores in the morning and spend the rest of the day talking and spending quality time with our daughter.

CHAPTER TWENTY

After breakfast, the horses were cared for, and household duties complete, we had lunch. Alex was down for her afternoon nap. I filled a couple of goblets of wine, and we sat on the front porch swing. We talked about our childhoods, marriages, likes and dislikes, fears, and hopes, reaching a better understanding of each other. We moved into the bedroom and made love until Alex woke up.

Our evening was just as relaxing, playing with our baby, bathing her, and reading her stories. Finally, Alex was ready for bed, and so were we. It was our last night together until who knows when. Our loving was slow and gentle; at other times, it was frantic and needy. We got little sleep that night. We didn't want to waste a minute sleeping while storing up intimacy for the separation coming our way.

Bleary-eyed, we had breakfast, and I helped Ben repack his suitcase. He pulled out a couple of packages from his luggage and asked me to open them later after his departure. Alex and I took Ben to the airstrip. His plane was waiting. We kissed and hugged goodbye with words of love for each other. My daughter and I watched as the plane took off and disappeared into the sky, heading west toward the land of make-believe.

Back home, I fed Alex as I cried. Then I opened the packages that Ben had left us. There was a little ballerina dress with *Daddy's*

Girl printed on the front of the top and a pink stuffed bunny for Alex. I opened the second package, holding a small black velvet box, opening the lid to find a necklace with two intertwined hearts sparkling with diamonds. I put the chain around my neck as more tears poured down my face. Since becoming involved with Ben, I had turned into a total watering pot. My emotions were so close to the surface it manifested in tears more now than any other time in my life. Was it hormones? Was it aging? Or my inability to have complete trust where Ben was concerned?

Alex and I slept the afternoon away. Partings might get easier as time goes on for us. It wasn't the physical separations, but the emotional partings. I didn't trust Ben. It's as simple as that—out of sight, out of mind? I don't know if I could handle the continuous fluctuation of my emotions.

*   *   *

I kept myself busy for the rest of September into October. Sam got the estimate to me for the coop, and I gave him the go-ahead. I called all the family to come over and pick through the barn, carting off whatever they wanted to take. All the leftovers were trash that Sam took away with the demolition debris. The weather held, and Sam's crew completed the renovation of the coop by mid-October.

Ben was flying in for seven days, the third week of October. We fell into our old pattern of chores, lovemaking, and spending time with our daughter. Ben was ready for a break. The film had wrapped and was now in the editing and music scoring stage. If all progressed well, it would premier around May in Los Angeles, then open nationwide with the international opening to follow.

We walked out to the coop. It was perfect and another great job by Sam and his crew. I had Sam build a 15-foot table below the windows that faced the yard. There was ample electrical service for anything we would need for a potting shed or alternative use. The old nesting boxes looked great, refinished, and ready to hold heaps of art supplies. You never know when the urge to bedazzle something might hit.

Sam installed a small sink in the corner, and a vinyl covered floor for easy cleanup. The exterior had the same siding as the house with a small bit of Victorian detail. The coop looked like it had always been a part of the house construction. I had a sign made to be placed above the door, "The Coop", in Victorian-style lettering.

My next project was to get the barn ready for the horses. Winter would be on us before we knew it, with the mid-west plains resembling the frozen tundra. As long as the weather cooperated, Sam would put on a new steel roof, and the barn would get a coat of bright red paint with white trim. Every farm needed a big red barn trimmed in white, or it wasn't an official farm to my way of traditional thinking.

Ben worked with Sam during his brief visits home to get the barn completely cleaned out. Then, they sat down at the kitchen table with heads together, drawing out plans for the new stalls and tack room. I was a little nervous that Sam hadn't given me an estimate before the work started. After questioning him, he told me to ask Ben.

Confronting Ben, I asked, "What's the deal with the barn? I need the estimate so that I know it will work with my budget."

"It's your early Christmas present from Alex and me. I wanted to do something special for you and knew this would be precisely what you wanted. You're not the typical diamonds and furs kind of girl, and that's what I love about you."

"That's playing dirty, putting Alex in the mix. Now, how could I say no? Thank you. I guess I will have to give you your Christmas present early then, too."

"I don't need things, Brenna. I just need you, Alex, and Chase. You're my family now."

"With that in mind, we need more time with you. I did The Coop for you as your office away from L.A. Welcome home, darling."

Ben picked me up and hugged me with tears in his eyes. "I knew the day I first saw you, you would change my life and make my every dream come true. How can I ever thank you?"

"Giving me, Alex, and loving me is thanks enough. We cried together, knowing what we had was a miracle. Something has preordained this turn in life when we found each other not once, but twice. Was divine intervention guiding us together? We may not follow the same paths, but we came together to enrich each other's lives. We jogged over to The Coop so that Ben could plan the placement of equipment he would need to conduct his business remotely.

"Do you mind if I order the equipment and furniture? I could have it delivered here and stored in The Coop. Then I'll deal with it when I get back."

"No problem. I'm more than happy for someone else to do the heavy work."

We spent the rest of our time working around the farm and visiting in town with Maggie and Ted. Ben met their two teenage daughters. The girls giggled and asked for autographs and had their pictures taken with him. Ben was very accommodating, and the girls were a chortling pile of star-struck teenage hormones.

Ben was no longer a secret in town as a frequent visitor to the farm, and rumors had circulated that Ben was my daughter's father. No one had the nerve to ask me directly if the rumors were true. I moved about my business and let everyone wonder. That's what small towns do; they may speculate between themselves but protect their own from outsiders.

Every once in a while, vehicles on the road would slow down and look toward the house; thankfully, no one stopped to investigate further. I was getting used to the fact that people would be curious, and I would have to deal with it. Then, while talking over supper one night, Ben had something he wanted to discuss with me.

"Is Chase coming home for Thanksgiving?" he asked.

"No, not this year. He has classes the day before the holiday and the following Monday. He would only have about a day and a half to spend here with the travel, and I thought it would be too exhausting for him, with finals coming up. So we planned on making up for it at Christmas."

"Have you heard anything from Gage?"

"Chase has talked with him, but I have heard nothing directly. Gage can hold a grudge for a long time and can be as stubborn as a mule."

"Wonder where he gets that?" Ben grinned.

"I'm going to ignore that remark. Why did you ask about Thanksgiving?"

"My mom and dad would like to meet you and Alexandra. They know all about our relationship and think it's high time they met their newest grandchild. What do you say about going to Hutchinson for a couple of days?"

"Have you ever brought any other women home to meet your parents?"

"They met my two wives once and made their feelings known. Not impressed."

"What do you think they'll say about me? That scares the bejesus out of me if I didn't live up to their expectations?"

"My parents are going to love you. You're genuine, warm, and loving. How could they not?"

"If you think it won't be awkward, I would like to meet your family," I said.

"Will your Guncle John look after the horses if we take off early Wednesday morning and return on Friday afternoon?"

"I don't think it will be a problem. The horses will have their new home by then. With all the feed handy, he won't have to do much. I'll check with him and see if he's available."

"My parents are going to love you and Alex. No need to worry."

"Easy for you to say. I have to go shopping and get Alex some holiday clothes."

"Speaking of Christmas. Where have you stashed the Christmas decorations?" Ben asked.

"I put them in the washhouse. I have my eye on a tree in the grove in front of the house I want to chop down and decorate. This will be Alex's first Christmas, so I want to do it up right for her. I thought I would place the tree in the big entryway by the front door. That way, we can see it while lying in bed, the living room and the dining room."

"Are we going to have stockings on the mantle, too?" chuckled Ben.

"Of course, with plenty of room for carrots for the reindeer and cookies and milk for Santa."

"God, I love you, woman. Know where I spent last Christmas?"

"No, I don't. Home with your family?" I asked.

"Las Vegas, watching a strip show and getting hammered."

"Why didn't you go home?" I asked.

"I wasn't in the mood for festive. I couldn't get you to talk to me, and I didn't want to listen to my parents harangue me about my superficial life. What did you do?"

"I was sorting through stuff here and supervising the remodeling. My sons were in Asia, my friends in Chicago were busy with their families—not that they didn't invite me for a visit—but I wasn't feeling up to it and treated the holiday like any other day of the week. I had dinner in town with Maggie and members of the clan, but that was about the extent of the holiday."

"Well, this year will be vastly different. I can't wait. Are you going to make Christmas cookies and fudge?"

"Of course, what's Christmas without a massive ingestion of sugar and chocolate?"

Our week together came to a close. Alex and I took Ben to the airstrip. Another goodbye and more tears. I made peace with the way our life together evolved—the frequent trips to L.A. or New York were inevitable with the passionate returns to the farm. I kept my days busy taking care of my daughter and chores that needed attention, while my nights were empty and cold in my bed alone.

Alex was crawling and eating regular food. She was changing so much, meeting and exceeding every baby milestone. Chase was eager to return home to see his baby sister. We continued to FaceTime twice a week.

Chase was filling out applications for Grad School. His first choice was MIT Sloan School of Management in Cambridge, Massachusetts. He had the top grades required, spoke multiple languages, and did loads of volunteer work in New York while at Columbia. Acceptance, I knew, would be a certainty. As for Gage, I didn't have a clue what his plans were.

Maggie and I set a date to do some shopping in Grand Island. I needed to get some dressier clothes for Alex and me for our trip to Kansas. Nothing over the top but more than our customary jeans and sweatshirts. Alex was growing like a weed and needed new clothes, anyway.

Maggie, her two daughters, Alex, and I packed ourselves into Maggie's big SUV and journeyed to the city for a girls-only mega shopping spree. Soon the teenagers were off on their own, agreeing to meet at a specific time in the Conestoga Mall. I get it. They didn't want to be seen with the ol' folks—so not cool.

Maggie, Alex, and I hit J. C. Penney's and Dillard's first. I bought a ton of new clothes for Alex, finding the perfect Christmas dress of red velvet trimmed in white rabbit fur, white tights, and sparkly red shoes. Alex was all set for the season after adding a couple more holiday dresses, play outfits, winter pajamas, sleepers, and a snowsuit.

Maggie was looking for a holiday cocktail dress for Ted's office party. She fell in love with a midnight blue lace sheath that looked wonderful on her. For a holiday dinner, I found some silk trousers and a sweater in a warm cream color. I found some other slacks and paired them with knit tops for my Kansas visit. I wanted to get something as a hostess gift for Ben's mother, but not knowing her, I didn't have a clue on what to purchase.

"You can never go wrong with a nice silk scarf and shoulder pin," suggested Maggie.

I put in a quick call to Ben. "What hair and eye color does your mother have?"

"Blond and brown."

"Do you know what color winter coat?"

"She always goes for navy blue. Why?"

"Oh nothing, bye."

We headed for the scarf display and found a beautiful silk scarf with a bit of color in an abstract design and a Vera Wang shoulder pin. It was 1 PM, and hunger made our bellies sing. Maggie called the girls on their cell to meet us at the Food Court in fifteen minutes. We filled ourselves with Arby's beef, fries, and milkshakes. Now that Alex had two top teeth to go along with the bottom two, she happily sampled the fries, tiny pieces of beef, and bun. I filled her sippy cup with a melted milkshake, and she was in baby gourmet heaven. I'm never going to get her to be satisfied with her baby food again. After lunch and a little more shopping, we headed back to Sanders with our purchases. Alex slept in her car seat the whole distance. The girls chatted in the back seat while Maggie and I talked about my upcoming trip to meet Ben's parents.

I was getting nervous. Ben's father was a retired police detective and now free-lanced, doing investigations for private agencies and occasionally his former police department and his mother a middle school English teacher. Ben's three brothers were all married with children and lived in the area.

I would be meeting so many people for the first time with them knowing I had given birth to Ben's child. I didn't know what to expect. Would they treat me like a scarlet woman? Or some strumpet after his money and fame? Just the thought of what they might think was giving me hives.

Back in Sanders at Maggie's house, I loaded my SUV with my purchases and took Alex and my neurosis home. Ben called later and wanted to know about the phone questionnaire. "I wanted to get your parents a thank you gift for the Thanksgiving invitation. I got your mother a scarf and pin, but I don't know what to get your father."

"That's easy, aged scotch. I'll pick up a bottle of his favorite. Do you want to fly or drive to mom and dad's? It's 314 miles, according to Google, and would take about five hours to drive if we fly private, about two, and then we'll have to rent a car. So I'll leave it up to you."

"Why don't we drive? Then we can see the countryside and have our car, and I can make a fast getaway if they hate me. And what about sleeping arrangements? Crap, crap, crap," I groaned.

"Would you calm down? My parents are going to love you. You have to relax, Brenna. Promise me you'll pour yourself a glass of wine and chill. I'll be home next week. I'll be at your side the entire time. How did the shopping go for Alex?"

"She should be set for the winter, and I got her an adorable dress for Christmas. Your little princess will be at the height of fashion. I better let you get back to work, sweetheart. I need to fix dinner and then get Alex ready for bed. Then I'll take your advice and have a really enormous glass of wine and a nice long bubble bath. Goodnight darling, love you."

Ben was coming home the weekend before Thanksgiving. All his office equipment arrived, stored in The Coop. Finishing the barn was the last thing on Sam's agenda on my farm. Connecting the lights by running a wire to the electrical box in Ben's office was the only task remaining on the punch list to complete the project. So I carried out my chores and started the holiday baking I would store in the freezer.

The following morning, Alex and I drove into town to do some grocery shopping for baking supplies, remembering to lock the car before entering the store. Usually, no one locks their car in our little community unless it's fall. So if a vehicle isn't locked, the owner is likely to come back and find their vehicle full of bags of zucchini and squash, courtesy of the produce fairies that sneak around before the first freeze.

Back at the farm, I hauled all the groceries into the kitchen and got out all our favorite holiday recipes. If I do one or two items every day, I would have the Christmas foods ready in no time. Next, I checked on the horses, feeding and watering them; as the evening closed in. After supper, I gave Alex her bath, and she was asleep by 8 PM.

I took a couple of minutes to email Betsy and Michele in Chicago and Chase at school. My nights were quiet and lonely. I had to find something to do, or I would go stir crazy once the crops wither and the land wraps itself in shades of brown and naps until spring.

After the beginning of the new year, perhaps I'll contact Dr. Michaels and see about the possibility of working remotely for the college. I couldn't base my life on visits from Ben. Nor did I want to be someone who waits at the door in a housedress and pearls for her man to return home. The June Cleaver days are over, and "The Beaver" wouldn't be sitting on the couch. I wanted to establish more of an independent life for myself.

I was still a person who enjoyed interacting with adults in the academic world, missing the satisfaction of completing a curriculum project and exercising my brain. The multiple dimensions of my life were disappearing. I love being a mother and my farm. I just don't want to hang too much of my life on Ben as he works me into his schedule.

CHAPTER TWENTY-ONE

As the days moved on, I made my infamous lists. I had to decide what to pack for Alex and me for our trip to Kansas. When I had a spare minute, I searched the washhouse for the Christmas decorations and carried them to the house. I hoped Ben would join in the decorating when we got back from his parents' home, starting our own holiday traditions with our daughter. I was trying to keep my mind off the visit. This trip might make or break our relationship if Ben's parents didn't think I was worthy of their son.

I had worked myself into a tizzy when I drove into Sanders to pick up Ben at the airstrip. Ben seemed to be happy to come home to us. He kissed me with passion and held Alex in his arms as she giggled and cooed with delight.

"Darling, you have to relax. It's no big deal to meet my parents. They're probably as nervous as you are," said Ben with some irritation.

"I'm trying, Ben. But I feel incomplete at loose ends between missing you with the long separations and Gage's estrangement. Sometimes I feel like a failure. I know that this might be hard for you to understand; you have a mission, a focus. Maybe I'm having the winter blues or a mid-life crisis."

"Honey, I am going to be around much more from now on. I will work out of my office here. The lease on my house in L.A. is up, and I let go of my Malibu beach house months ago. My home is now with you and our child. I'll be able to do the vast majority of my prep work from here. I know that the farm takes a lot of work, along with caring for Alex primarily by yourself, but I'm here now to share the burdens and the joys. You're not alone; we're a team.

"I have something you can help me with if you're interested. I have three books that I might consider for my next foray into directing and knowing how much you love a good story. If you have the time to read through the books and then critique them for me, it would be a big help. I value your opinion and character insight."

"I would love that, a chance to exercise my mind again."

We drove back to the farm, with my heart feeling lighter. The sense of family having a close unit was so important to me. Ben had a massive amount of luggage to take into the house. Thank goodness I had a huge walk-in closet in our bedroom. After getting organized, the three of us moved over to The Coop. Ben was excited to see that all the office equipment and furniture had arrived.

"I'll get to unpacking this and setting everything up, but now I have something more important. How about some lunch? Get Alex down for her nap, and we can have some alone time. I've missed you so much and can't wait to make love to you. Sound like a plan?"

"It's about time." We headed back to the house. After lunching with Alex, I changed her, and she was down for a nap in record time. We came together in our bedroom, tearing the clothes from each other until our skin meshed together. We fell on the bed and mated with a frenzy of need nurtured by our separation. Ben came as soon as he entered me, and my muscles contracted around him until I milked him for every drop of his seed. Our bodies held each other in a fierce grip and urgent hunger as I pushed my hips forward, wanting to prolong the exquisite filling of my body.

Ben whispered, "Next time, we go slow and savor."

I could only nod. We lie together with moisture, sheening our bodies as we met our immediate needs, but only temporarily. I took in Ben's unique scent, touching the skin covering the length of his body and running my hands through his thick hair. How I loved this man, my partner, the father of my daughter—speaking of daughter, Alex was making her waking up noises.

I poked Ben, "Your turn."

"I'll take care of the baby this afternoon. Why don't you take a nap?"

"Don't mind if I do," as I turned over and fell asleep.

I woke up covered in a fuzzy blanket that Ben must have spread over me. After dressing, I started supper and walked over to The Coop to see what was happening. Ben took the new equipment out of the boxes, and Alex was busy crawling in and out of the discarded cardboard.

"You're getting there, sweetheart. Ready for supper?" I asked.

"Alex and I were about to call it a night. It's getting dark early these days."

We walked back to the house. The casserole was ready. Ben set the table, put Alex in her high chair, and prepared to dig in. After supper, Ben did the bath duties with Alex, and I cleaned up the kitchen. Alex was then ready for her snack, milk, and bed. I liked the sharing of chores. I didn't feel that everything was on me anymore, that there was someone I could share everything with and seemed to know what had to be done without me acting like a taskmaster.

"Mind if I start a fire in the living room fireplace?" Ben asked.

"This is now your home, too. So you don't have to ask. How about some wine?" I offered.

"You read my mind."

I spread a blanket on the floor before the fire with a couple of pillows. I put on some soft music and handed Ben his glass of wine. Then we sat down to talk.

"Who would have thought eighteen months after we met, we would find ourselves sitting in front of a fire, drinking wine in a farm-house in Nebraska?" Ben mused, staring into the blazing glow of the fire.

"With a seven and a half-month-old daughter. Life sure holds its share of surprises."

"The best surprises and the best gifts. I love you so much, Brenna. Every day away from you and Alex is an eternity. You are the woman of my dreams. You gave me a child. I want to spend the rest of my life with you. Will you marry me?"

"Do we know each other enough to move to that next stage? We are living together for the first time now that you're moving in. Total commitment is the most important aspect for me, both physically and emotionally. There's no forgiveness in me for a slip. I have to have faithfulness from my partner and be able to trust the man I marry. My trust has to be earned."

"I know my reputation isn't the best. I was young, like a kid, in a candy store, and I indulged. Now that I'm forty-four years old, I know what is important and of value. I know what's real. I promise you a faithful and loyal husband and friend if you marry me and I will protect you from hurt and disappointment. We can build a life together, growing old and raising our daughter in a loving home. Marry me, Brenna."

"I love you with all my heart. I will place my heart in your hands. Yes, I want to marry you."

Ben took a small Tiffany blue box out of his pocket. "I know you wouldn't want anything ostentatious. But if you don't like it, we can find something else." Ben opened the box and took my left hand in his. He slipped a diamond solitaire ring set in yellow gold on my finger. "You set the date, and I'll be there to have and to hold forever and ever."

I looked at the beautiful ring. "It's perfect. I wouldn't want anything else. How about May when my son will be home and the 2nd anniversary of the day we met?"

"I wish it were tomorrow, but if you want May, then May it will be. I'll leave all the details and plans up to you. I don't care if it's just you, me, a judge and a witness in Las Vegas, or a big extravaganza, whatever you want to do. I just want to marry you."

We toasted each other with our wine, kissing with renewed passion. We made love on the floor before the roaring fire with a new feeling of commitment and intimacy. Before we ended the evening, we FaceTimed Chase, who was elated and offered his congratulations on our engagement. Ben planned on calling his parents tomorrow. We headed to bed and made love again. Just knowing that we were there for each other side-by-side now and in the future added to our happiness.

I looked at my ring the following morning in the light of day. It was so beautiful; the stone might be a little bigger than I would prefer, but Ben picked it out, and I would cherish it as is. I called Maggie and asked her if she and Ted would like to come to dinner tonight. She accepted, and they would be at the farm at 6 PM. I emailed my friends in Chicago and announced my engagement to one Benton William Langford wedding in May, and I would be thrilled if they could attend. It wasn't over five minutes after I sent the emails that my phone rang with a three-way call with Betsy and Michele. Their reaction ran the gamut of emotions—surprise, joy, astonishment, and pique that I left them out of the loop with the details of my love affair.

Betsy was screaming with excitement, and Michele was just as thrilled. "I am so happy for you. Is this the same Ben Langford, the movie actor and hottest man on earth?" asked Betsy.

"Yes, it is. Ben's the man I fell in love with in Italy and Alexandra's father. We are very happy and now live together on the farm. I hope you'll be able to come here for the wedding. Both of you were my rock and got me through the tough times. I couldn't think of getting married without you."

"We can't wait to meet him, and we are so happy for you."

"You may not have met him face-to-face yet, but you've talked to him on the phone. Ben made the 'Bob Smith' calls to our office."

Betsy about lost it. "OMG, I almost told him to 'fuck off' the last time he called."

"I have one favor to ask. Could you keep tight-lipped about this? I don't want to deal with any press or make our location public. It's bad enough that people in town know that he's here; so far, it's been controllable. I want a quiet wedding with my closest friends sharing in our happiness."

Michele and Betsy said it would kill them to keep such a delicious secret, but they would do their best in order to preserve their attendance at the wedding. So, with squeals of delight and many congratulations, I promised to call them again soon.

Ben called his parents to announce our engagement. They offered congratulations, but were a little more circumspect. "They're reserving their support until they know that you're not another one of the 'bimbo brides'. You don't have to worry. They will love you as I do," reassured Ben.

*　*　*

I prepared an Italian supper, homemade lasagna, garlic bread, antipasto salad, wine, and tiramisu for dessert. I set the table in the dining room as Maggie and Ted drove into the driveway. Maggie bounded into the house, asking if I needed any help, then stared at me with astonishment.

"What do I see on your finger?" she asked.

"Just a little engagement ring," I answered casually.

"TED! Come here; you have to see this," yelled Maggie, grabbing my hand. Ted and Ben came into the kitchen as Maggie hugged me and Ben. "I'm so happy for you both. This is a real occasion for celebration. Congratulations, you two," as tears spilled from Maggie's eyes.

"Don't expect a kiss from me, Ben," commented Ted drolly. "But I will not pass up the opportunity to kiss Brenna."

We spent the evening with an aura of happiness surrounding us. Many glasses of champagne were raised in our honor. Maggie joined me in the kitchen as I cleaned up after supper.

"Are you as happy as you seem to be? Any reservations?" she asked.

"I am; my only concern now is meeting his parents at Thanksgiving in Kansas. What if they don't like me or turn their backs on Alexandra? Frankly, I'm terrified."

"You don't have to worry about that. You're the best thing that ever happened to their son. How could they think anything otherwise?"

"I'll find out soon," I said.

"I'll be waiting to hear when you get back or send me a text."

Ted and Maggie took their leave with hugs and kisses. Maggie gave me an extra squeeze, full of reassurance.

That did little for my reemerging nerves for the upcoming visit. The following day, I got out the suitcases for our three-day trip. I laid out the clothes I planned to take and asked Ben's opinion of what I had chosen was proper. I certainly didn't want to commit a fashion faux pas. Ben said that everything was fine and suggested adding jeans and tee shirts.

Since the boys were infants, I forgot how much stuff babies required to travel. So I drove into town and purchased a Pack-n-Play for Alex to sleep. I packed blankets, a box of diapers, and many changes of outfits and her best dresses.

"Honey, mom and dad have twelve grandchildren in the house at different times. So they have all the stuff we'll need to keep Alex comfortable."

"I want to be sure. I know I'm overdoing it; I'm just nervous."

"I wish I could reassure you. My parents will love you and Alex as soon as they meet you."

We were leaving early the following day with the car packed to the roof for our five-hour drive. During our visit to Kansas, Guncle John would look in on the horses. The night before we were going to leave, Ben took me in his arms as we cuddled in bed. "I know how to make you relax." He proved it to me more than once!

CHAPTER TWENTY-TWO

It was nice to be on the road, enjoying the beauty of the countryside as fall took a firm hold. Alex was an angel sleeping most of the time and only crying when hungry or wet. The miles rushed past us furiously with my stomach in a knot as we got closer to our destination.

We drove up to a lovely, well-maintained ranch-style home in the Hutchinson suburbs. Ben's parents were at the door as we got out of the car. Ben held Alex in his arms as his parents walked up to us, with Ben making the introductions. I shook hands with Ben's father and turned to his mother; she gave me a big hug, much to my surprise.

"We are so glad you're here. It's so nice to meet you, Brenna. Ben has told us so much about you; I feel I know you already. Now, let me hold that beautiful baby." Vickie took Alex and started cooing to her. "I'm your grandma, my darling. Aren't you the cutest little thing?"

Alex put her hands on Vickie's face and gave her a big smile, and Vickie melted right before my eyes. Then, while Vickie and I walked into the house, Ben and his father hauled in the luggage and baby paraphernalia.

Ben's parents were warm and welcoming; I soon felt comfortable shedding my concerns. We walked into the kitchen. Vickie had prepared lunch for us and had a high chair set up for Alex. Ben's father,

Will, asked me about the farm and how I found myself there after living in Chicago. They inquired about my career at the college and my sons. Ben told them how we met and all the tricks I pulled on him in Florence. They laughed with glee. The men took Alex off to get her ready for a nap, leaving Vickie and me in the kitchen.

"I am so happy you're here, Brenna. But, just as important, my son is happy and content. I haven't seen Ben this settled down ever before. It's no secret that we didn't approve of Ben's previous wives. When you see your adult son making a mistake, heading for heart-break, your own heart breaks for him, and there's nothing you can do to head it off. A parent has to sit back and be there for them when their life comes crashing down. Celebrity is heady stuff. It cripples and destroys lives. I am so happy that you and Ben found each other. I can see how much he adores you and Alex. He has always wanted children, and this time he's made the right choice," said Vickie as she smiled at me with warmth.

"Thank you, Mrs. Langford. That means a lot to me."

"Please call me Vickie or mom, whatever you feel comfortable with. Have you set a date for the wedding?"

"I thought May, the second anniversary of our meeting. My son, Chase, will be home from college. I couldn't get married without him."

"Ben told us that your other son was not very accepting of you, Ben, and the baby. I hope he'll come around. Sometimes our children get this wild idea in their heads and can't see that their parents are as human as everyone else. It must be hard for you, I'm sorry. Ben, like his brothers, has given Will and me more than a few moments of distress, but a parent still loves them, and eventually, things work out. Now on to better things.

"I asked that my other children and their families to wait until tomorrow before they descend on you all at once. It's going to be chaos, but I love every minute as long as they all go home," Vickie laughed.

"What can I do to help you get ready for tomorrow?" I asked.

"Ben tells me you're a superb cook, something I am not. I'm adequate, but not outstanding. If you would like to make the stuffing, we can get the turkey prepped and then relax for a while."

I made my grandmother's special recipe for turkey dressing. Mouthwatering aromas soon filled the kitchen as Vickie baked the pumpkin pies, and we worked in companionable ease. Will and Ben took charge of Alex, and they ordered pizza for supper. After Alex ate and bathed, she was ready for bed. I noticed the men had moved our luggage into one bedroom. I looked at Ben with a question in my eyes.

"Honey, we're both over forty with a baby. So it's no big deal for us to sleep together at my parents' house."

"If you think it's alright."

"It's fine. Nothing to worry about except your virtue," Ben grinned. "It's payback time."

"You wouldn't, not in your parent's home."

"Wan' a bet?"

*　*　*

Ben's siblings and their families started arriving on Thanksgiving morning. They introduced me to so many big and little people I couldn't keep all the names straight. Ben's sisters-in-law at first appeared reserved and then warmed up to me as we danced around each other in the kitchen. Finally, serving the meal, it seemed like everyone was talking simultaneously. Ben was just Uncle Ben, home for a visit. The only reference to his high-profile career was when a niece asked him if he knew Lady Gaga.

We ended the evening with many asking if they could visit us at the farm. I invited all and truly felt they entirely accepted Alex and me into the Langford family. We left for home early the following day with sincere wishes from Will and Vickie for our return soon.

Once on the road, Ben looked over at me. "See, you had nothing to worry about. They love you and Alex, or else they wouldn't have asked to come to Hartsuff to visit us."

"You were right, darling," I said.

"What did you say? Can I hear that again?" Ben laughed.

Our drive was relaxing, and we chatted about this and that, nothing of major concern. Ben had been mulling over the idea of purchasing a truck for use on the farm. Unfortunately, it wasn't always convenient to use my vehicle when we both had somewhere to go, and Chase's little two-seater car that he kept at the farm wasn't of much use.

"We have to haul stuff regularly, and it would be more convenient than cramming stuff in your SUV and getting it all dirty and stinky. What do you think?"

"That's a great idea, and you can come and go as you please," I said.

"I noticed when we drive around town and back and forth to the airstrip every truck or car we pass, the driver gives a kind of flick of the wrist wave. Do you know everyone in the county?" Ben asked.

I had to laugh, "That's 'Highway Howdy'. It's a habit we have around here. If you don't wave, we know that you're not local. If that's the case, we check out the vehicle's license plate. Most of the locals can tell immediately where someone is from. If an out-of-state plate appears, we know someone has company before they even hit town. That's life in the country. Nothing is a secret for long."

"I'll have to keep my hand at the ready on the steering wheel when I get my truck. I want to be considered a local. I'll do some research on the internet or ask Sam what vehicle he thinks will work best," said Ben. "Ted and I can go out to some truck dealerships. It wouldn't hurt to have an attorney along for the negotiations." We were home in less than five hours, having talked the entire way.

Later the following day, we took Alex out to the front of the property, and we cut down a Fraser Fir for our first Christmas tree. I had the tree stand ready, and we positioned the tree in the large front entryway just as I pictured, and the outdoorsy smell of the freshly cut tree filled the house. Other than the religious significance, nothing says Christmas more than that fresh piney smell.

Ben spent an hour untangling the lights while I got out the ornaments. Alex sat in her walker, taking everything in. Plugging in the lights, her eyes lit up. We spent the afternoon placing the ornaments as I told the stories to Ben of each one. Some of them were homemade ones that my sons had made through the years. It wouldn't be long before Alexandra would have her own to add.

* * *

The next couple of weeks were relaxing as Ben worked for hours in his office, and I read the three books he was considering for his next directorial project. Unfortunately, he had removed the covers and only identified the manuscripts as number one, number two, and number three. However, after carefully reading each and analyzing them, there was one outstanding amongst the others.

I ran over to Ben's office in The Coop. "It's door number two," I said. "I love this book, and I think it has all the elements for a good movie. It's not just 'Chick Lit' or 'Dick Lit' but a combination of both, so it will appeal to a wide audience."

"Interesting word use in your analysis," chuckled Ben. "That was my thought, too. Thanks, honey, for taking the time to read through them. That's a big help to me."

"Glad I could be of service, Mr. Director, sir," as I saluted smartly.

"Don't forget, my soon to be my wife, you are much more than that; a helpmate, my lover, and the mother of my child. Do we have to delay getting married until May?"

"I thought that would be the best time to get everyone we love together when the weather is good, making traveling easier. I'm hoping that Gage would be around to join our celebration."

"I hope so too, darling. I'll come home in a couple of minutes. There are at least one or two more things to finish."

I walked back to the house, waiting for Alex to wake up from her nap. I wanted to drive into town and do some Christmas shopping. However, I had a feeling that our rural town wouldn't have what I was looking for, and the Amazon sleigh would have to make a few stops at the farm.

Chase will be home next week for the holiday break from school. I strived to have everything ready for his homecoming. Ben also needed to go to New York the week before Christmas to help with securing funding and insurers for the new film. He planned to be away three days, back home in plenty of time for Christmas.

After Alex was in bed for the night, Ben and I sat down at the laptop and did a massive amount of Amazon shopping for the children and his family. Everything for our first Christmas was coming together. I decorated the inside and outside the house, including The Coop. I was getting excited, a world of difference from the Christmas I spent pregnant and alone the year before.

Chase arrived home, immediately taking his sister in his arms. Alex slapped his face and giggled every time she saw him, gifting him with the biggest smiles and holding out her arms. Chase took charge of the horses and thought the barn renovations were perfect, making caring for our three horses more efficient and certainly more shelter for the animals during the harsh winter months.

Leaving brother and sister together at the farm, I drove Ben to the airstrip for his flight to New York on the production company plane. Ben had ordered a new truck from the local Dodge dealership, delivery expected in January. The roads were snowy, and an ice storm predicted for late evening; I was used to this kind of driving and took my time getting Ben to his plane.

"Darling, be careful driving back. These roads are treacherous; call me when you get home," asked Ben.

"I will, honey, safe flight. I'll pick you up in four days." We kissed and hugged as if this temporary separation was months instead of days. Unfortunately, by the time I reached the farm, the snow and ice storm were on us in full force as I texted Ben of my safe arrival. I hoped his plane could fly above the storm; I held my breath until Ben called to say he had landed safely in New York.

The days whirled by with baking, gift wrapping, and spending time with Chase. We banked the Christmas tree with sparkly wrapped boxes that continuously caught Alex's eye. I was on constant alert when Alex was crawling around the house. She immediately headed for the tree if I turned by back. As hectic as the holiday season is, I loved every minute. The only missing piece for complete happiness was Gage.

Ben was on his way home. Chase would look after Alex while I navigated the icy roads to the airstrip. I left a little early to return a large crescent wrench to the hardware store before Ben's plane came in. Caution was the word for the day while driving our road to town. When rounding a curve; one of the Warchekski's steers was in the middle of the road again. I stomped my foot down, causing the brakes to lock, throwing my SUV into a skid, and then a spin. Losing control, I couldn't help but hit the animal. The car careened across the road, hit the gully, turning my vehicle on its side. The five-pound wrench I had placed on the passenger seat flew through the air and whacked me in the head as airbags deployed and I lost consciousness.

CHAPTER TWENTY-THREE

B en called the house phone after getting Brenna's voice mail on her cell. "Chase, has your mother left to pick me up at the airstrip yet?"

"Ben, she left an hour ago. She was going to stop at the hardware to take something back before picking you up. With the road conditions, it might take her some extra time. I have Alex here, so I can't go out and look for her. Let me call the hardware store and see if she made it there. I'll call you back." Chase called the store; they hadn't seen Brenna in today. After he hung up, the house phone rang again. It was the sheriff's department.

The Valley County Sherriff's deputy told Chase that Brenna had been in an accident and was now at the hospital. She was in stable condition and receiving treatment. Chase called Ben's cell phone in a panic. "Ben, Mom's been in an accident. She's at the hospital in town. All the deputy would say, she was in stable condition. Can you get there?"

"On my way. I'll flag down a car and get there as soon as I can and call you back." Ben disconnected and ran for the main road outside the airstrip. Maggie's husband, Ted, was driving down the road and recognized Ben waving frantically. After explaining the situation, they sped to the hospital.

Ben ran into the emergency entrance, causing quite a stir. "Is Brenna Herrera here?" asking the desk attendant on duty.

"Are you family?" she asked.

"Brenna is my fiancé. Where is she?" asked Ben in an agitated state, not noticing the attendant's shocked expression.

"Exam room three," she said as Ben ran into the Emergency Department.

Brenna's physician, Dr. Krason, stopped him before he could reach Brenna's side. "Mr. Langford, isn't it?"

"Yes, ma'am. How is Brenna? Is she going to be okay? Can I see her?"

"I'm Doctor Krason, Brenna's family doctor. She's going to be fine. A little knock on the head and a bruised face. It could have been a lot worse. The car's airbags kept her from more significant injury. I think it's a draw between her and the steer. I want to do another head x-ray and run a couple of tests, and then I think she'll be able to go home. Let me check with her for a moment, then the two of you can see her."

The doctor disappeared behind a curtained-off section of the emergency room. After some mumbled conversation, Ben walked to Brenna's bedside.

Ben took her hand and kissed it. "Are you okay, darling? What happened?"

"I'm fine, but I don't think the Warchekski's steer is doing so well. He was on the road, and I couldn't stop; it was too icy." I looked over for the first time, noticing the other visitor in my cubical. "I must be dying. Is that Gage, or am I hallucinating?"

"Hi, mom," Gage hesitantly stepped forward to hug me. "I'm so sorry for the things I said to you. Please forgive me. I love you," he said as he cried.

"I love you too, Gage. Let's not dwell on the past. I'm so happy to see you." I looked at Ben. "Is this your doing?"

"Gage and I had a little heart-to-heart. No big deal," Ben admitted.

"It is a big deal, a very big deal. Thank you, darling. I love you so much," I said as Ben leaned over the bed, meeting my lips.

In the next minute, Doctor Krason came into my space. "Okay, break it up with all this mushy stuff. I want to go over a few things with Brenna. If you gentlemen will excuse us."

Ben said, "I'm going to call Ted for a ride back to the farm. Gage and I will see you in a couple of minutes."

After the men exited the examination room, Doctor Krason sat down on the chair next to my bed. "Brenna, I ran some general blood and urine tests on you and found a little something. It seems that lightning can strike twice."

"What do you mean?" I asked.

"Your hCG hormone levels are elevated."

"What does that mean?" Asking again for clarification.

"I believe you are in the first couple weeks of pregnancy," Doctor Krason grinned.

"Are you serious?"

"Yes, I am. Let's wait a couple of weeks and take another test. Is this something planned or an oops?"

"If I'm pregnant, it's neither. Not planned, but welcomed. I want to keep this to myself, so say nothing to Ben."

"I'm not even going to note it on your chart. Come see me in a couple of weeks. Take care of yourself. Rest for today and put some ice on your facial bruises. If you have any further head discomfort, call me. X-rays are clear, so you can go home. Congratulations."

"Thanks, Doctor Krason. See you in two weeks." Shocked beyond belief but so happy, it would be hard to keep this unexpected news to myself.

Ben called Ted. He arrived back at the hospital to take us home. I promised Ted to call Maggie as soon as I could. I was on cloud nine. Not only was Gage home, but I was giving Ben another child. The best Christmas ever.

Ben insisted I go to bed as soon as we got home. I wasn't going to argue. I was exhausted. But, first, I wanted to introduce Gage to his baby sister. As Gage picked up Alexandra and hugged her close, there were tears in our eyes. Alex looked with confusion at this new person, who looked just like her other brother. She smiled and gurgled with glee to have two playmates.

It was getting late when everything settled down. Chase moved to the kitchen to make supper while I showered and got ready for bed. Ben sat on the side of the bed. He told me about going to Gage's frat house and sitting down with him and having a man-to-man talk. "I told him how much I love you and that we were getting married. If he wanted to hold a grudge, that was up to him, or be part of our family—his choice. I made him an offer. If he wanted to come home and apologize to you, he could come to the airport and fly home with me. I gave him the time and location of the flight. Either be there or not, and the rest is history. Merry Christmas, baby."

"How can I ever thank you for bringing our family together?" I cried.

"Well, I can think of a couple of things, but first, do we have to wait until May for our wedding?"

"What are you doing on New Year's Eve?" I asked.

"Seriously? Can we get something together in less than two weeks, or is this just a reaction from the knock on the noggin?"

"I'm very serious. My family is here; I want something small and intimate with your parents here at the farm. Do you think they would come on such short notice?"

"You wouldn't be able to keep them away. My family loves you and Alex."

"Let's keep our secret until Christmas night, and then we can work out the details. I already have a dress, and you have a suit. We get a license, order a cake, invite a few people, and we'll have a wedding."

"You've made me the happiest man in the world. I'm going to let you sleep, so you don't have a chance to change your mind. I love you. Rest. I'll take care of the children—all our children, the big ones and the little one."

Ben held me close, and I got a good night's sleep. I had a minor headache and slight bruising when I got up to fix breakfast. My family was all together again. I placed a hardy breakfast on the table. My sons struggled out of bed, finding their sister already sitting in her highchair and banging her spoon on the tray. Ben was awake and talking on the phone with the local car dealership. He arranged for a vehicle to use while mine was being accessed for damage. The Warchekski's called to say how sorry they were that one of their herd had gotten in the road.

They had it butchered and would deliver the meat as an apology, all wrapped, ready to fill up my chest freezer in a couple of days.

Chase took Gage out to the barn, showing him how to care for the horses. When we had a minute alone, Gage and I sat down for a talk.

"Mom, again, I want to apologize for all the nasty things I said to you. I didn't mean them. I think I was in shock. I always thought that Chase and I would take care of you. You are MOM; I guess I lost the understanding that you're a woman too, not just the mother whose life revolved around us. I missed knowing my little sister for months, and I deeply regret that. I should have been here for you emotionally, and I wasn't."

"I know what you're trying to say. I didn't have a separate life while you were growing up and never dated, so I did not expose you to that side of me. Now that you're here, that's all that counts."

"Ben came to see me at my fraternity house on campus. Boy, did he create a riot, and then when he asked for me, the frat house exploded. Ben's a good guy, mom. We talked, and he told me how much he loved you and how unfair my treatment of you was. He told me the story of how you met and how you both fell in love.

"Ben made me realize you're a woman, not only a mother. You deserve to love and be loved. Ben pointed out that my dad died while you were so young, and I couldn't expect you to be alone for the rest of your life. If I could accept that, he wanted me to be part of his life. I have to say that having a baby blew my mind."

"You and me both. I thought I had a terminal disease when I wasn't feeling well."

"No kidding. That must have scared the hell out of you. Why didn't you tell us?"

"I didn't want you guys to worry about me when you were so far away, and I was just getting over the shock myself. Can you imagine? My sons were in college. I was pregnant, and a tad embarrassed."

"Is that why you quit your job and moved here?"

"Partially. I wanted to come home. I was lonely, and I felt it was time to leave the city and come home to family. What do you think of the house?"

"It's great. You really did a lot to it. Grandma would have loved it."

We hugged and kissed as if there had never been a painful separation. The three of us had been a unit for so long. It would take some adjustment for all of us to gel as a family of five, but we were up for the challenge.

Christmas Eve was finally here. I invited Maggie and Ted with their girls, Sam and his date, Guncle John and Aunt Rose, over for wine and food. No one seemed to realize I was drinking sparkling white grape juice. Chase and Gage took Maggie's two giggling girls out to see the horses. My sons seemed to be a hot topic in town with the teenage population.

Our guests left as the snow fell; a White Christmas was never in doubt. Gage and Chase showed their sister how to set out carrots for the reindeer and cookies and milk for Santa. The boys had more fun than Alex, who was just interested in eating the cookies. The stockings hung by the chimney with care when the boys moved upstairs, and Alex was snug in her bed. Ben and I sat down in the living room with cups of hot chocolate.

"Well, Santa," I said as I looked at Ben. "You better drink the milk and eat a couple of cookies. I'll put the carrots back in the refrigerator."

"HO HO HO! First, I want to kiss my fiancé," Ben spoke in his best Santa voice.

We moved into each other's arms. We fit so well together. My love for this man was overwhelming; it filled my world with joy. I continued to keep my special secret; I was sure that I was pregnant. All the early signs were there. I hoped I could keep the secret for a couple more weeks.

"Before we get carried away, let's stuff the stockings and get the presents out. Then I want to make love to you," I said as we smiled at each other. We got busy and set out the Santa gifts, and the stockings were full. We climbed into bed and had our intimate celebration, enjoying our closeness to the fullest, filled with joy as a reunited family.

Christmas morning came early courtesy of my sons, who were as excited as little kids. They got Alex up, changed her diaper, and woke Ben and me. They were jumping up and down with Alex in their arms.

"Look, Alex, Santa was here. He brought you all kinds of things to chew on and throw," laughed Chase.

"She will probably still like putting her toes in her mouth as much," chuckled Gage. "I wonder who she got that from—Chase? You're always putting your foot in your mouth."

Soon wrapping paper was flying. Chase and Gage got sweaters, gift cards, and monogrammed briefcases, and a bunch of gag gifts. I opened a small box from Ben. Inside was a set of keys with a note: *Look out in the backyard.* We all ran to the backdoor. In the driveway was a brand-new Premium Luxury Cadillac Escalade in the blue color I loved, with a big red bow on top. My mouth dropped open; it was way too much.

"Honey, your SUV wasn't worth fixing, and I wanted you and Alex to be safe should another bovine sashay down the road again."

"Thank you, sweetheart. I love it. Now it's time for your present. Let's run out to the barn." We donned our coats and hurried to the barn where our extra shall now held a black stallion. "Sorry, honey, it's only one horsepower. Merry Christmas," I laughed.

"He's beautiful. I can't wait to saddle him up and take a good long ride. Thank you, my love. This sure beats the pony I wanted as a kid," Ben laughed. "I thought we already gave each other presents—The Coop and the barn?"

"Yeah, what happened to that?" I asked with a grin. We walked back to the house, and I prepared a big Christmas morning breakfast of chocolate chip pancakes, eggs, and sausage. It warmed my heart to see the people I loved, having a good time laughing and joking around the table. My sons seemed to accept Ben fully. Soon everyone was on their phones, and Alex was having a great time ripping the discarded wrapping paper to bits. Ben called his parents to wish them a Merry Christmas.

Will and Vickie loved the gifts we sent, and they would pass on holiday greetings to the rest of their clan. They wanted to drive up for a visit soon. I said we would call later and arrange a date. They didn't know it would be in a week, as Ben and I grinned at each other.

We relaxed and enjoyed being together as a family unit. Once we cared for the horses and everyone parked themselves in the living room, Ben and I were ready to make our declaration. I looked at my handsome sons. "Ben and I have an announcement. We're getting married on New Year's Eve here at the farm."

Chase and Gage looked at each other in harmony, said, "It's about time."

"It's going to be a small wedding, with probably twenty or fewer guests. We want to keep it low profile, so keep it close to the vest until it's over so the media can't invade our privacy. We're inviting Ben's parents and siblings, Cousin Maggie and her family, Sam and his guest, and Guncle John and Aunt Rose. That's it. Small and personal is what we want," I said.

"If you guys want to go away for a couple of days, Chase and I can take care of Alex," offered Gage. "We aren't leaving for school until the 4th."

"That's generous of you," I looked at Ben. "I don't know if it would be possible with Ben's parents here. We might have to plan something for later."

Ben and my sons took off to the barn to feed the horses and look over the recent addition. I called Maggie and told her of our plans and asked her for covert help with several details. Maggie was thrilled. We discussed all the things we would need to pull off this short notice wedding. After talking to Maggie, I asked to put Ted on the phone. I made an appointment to meet him in his law office the following day. There were things I wanted to do to ease my mind before I took the next step with my marriage to Ben.

I googled the information for a marriage license. We could get a license anywhere in the state to use at our home. Maggie's husband would have the County Magistrate come over on New Year's Eve to perform the ceremony. Maggie offered to make the wedding cake and get the flowers for the house and my bouquet. Ben and I planned to drive to Grand Island the day after tomorrow to get our license and buy wedding rings as surreptitiously as possible. We'll need some luck to pull that off.

That evening, Ben called his parents to announce our plans for the wedding. They were excited and said they wouldn't miss it for anything. They planned on arriving the day before the wedding to help. We stressed it would be low key since it was Ben's third marriage and my second. I invited them to stay at the farm. Gage and Chase could bunk together upstairs, and Ben's parents could stay in the other bedroom. If Ben's siblings wanted to come, I would make reservations at Sanders' only motel. We tried to keep this as quiet as possible. I called the other invitees and told them it was a New Year's celebration.

I had my dress; Ben had a suit, as did my sons. I would dress Alex in her red velvet Christmas dress. Maggie would serve as my Matron of Honor, and Ben asked his father to be his Best Man. Things were moving right along; everything was falling into place. Even for a simple wedding, there were a slew of details to see to. The following day, I met with Ted while everyone else was busy with farm chores. Ted addressed my concerns with merging Ben's and my life together.

Gage and Chase took care of Alex while Ben and I drove to Grand Island the next day. Ben put on a hat with dark glasses when we applied for the license. It didn't fool anyone. Next, we purchased two simple gold rings when I asked, "Ben, is this going too fast for you?"

"It can't go fast enough for me. I like the plans for something small. I'm sorry that we can't go on a honeymoon with my parents and the boys here. What do you think about someday going back to Santorini? But in the meantime, anywhere I'm with you is a honeymoon."

"Good answer. Is there anything you want to add? I don't want it to be only what I want for the wedding without your input."

"I'm not good with this kind of stuff. It's all yours, honey. Just point me to the where and when, and I'll be there."

We arrived back to the farm as the Warchekski's delivered the meat from my beefy road collision, all six hundred and twenty pounds. It filled the chest freezer in the mudroom and the kitchen freezer.

The following two days, Maggie and I ran around like crazy, getting the food ready and freshening the guest room upstairs for Ben's parents. My sons took charge of their sister. The next day, the day before the big event, would keep us busy arranging the flowers, ensuring that everyone had clean and pressed clothes, and dealing with just plain nerves.

As we checked the liquor supplies, I made sure that there was one bottle of non-alcoholic sparkling white grape juice. Maggie gave me a quizzical look. I looked around to make sure no one else was listening. I told her my secret.

"Does Ben know?" she asked.

"No one, only you. I'm keeping it a secret for a couple more weeks."

"Mummy's the word," said Maggie. She's such a comedian.

Ben's parents arrived with Ben's youngest brother, Jordon, and his family the next day at noon. I showed Will and Vickie to their room and told Jordon that a room for him and his family was ready for them in town. Maggie and Ben's mother took over the kitchen and prepared the food for friends and family.

Vickie pitched right in and put the flower arrangements together. We shoved the men out of the house, spending their time in the barn and The Coop. As the evening progressed, the men removed them-selves to Hartsuff to the little hole-in-the-wall bar for a mini-bachelor party, leaving the women with a bit of peace. My sister-in-law-to-be

Carol took charge of Alexandra, along with her three children. When Vickie and I got a few minutes to sit down, I poured her a glass of wine and myself a glass of ice water.

"Brenna, I am so happy to have you in our family. You're the woman I always hoped Ben would settle down with. I love my son, but I know his weaknesses. Ben was the definition of a wunderkind. Celebrity came to him early after the phenomenal success of his first film when he was nineteen. He sowed more than his share of wild oats and married twice to my distress. Will and I called them Bimbride one and Bimbride two. Thank God they didn't last long. We tried to keep Ben grounded in reality, but it's almost impossible when there are hordes of people seeing to his every whim. Now that Ben is in his forties with a child, I hope he knows how lucky he is to have you. Can I ask you a personal question?" said Vickie.

"Of course," I said.

"Are you pregnant?"

"Yes, I am, about five weeks. What gave me away?"

"I noticed that while the womenfolk were working today, everyone was sipping wine, and you stuck with water or a soft drink."

"No one but Maggie knows, not even Ben. I want to keep it to myself for a couple more weeks until I'm over the fragile first trimester."

"Your secret is safe with me. I'm so happy for you both." Vickie gave me the biggest hug and kiss. "Please know that you can call on me anytime. Ben will travel a great deal of the time as the new film gets underway. If you feel the need to talk or just want a friendly chat, I am here for you."

"Thank you, Vickie. I never had a mother; my grandmother raised me. It'll be nice to have a real mom."

By the time the men came home in high liquor-infused humor, the tables in the dining room were set with plates, glassware, and silverware ready for the celebration. Ben grabbed his clothes for tomorrow and joined his brother and family at the motel in town for the night. As silly as it might be, I was sticking with the tradition of not seeing him or he me before the wedding.

CHAPTER TWENTY-FOUR

The morning of the wedding was a flurry of activity. My sons got the horses taken care of, the food was ready, and the flowers put in the living and dining rooms. We arranged my bouquet, then Maggie started on me with hair and makeup. She did a great job covering the bruises still visible from the "moo mow down". Vickie got Alex up, fed, and then dressed her in the red velvet dress, white tights, and sparkly red shoes. We scheduled the ceremony for 11 AM.

Everyone was dressed, the guests arrived, and the magistrate was ready. Maggie and I stayed in my bedroom with the pocket doors closed. Gage started the recorded music as our guests assembled in the living room, and Ben standing with his father. Maggie came out of my room and walked across the entryway toward the front of the living room. I followed in my tea length off-white lace dress, flowers in my hair with a bouquet of roses in my hands to meet my groom. Maggie's husband, Ted, took pictures by the dozen as Ben and I faced each other. Ben had the biggest smile on his face, and the warmth in his eyes melted my heart and calmed my nerves.

The magistrate spoke the traditional words as we slipped the wedding rings on our fingers. As he pronounced us husband and wife, our daughter started clapping her hands. Everyone was laughing as Ben sealed our union with a kiss. Maggie moved our guests toward the dining room for a toast with champagne and fruit punch for the children.

Chase asked everyone to raise their glasses, "Ben, welcome to our family. All I ask from you is to take care of and love our mother because she sure loves you. When you look at each other, I can tell that's what true love looks like. Congratulations. Cheers."

Our little party of twenty heaped their plates with finger foods. Will and Vickie put all their focus on Alexandra, to her delight, making sure she was fed, changed, and put down for her nap. Gage put on some music so that Ben and I could have a first dance as Maggie and Vickie got out the wedding cake.

Maggie is a true cake artist, and she outdid herself for our wedding. The two-tier red velvet cake with chocolate gnocchi between layers and buttercream frosting was a work of art. Maggie made edible flowers for the top and had miniature books, snips of film, a small David statue and horses circling the bottom layer. It was the most beautiful and delicious cake imaginable as Ben and I fed each other a bite.

Ben called for everyone's attention, "Brenna and I want to thank you all for celebrating with us today. I am the luckiest man in the world to have the most beautiful woman I have ever known as my wife. Not only is she stunning to look at, but she has a beautiful spirit and an abundance of kindness. I am truly blessed to have her in my life. To you, Brenna."

Tears ran down my face while I kissed my husband as our guests cheered and raised their glasses. Ben's father, Will, then added that he and Vickie were so happy to have two more handsome grandsons and hoped Chase and Gage would always think of them as their grandparents. My heart was so full of love for this group of people surrounding us on our special day. The Langfords welcomed us, including all my children, with great affection into their family circle.

Chase got his sister up from her nap so that she could have her bite of cake. She enjoyed getting to know her cousins and playing with her grandparents. People left about 4 PM as our celebration wound down. Maggie and Ted stayed behind to help clean and get the house back in order. After changing clothes, our more intimate group cooked some hamburgers for supper and talked about plans for the coming year. The Langford parents were very impressed with Chase and Gage, their field of study, travels, and language skills.

Ben told his parents about the final cut of his first directorial effort and plans for the next. The evening was relaxing and everyone seemed to enjoy getting to know each other better. Will and Vickie stayed for another day and then hit the road with Jordan, Carol, and their children. Life was back to normal within days.

*　*　*

Ben had to go to New York to meet with the screenwriter he had hired to prepare a treatment and a rough script from the book he purchased. He would be away for two days, and he would have the boys fly with him in the production company's private plane back to school.

All our guests left for home, and the boys were off to school with Ben in New York. My life was back to a daily routine with my daughter and the farm. Winter reared its ugly head, and we were snowbound for a couple of days. I fed the horses and spent some time brushing them down while Alex took her afternoon naps.

Ben was back, and we spent some quiet time together. He had me read the rough screenplay, and I thought it was great. Ben also brought home the final print of *Galway Gone* to watch on the DVD player, his first film as a director. The film was one of the most wonderful films I have ever seen. Ben captured all the emotions. The actors were marvelous, and the cinematography was breathtaking. I cried when it was over.

"Ben, it's incredible. I couldn't see a flaw in anything. It's perfect. I'm so proud of you."

"Thank you, darling. It was a lot of hard work; everything came together with a great cast, crew, and talented pre and post production staff. There's going to be a premiere in Hollywood. Will you consider coming with me to L.A.?"

"I think I can probably work it into my schedule. I want to be there for your big moment. How does it feel behind the camera instead of in front of it?" I asked.

"It's OUR big moment. In a way, it plays a big part in our story. Your comments and opinions on the project were invaluable. I love directing. It's like taking the pieces of a puzzle, putting them all together for the perfect picture."

The following two weeks, we had our honeymoon at home, making love, playing with our daughter, and Ben had a chance to relax before the new film got underway. He spent hours in The Coop going through audition tapes that his casting crew thought were worth considering.

Ben took delivery of his new truck, and he took pleasure in driving around town, picking up supplies for the farm, and practicing his "Highway Howdy". When not doing farm duties, I could find him in The Coop, arranging meetings with a score of film professionals before his upcoming trip to L.A. Ben's trip would be of unknown duration. Still, he reassured me he had assembled a great staff to do the grunt work, and he could make many of the decisions by holding meetings over Zoom remotely.

I helped Ben pack for his trip; he was leaving in two days. He insisted he drive his truck to the airstrip and leave it in the hangar so I could avoid the icy roads with Alex. If I needed the truck before he got back, Ted or Sam would bring it back to the farm.

We spent our last night together before his trip making love. I would miss his gentle touches and passionate journeys over my body. I couldn't get enough of him, the texture of his skin, his essence, and his strength. Our ardor seemed to grow since we spoke our marriage vows. I felt Ben's total devotion and commitment to making our union work.

While Ben was taking his morning shower, I slipped a small wrapped box into his coat pocket with a little card telling him how much I loved him. The box held a pregnancy test stick that plainly said—PREGNANT. I couldn't wait for him to find it after he left and hear the excitement in his voice on the phone.

I fixed breakfast like usual. We sat down and shared our meal with our daughter, knowing that it would be awhile before we were together again. Ben picked up Alex and smothered her in kisses as she grabbed his hair. He kissed me fervently while I tried not to let my emotions make his leave-taking more difficult. Ben warmed up his truck and placed his luggage in the cab. I stood at the door as Ben ran over to The Coop to grab his briefcase. As I turned to close the door, I noticed the manuscript he had been making notes on laying on the kitchen table. After I secured Alex in her highchair, I ran to The Coop to add the book to his other materials that he needed to take with him. Ben had his back to the door while talking on his phone.

I opened the door silently and stood frozen in place as my carefully shaped, beautiful new life imploded in front of me.

CHAPTER TWENTY-FIVE

"I can't wait to get back to you, baby, and resume what I started when we were together in New York. I'm going to crawl back up those long legs of yours and screw you seven ways to Sunday," said Ben as he chuckled with the voice on the phone.

After hearing his side of the conversation, I must have made a sound. Ben whipped around, looking at me with a shocked expression, knowing I had listened to every word of his side of the conversation.

"I thought you might need the manuscript." I laid it on the table, turned around, and left as he called out my name. I hurried into the house and moved the steel tornado bar across the door, preventing his entrance. While I looked out the window, I saw him pause at the gate to the yard. I could almost see his thought processes with this crisis of conscience. *Do I stay and try to fix this, or do I go and make my flight?* Ben stared at the house for minutes, shook his head, and turned away. Making his decision, he got into his truck, drove down the driveway and out of my life.

* * *

I sat down in a chair in the kitchen. I handed a graham cracker to Alex, keeping her busy. Devastation didn't cover what I was feeling;

The pain of his betrayal filled me with a frisson of towering rage that I had never felt before. My phone started chirping; the caller ID showed it was Ben. I turned the ring tone off. I didn't want to hear the lies or excuses that I was sure he would use to explain his phone conversation. The words would forever echo in my mind. The saddest thing about it—not a shock. In the recesses of my heart, I knew it would happen with Ben eventually, just not this soon after our wedding.

After I was sure that her daughters had left for school, I called Maggie, asking her to come out to the farm. Maggie pulled into the driveway and ran to the door. She had heard from my voice on the phone that something horrendous had happened. By the time she arrived, I was crying. I let her in and grabbed onto her as I cried in choking, agonizing sobs. Ben's treachery so wholly overwhelmed me; my legs could no longer hold me up. Maggie guided me to a chair and held me until I could speak. I told her about the phone exchange I had overheard.

"He must have been screwing someone the entire time we were engaged. Why would he do this to me? I asked.

"I can't tell you what was in his mind, Brenna. But calm down, or you're going to bring on a miscarriage."

"Oh God, I put the pregnancy test stick in a box and put it in his coat pocket. I thought it would be a cute way to surprise him with the pregnancy we thought would never happen. He always wanted more children, and it thrilled me to get pregnant again. What am I going to do, Maggie?"

"Do you think you want to hear him out?" She asked.

"What can he possibly say? There was no ambiguity in his words. I don't even care who he was talking to. If not this woman, it would be someone else. I feel like such a fool; within a month of our wedding, it's over."

"I don't know what to think or say. You've lost two men that you loved. It may be in different ways, but the hurt is the same—a death of your life as you knew it. You'll get through this as you did when Marco died and come out stronger. You have a baby to take care of and another on the way. That's why you will survive. With any kind of grieving, the sharpness and rawness will soften as time moves on. Family and friends are here to support you. You're not alone. You will get through this."

* * *

Maggie and Ted helped me box up Ben's things from the house and The Coop. I had Sam change the locks on both buildings. I made arrangements with a Grand Island Cadillac dealership to get rid of the ridiculously expensive SUV Ben had bought me for Christmas and find something less flashy. The one thing I didn't have to do was change my name.

I had changed nothing after the short duration of my marriage and not petitioned for Alexandra's last name to be changed. The days moved on as I adjusted to Ben's betrayal, another catastrophic change in my life. My emotional tank ran on empty. I didn't cry. I didn't laugh, but just moved through the motions of living. The calendar page flipped to February, and it was soon Valentine's Day.

After avoiding Ben's phone calls for weeks, I knew we had to speak. So, as my phone rang one more time, I picked it up and pressed the talk key. "Hello, Ben."

"Hello, Brenna. How are you?"

"I'm doing okay."

"I can't tell you how sorry I am for what I did."

"I know you are. But I want you to know that it's not all your fault. I knew from the beginning we were from two different worlds that could never mesh. You tried so hard to become part of mine, and I thank you for that, but I knew you weren't happy. You knew I could never be part of yours, and I didn't even try.

"I sought to make you into someone you weren't, and that was wrong of me. I couldn't change, and I shouldn't have expected you to. We can't transform who we are, or else neither one of us would be happy.

"You love the limelight, your fans, and the fame that goes with it. You deserve all the acclaim and accolades that go with the business you love. But, unfortunately, country life isn't for you; I know that now but you tried for me, and I appreciate that.

"I'm checking into an annulment or divorce, whatever is easiest for each of us unless you want to file. I've packed up your stuff and will have it shipped out to your agent or any other address you want. What do you want to do with your truck and horse?"

"Brenna, I don't want a divorce or annulment. Can we work this out?"

"We can't change who we are. Putting our parting off would delay the inevitable and make it more painful for both of us. At least this way, we can try to remain friends for the sake of our child."

"Brenna, I never meant to hurt you. You're the best thing that ever happened to me. When I opened the box, you put in my pocket, it broke my heart. Are we really pregnant, Brenna?"

"Yes, Ben, I am; we are not."

"How far along are you?"

"Twelve weeks."

"Why didn't you tell me sooner?" Ben asked.

"Would it have made a difference?"

"Probably not," Ben sighed in all honesty. "I love you and Alexandra and now the new baby. Will you let me see them?"

"You will always be their father. You can visit after we set up a schedule. I will never malign you to them or keep them from you. I'll send pictures, tell you how Alex is, and notify you when the new baby is born. That's the best I can do, Ben."

"Please, please give me another chance. I need you in my life, Brenna."

"I will always be in your life, just not like you want me to be. I can't be with someone I can't trust. The vows we took six weeks ago to be faithful to each other are broken. There are no 'do-overs' when it comes to faithfulness. You knew going into this marriage that was the one thing I had to have from you. You may have thought that the idea of marriage and fatherhood was something you wanted, but in reality, you are not suitable for the role.

"I wish you every happiness and success with your career. I hope you can find what you're looking for and achieve contentment. It's not here with the children and me. We both know that now."

"I love you, Brenna."

"I love you too, Ben. That's what makes this so sad." I whispered, "Goodbye, Ben," as I softly disconnected.

CHAPTER TWENTY-SIX

Alex sent chocolate-covered strawberries to her brothers for Valentine's Day. I sent a Valentine to Will and Vickie and signed the card with only my name and Alex's. I sent back the heirloom quilt Ben's grandmother had made that Vickie had given us as a wedding present only weeks before. Including a note that I had filed for an annulment, which precipitated an emotional phone call from Will and Vickie. That was a tough conversation. The only thing I could say was it didn't work out and they should talk with Ben if they needed answers.

"Darling Brenna, I can guess what happened. I know my son and what kind of life he has lived. When he entered his forties, I hoped he would realize what was real and what was an illusion. I am so sorry for the hurt you are going through," said Vickie. "Please know we are here for you. Will and I will always think of your family as part of ours.

"I have concerns about your pregnancy. It's hard enough to be pregnant with a toddler running around, but you have the farm and the added emotional turmoil. Take good care of yourself. We are here for you if you need us, and we'll keep in touch."

"Thank you, Vickie; I appreciate your kind words. I will get through this and keep you posted. The baby is due August 15th; you and Will will always be in your grandchildren's lives."

I sent Chase and Gage emails, telling them that Ben and I were no longer together and that we would talk about it when they were home for the summer. They said they couldn't wait that long and were coming home for spring break in a couple of weeks.

*　*　*

This pregnancy wasn't going as well as my previous two. I was sick most of the day and half the night. My energy was in the basement; I could hardly drag myself out of bed in the morning. But, of course, at forty-two years old, age made all the difference. I hired one of Guncle John's grandsons as a hand for the horses and maintenance around the farm. I couldn't handle it all on my own.

My doctor scheduled an amniocentesis in Grand Island for the week my sons would be home in March to babysit for Alex. I heard nothing further from Ben. I sent pictures of Alex with captions to him with no further dialog. Whenever I shopped in the grocery store, I would see his picture on gossip rags or hear snippets on entertainment programs. The premiere for his film would be in May at Grauman's Chinese Theatre and promised to be a big star-studded event. Filming would start with his second directorial effort in July.

Ben seemed to have quickly moved on. I sent annulment papers to fill out to his manager, the only address I had for him. After that, our only exchange was through regular deposits of child support he put into my personal account at the bank in Sanders. Perhaps it was his way to make some sort of amends—who knows how long that will last?

In March, Alex and I picked up my sons at the airport in Grand Island. My appearance appalled Chase and Gage. I couldn't dispute it. I had purple circles under my eyes, my hair was dull and limp, and I had lost weight. When asked about Ben, I only said that he wasn't the marrying kind, or rather he didn't hesitate to marry, but just didn't know how to stay married. My sons weren't stupid; they deduced what had happened. It was difficult to tell them I was pregnant again.

That bit of news heightened their ire and confirmed their misgivings. It's a good thing that Ben was far away, or they would have kept their promise to go after him. It wouldn't be pretty. I tried to calm them down. Retribution was no solution and we would carry on like before. I appreciated their desire to protect me, but I needed to put my relationship with Ben behind me in order to move on.

Chase and Gage made it their mission to pamper me during their visit home. They ushered me to bed while caring for Alex and did all the cooking and housekeeping chores. I rested most of the week and felt better physically, but nowhere near my old self. Nothing would return me to what I was before Ben's duplicity. He delivered a fatal blow to my ability to ever trust him again.

Gage and Chase planned an early birthday party for Alexandra since they wouldn't be here on April 4th. They were planning a surprise for me they had been working on since they came home. I baked a pink princess cake and a special smash cake for Alex's celebration. Maggie and her family and Sam were honored guests at the party.

The invitees gathered as we had Alex's favorite dinner—hamburgers, french fries, and milkshakes. When Alexandra's tummy was full, she tackled her gifts—building blocks, dolls, and storybooks. I got her a swing set that would go up in the yard as soon as the snow disappeared and the ground softened. Sam volunteered to help put it together. Now for the surprise.

Gage picked up his sister from her highchair and stood her up on the floor while Chase filmed. Then, with a big smile, Alex walked with a couple of wobbly steps with her hands stretched out for me, jabbering "mama" as she crossed the floor into my arms. What a precious baby! As tears ran from my eyes, and our guests clapped with delight at her achievement.

Cake time as Alexandra took hands full of her smash cake, shoving them into her mouth as we sang Happy Birthday. After everyone had devoured their slices, the party was over. Alex was high on sugar and covered in frosting, with Chase capturing every moment on video. After a bath, she was ready for bed.

Later, when Alex was fast asleep, my sons and I sat down to talk. Graduation was coming up in May from Columbia for both my sons. They didn't plan on walking at the ceremony, saving that rite of passage when completing their Master's degrees, or so they said.

Chase was accepted to MIT Sloan and Gage at The Wharton School. Both had applied for multiple scholarships and grants and received enough money to finance most of their advanced education. Their tuition and housing were taken care of, with what their father had invested for their education. I know they did this for me. Worrying about my finances, I tried to reassure them that was one thing they didn't have to worry about. I had most of the money from the condo sale in Chicago after the farm renovations, but they still worried.

After we discussed their plans, Chase got down to the nitty-gritty. "Mom, what happened with Ben?"

"He was seeing someone else."

"He was cheating on you?" questioned Gage.

"I walked in on a conversation Ben was having with another woman, leaving no doubt in my mind that they had an ongoing physical relationship," I said.

Chase ventured to ask, "Does he know about the baby?"

I confirmed he did. "It wasn't all his fault," I admitted. "I knew that the farm life wasn't for him. He tried, but it didn't work out. I am getting over it, and you should too. Please don't hold it against him; he's still Alex's and the new baby's father. We have to respect that."

Chase continued, "I would never say anything to Alex or the baby, derogatory about Ben. That doesn't mean I wouldn't say something if I ever run into him again. I could see it coming. When Ben gave us a ride back to New York, you wouldn't believe how people, as in women, threw themselves at him and everyone else kowtowed. His butt must have been chapped, with all the ass kissing going on. It's a whole different world."

"As much as someone says they want a different life, a normal existence, it's hard to give up what you're used to and deep in your heart enjoy. I understand that. I have to move on, and I am working on it," I said.

Gage added his comments, "Mom, how are you feeling? You don't look well."

"I'm okay. I'm older, and that takes a toll on this old body, but it'll be over by mid-August."

"We'll be home in five weeks to take care of things for you. Please don't ask us to deliver our baby brother or sister," laughed Chase.

"Whoa, that's a visual I don't want stuck in my mind," said Gage.

The following day, Maggie took me to Grand Island for my amnio while my sons watched their sister. This time, I wanted to know what I was having. I had enough surprises lately.

We were on the road early and arrived at the hospital for the test. Maggie came into the exam room with me and saw the baby on the ultrasound screen. My heart burst with love as Maggie held my hand. The doctor extracted the fluid that was needed for the test. The technician noted a significant appendage and informed me I was carrying a boy.

The baby rolled around in the amniotic fluid. His little arms were waving at us. This moment made everything I tolerated with Ben worthwhile. It's sad that Ben would never see this miracle develop and grow. Perhaps he'll have more children if he settles down, but right now, this is my miracle. I wouldn't regret this pregnancy for one moment.

When we got back to the farm, I rested for the remainder of the day. Chase took steaks out of the freezer for supper, baked some potatoes, and made a salad. After we sat down, they looked at me expectantly.

"You have a brother on the way," I announced.

Gage asked, "Are you going to tell Ben?"

"Not unless he asks."

The boys did a high-five, adding a fist bump, the baby was the tiebreaker. A baby brother moved the lead in the testosterone versus estrogen scorecard. Our days together ended. I took the boys to the airport for their return to college. Our separation before break wouldn't be long. Alex and I were excited to have Chase and Gage with us for the summer. Alex has become so attached to her big brothers. She would look up the staircase and call out "Cha" or "Gag".

I drove to my doctor's appointments in town. Dr. Krason had some concerns. She had gotten the amnio results that were normal, but I presented with elevated blood pressure. The doctor wanted to monitor that closely and sent me home with my own blood pressure cuff. I would go into the office every Monday for a blood pressure check and urine test.

March turned to April, with the temperatures rising, as did my blood pressure. My doctors suspected I was developing preeclampsia. They have instructed me to avoid salt, drink plenty of water, and lay down on my side as much as possible. Maggie came over every day so that I could rest while she took care of Alex. I was going to the doctor every other day now. I didn't want to mention anything to my sons, especially during exam week at college. They had enough on their minds with finals and dealing with Ben's betrayal.

My blood pressure was steady but still too high by the end of the month. My doctor added low-dose aspirin to my bed rest. Maggie worried. She would take Alex with her during the day and leave me in bed with my cell phone within reach.

Chase and Gage arrived home from college. When they saw me, my appearance horrified them further. I had dark shadows under my eyes and my fingers and feet were swollen. On my next doctor's visit, Chase joined me while Gage stayed with Alex.

Doctor Krason wanted me on a diet of vegetables and fish, omitting any salt, sugar, carbohydrates, and added complete bed rest with plenty of water. In addition, they prescribed blood pressure medication. Finally, the doctors monitored my kidney and liver function with every visit. "We have to get you into your seventh month at your current health levels and may have to deliver this baby early if your condition worsens. If you have any headaches, dizziness, or difficulty breathing, call me immediately," Doctor Krason cautioned.

I ventured to ask, "What would happen if my condition worsens?"

"You're at increased risk of seizures, placental abruption, stroke, and possibly severe bleeding; there's also a higher risk of stillbirth. Headaches, blurred vision, inability to tolerate bright light, fatigue, nausea/vomiting, urinating small amounts, pain in the upper right abdomen, shortness of breath, and tendency to bruise easily are all signs to look for. If you experience any one of these things, it will force me to hospitalize you and move to delivery. Unfortunately, our hospital can't handle a preemie at that stage, and you would have to be transported to Grand Island," Doctor Krason said.

"I'm scared, Doctor Krason."

"We will keep a close eye on you. I want you healthy and deliver an equally healthy baby boy. Please follow my instructions. We will go day by day until we get you to a safe delivery date. Don't be surprised if you deliver by the end of June or the 1st of July. I will see you in a couple of days."

On the drive home, I told Chase about the preeclampsia diagnosis and what I had to do to counteract it. I felt so guilty putting this burden on my sons. But I knew Chase would be on the internet researching my condition as soon as we got home.

"Mom, you've taken care of Gage and me for over twenty years; now it's our turn to take care of you."

I turned into a complete slug. Chase, Gage, and Kevin, my hired hand, planted the vegetable garden and took care of the horses. My sons spent every waking minute with their sister. Gage and Chase became adept at cooking, cleaning, and changing Alex's dirty diapers without gagging.

Maggie came over to help me in the shower and wash my hair regularly. She sat with me while I lay in bed. I had the small television on in the bedroom during one of her visits when some entertainment program came on to report on the gala premiere of Ben's movie. The reporter interviewed Ben on the red carpet with some nameless bimbo plastered to his side, making saccharine-filled idiotic comments.

"Sounds like her bra size far exceeds her IQ, and it looks like her lips are about to explode. Take a gander at those dagger-like fingernails. I have to wonder how she goes to the bathroom and finishes the job?" said Maggie.

"If not her, it would be someone else. It's who Ben is and the life he enjoys."

"Did you partition for the annulment?" Maggie asked.

"I have the paperwork on my desk; I haven't been able to get it filled out and mail it to Ben yet."

"I see he is still wearing his wedding ring," as she glanced at the television.

"I am, too, only because I can't get it off my fat finger."

"Is that the only reason?" Maggie asked.

"What else could it be? I still love him, but I don't like the person he turned out to be. I can't be the wife he needs, and he can't be the husband I need. Delivering this baby safely is my priority; anything else now is irrelevant."

Sam came over one afternoon; he, Gage, and Chase got the swing set together and set up in the yard. Sam also brought a plastic sandbox with filtered sand. Chase filled him in on how sick I was and I would be on bed rest for the duration of my pregnancy. Chase told me later that Sam left really pissed. Sam had never really liked Ben from the beginning, just tolerated him for my sake.

May passed into June with little change in my condition. The only time I got out of bed was to pee, and I did a lot of that. I FaceTimed with my friends in Chicago, Nonno and Nonna, and Giorgio and Carlo in Italy. I talked with Will and Vickie on the phone but didn't tell them of my pregnancy complications, fearing they would tell Ben. I hadn't passed on that I was having a boy, either. If Ben wanted to know anything, he would have to make an effort himself. He didn't remember Alex's first birthday, so why would he want to know anything about another child he could and would probably ignore?

I was being driven into Sanders to the doctor's every other day. Doctor Krason did an ultrasound to measure the baby's growth. He was small, at about two to two and a half pounds. I was holding with the blood pressure, but I presented with abnormally high protein in my urine, atypical liver enzymes, and a low platelet level. If I can get through the next six weeks without stress on the baby, I'll feel like we'll make it to a safe early delivery. The doctor recommended I eat a steak every night to counteract the high protein count in the urine. It sounds contradictory to me, but that's what the doctor ordered.

Chase was grilling every night for dinner. No shortage of beef in my freezer. I encouraged Chase and Gage to catch the horses in the pasture and take a long ride when Alex and I were down for our afternoon naps. They took turns going into town for a beer with friends at night. I felt guilty that they had to spend their summer taking care of Alex and me. I noticed that the boy's phones rang frequently, and they had long, quiet conversations, suspecting the girls in town and some of their college friends kept in touch.

I had four weeks left of my pregnancy by mid-July. The blood pressure numbers were inching up, and my doctor scheduled a cesarean section delivery in two days at the Grand Island hospital. While the baby was small, it was best for both of us to deliver early. We had a celebration dinner that night. Gage grilled steaks and made a salad from the vegetable garden. Maggie and Ted drove out to the farm with cartons of low-carb, sugar-free sorbet. We sat in the yard and spent the early evening enjoying each other. I got up to go into the bathroom when I felt dizzy, and a severe, stabbing pain pierced my skull as blackness closed over me.

CHAPTER TWENTY-SEVEN

Maggie screamed as Chase dialed 9-1-1. The paramedics from Sanders arrived in fifteen minutes. Gage called the doctor, who ordered a Life Flight helicopter after getting an assessment from the paramedics. The chopper landed on the road next to the farm driveway, and within minutes, they transported Brenna to the Grand Island Regional Medical Center. Ted took charge of Alexandra while Chase, Gage, and Maggie jumped in the car and drove at top speed to the hospital an hour away.

After arriving at the ICU on the delivery floor, the doctors indicated to the newly arrived family that Brenna was being stabilized and prepped for surgery to deliver the baby. The doctor didn't mince words. "Mother and baby are under stress, and delivery is our only option. Who is the next of kin that might have to make medical decisions?"

Gage and Chase stepped forward when the doctor asked about Brenna's husband. Still married, Ben was legally the one who had the right to make any necessary decisions. Chase took out his phone and placed a call to Ben.

"Hello, Ben. This is Chase Herrera, Brenna's son, if you remember. I wanted to let you know in case you give a shit; Life Flight took my mother to Grand Island Regional Medical Center in critical condition. If she dies giving birth to your son, her death and the baby's will be on you." Choking to get the words out without breaking down, Chase continued, "It pains me to tell you, you are the next of kin, legally, if medical decisions have to be made. If you want to see your son before he dies or my mother, you better get here as soon as possible. If not, I guess that leaves no doubt in our minds the type of man you are and always have been."

"I'm in Colorado, and I can get on a plane within minutes. I'm on my way," as Ben disconnected. He arrived in two hours and muscled his way into the ICU. "I want to see my wife." They led him into Brenna's room with tubes and monitors attached to every part of her body. The staff had attached a fetal monitor to her distended belly. The surgeon indicated the baby was under stress. It's time to get the baby out. They wheeled Brenna into the surgical/delivery room while Maggie, Gage, Chase, and Ben remained outside the door in the waiting area.

Chase could no longer hold himself back and faced Ben. "You made it. That's a fucking surprise. Where have you been for the last six months? Was it guilt that drove you to leave your world of make-believe for a dose of the real life? I prepared myself to like you when we met because my mom loved you. And I did like you until you broke her heart—again. Something my Grandma Vernie used to say fits you to a tee, 'You can put a brass handle on an outhouse, but it's still an outhouse.' And let me add—full of shit.

"I want to tell you something about the woman my mom is. After my dad's death, my mother was everything to Gage and me. We had the hottest mom by far in school, but mom didn't give anyone a passing thought. She always put us first, never letting us feel we were in the way or she was sacrificing her youth for us. Instead, she unselfishly gave us the courage to soar and reach for our dreams.

"Now she has sacrificed her health and maybe even her life to give your baby a chance to live. She wouldn't have it any other way. Did you know Mom has been on bed rest with Preeclampsia for the last four months? That her kidneys and liver are malfunctioning, trying to hold on long enough so that baby boy can live? That's love, not that plastic world you live in where a starring role or self-indulgence is at the top of your priority list.

"If my mother doesn't make it, Gage and I are guardians of Alexandra—remember her? She's walking and talking now, and she doesn't even know you. Gage and I will also take the new baby if he makes it. We will see that he and Alex know who their mother was and how much she loved them. Eventually, Alex will figure out what a fucking prick you are.

"I do not doubt that you'll go on as if this is a minor inconvenience and even some adverse publicity for you, but I have no doubt that you'll work it to your advantage. You'll get over it, a mire blip on your perfect life, and all indications are you already have. You may play the part of a big macho man, the hero in your films, but in that operating room is the bravest and most honorable person I know; my mom is the genuine hero.

"Some of us grow up to be heroes, and some of us live their life faking it. What do you see when you look in the mirror, Ben? You can go to hell." Chase dissolved into tears as Maggie wrapped her arms around him.

Gage glared at Ben. "It pisses me off you are the one who legally has a say to what happens with my mother and baby brother. You may be married to my mom, but you have never been her husband or a father to Alexandra. Our mother loved you, and why is beyond me. You have no redeeming qualities, I can see. Alexandra, a child you conveniently forgot, is your only valuable contribution to our family. Was my mom someone you played with until you tired of it? I don't think you are capable of loving anyone but yourself. Once this is over, I hope I never see you again."

Ben sat down in the waiting area, covering his eyes with his hands, not responding to anything Chase and Gage had to say. Close to midnight, a doctor finally appeared to update the anxiously waiting family.

"I'm Doctor Finlay. We delivered the baby. He's small but gave a robust cry when born and is breathing on his own. He'll be in the NICU, and you'll be able to get a look after we have evaluated him. Brenna is in recovery and survived the surgery. We will have to deal with her pregnancy complications and get her stable before you can see her. Her condition is serious. We have to determine what brought on her episode of unconsciousness. I won't sugarcoat this. We haven't ruled out a stroke or brain bleed, but she's strong. We'll do everything we can for her. Any questions?"

"Can I see Brenna for a minute? I want to let her know I'm here for her," asked Ben.

The doctor was a little taken aback as he recognized Ben. "Ben Langford? What's your connection to the patient?"

"Brenna is my wife, and that is my son that you delivered. These young men are her sons, and Maggie is her cousin and close friend."

"You'll need to gown up, and I'll take you in for a minute. Brenna is still unconscious, but if you talk to her, she might respond."

After Ben was scrubbed and gowned, he was escorted into the ICU recovery room to Brenna's bedside. Only her hair looked like his wife. Monitors were beeping and tubes were attached to multiple sites on her body. She was pale and bloated.

Lifting her hand, "I'm here, Brenna. Please wake up; I love you so much. Be strong for our baby boy and our daughter. I need you, my love. Please wake up. Chase, Gage, and Maggie are waiting to see you." With no response after twenty minutes, Ben left the room and walked down to the NICU with the doctor.

In an incubator tagged Baby Boy Herrera, Ben looked at his newborn son with tears in his eyes. The doctor lifted the baby out of his confines and handed him to Ben.

"He's so light," Ben marveled.

"Baby weighed a little over four pounds, and that's big for a preemie with maternal pregnancy complications. He's getting supplemental oxygen, but he's alert, urinating, and has a strong sucking reflex. The baby has a little fluid in his lungs, but that's normal for a C-section baby. There's no sign of brain bleed or blood anomalies so far. We will continue observation and monitor his weight."

"Thank you for everything you're doing for my son and my wife," said Ben.

"That's our job to bring into the world healthy babies and send them home with healthy mothers." The doctor shook hands with Ben and guided him back to the waiting room.

Ben faced Brenna's family. "I know you don't think much of me, and I don't think much of myself, but I love your mother and our babies. I know how much I let them and you down. There's nothing I can say to make up for it, but I am sorry. Does your mother have a name picked out for the baby?"

Maggie spoke up. "She was thinking, Robert William, 'Robbie' after her father and yours."

"I have to call my parents and let them know," said Ben as he walked away from the others. Then, returning, "They'll be here in about four hours."

"At least there'll be two people here on your side," said Gage. "Sorry, won't cut it with us. Save your worthless words for someone who gives a damn if you can find anyone, because I sure don't."

Maggie called Ted with the news. He had taken Alexandra to their house so that his girls could help him care for her. Gage and Chase stretched out on the couches to rest as Maggie and Ben went downstairs to the hospital cafeteria for some coffee. Ignoring the quizzical looks and whispering from the nurses and doctors, Maggie started in. "Where the fucking hell have you been? Brenna went through hell in the last couple of months? You forgot your daughter's birthday and forgot about the woman you married. What the fuck is wrong with you? Did you trade in your decency for fame and fortune? Sell your soul to the devil? What will you have in the future but dusty old movies on the classic movie channel? Your children will be grown, never knowing you and the wonderful woman who loved you, gone. I can't understand how you think. When Brianna recovers, it is my sincere hope she can rid herself of any feelings for you and find someone who deserves her." Maggie marched out of the cafeteria, leaving Ben alone with his thoughts.

Will and Vickie arrived at 7 AM. Maggie filled them in on all the information on the baby and Brenna's condition. Vickie didn't know that Brenna had been so sick with her pregnancy; Brenna never told her. Neither did Brenna tell her she hadn't heard from Ben in over five months, which was a blow to Vickie. When Ben returned to the waiting area, he could see the disappointment on his parent's faces. Vickie was crying and didn't even speak to her son. Finally, his father shook his head and said he would talk to Ben later.

The doctor appeared at 9 AM. Brenna was waking up. The medical team had determined that Brenna did not have a stroke, her brain was functioning normally, and her kidney and liver functions were recovering. Instead, her rising blood pressure alone seemed to be the culprit for her collapse. In a silence that was thick with unspoken thoughts, Ben left the waiting area for the recovery room and Brenna's bedside.

* * *

"Is the baby okay? Did he make it?" Brenna choked out her question while she felt the change to her stomach.

"He's beautiful, Brenna."

"I need to see him for myself."

"I know you do, darling," said Ben.

"Don't call me that. What are you doing here?"

"I wanted to be here for you. I didn't know what you were going through."

"How could you with your busy schedule of poseurs, premiers, and parties?"

"I tried to keep in touch, but you won't talk to me. So, what was I supposed to do?"

"How about keeping IT in your pants, thinking with your brain, not your dick?"

"I deserve that, and a lot more. I'm sorry, Brenna, for treating you like I did. Could you ever forgive me?"

"I forgive you, but we don't belong together; we never did. You have a longer and more faithful relationship with your fans; that's where you belong. Please leave. Don't make this any harder for me. I've been through enough when it comes to you."

Ben turned away and left the room. He signaled to Gage and Chase to go in and see their mother. Ben said a few words to his parents, left the waiting area and walked out of the hospital with tears running down his face.

CHAPTER TWENTY-EIGHT

I was in the hospital for a week. I stayed in town for an additional week to nurse the baby until the doctors released him. Finally, we returned to the farm to a house full of people welcoming me home with gifts for Robbie. Everyone but my sons, daughter, and Maggie left after an hour.

It peeved Alex that she hadn't seen me for a couple of weeks and another person was in her room. I was sore from the surgery but felt better than I had in months. I was feeling my energy slowly returning. It would take all my powers of motherhood to keep up with a seventeen-month-old and a new baby. Thank God for Maggie and her mother coming over twice a week and letting me sleep while they cared for the baby. Gage and Chase entertained Alex.

August moved on, and we were almost back to normal. Gage and Chase were getting ready to go to their post-grad schools. The second time, it would separate them. I took my sons to the airport in Grand Island for their flights to Cambridge and Philadelphia. Chase and Gage had been so supportive during their summer break, doing all the cooking, cleaning, and outdoor work. I don't know how I would have done it without them. We had always been close; this summer strengthened our bond.

Ben would email every couple of days, and I replied with pictures only. I remained close to Will and Vickie with FaceTime updates with their grandchildren. I invited them to stay with us as soon as Robbie slept overnight.

* * *

Glorious fall burst upon us. Time to pick apples and get all the vegetables out of the garden before the first freeze. Maggie and I got together to can some tomatoes and applesauce. I made all my apple recipes with the bounty from the orchard; pies, cake, butter, and muffins for the freezer. I kept on my hired hand to take care of the horses and the outbuildings during the winter. The airstrip in town notified me they wanted Ben's truck removed from the hangar. It had been there for nine months. Maggie and I retrieved it, and I put it in the garage.

"When are you going to get the paperwork filed to annul your marriage?" asked Maggie.

"I'm almost finished with my part and will have it in the mail to Ben's manager this week. After that, I need to find out what he wants done with the truck, his horse, and the large office equipment in The Coop. I shipped out all his personal things ages ago. So not much left that's his."

"How do you feel about it?" Maggie asked.

"I told him at the hospital we would never be together again. It just wouldn't work. He needed to move on, and so do I."

"But have you moved on?"

"Not with two children under the age of two. I hardly have time to go to the bathroom, much less move on with my life."

"I almost forget how hard it is with little children. If that ever happened to me, I'd give Ted a vasectomy myself," quipped Maggie.

"Well, this funhouse is closed for business. My ovaries have had their last hoorah. I had my tubes tied after Robbie's birth. Never again. I'm praying for menopause to hit any day now. I'd trade morning sickness for a hot flash any day."

"Do you know what Ben has been up to?"

"Just what People Magazine and the grocery store rags have to report. His new film finished shooting, and he's probably dicking his way through Hollywood as we speak. No longer my concern."

Maggie packed her car with crates of apples, produce, and some roadkill beef. The children and I prepared to settle in for the winter. Will and Vickie came to visit in mid-November for three days. Everyone made a determined effort, not to mention Ben's name. Grandpa and Grandma Langford spoiled the kids with gifts and played non-stop with them. I don't think Alex's feet hit the floor once during their visit. Someone was always carrying her around. The Langfords left for Kansas, asking that we plan a visit as soon as spring came to the country. I promised we would.

Thanksgiving took us over to Maggie's for a big dinner with members of my extended family. I was in charge of the apple pies this year. It was great seeing everyone, and they made a big fuss over the children. Finally, after an exhausting day, the children and I left for home. As we pulled into the driveway, my security lights were shining off an unfamiliar car parked by the gate to the backyard. Sitting on the hood of the vehicle was Ben. Robbie and Alexandra were asleep in their car seats. I got out of the car and silently closed the door.

"What are you doing here, Ben?"

"I came to see you and my babies."

"Do you think you have the right to call the children YOUR babies? You were certainly more interested in contributing to their creation, but not after their birth. We didn't hear from you when Alexandra had her first birthday or around for her milestones-walking and talking. You knew I was expecting another baby and couldn't even be bothered to check in. You haven't seen to their financial support for months. Let me reassure you. We don't need your money or your empty promises. I can support my children comfortably without you. For a man who preached about how he wanted children and a family to come home to, you're a miserable failure as a husband, a father and a man. Shocker.

"You should have called or emailed first. I don't think this is a good idea for you to be here. You can't be a revolving door father popping in whenever the mood strikes. It will confuse the children as they get older. Now I have to get the kids ready for bed and feed Robbie. Please go."

"Let me help you get them inside before I leave."

Big neon signs were flashing in my head. *CAUTION: MAY CAUSE FATAL STUPIDITY AND SELF LOATHING! Don't let him put his lying, cheating foot in your home.* I knew my strengths and knew my weaknesses, and he was most certainly my biggest weakness. Ben was like my drug of choice. After the first hit, it was never enough, even though you know it's bad for you and not being able to garner the strength to quit as you slowly fell deeper and deeper into its unbreakable clutches.

I unlocked the back door and turned on the lights; returning to the car. I had Ben take a sleeping Alex while I picked up Robbie and the diaper bag. We took the children to their room, changed diapers, and got them into their night sacks. Robbie was hungry, and I sat down in the rocking chair, unbuttoned my top, and put Robbie to my breast. Alex returned to sleep without a whimper as I nursed the baby, trying to ignore Ben's presence.

"You're more beautiful than ever, Brenna. Robbie has grown so big since I held him at the hospital. I've missed so much watching them grow, and I regret that more than you could know. I miss you even more. My thoughts are with you every day and night."

"That's empty lip service with no substance. Were you thinking of me when you told a woman on the phone you were coming to screw her brains out? Ben, do you think you miss us because you can't have us? You have always gotten everything you ever wanted, and it came easy to you. We are the one thing you couldn't have at your command. A bruise to your ego isn't enough of a reason to allow you to disrupt our lives when the mood strikes. You're a perfect image on the outside, but you are an empty vessel. No feelings for others. No interest but your own or capable of caring about the hurt you leave in your wake. I don't know you, nor do I want to."

"I've made so many mistakes with you and with our children. I could never make that up."

"No, you can't. But, since you're here, let's take care of one of those mistakes. I completed the paperwork for an annulment. So, if you would sign them, we can all move on."

"Brenna, I don't want an annulment or a divorce from you. Don't you think we owe it to our children to try again? I will do anything to make our family work."

"I don't believe you, Ben. We have never been a family. Where were you when I needed you the most? I was very sick when I was pregnant with Robbie, and you appeared on television with some airhead. You rubbed my nose in your infidelity for all the world to see." Robbie finished nursing, and I put him to bed. Ben and I moved to the living room. "Here are the papers; please read them, sign and then go."

"Is this what you want, Brenna?"

"It's never been what I wanted, but it's what I need. Ben, I am tired, emotionally and physically. I have to move on; I can't have my heart broken again. A broken heart can only mend so many times when it gets to a point it can't recover and function anymore. How could I ever trust you? I knew deep down in my heart you would never be faithful to me, or anyone, not even yourself. You're not the person I thought you were and probably never was. You're not capable." I cried. All my hurt came pouring out in torrents of tears. He wrapped me in his arms and held me tight, kissing my head as I sobbed. I finally got myself together and stood up, away from his comforting arms. "Don't you have to be somewhere?"

"This is where I have to be, for you and our babies. It has taken me a long time to realize what's important and over forty years to grow up. I want to be a good husband to my wife and a good father to my children. You and the children are the most important thing in life, not my career or the fame. That means less than nothing now if I don't have you. Chase said something to me in the hospital when Robbie was born. 'What kind of man do I see in the mirror?' What I saw was not someone I could be proud of. You need to go to bed. Would you mind if I stayed? I'll sleep upstairs."

"The roads are too icy for you to drive tonight. A blizzard is coming in from the north. That's the only reason I will let you stay.

You can sleep—upstairs. It seems every time we sleep together, I get pregnant. With two children under the age of two, I had my tubes tied. I'm done having babies, and I'm done sleeping with you."

*   *   *

The day starts early with two young children. Alex woke up first, and I got her dressed and in her highchair. Robbie was still sleeping when Ben came downstairs. Alex looked at him without a sign of recognition. I left Ben in the kitchen with his daughter while I got Robbie up and dressed for the morning. We walked into the kitchen; I fixed breakfast and brought everyone to the table. I nursed the baby while trying to get some food into my stomach. Ben made a pot of coffee, offering me a cup. I declined, saying that caffeine kept Robbie awake.

"You give a whole new meaning to multitasking," Ben commented.

"That's life as a mother of two young children," I said.

"I noticed last night that you don't have the SUV I bought you. Did you run into another cow?"

"It was a beautiful car, but it was too flashy for me. Too many bells and whistles, and it was conspicuous when I traveled to town, and I felt guilty if I had to haul natural fertilizer in it. I traded it in and got something more practical. As for vehicles, your truck is in the garage. The airstrip wanted it moved, so I brought it here. You need to decide what you want done with it."

"I'm sorry I didn't take into consideration your needs and feelings. I understand my shortcomings. My parents raised me entirely different— to be considerate of others, empathetic, and think of others before myself. For over twenty-five years, I lived in a make-believe world. I looked back on my behavior, and I didn't recognize myself. I failed you, the children, and myself."

"Yes, you did. What brought all this on? Why now this examination of consciousness?"

"It was more than one thing, my parents, your older sons, and the people I associated with the last twenty-five years. I didn't know the object of living a pointless life any longer, not holding on to what was important. Could be my mid-life crisis; I don't know. One day, I thought about what was important and real and what was a mirage.

"Now that I am here, I want to give you a day off. If you let me, I'll take care of the kids and do any chores while you take a long bubble bath and sleep or anything else you want to do. The only thing I can't do is feed Robbie, but I want to do everything else. What do you say?"

"Have you thought this through? Alex runs now and is fast on her feet, getting into everything, and it usually ends up in her mouth. You'll have to watch her every minute. Alex has a nap in the afternoon and Robbie in the morning and afternoon. Alex eats regular food now. Just make sure you cut it up into small pieces. Since it is regular food, diaper changing may gross you out. Are you sure you're ready to play daddy? If you turn tail and run, I won't be surprised. That's what you're good at."

"Go take a bath and relax. We'll be fine."

I didn't give him a chance to change his mind. Let him have a dose of parenthood for a change. I took a book into my bathroom and filled the tub. I sat in the swirling water and read for an hour. Finally, I slipped back into my nightgown and crawled into bed. I was asleep when I heard Ben tiptoeing into the nursery to change Robbie and put him down for his morning nap. I had to silently laugh when Ben took Robbie's diaper off. Ben took a direct shot of urine right in the face. Did I forget to tell him that changing baby boys differs slightly from changing girls? Oops, my bad? I turned over, going back to sleep.

Ben was tapping me on the shoulder about an hour and a half later; Robbie was hungry. I nursed the baby while Ben chased after Alex. She thought it was great fun throwing her toys all over the house. Ben brought Alex into the nursery for a diaper change. I could tell from a distance that it would test Ben's tolerance. I could hear him choking and coughing as he cleaned her up. Robbie finished nursing as I tried to hide a snicker.

I got up. There was no use trying to sleep and miss the comedy show going on in the other part of the house. I sat in the living room with my book while Ben chased Alex and tried to keep her out of the cupboards and house plants. I calmly mentioned to Ben that laundry had to be started before lunch. After an hour, I walked toward the kitchen after stepping over toys and finding Alex unrolling the toilet paper in the guest bathroom while Ben was loading the washer.

Robbie was in his bouncy chair and had spit-up. I pointed that out to Ben as he wiped off the baby and searched for Alex. When Ben found Alex, I heard a very audible "Oh, shit".

Not long after his vocal exclamation, a little voice mimicked, "O sit Da Da." I couldn't contain myself any longer; I laughed like I hadn't laughed in ages.

"Had enough?" I asked. I never saw Ben more frustrated.

"You do this every day?" he asked.

"Think what fun it was with twins."

"I have to call my mother and thank her for everything she endured with four boys," Ben said.

I changed diapers and fixed lunch, giving Ben a break. Alex was eating in her highchair as I fed Robbie some bananas and nursed while we had lunch. Finally, everyone was ready for a nap. Ben laid down on my bed and fell asleep immediately while I put the children down. I sat on my bed, wondering if I was asking for trouble, as I covered myself up with a blanket. I was lightly dozing when I felt an arm gathering me around the waist. He turned me toward him and kissed my ear, then moved to my neck. I let myself enjoy the pleasure of his lips on me again. Our lips met in a passionate struggle for access. My hands wandered to his chest as our bodies pressed together. Why did I allow myself to succumb to his touch? What was the matter with ME? Was I so pathetically lonely and devoid of self-esteem? Was I content to settle for a roll in the hay with the one man I had allowed to break my spirit yet again?

"You're still my wife, and I'm still your husband," said Ben, just as our children woke up from their naps. The babies saved me from going down that path any further.

"I can't do this, Ben. I can't let you ingratiate yourself into our lives again and then ride off into the sunset, unencumbered. It's a proven fact when the chips are down, you disappear, leaving me with the cleanup. I CAN'T DO THIS AGAIN."

"I'm not going anywhere. My film finished, and I concluded that directing wasn't for me, and acting has lost its bloom. So, I thought I might write a book about my life in showbiz. What do you think?"

"You're not listening to me. Wake up, Ben, and listen for once. This isn't all about YOU. Are you saying the children and I are your last resort until you figure out who you really are? How long will it take for you to get bored this time—with me—with the farm? Ben,

I won't ride that roller coaster again while you're trying to figure out your life."

"I've never been bored with you. The life I was leading was exhausting. I missed you and the children. I have always wanted a family to come home to. You are the woman I want for the rest of my life. I was leading a valueless existence without you. The last film made me realize that my life lacked what was truly important—a meaningful love between a man and a woman—you and me. I won't say I may never want to accept an acting role again, but it would be a short stint that would take me away for days, not weeks, taking my family with me.

"I don't want to be away from you and the children again, missing their milestone moments, watching them develop their personalities. I don't want my children to grow up without their father and my wife without her husband."

"Very pretty pile of platitudes you're spouting. It all sounds very good in theory, but how can I trust you again? I can't do whatever this is again. You destroyed my faith in you and my peace of mind."

"Day by day, I will prove to you I will be the faithful husband you deserve if you give me a chance."

"Another chance? You've been married three times and failed three times. What's the common denominator? You, Ben. You can't do the same thing repeatedly and expect a different outcome if you can't or won't make a permanent change. I don't think you're capable of changing, nor have a genuine desire to do so."

I got the children up, changed them, and moved to the kitchen for an afternoon snack. Alex was in her highchair with a graham cracker and milk while I nursed the baby. I had a lot of thinking to do, not just for me, but for all my children. Chase and Gage would be home in a week for winter break. I could see them squaring off against Ben, trying to protect me from another disappointment. Ben will have to realize he has fences to mend with them as well as me. Unfortunately, some fences are too damaged to be saved, no matter how hard you try, even before the pasture is empty.

CHAPTER TWENTY-NINE

Chase and Gage were more than a little shocked to see Ben back at the farm. Tensions were running high for more than a few days. Ben took them aside with some man-talk. They seemed to give him a limited benefit of the doubt. The holidays passed with a guarded truce. My sons returned to school, and Ben and I settled into a more relaxed routine. He didn't slack off as a helpmate, and we resumed our physical intimacy.

Maggie, Ted, and Sam reluctantly accepted Ben back in my life, but remained cautious. Then, finally, spring came to the sandhills. Ben was spending a lot of time with the horses. Larry, Moe, and Curlie were feeling their years. Ben's horse, Midnight, was a spirited animal, and Ben did some research and bought a couple more horses from the Pfizer Breeding Ranch in our area.

He expanded our herd and took great pride in building our stable into a reputable breeding business. Ben's celebrity status didn't hurt promoting our farm, giving the nationally known Pfizer Ranch a run for their money. Nick Pfizer became a regular visitor to our farm, and I enjoyed talking to him as he and Ben planned out different insemination plans for breeding the mares.

Ben was happy and said he didn't miss the Hollywood life. He would appear on late-night talk shows every once in a while, but had no interest in leaving for more than a night or two with our family along for the ride. Eventually, we changed the younger children's last name to Langford as I did mine, showing Ben my renewed trust in him.

Our life together was everything I had hoped for, filled with the people, places, and things we loved. Will and Vickie made regular visits with Ben's brothers and their families. We decided with so much family company and visiting buyers for our horses; we built a couple of small comfortable guest cabins next to our home. There were now three barns and a huge stable with The Coop turned into the business office. We now employed two full-time grooms and two trainers. Grandma Vernie would have been proud to see the farm revive with new life.

*   *   *

A couple of years rolled by as our family business grew in leaps and bounds. We were becoming nationally known as a world-class breeding farm. But, while Ben and I enjoyed a close and intimate relationship, the time on this earth ended with Guncle John and Aunt Rose. Guncle John was grandma's youngest and last of her surviving siblings.

Guncle John had been there for me when I needed him in the rough times and the joyful. He was my connection to Grandma, telling me stories of their youth on their farm and stories of my dad that I had never heard. With his and Aunt Rose's passing, it was the close of an era from where my love of a slower, more traditional life grew. Family values and a purer existence were to be proud of, passing on to our children and future grandchildren as the world seemed to change so rapidly all around us.

My dear cousin, Maggie, battled breast cancer. I was there for her as she had been for me. I took her to her chemo treatments and nursed her through the after-effects of the medication. After a year, she beat it and remained healthy as we shared our lives as sisters.

My wonderful friend, Sam, finally found the love of his life, Sandy. I had never seen him so happy. Sandy had been a widow for several years, giving Sam a chance at fatherhood with her three children. Sam continued to be our contractor, becoming an expert at stable construction as our business continued to prosper.

Chase and Gage graduated with their advanced degrees with honors. Our family traveled to both graduations, cheering on their achievements. Chase introduced me to Harper Lindstrom. A lovely young woman from his graduating class. They announced they were moving in together to New York, where they planned to launch their careers in International Finance. Gage was still playing the field with a bevy of young women listed in his little black book. I hoped he remembered my hurt when a man playing the field broke my heart and all the pain that followed.

My older sons came home at Christmas and in the summer like I did when Grandma was still with us, keeping her legacy alive. Both Gage and Chase adored their younger siblings, but Alexandra was special, their only sister. She was their baby, the child that they diapered, bathed, and rocked to sleep.

The next couple of years seemed to fly by, with our business growing by leaps and bounds. We bought Guncle John's farm across the road, adding to our acreage and barn space. We had a full-time manager for our stables, and Ben was making regular trips to Virginia, Kentucky, and Montana, purchasing mainly Arabian, American

Quarter, and cutting horse stock. Our herd grew to over two hundred horses, and we offered stabling, breeding, training, and sales.

Our children were riding as soon as they walked and learned to take care of their animals. At age six, Alexandra trained her quarter horse, an appaloosa, for barrel racing. She practiced every day, hoping to be on the rodeo circuit when she was older. She looked like a Native American princess riding like the wind, with her long black hair and dark eyes. Her thoughts were always with the horses, and I never had to remind her about stable chores.

Robbie, at age five, was as enthusiastic about the business and his love for the horses as his sister. Ben was in his element. Our horses took part in shows all around the country, and our farm was recognized as an award-winning breeding and training facility. Sam, our contractor, built a massive show ring across the road on Guncle John's old farm, a foaling barn, and a wash stall with warm water and heaters. Our horses had a visiting farrier/blacksmith for horsy pedicures, comfortable hoof wear, and an equine veterinarian on retainer for injury, vaccinating and floating the horses yearly. Floating is hard on the horses to have the rough spikes on their teeth filed down. Even horses hate a visit from the equine dentist.

With Ben's Hollywood connections, we would frequently have actors with us to learn to ride for their roles in movies and television. It was exciting to have the famous or almost famous stay with us for lessons. There was always someone coming and going through our gates.

I concentrated my efforts in marketing, making sure we had a significant online presence and that our name, The Souchek-Langford Breeding Farm, was visible at horse events all over the country. In addition, I started a Western/Equestrian Wear and Tack Shop in town. Maggie was the manager and developed the online sales. My life was happy and content, and so was Ben's. We enjoyed our children, and they thought their father hung the moon. We enjoyed the regular visits with Ben's parents and siblings, and my older sons and their families.

My love for Ben seemed to grow. Our love life was as healthy and frequent as ever. We never tired of each other, even after spending so much time together. Ben did guest shots on movies and television periodically. Now his desire for the farm was more potent than the draw of Hollywood. He found his niche and was loving it. He would drive to Virginia frequently to buy and sell horses, and I would accompany him whenever possible. We attended the major horse shows together. Our family saddled up and rode in parades in the towns and cities nearby, even riding in the Grand Entry yearly in the town of Burwell for Nebraska's Big Rodeo.

Chase and Gage married and had little ones, making Ben and I, grandparents. They enjoyed coming home to Hartsuff, and they oversaw our business affairs and investments along with a CPA that they recommended and consulted with regularly. Chase continued his career in New York while Gage lived in London.

During the slow winter months, I did some remote work for Dr. M for the Chicago College. The school had offered the Italian travel course I had developed three times since I retired. The instructor and chaperones did an outstanding job facilitating the course. It was becoming one of the most sought placements in the curriculum. Dr. M had concerns when told that the current instructor would retire within the next two years. A replacement had to be found and prepared if the program was to survive.

Dr. M ventured to ask if I would be interested in going over resumes and evaluations for the replacement remotely. After candidates were selected, he wanted me in Chicago for the final interviews.

I had to think this over before I committed. The children were still young, and I had responsibilities at the farm. I would have to get input from Ben. Also, at this same time, certain red flags appeared in our business dealings. Nothing overt, but a word here and there; I was getting some disturbing vibes from some of our vendors.

CHAPTER THIRTY

Chase took me aside during one of his visits. He voiced some concerns about the amount of money Ben was spending on horses and improvements on the outbuildings on the farm, along with Ben's frequent travel. Our business expansion had taken off at a whirlwind pace over the last six years, which made me a little uneasy. Our friend, Nick Pfizer, also mentioned that Ben had made some less than wise livestock purchases, buying some older, rank horses that were virtually worthless. Ben bought horses from the slaughter ring instead of buying prime stock in the sale ring at auction, inflating their value on our books.

The slaughter ring offered animals that weren't fit for prime sale, and the owners wanted the animals disposed of, mainly sick or old, unbroken stock. Ben was associating with people in Virginia and Kentucky who were less than reputable in the breeding business.

Our vet also mentioned the inferior, cheaper hay that we stocked in the barn. Ben bought a stockpile of sorghum and sudan hay while the invoices billed us for the more expensive and recommended orchard and timothy grasses.

After finding more than a couple of inconsistencies in our business practices, I authorized Chase to have a thorough independent audit of our books done as soon as possible. Within a couple of months,

I knew we were in trouble. Ben had highly leveraged our herd's inflated value to build more and more stables and barns that we didn't need, without my knowledge. I had to kick myself. With my accounting background, I should have seen the warning signs. But I had placed my faith in Ben's growing expertise and the answers he offered when I questioned the changes he wanted to make for the business.

I had been busy with the children and the store in town. I paid little attention to the breeding farm business, leaving it in the hands of Ben. With the audit, it came to light that more than a few of the stock purchases Ben negotiated were listed at high purchase prices, well over market value. I suspected Ben was taking a kickback from the sellers and pocketing the money. This anomaly wasn't a random incident, but had been going on for some time to the tune of hundreds of thousands of dollars. It mortified me with my stupidity in placing my trust in the least trustworthy person ever to come into my life.

If I was honest with myself, there had always been a niggling thought in the back of my mind that our life together was built on a foundation of quicksand. I was waiting for the inevitable sinking into the abyss. I collected all the documentation from the audit and prepared myself to challenge Ben and get the answers to this mounting debacle.

After the children were in bed and asleep, I didn't mince words. I confronted Ben with the documents on his recent horse purchases and the fair market value of comparables sold simultaneously. Ben had paid far above the value of the horses, and our Equine Insurance agent evaluated the horses at a much lower amount. "What's going on, Ben? You're not stupid. You paid too much for these horses and pledged our herd as collateral for loans without my knowledge. I want an explanation, and don't insult my intelligence with a bunch of lies. I know about the kickbacks. Where's the money, Ben?"

"It's not what you think, Brenna," he said.

"Where have I heard that before? Excuse my sarcasm if I don't believe a word you say."

"I had loans to pay off for the improvements in the stables, not wanting to bother you with the details. I have it handled, so you don't have to worry."

"That's crap, Ben. I commissioned an audit on our books, and there seems to be a lot of money missing. You have put us in a precarious financial position. We will have to sell some horses and the property we bought across the road from Guncle John's estate. What else have you been hiding from me?"

"Where are you getting all this from? I may have overextended a bit, but it was for our family. I wanted to make this farm into something you could be proud of."

"SOMETHING I COULD BE PROUD OF? Are you serious? I have always been proud of where I come from and this farm before you came along. It was you that was too proud to live on a simple farm. You, Mister Hollywood, couldn't stand the thought that you weren't the center of attention and the universe didn't revolve around you. It was you that put this farm in financial jeopardy. Go back to Kentucky and cancel any contracts to buy stock and sell some of our horses. I am going to find a way to get out of this mess you created."

"You're blowing this way out of proportion. I don't know what you've heard. Sometimes shit happens, but it's not that bad."

"Don't treat me like an imbecile. The horse-breeding community is very small. Everyone knows everyone else's business. Nothing stays a secret for long."

"I get it. Has Nick Pfizer been whispering in your ear, trying to make me look bad? Trying to get in your pants while I'm away?" Ben questioned with a sneer.

"You're disgusting. Just because that's how you lived your life doesn't mean I would stoop that low. Now get on the phone and make whatever arrangements necessary to sell off a good portion of our herd. I want a list of who we owe and how much, including your off the books deals, down to the last damn penny," I said.

Ben left the house and walked over to The Coop. I was so angry. I called Ted and made an appointment at his law firm to see how we could protect ourselves. I shuffled off to bed but couldn't sleep. Ben came in a couple of hours later. I feigned sleep. I didn't want him to lay a finger on me. Sex would not lure me into forgiveness this time.

Ben took off with a four-stall horse trailer with our top breeding mares the next day. He left me a tally sheet of our debt; it was worse than I thought. We'll have to liquidate most of our herd, equipment, vehicles, and the property across the road. While Ben traveled back to Kentucky, I had an unexpected visit from Nick Pfizer.

"Brenna, why didn't you tell me you were selling your farm?"

I was dumbstruck. "I'm not selling the farm. What gave you that idea?"

"I heard from a couple of friends in Kentucky that Ben was shopping around for a buyer for the farm and your business. These are reputable sources, so I did not doubt that the information was legitimate," said Nick.

"I can't believe he would do that to me. It's not his farm to sell. Could you get me some more information and see what he is up to? I hate to put you in this position, but I have a feeling that I may be in deep trouble. Nick, I'm scared. I have to know what I'm facing."

"You know that I have always thought highly of you. You've worked so hard to make your business prosper. I have heard over the last couple of years rumblings about Ben. I didn't want to pass on hearsay or gossip without proof to you.

"Ben is not very well thought of in our business. He seems to have gravitated to doing business with some of the shadier characters in the breeding community. I'll see what I can find out and let you know soon as I can. You're a good friend, Brenna. I am sorry for bringing this up. I thought you had every right to know."

"Thank you, Nick, for your support. You may be the only person who dared to tell me what's going on. I've been a fool to believe in Ben, but that stops now."

I tried to carry on as normally as possible in public while I seethed in private, wordlessly screaming with the unbearable pain of treachery. I didn't want the children to worry that something was wrong. Ben planned for a week away, which gave me time to figure out how to extract myself from this situation. If Ben was doing everything Nick had alluded to, our marriage and partnership in the business would be in ruins.

Nick came to see me within two days of our discussion. "Brenna, I have some disturbing news for you. I talked to two breeders in Kentucky I know very well and have dealt with for years. They both signed agreements to buy your property and business. I had them send me copies of the agreements and the checks Ben requested for an earnest money deposit made out to him. Ben sold the four horses he took with him for a check made out to himself also, not the farm. The copies of the agreements to sell appear to have your signature on them."

I looked at the documents. "That's not my signature; it's a forgery."

"Brenna, I am so sorry. If there is anything I can do, please let me know."

"Thank you, Nick. You've helped me a lot. I know where I stand, and exactly what I have to do. I will call you later." That's all I could say. Nick left me with a look of anguish in his eyes. I was too enraged to cry. I would not shed another tear on a man who, for the third time, played me for a fool. The time for unproductive emotional outbursts was over. I stepped into the house and called Ted and requested an emergency meeting. The kids were in school when I drove into town to Ted's office.

I spilled my guts and filled him in on all the details of Ben's efforts to sell the farm, including forging my name and pocketing the earnest money, supplying him with the copies of the documents I had received from Nick. Laying out my plans for what I wanted done, I had come to the end of the road with Ben. Whatever love I had for this man blew up in a puff of smoke. It may have taken me years to see the light, but now I could see Ben for what he really was and always had been—out for himself. I had to ask myself where he thought his children and I would go if we lost the farm? Was this machination a part of his master plan for our family to move to California, or was Ben going to leave us homeless on the side of the road?

*   *   *

I lived my life molded by a code of conduct as a Sandhills woman. My people gave solace to the suffering, lend a helping hand to those in need, living life with integrity and the most important aspect—family was everything. We may give "the stink eye" to those who might engage in lying, cheating and stealing on a small scale, but when it came to Ben, he had hit the trifecta big time. My days acting like a milquetoast were over. It was time to release the Kraken on his sorry ass.

CHAPTER THIRTY-ONE

Ben was due back home in two days. I texted him to meet me at Ted's office to discuss our situation when he returned to town. Ben was a little mystified about a meeting but promised to text me the time of his expected arrival.

I drove back home and called Chase and Gage before the children came home from school. I told them what had happened and my plans to take back my life. Then, I called Sam to once again change all the locks on the buildings at the farm. Sam came out and fulfilled my request. He didn't ask questions, and I didn't enlighten him, but he had a smile on his face when he left.

The following day, while the children were in school, I packed up Ben's belongings and took them out to the garage. Ben phoned that evening, and we talked as if nothing was amiss. He spoke to the children for a couple of minutes, and I reminded him to stop at Ted's office when he returned to town. Sleep evaded me the night before Ben's return. I tried to act as if it was any other day for the children as I saw them off on the school bus in the morning.

I dressed carefully for our meeting in conservative business attire. I drove to Ted's office, and we reviewed all the details of what I wanted to cover. Ted's law partner, Abe Corsky, joined us to handle some elements that were out of Ted's realm of expertise.

Abe had a few words of wisdom. "Brenna, I will make this divorce as easy as possible. While divorces are never without tensions, you are the wronged party. To put it in the words of a very wise man, 'This will be a donkey barbeque, and Ben is supplying the ass.'"

I couldn't help but laugh, relieving a bit of my anxiety. Finally, Ben arrived for our meeting in the conference room. I seated myself away from Ben's reach.

"Brenna, what's going on?" asked Ben, a quizzical look on his still handsome face.

"Sit down, Ben, and we'll get started," directed Ted. "Brenna has retained my partner, Mr. Corsky, and me, to handle several actions regarding you and the farm. First, this is a petition for dissolution of your marriage to Brenna Maureen Souchek-Herrera Langford." Ted handed the document to Ben. While Ben sat speechless, Ted continued, "Next, this is a document giving up all your parental rights to the two minor children listed."

"THIS IS AN OUTRAGE. What are you trying to do, Brenna?" said Ben as he rose out of his chair. "THIS IS BULLSHIT! We are not getting a divorce, nor will you take my children."

"Shut up, Ben, and sit down. This is just the beginning," I said in a cold, controlled voice he had never heard before.

Ben sat back down, stunned, as Ted continued, "I have applied for and received, signed by the judge, a Personal Protection Order for Brenna and the children. This order forbids you from going to the farm without a police escort, contacting the children and Brenna, or coming within one hundred yards of them. Furthermore, the farm bank accounts are frozen, and I have canceled the credit cards."

Ben looked at me with undisguised hostility. His fury and hatred were clearly evident. "You can't divorce me and keep the farm and everything I put into it. I will take half as my marital right. I will fight you every inch of the way and drag your ass through court until I get what I deserve."

"You'll get what you deserve, all right. You should have done your due diligence when building your house of cards. It gives me great pleasure to tell you, I don't own the farm."

"SINCE WHEN?" Ben roared.

"Since BEFORE we got married, I deeded the property to my sons, Chase and Gage. They are the legal owners, not me. As your landlords, you owe them, to my calculations, a bucket load of money for rent over the last six years. You get no compensation for improvements on land you didn't, or I didn't own," I continued looking straight at Ben. "The only property we own together is the farm across the road, and I am prepared to buy your half at fair market value, of course."

"You conniving slut, you're trying to cheat me out of everything I have built, YOU FUCKING BITCH!"

"That's enough. Please watch your language. This meeting is being recorded for Brenna's and your protection." Ted continued in a much sterner, more professional voice. "I understand your concern, Mr. Langford, but we haven't gotten to the most serious part yet. And that's your attempt to commit Grand Larceny, the fraudulent sale of property you didn't own, and the retention of the earnest money you accepted from two different parties, which is Felony Grand Theft. The rightful owners, Chase and Gage Herrera, are filing a suit that charges you with your attempt to swindle them out of the property. I have also conferred with the attorneys for the two parties you agreed to sell the property to, to sue for a false and fraudulent sale. Brenna is also suing for forging her name to the Agreement to Sell, a criminal act.

"I have secured affidavits from the affected parties regarding your unlawful actions. I suggest you engage family and criminal attorneys as soon as possible. A deputy is standing by to deliver the vehicle and horse trailer back to the farm. A judge has frozen all assets until a determination of the court discerns ownership. Brenna will remain at the farm per the registered owners with full custody of the minor children unless or until the family court determines permanent custody. You are welcome to pursue supervised visitation with the minor children and child support payments will be assessed through the family court.

"I notified the minor children's school that you are not to have access to the children until determined by said court."

"What about my belongings? I need my property and living expenses until I can get this to court," fumed Ben.

"Brenna has packed up your personal items and are available for pick up in the deputy's presence who will drive with you to the farm. The truck you purchased is yours. You can use it to remove your personal property. As for living expenses, that's your problem. Perhaps some of the money you have looted from the business can service your living expenses. Again, I will remind you to take these matters seriously and not violate the Protection Order. I believe that concludes our meeting. Any questions?"

"How could you do this to me, Brenna? To us?"

"Shit happens, doesn't it, Ben? You fed me a plate full for too long. Now it's your turn. Buon Appetito."

Ben looked at me with a mix of humiliation and anger. "I trusted and loved you, Brenna?"

"You trusted me? To do what, Ben? Should I have turned a blind eye while you stole from the business? That you put the children and me in financial jeopardy? You don't know the meaning of the words trust or love. Someone has always shielded you from real life and its consequences with your gaggle of protectors bowing and scrapping to fulfill your every wish. You were so used to getting away with hurting people without considering the aftermath. Now you know how it feels on the receiving end. Not a good place to be, I know from experience," I said as I continued with the coldest, most unemotional stare at Ben. He looked at me, and I didn't recognize the man I had married. The man I had two children with—the man who promised to care for me, to be a family.

"You were my addiction, Ben. Stronger than any opiate. I overlooked your infidelity and swallowed my pride, giving you chance after chance. I am no longer addicted. I've kicked the habit."

Ben turned away and left the room with the deputy.

After Ben's exit, Ted, Mr. Corsky, and I remained in the conference room. "Thank you, gentlemen, for your support. I think I have been preparing for this for several years. I didn't know Ben's arrogance would reach such crushing depths. Unfortunately, now I have to go home and tell the children something," I said.

"I know you'll come up with the right words, Brenna. I've known you for a long time and seen you go through a lot with Ben. This is for the best. You're a strong woman, and I am proud of you," said Ted.

Mr. Corsky added, "My impression is that Mr. Langford knows he is in a heap of trouble, both criminally and civilly. He will have to engage attorneys for both Nebraska and Kentucky, and who knows, there could be other things that might come to light before the court cases are resolved. You are in an excellent position. Smart move, deeding the farm to your sons before you got married."

"That was Ted's idea, along with setting up a trust with the money I got for the sale of my condo in Chicago and other investments left to me from my late husband. Ted looked into his crystal ball and saw the future clearer than what I could. It's said that love is blind and I guess it's true," I said.

"You always think the best of everyone, Brenna. In our line of work, Abe and I see people at their worst and prepare for what might happen. I'm glad we could be here to keep you and the children safe and secure," said Ted.

"Thank you again, gentlemen. I'm sure we'll be in touch."

CHAPTER THIRTY-TWO

I grieved for what I always knew deep down was inevitable. I didn't think Ben was so cruel as to deprive the children and me of our home for his selfish purposes. *Wrong again, Brenna—you sap. You have only yourself to blame.*

When I got home, I sat down with the children and reassured them they were loved and secure in the home they had always known. It was hard to explain to them that daddy wouldn't be living with us anymore, and it might be a long time before they would see him again. I answered all their questions, not denigrating their father but clarifying that he had made some serious mistakes that he had to take care of. As the children get older, their questions will need more detail and be more difficult to explain. In addition, they are bound to hear from other children in school about the circumstances of Ben's exodus. A bumper crop of gossip would make the rounds of coffee klatches for a long time.

The first holidays without Ben were difficult for the younger children. Chase and Gage came home with their families for a visit. They were fully apprised of the legalities of the different lawsuits filed against Ben. Ted kept all of us informed.

Law enforcement officers arrested Ben in the Kentucky matters and he was eventually found guilty of attempted fraud. It wasn't a surprise to anyone that Ben hired a top-notch legal team. With his charm and celebrity, he managed to avoid significant jail time and made deals with the star-struck prosecutors for most of his charges. His cases settled with minimal personal inconvenience. He made restitution to those he had received money from in the attempted land swindle. The gossip rags were having a field day with the titillating details of his criminal endeavors. The intense publicity seemed to enhance his reputation as a bad boy, and he was in demand once again for movies and television talk shows.

Why is it that people are attracted to "bad boys" and not empathetic to the victims of their misdeeds? As my son Gage would say, "You can wrap up a turd in sparkly paper, but it's still a turd."

I made my deal with Ben's attorney that I would not pursue a monetary award with the lawsuits at this time, keeping it in abeyance, if Ben kept my name and those of the children out of any publicity he generated due to his maleficence. I will not stand to have my name dragged through the mud for something Ben was entirely responsible for. If there was ever a whiff of talk that Ben would try to make me into the villain in this fiasco, I would make it my mission to ruin him financially. The lesson to be learned: Never make a Nebraska girl mad.

*   *   *

Our divorce was final a year after I filed. I bought out Ben's share of the property across the road and sold most of our stock. I kept six of the horses, my store in town, and played around with a few ideas for the future as life settled down to a new normal.

After the various court proceedings concluded, I petitioned to change my name and that of my minor children from Langford back to Herrera. Ben did not offer any protest. The Langford grandparents were upset, but understood my need to erase the shame Ben brought to our family and for the well-being of the children. They were more upset with their son than with me.

Vickie and Will didn't escape Ben's negative notoriety either, with the press hounding them for months as the court cases ran their course. The once pride filled parents were now keeping silent when asked about Ben's difficulties, enduring their embarrassment in private.

The farm was now The Souchek-Herrera Farm, back to where I started when I sought succor when I was pregnant with Alexandra. I was at peace again—content with a smaller farm that I could handle with only one part-time hired hand. The children continued to thrive and asked about their father rarely. Unfortunately, Ben didn't keep in touch with them after our divorce was final, but their Langford grandparents kept in regular contact with the children.

I was happy again, and the children were well-adjusted and content. My children are my redemption. I am grateful to Ben for giving me those two bright lights. My youngest, Robbie, is the only one of my four offspring who looked like me, with strawberry blond hair, green eyes, and the kindest, most gentle soul.

I slowly gained my self-respect back and realized my strength as a woman who made it on her own, overcoming challenging times and coming out stronger for it. Sure, I missed not having someone to cuddle up to on the cold winter nights. The joy of physical love was missing. I had two great loves, and that was all I could expect. I guess I will have to go back to reading Sandra Brown novels. I was approaching my fifties, and that was enough for me.

As the children got older, I thought of things to do to keep involved and my mind alert. The guest cabins stood empty since the breeding business's dissolution. I gave some thought to starting a small riding business, giving lessons to adults and children with overnight accommodations available. My own little Dude Ranch B & B.

Since my divorce, Nick Pfizer and I have kept in touch over the last couple of years. I offered to sell him the property across the road that he had shown an interest in. The Pfizer ranch continued to grow and was one of the country's most highly respected breeding farms, serving equine enthusiasts from all over the world for half a century.

Nick had been running the family ranch for the last five years since his father's retirement and had grown up in the business. He married briefly and had a grown daughter, but had remained unshackled for over twenty years. Every single woman and possibly some married ones tried their hardest to bring him to ground with no success. Nick was every woman's 'wet dream'. He looked like young cowboy Tom Selleck, complete with old-world manners, a work-hardened body, and an innate kindness and caring for others, not to mention a sharp mind.

Nick stopped over to the farm frequently to talk about purchasing the facilities across the road. I made a simple supper for Nick and the children on one of his visits. While the kids were doing their homework, I took Nick out in the yard to pick his brain about the feasibility of developing the riding business sometime in the future.

I showed him the guest cabins, the stables, and the barns. First, he looked over the six horses I still had. Then, after some consideration, he thought the idea might have merit when some income/expense projections could be calculated and a firm commitment to a new enterprise established.

We walked across the road, and he looked at the training arena, wash stalls, and fouling barn that Ben had built. "Are you sure you want to sell, Brenna?" Nick asked.

"I don't need it, Nick. Guncle John's house is down the road, part of the package and the acreage. I don't want to oversee something of no use to me. I want to downsize to something I can control comfortably. Bigger isn't necessarily better. The children are eight and seven, and before I know it, they will be on their own in a few years. After twenty-five plus years of mothering, I think it's time for me to do the things I enjoy without guilt. I found my place and know my limitations. A smaller life is right for me."

"Can I ask you a personal question?"

"Of course," I said.

"Do you ever hear from Ben?"

"I don't, and that's fine with me, but he doesn't seem to remember that he had children even after supervised visitation was granted. It breaks my heart for them. Someday they may feel the need to contact him and I hope he will respond. Meanwhile, it doesn't seem to bother them too much at this age. They know what their father had tried to do to our family. If they ask questions, I strive to answer honestly, not disparaging Ben. He is still their father, even if he shows no interest."

"You've done a fine job raising them. They're smart kids, and they certainly adore you."

"Thank you, Nick. I try my best to make them feel secure and loved. I was a single mother before, and I knew I could do it again. I didn't come out a loser in this deal with Ben. I have the little girl I had always yearned for and Robbie, who is such a bright, loving little ray of sunshine. I'm happy again and more than content with the road I have traveled."

"I better hit the road myself, always chores to do at home. I will have an offer for you on the property in a couple of days. Thank you for dinner. I enjoyed it and seeing the kids. Ah. . . . . Brenna . . . . would you consider going out to dinner with me?"

"I would love to, Nick."

CHAPTER THIRTY-THREE

Nick and I became a couple, enjoying each other's company with so many interests in common. The younger children referred to him as mom's "boyfriend". That designation was fine with me. I knew I would never marry again, but that didn't stop me from having a loving, fulfilling physical relationship with a man who understands me and respects my need for independence.

Robbie and Alexandra thought of Nick as a surrogate father, and Nick took to the children in a genuinely caring way. He backed me up concerning parental direction, never intrusive with my mothering instincts and my children. Nick trusted me to live my life as I saw fit without interference, knowing I was strong enough to handle today and tomorrow.

Chase and Gage fully approved of Nick and enjoyed every minute they spent with him at the farm. We would saddle up and ride over the sandhills and the open ranges. The kids spent time at the Pfizer ranch marveling at a well-run breeding business, much bigger than we had ever been. Nick's father, Charlie, lived in the ranch house with Nick.

It seemed to give Charlie a needed purpose in life since his retirement to have my children around, and he asked them to call him grandpa. Charlie was always ready to take Robbie fishing or hunting and answered his many questions about horse breeding. Robbie spent as much time at the Pfizer ranch as he did at home. Grandpa Pfizer and Nick were frequent guests for dinner, and Robbie would even spend the night at their house when one of their prize mares was near to dropping a foal.

Maggie, Ted, Nick, and I became a regular foursome around town, going to dinner, dances, or the movies. Grandpa Charlie was more than willing to babysit whenever I needed him, and the children couldn't wait to be in his care. We became a family, not by the traditional definition, but a family nevertheless. We celebrated holidays and birthdays together with Maggie's family, knowing we were a unit not united by blood but by love.

I sold Maggie my tack shop in Sanders. She had managed it for so long, loving every minute now that her daughters were grown and on their own. Another item off my plate of responsibility. Instead, I concentrated on formulating plans for the B & B Dude Ranch and working remotely for Dr. M at the college in Chicago.

I had time to sit back and smell the roses and enjoy my family, home, and interests. Dr. Michaels would have me confer with him in Chicago twice a year to discuss the upcoming Italian study program plans. Nick even traveled with us during one of the winter meetings and had won the affection of my Chicago friends.

Betsy and Michele would take charge of the children while I attended the biannual meetings. Dr. M had some concerns with the new instructor he hired to facilitate the tour. After four tours, the previous instructor had retired, doing an excellent job as an extraordinarily knowledgeable and competent expediter. While having the teaching credentials, the new instructor did not have the same skill to maintain her predecessor's discipline and organizational talents. Dr. M asked, and I agreed to mentor the new instructor with twice a week Zoom meetings and go over the itinerary, curriculum, and a step-by-step script of best practices. We had twenty weeks in preparation before the next tour was to begin.

After one of my in-person meetings with Dr. M concluded, I took the children to some of the same attractions Chase and Gage visited when they were younger. They enjoyed the city's delights but were ready to go home to the people and place they loved.

Nick would meet us at the Grand Island airport, ready to take us back to the farm. When Alexandra and Robbie spotted Nick waiting at the luggage carrousel, they ran to him with outstretched arms and shrieks of joy. Someone would think we left for weeks instead of five days. After kissing and hugging the children, Nick took me in his arms and welcomed me home with mind numbing kisses. When Nick gathered us close, I could see the faces of the women in the airport looking at us with envy.

"I missed you, woman. I was counting the minutes until I could see you again and hold you," said Nick.

"I missed you too. Take me home." My Chicago trips were the few times we had not seen each other daily for the last two years. He had become such a big part of my life; our relationship was so comfortable. He lifted my spirits and healed my heart. Nick is a good man through and through, someone I could count on and trust. He made me whole again. Our physical relationship wasn't the explosive highs and lows I experienced with Ben but a steady burn for each other, always needing to touch or look into each other's eyes.

I told Nick about my meetings. I would mentor the new instructor through the winter and spring. Nick could tell how excited I was to have a new purpose separate from the children and the farm during the slow months of the year.

The holidays came with visits from Chase and Gage with their families. Grandpa Charlie and Nick stayed for all the feasting and getting ready for Santa, and Susan, Nick's twenty-six-year-old daughter, joined us. She was such a pleasure to add to our family, joining right in with all the pranks and joking, a trademark behavior with my older sons.

January was soon on us with ferocious winds and biting cold. It was all I could do to get out to the barn and make sure the horses were fed and cared for. When Alex and Robbie were in school, it was Nick's and my time for intimacy. We spent hours in bed making love, exploring each other, and achieving mutual fulfillment, cuddling under warm quilts as the snow and ice coated the landscape.

The Zoom meetings were going well. I gave the new instructor all the advice I could think of. In addition, I gave her the contact information for Georgio in Florence in case she ran into trouble. Another thought was familiarizing the students with the difference between Fahrenheit and Celsius, distances in measurements of feet and miles to meters and kilometers, and dollars to euros, but it was a new day and the students probably had apps on their phones now. Not like the old days when we had to make calculations in our head, but it wouldn't hurt to have the knowledge in case, heaven forbid, their phones didn't have service or were low on power.

I contacted Carlo and Georgio, letting them know a new team would tour in June. However, my Italian friends kept up their nagging about my return to Florence. We FaceTimed regularly, and they got to know the children as we practiced our language skills. Perhaps someday, when the children are more independent, I would approach

Dr. M to take over the tours or investigate different countries for an expanded program.

Spring was just around the corner, and I spent a lot of time in The Coop nursing seedings for my vegetable garden and annuals for the hanging baskets under the warm plant lights. Ben's presence was no longer in evidence, and I spent many relaxing hours in my 'She Shed'.

In April, Alexandra celebrated her tenth birthday with a party of friends riding the horses, roasting hotdogs, and making smores over a campfire. Grandma and Grandpa Langford visited to add their birthday wishes and met Grandpa Charlie and Nick.

Vickie took me aside to ask, "Are you happy, darling?"

"I am, Vickie. I am so blessed to have happy and content children and equally blessed to have you and Will in our lives."

"I can see how much you care for Nick and he you. I am so happy for you. Will and I wish you all the happiness in the world. Thank you for letting us be part of the children's lives."

"You're family Vickie. We love you and hope you will always think of us as family." I could see sadness in her eyes for what should have been, but could never be. Vickie or Will never mentioned Ben during their visits, but if the celebrity magazines were to be believed, Ben remarried frequently and divorced just as regularly. Alex would sometimes take Vickie aside and ask about her dad, and Vickie would diplomatically answer her questions. I could understand Alex's natural curiosity regarding her father, but since I had no contact with him, Vickie was her only source of authentic information, and I was okay with that. Vickie wasn't blind to her son's faults and tried to shield the children from any hurt. Ben had not only fractured our family, but his own.

By mid-April, I had my garden in and set up a schedule for exercising the horses. It helped to have the children riding the horses on their own so that I wouldn't have to ride for hours by myself. Sam came over for the yearly check on the outbuildings so they could be adequately maintained. "Uncle" Sam was another favorite in the children's orbit, and it thrilled them when he had the time for visits. He was another male figure for Robbie, teaching him how to scope out and repair minor plumbing issues and do small repairs to the buildings while wearing his own little tool belt.

My mentoring assignment for the college was drawing to an end, going so-so. It concerned me that the new instructor was reluctant to take my advice, since I did not have the teaching credentials she did. In addition, this trip had expanded, accepting ten boys and ten girls and would have two female and two male chaperons under the instructor's supervision. I could sense an attitude of dismissiveness on her part for my guidance. I passed on my concerns to Dr. M and let him know that the college could call me if they had questions.

In another month, Alex and Robbie would be out of school. Nick and I would have to be creative to continue our romantic life. The kids were used to us kissing and hugging, but I didn't feel that we could share a bed while they were this young. Our passion was strong, and Nick told me frequently that he loved me. I loved him too, but I couldn't say it out loud. My inability to say the "L" word hurt him. I told him I cared for him; it was commitment phobia on my part. Perhaps I was afraid to jump over that last hurdle, feeling I was diminishing my hard-won independence and self-confidence. I was reluctant to let myself become vulnerable to heartache again.

Nick's workload was picking up with many mares foaling within days of each other, and others were in season. The Pfizer foaling barn across the road was a hive of activity. The kids were running over there constantly. Sure will make the "birds and bees" talk easier for me in the future.

The children witnessed the birthing process, insemination, and understood the need to abort a fetus if a mare was carrying two foals. If that procedure wasn't performed, the mare's chances were high to become sterile or die. The children took all this information in stride as nothing unusual.

Spring burst out over the plains. The farmers were plowing and planting their fields, and ranches were busy with calving and foaling. I nurtured my vegetable garden, made mirror repairs around the farm, and did the usual chores of parenthood and farm life. As busy as spring is, Nick and I made time for each other whenever we could. The town folk recognized us as a stable family unit. Nick and Grandpa Charlie often accompanied the children and me to school events in town and other assorted public activities or family get-togethers. No one ever ventured to ask me about plans for marriage——except Maggie.

"When are you going to marry this man so he can make you an honest woman?" asked Maggie.

"Number one, he hasn't asked me, and number two, I don't want to get married again."

"Nick is not Ben, even though Nick is just as pretty. Ben sold you a defective bill of goods. Don't let that buttfungus destroy your chance for happiness. Nick is a good man. He doesn't screw around; he's trustworthy and loves your kids. Nick has plenty of money, so he doesn't need yours, and I bet he's slap-your-mama hot in bed. You and Nick perfectly complement each other. What more can you ask for?"

"I'm fine with the way things are with us. We are together when we want to be and apart when we need to be. I've gotten used to being my own person and making my own decisions. So why rock the boat?"

"How about rockin' the sheets, sleeping together every night instead of sneaking off like a couple of horny teenagers? What if you found Nick gone tomorrow? How would you feel? I know you love him, and he loves you. What if he wants more?"

Maggie gave me a lot to think about. The thought of Nick walking out of my life was scary. No, more than that, it would devastate the children. I did "devastating" before and didn't want to do it again. Was I being selfish? Nick didn't want to change me, and I didn't want to change him. We had our fun times and quiet times, and I knew I could talk to him about anything. Nick didn't tell me what to do, but let me be myself. I don't know why I'm even thinking about the "M" word. It has never come up for discussion.

June was well under way. The kids were out of school, busy caring for our horses and helping with the garden. They were across the road at the foaling barn or spending time with Grandpa Charlie in their spare time. The cultivated fields were full of waist-high corn nurtured with the heat and plentiful rain. The sandhills were again alive with blue-green bluestem grasses and yellow prairie flowers. Large herds of Black Angus, Hereford, and Longhorn cattle were peacefully grazing the days away, getting fat and ready for the market by fall. Then, our calm days of summer on the prairie came to a screeching halt with a phone call from Dr. Michaels in Chicago.

CHAPTER THIRTY-FOUR

"Brenna, I desperately need your expert help," said Dr. M. "Professor Wells has run into several problems on the Italian tour. Two chaperones are threatening to quit and students are going off on their own, drinking to excess, and defying all the rules set forth for behavior and academic standards.

"I have to ask you a huge favor. Can you fly over immediately and straighten this out before a tragedy occurs? I wouldn't ask this of you unless I thought the students weren't in serious jeopardy and our school's reputation at stake.

"Of course, I will pay all expenses that you deem necessary to get the tour back on track. I need your answer within a couple of hours, or I will have to recall all the students and refund fees, not to mention the severe damage to the school's reputation. I will call you back in one hour and fifty-seven minutes for your answer," said Dr. M as he disconnected.

I called Nick on his cell and said I had an emergency and asked him to come over to the farm as soon as he could. As Nick's truck roared into the driveway, I explained the situation to the kids. He ran in the door and joined us in the living room.

"Is anyone hurt? What happened?" he asked in a state of acute anxiety.

I explained what was happening in Italy and Dr. Michaels' request to go over to Florence to straighten everything out; I would take the children. If Nick could watch over the hired hand, we could get on our way. I felt I had to do this to save the program for Dr. M. I owe him for everything he had done for me and as my friend. Alexandra was excited, Robbie, not so much.

"But Mom, I can't leave now. My horse will have her foal any day now. I have to be here. I don't want to go. I want to stay here with Ginger. Can't I stay home with Nick and Grandpa Charlie?" begged Robbie. I looked at Nick.

"I can take care of Robbie. It's no problem. How long will you be gone?" asked Nick.

"About two weeks. Are you sure about keeping Robbie for that length of time? I don't want to impose."

"You're not imposing. This is an emergency. Grandpa and I will keep Robbie busy and watch over everything here, so don't worry. Make your arrangements, and we'll get you and Alex to the airport. Everything will be fine when you get home. What can Robbie and I do to help?" asked Nick.

*   *   *

I immediately got online and found a flight to Chicago from Grand Island departing in four hours. Next, I called Dr. M and let him know I was on my way with Alexandra and would arrive in Chicago at 6 PM. Then, I requested that Dr. M find the biggest, burliest, no-nonsense college security guard to accompany us to Italy and book the three of us on the United Airlines direct flight to Rome with a connecting Alitalia flight to Florence, all flights in first class. I wasn't above demanding a perk or two in this emergency.

I asked Nick to pack up my laptop while I got out our suitcases grabbed what I thought I would need for the trip. Alex was next as we tossed her things together, and I had her get some books to read during the long flight. Finally, Nick and Robbie drove us to Grand Island in time for our flight to Chicago with passports in hand.

Alexandra was so excited she was almost sick. Robbie had a big smile on his face, knowing that he would be the man of the house with Nick's help.

I was running on pure adrenalin, thinking I probably forgot half the stuff I would need. Nick was steady as a rock, getting us to the airport in plenty of time. Alex and I checked in, and I hit the ATM for some cash for incidentals. Nick and Robbie walked us to the security gate.

I gathered Robbie in my arms and hugged the stuffing out of him, telling him I was so proud of him for volunteering to take care of our home while Alex and I were away. I promised to call every day to let my men know how everything was going, and I would bring them back something special from Italy. Nick took me into his arms for the longest kiss and hug of my life. My eyes welled up, and I tried not to cry. This separation was the first for Robbie and me and the longest from Nick, since we had become a couple.

Separating, I look into Nick's eyes filled with longing as he said, "I love you, my darling. Stay safe, and don't worry. Robbie and I have it handled. We will see you in two weeks." Nick kissed and hugged Alexandra, and I could only nod after one last kiss for my men. Alex and I turned and moved through security and waved until they were blocked from our sight by corridor walls.

Borrowing from Alexandra's well of delight, my stress was lessening, and I was getting excited about the task ahead and seeing Georgio and Carlo again. While waiting to board our flight, I texted Georgio asking if a room was available for Alexandra and me for the next two weeks with our arrival in the morning. I received a text from Dr. M.

He was sending a man named Trevor Noble, a college security officer, to Italy with me. Mr. Noble would meet Alex and me at O'Hare for our night flight and included a picture of the six-foot eight-inch, 280-pound former football player. Also included in the text was the information for our electronic tickets on United Airlines. Sleep would be a priority on our ten-hour flight. Considering the time change and connection from Rome, we would arrive at the B & B at about 11 AM.

Trevor was a godsend, handling all the baggage. Alex and I got a lot of curious looks—Trevor looked every inch a bodyguard. Our flights were smooth, connections perfect, and we arrived at Carlo and Georgio's at noon. I introduced Trevor to my friends, who had astonished looks on their faces. Thank goodness Trevor didn't speak Italian, or he would have blushed right down to his toes.

Trevor would stay with the students and chaperones at the hostels. I texted Professor Wells as soon as I got Alexandra settled with Georgio and Carlo for the afternoon and asked for the current location of the tour group. They were about to enter the Galleria dell'Accademia.

Trevor and I walked the three blocks to the gallery. I talked to him about our approach. We would observe the students' behavior and then talk with the individual chaperones and Dr. Wells to get their feedback.

It thrilled me to see that Piero Rossi and Antonia Bianchi were still in charge of the gallery. We greeted each other like long-lost friends, hugs and kisses in a flurry of Italian, much to the amazement of the students and Dr. Wells. I heard a few students commenting, "The calvary has arrived". Trevor stood in the back of the group as the tour started. While the students appeared to be avidly listening to Antonia, I quietly spoke with the chaperones.

Between the four chaperones' remarks, I pinpointed two students that seemed to more than test the boundaries set for student behavior and the instigators of the conflicts. These young men didn't seem to think that the curfew hours applied to them since they were over twenty-one. Nor did they believe that coming back to the hostels highly inebriated was a big deal. Checking with the instructor, the dynamic duo didn't feel that completing reading assignments or taking the tests was a necessary part of this tour for their grade. Their continuous efforts to disrupt and constant insolence tried the patience of the chaperones and the instructor at every turn. After the day's activities concluded, I called a meeting for all the students, Dr. Wells and the chaperones at the hostel.

In the common room, the students assembled with their iPads. I introduced myself and announced that Mr. Noble and I would join the tour to evaluate the content and stay until the conclusion in two weeks. I asked the students to open up their class notes on their iPads and open the file labeled Student Code of Conduct and Disciplinary Action.

"This document is the Code of Conduct you signed and agreed to follow during this foreign study tour. Specifically, number four applies to set curfew hours while under the supervision of The School of Art and Architecture of Chicago.

"I highly recommend that you revisit this document to refresh yourselves with every aspect. These are not suggestions, but rules for you to follow without deviation. These rules are for your protection. You are in a foreign country, not knowing the laws or the language. The Italian jails are a place you do not want to spend time should you run afoul of the law. Please look at image one of a typical Italian jail.

"Jails are old buildings, crowded and unpleasant. You will have to buy your food, and the wheels of justice move slowly in Italy. The school will not intervene on your behalf in a justified action taken by the polizia. An occurrence such as that will culminate in your suspension from further classes until your appearance in front of the Student Disciplinary Board, where expulsion is a possibility. There will be no refund of tuition for this foreign study tour. Any serious infraction will result in your removal from this program, and I will send you home.

"As for your classwork, reading assignments, tests and quizzes are required to pass the requirements for a grade. Failure to participate may result in a failing grade, which will affect your GPA. Have I made myself clear? Are there are questions?"

The students were appropriately cowed, except for one of the "bad boys" who raised his hand.

"Devon Larsen, isn't it? I asked.

"Some of us are over the age of twenty-one. We're adults, so you can't hold us to this curfew rule."

"Oh, but I can. Your majority does not supersede the Code of Conduct Agreement that you signed. That is a binding contract between you and the college. As a representative of the school, I will take any action necessary to ensure the safety of all students, chaperones, and instructors while safeguarding this program's integrity. Does that answer your question?"

"Yes, ma'am," said Mr. Larsen, as he saluted with a cocky smile on his face.

"If there are no more questions, you have free time until curfew. So please be vigilant, travel in pairs, use common sense and enjoy this wonderful opportunity in Florence."

Following the meeting, Trevor and I met with Professor Wells. She was a little more circumspect about her ability to handle the program. The itinerary had flipped since its inception, and the students had already spent time in Rome. They now concentrated on Florence, Pisa, and Venice. Professor Wells indicated that Mr. Larsen and his cohort Mr. Scott had been acting up the entire trip. Mr. Scott was more of a follower than a leader, but just as culpable. Mr. Larsen was obviously the ringleader.

I asked the instructor to continue to give out assignments and record test scores, giving the students the marks they deserve. Trevor would shadow the students as added security until the end of the tour. I confirmed that both of them had my cellphone number should they need my assistance. Trevor reassured me that our "problem children" would probably toe-the-mark for the next couple of days until they felt comfortable again. I took my leave and walked back toward Georgio's B & B, hoping to have a quiet evening with Alex and my friends. As I walked over the Ponte Vecchio through the Piazza di Santa Croce, I remembered my favorite leather goods shop right on the piazza. Entering the store, the scent of tanned and tooled leather was overwhelming and stopped me in my tracks. It was the masculine scent that surrounded Nick. Tears sprang up in my eyes, and my love for this man filled my heart. I knew that my life wasn't complete if he wasn't in it. Even though I had left him a couple of days ago, I missed Nick's gentle presence at my side. I picked up a leather vest and hugged it to my chest as if I could feel his embrace. I bought the buttery soft brandy-colored vest and a smaller one for Robbie. In twelve days, I would be home, never to be separated again.

Alexandra was in seventh heaven, having spent the day shopping with "Uncles" Georgio and Carlo. They spoiled her with a suitcase full of new clothes and shoes, then treated her to multiple gelato flavors. She was now getting a cooking lesson from Carlo about preparing pasta.

Alexandra didn't seem jet-lagged, but I put her to bed in our apartment after we finished dinner. Then I joined my friends for a glass of vino, when the questions began with Georgio.

"I am sorry that things didn't work out with Ben, but at least you have that darling girl and Roberto. Cara, are you sure it is over? I know you loved him, and he loved you," said Georgio.

"Yes, it's over. Ben played me for a fool and tried to rob me of my farm, putting my family in financial jeopardy while screwing his way through Hollywood. He was never the man I thought he was or wanted him to be. The saddest part is he seems to have forgotten that he has children. They never hear from him. Perhaps someday Ben will realize what he lost, not knowing our beautiful children. It has taken me a while, but I am over him. I forgive him for what he did to me, but not what he's doing to the children."

"It's been a few years now. Anyone new in your life?" Carlo asked.

"As a matter of fact, there is. His name is Nick, and he runs the biggest horse breeding ranch in the state. We have been together for two years, and he's wonderful. Robbie is staying with him and his father while I'm here."

"Is he good to you, cara?" asked Georgio.

"The best. Nick likes me for me, the person I have finally grown into. I'm happy again, Georgio."

"We can't wait to meet him. In the offseason, we will come to visit this farm of yours. We haven't taken a vacation for years."

"You and Carlo are welcome any time. I would love to see you as cowboys."

"Oh Signore, aiutami—Oh Lord, help me."

After telling Georgio and Carlo my plans for the following day, I kissed them goodnight and joined Alex in our apartment. I took a couple of minutes to email Dr. M going over the situation and request a copy of the application submitted by Devin Larsen for this course. Because of the time difference, I should know something by morning. Next, I called Nick's cell phone to talk to my guys. Everything was quiet on the home front. Ginger still hadn't dropped her foal, and Robbie was anxiously waiting.

I was exhausted after our flight and a full day of student review. I was asleep as soon as my head hit the pillow. The next couple of days were relaxed, and the students were well behaved and enjoying the wonders of Florence without the stress created by our problem children. We visited many of the lesser known museums and toured the many Medici palaces. Next on the itinerary was Pisa.

* * *

After breakfast, Alex and I joined the student group for a bus ride to Pisa. I had received the application I requested from Dr. M. Devon Larsen was less than an academically gifted student. Then I found it. His mother was on the mayor's Educational Council and a significant contributor to the school. I admire Dr. M, who told me to treat young Mr. Larsen the same as any other student. If dismissal from the program was warranted, he would stand behind my decision.

I spent the day observing and chatting with Trevor. The students were following all the rules to the letter. Alex and I circulated and practiced our Italian. My daughter loved spending time with the female students becoming their pet.

The weather was beautiful as the students climbed to the top of the leaning tower for a panoramic view of the city. Next, the cathedral and baptistry, these three buildings together, make up one of the most beautiful and famous ensembles of 12th-13th century artistry to be found anywhere in the world. Finally, we had enough time to visit the Piazza dei Miracoli, the Square of Miracles, recognized as an important center of European medieval art. After a wonderful meal in the Tuscan Hills on the way back to Florence, the students were dragging, ready to crash for the night as Alex and I headed back to the B & B.

Alex and I hung out with the students for the first half of the following day. The plan for the students was to tour all the Medici gardens and visit the hills where Michelangelo selected and quarried his marble, with Trevor keeping order. I borrowed Giorgio's car so that Alex and I could drive to Siena for an afternoon visit with Nonna.

Nonno had passed away a couple of years ago, and Nonna now lived with her daughter. My Italian family knew about my brief marriage and children with Ben. Nonna was wonderful with Alexandra for their first face-to-face meeting, treating her as if she was a blood grandchild. I filled Nonna in on the news of Gage and Chase's lives while we shared a meal. We left later in the afternoon. Nonna seemed to tire easily, and we wanted to let her rest.

I checked in with Trevor. All was quiet on the student front. The following few days, students would concentrate on all the churches and galleries in Florence and then on to Venice for a three-day visit. The students seemed to take my review of the Code of Conduct seriously.

In the late afternoon, two days before our Venice tour, I gave a lecture to the assembled students in the common room at the hostel on the history of Venice and what they could expect to see. During The Q & A period, Mr. Larsen raised his hand.

"Yes, Devin?" I asked.

"Is it true that you're married to Ben Langford?" he asked with a wise guy sneer on his face. The room erupted in chatter as the students looked at me in stunned surprise, waiting for my response.

It took all my powers to maintain my half-smile and not let Mr. Larsen know that his question had thrown me. "Ben is my ex-husband, and we met here in Florence where he was filming a movie, now a closed chapter in my life. Are there any more questions about our tour of Venice?" The students were too dumbfounded to make any further queries.

I released the students for free time to shop or entertain themselves with a movie or dining. I conferred with Trevor, anticipating that Mr. Larsen was back to attempting to disrupt by trying to intimidate and embarrass me. If Ben taught me anything, it was how to handle narcissistic, immature, and enabled jerks.

I left the hostel for the B & B and invited Giorgio and Carlo to dine with Alex and me at one of our favorite ristorantes. The evening was mild, as we enjoyed a sumptuous meal and relaxed with a magnificent wine. As our party walked back to the B & B, we ran into some students having a great time wandering the streets of Florence.

Carlo gave the students tips on what to see in the neighborhood and charmed them with the power of his personality.

* * *

Alex and I bathed and settled in bed early after phoning home to talk with Nick and Robbie for a few minutes. No foal yet.

I was sound asleep when my phone buzzed at 4 AM. Trevor called to say that a belligerent Devin and his sidekick, Mr. Scott, had arrived back at the hostel after a night of drinking and fighting, in the custody of the local polizia.

CHAPTER THIRTY-FIVE

I took Alex over to Giorgio's apartment and explained the situation. Carlo drove me over to the hostel. I conferred with a bevy of officers to get the story. It couldn't be determined who started the fight between our students and the local ruffians. All parties were well into the vino. I persuaded the polizia to let me handle it and reassured them that the appropriate action would be taken. After the officers left, I sat down with Mr. Larsen and Mr. Scott, with Trevor unobtrusively recording my questioning with video and audio.

"Okay, Devin, what happened?" I asked.

"Aaron and I were minding our own business, and this bunch of cocksucking wops started bugging us, so we got into it. End of story. Now, if that's enough for you, I want to go to bed."

"It's not the end of the story. What time was curfew?"

"I don't give a shit. I'm an adult. I don't have to go by your brain-dead rules."

"What do you have to say for yourself, Mr. Scott?" I asked.

"What he said," as Aaron laid his head on the table and passed out.

"Mr. Larsen, you and Mr. Scott have been given numerous warnings to conform to the Rules of Conduct. Unfortunately, you have shown a grievous disregard for rules put in place for your safety and the others on this tour. Arrest and detention could have been a distinct possibility with your conduct tonight."

"Well, we weren't. Just shut up, bitch. You're nothing but a paid college chippy. Let me get to bed so that we can take off for Venice on time."

"The class will go to Venice. You and Mr. Scott will not. Instead, you will pack your things and be going to the Rome airport with a professional escort for a flight back to Chicago. College security will meet you at O'Hare and help you gather anything you have at school and then drop you off on the curb. You are expelled from the college, effective immediately."

"You can't do that. Do you know who my mother is? She'll have your fucking ass before the plane lands." Devin said as he rose out of his seat with a raised fist headed my way. Trevor grabbed his arm before Devin could make contact with my face.

"Does that fit the definition of assault to you, Trevor?" I asked.

"I believe it does, Mrs. Herrera."

"Did you get it all on video?"

"Yes, I did with full audio."

"Please stay with Mr. Larsen and Mr. Scott. I will make arrangements to pack their things and get them on their way to Rome." I had Trevor send the video to Dr. M as I placed a call to him. He confirmed my decision for expulsion and would have college security waiting at the airport when I texted him the arrival time for their flight. I arranged to have the professional escort service at the hostel within two hours and transportation to Rome.

The chaperons for the two young men packed up their room and had the suitcases waiting within the hour. By 7 AM, the two boys were on their way back home in disgrace. I gathered the other students together at breakfast, explaining that Mr. Larsen and Mr. Scott were on their way home because of their ignominious behavior. It didn't seem to surprise anyone, and many sighed with relief.

I left the students in the hands of Trevor, the instructor, and the chaperones for the last day in Florence before leaving for Venice. Later, back to the B & B, I felt relief with every expectation the rest of the tour would run smoothly now that the cancer had been expunged.

Carlo made me take a nap while he and Giorgio took charge of Alexandra. There were four other guests at the B & B, and Alex was excited to help serve them breakfast. Rest didn't come easy. Finally, I called Nick and told him about my early morning conflict. He heard me out reassuring me I made the right decision, but upset that the student had almost decked me, asking if I was okay. I replied I was fine and not to worry. It was part of the job when dealing with entitled, poorly parented students.

I gave up on any sleep. Alex and I joined the student group at the Uffizi Gallery. Everyone seemed to be more relaxed and in a much lighter mood. Late in the afternoon, I treated everyone to a double-dip of gelato. The students walked back to their hostel for the evening to prepare for Venice in the morning.

Alex and I packed for the three-day trip and dined with Carlo and Giorgio in their apartment. After calling home, Alexandra and I were ready for bed. Still no new foal.

The following day, after breakfast, our bus set out for Venice. The weather was again warm with azure blue skies and puffy white clouds. I practiced Italian phases with the students as the magnificent rolling countryside dotted with vineyards and olive groves sailed by our windows. The movie *Merchant of Venice*, filmed in 2005, played on the bus monitors on our three-hour drive.

Our bus pulled up to the parking area, and we had to walk with our bags to the hotel just off the Piazza San Marco. Since no motorized road vehicles were allowed in Venice, we were in for a lot of walking. After checking the students in at the hotel, we walked over to the piazza for an al fresco lunch in front of the Basilica di San Marco.

Crowded with tourists and hundreds of pigeons, the piazza was a melding point for people from all over the world who wanted to experience the art and architecture of an once world power from the Middle Ages. After everyone ate, a tour of St. Mark's Basilica was on the agenda. The instructor had prepared the students well with the history of Venice and the middle eastern/oriental design of the church architecture. It was fun watching the wonder on the students' faces, and Alexandra was just as excited. With the exit of the problem boys, the rest of the students felt freer to enjoy the tour, showing respect for the instructor and their chaperones. I guess that idiom of "one bad apple (or two) . . . ." was very fitting.

Moving on to the adjacent Palazzo Ducale, once the home of the Venice rulers, the evening was closing in. We grabbed some sandwiches and returned to the hotel. The common room offered the movie *Casino Royale*, a James Bond film from 2006 that was filmed in part on Venice's famed Grand Canal.

The following day was "Venice Canal Day". A water bus would take the group around the Grand Canal with a guide to explain how the buildings were constructed and the history of the iconic Rialto Bridge. I had reserved five gondolas for an afternoon tour of the narrower waterways touching on the history of the Bridge of Sighs and the many islands that make up Venice. We even talked one gondolier into singing "O Sole Mio" as we glided down the canals. To add to the local flavor, we watched a polizia water boat with siren and lights run down a speeding canal lawbreaker.

Exhaustion ran rampant by the end of the day. With Trevor's help, the instructor and chaperones had everything well in hand. I decided that Alex and I would have mother/daughter time the following day, our last full day in Venice. The students were going to numerous art galleries and churches, and I thought that wouldn't hold Alex's interest for long. She was such a trooper with the hectic schedule and shuttling her to Giorgio's care periodically. We would do everything she wanted to do for the day.

What an excellent way to strengthen the bond with my only daughter. Alex and I didn't have many opportunities to spend alone time together on the farm. Our days were always so busy at home, this girl time was precious. We ate our weight in gelato as we cruised the upscale shops around Saint Mark's Square and then took a water taxi over to the Venetian Island of Murano. We watched the glassblowers at work as they created magnificent pieces of art right before our eyes. Next, we took another water taxi to the neighboring island of Burano. The village contained dozens of brightly colored houses and shops that offered handmade lace items created by the local women. We chose a ristorante that I remembered from a previous visit that served the most delicious shrimp and avocado risotto. Alex and I sat down for an early dinner at the waterfront when we got down to some serious talk.

"Have you had fun, Alex?" I asked.

"Yeah, but I miss home and my horse."

"I know you do, and so do I," I said.

"I even miss my brother, but I really, really miss Nick and Grandpa Charlie."

"Me too. There's no place like home, is there?" I said.

"Mom, can I ask you something?"

"Sure, sweetheart, anything," I said.

"Are you going to marry Nick?"

"Why do you ask, Alex?"

"You guys are kissing all the time, and I want a dad, mom. Robbie and I never see our real dad. I don't think he loves us, and Nick does."

Out of the mouths of babes. How do I answer this one? Damn you, Ben, you did this, and now our children are hurting because of your self-absorption. "Sweetheart, I know your father loves you, and Robbie, he's just unable to show it. Some people are like that. You and Robbie have done nothing wrong, it's the type of person your father is. He has always cared about you and your brother. Never think that he doesn't. Your father is one of those people who can't reach out and show his feelings to anyone. As for Nick and Grandpa Charlie, they are family. Sometimes people make their own families like ours, related by love."

* * *

We took a water taxi back to Saint Mark's, visiting all the souvenir kiosks, buying sweatshirts, carnival masks and hats for our family back home. I took a dozen pictures of Alex as the pigeons in the square descended on her as she giggled with glee. We took one last gondola ride, just the two of us as the sun disappeared, saying goodbye to this beautiful city. We would return to Florence the next day as the students prepared to leave for home. Alex and I planned another two days to spend with Giorgio and Carlo. It had been a stressful trip for me, and I wanted a couple of days to decompress before returning home.

Dr. M had sent me an email to fill me on a meeting he had with the mother of Devin Larsen. Mrs. Larsen was all set to make an issue about her son's expulsion until she viewed the video that Trevor had shot. He reminded her that should she pursue any action, the video might become public. She backed down and stomped out of his office. Dr. M didn't expect any further opposition. He thanked me for taking care of this sensitive situation with minimal damage to the program. I was glad it was over without bloodshed, particularly mine.

Our bus took the group back to Florence the following morning for the last day before the students departed for home. The instructor, Professor Wells, could handle everything from here on out. The next morning, I walked back to the hostel to say goodbye to the students as they boarded the bus to Rome for their flight home. Travis would accompany them.

This mission for the college took a lot out of me. Like Alex, I missed my home as never before. Alex gave me a lot to think about with her comments about Nick. I had no one to lean on in a long time. I had to be strong after Marco's death and Ben's duplicity. Nick had shown me nothing but love and devotion ever since we became a couple. He was my rock in times of trouble and my soft place to land when I needed one. Those niggling thoughts I always had with Ben regarding trust were not part of my relationship with Nick. He was patient and loving with my children, and we had the same small-town values growing up. Making love with this man was everything to me—a steady burning flame. On paper, he was perfect. In practice, he was magic.

*   *   *

Alexandra and I slept in late the following morning. I planned a trip to Siena to see Nonna one last time before we left for home. Alex and I took the bus after breakfast for our visit, had lunch with Nonna and her daughter. After a tearful leave-taking, we headed back to Florence. We did a little window shopping, ogling all the gold jewelry Italy is famous for. Dinner was at the only fast-food place in Florence— McDonald's. Alex was having a serious burger Mc-mergency. Once the burgers, fries, and shakes were history, I texted Giorgio that we were on our way back to the B & B. Hand-in-hand, Alex and I walked down the narrow cobbled streets enjoying the warm evening and greeting other strollers.

People were out enjoying their friends and making new ones. Evening was the time for socializing, not on their phones or playing video games but talking face-to-face, getting to know others on a basic human level. The smells of the ristorantes and panificis—bakeries— perfumed the air as we walked toward our Italian second home. We were just yards away from our door when I heard a familiar voice behind us.

CHAPTER THIRTY-SIX

"Brenna."

I froze in place with a thousand images running through my head. It can't be. Was my imagination playing tricks on me? Was the stress of the last two weeks sending me over the edge? I slowly turned around as my mouth dropped open in astonishment and tears flooded my eyes.

"Mommy, mommy, I missed you, and I wanted to tell you that Ginger had her colt." Robbie ran toward me and I to him. I wrapped him in my arms and covered his face with kisses.

"I missed you too," laughing and choking out the words as I smiled up at the most beautiful man in the world—my Nick. Alexandra ran to Nick and jumped in his arms while I cuddled Robbie. Hearing the commotion in the street, Giorgio gathered up the children after assessing the situation with a big smile breaking out on his face. He herded the children inside as I threw myself into Nick's waiting arms.

"Robbie missed you . . . . . . and I missed you," said Nick.

I kissed him with all my pent-up love, the love I had always felt but could not express out loud—until now. "I love you, Nick. I love you," as I cried in his arms.

"Don't cry, darlin'. I love you so much and couldn't wait another minute to see you. I don't want to live another day without you or sneak around to make love to you. I want to sleep with you every night and hold you in my arms. Whether we live at your house, mine, or we build a new house in between, I want to be a father to your children and your husband." Nick got down on one knee. "Brenna, you don't need someone to complete you, you just need someone to accept you completely, and I do. I love your beautiful spirit and your boundless love for family, friends, and community. You're a strong woman, and I want to be strong with you and for you. I want to grow old with you and cherish every day by your side. I promise to make you happy and share life's moments with no more you and me—only us. I will be faithful to you today and every day of my life. Will you do me the great honor of marrying me?"

*   *   *

I said YES. Nick and I married three months after returning to Hartsuff with a big outdoor wedding at the Pfizer Ranch. Gage and Chase walked me down the aisle with Alexandra as the flower girl and Robbie as the ring-bearer. I promised Maggie this would be the last time she would be my Matron of Honor. Nick's daughter, Susan, was the Maid of Honor with Grandpa Charlie as Best Man. The ranch was overflowing with our family, friends, and some of Nick's business associates.

My friends from Chicago, Dr. M, Michele, Betsy, and their families celebrated our marriage with country music, dancing, and barbeque. Carlo and Giorgio even made the trip from Italy to rejoice in our union. I had never been so happy and so sure. I didn't have a minute of doubt. This was forever, and I had found the man who was my equal partner. Wait for it—it's cliché time—my "soul mate". Nick is the man I would grow old with, celebrate family, and love until our time together on earth ends. This is real, this is love, and this is my happily ever after—finally.

EPILOGUE

Over the years, I looked at my life as three different chapters. My first great love, Marco, my handsome Italian man who swept me off my feet, who took care of me before I could take care of myself. Pregnant and married by nineteen, mother of twin sons by twenty, and a widow at thirty.

The naivete of youth, a wondrous time when you think nothing bad can happen to you or to those you love. Youth is a special moment in life between childhood and adulthood where nothing is insurmountable, and we can reach every goal. It cloaked me in a world of security and love until brutal reality barged its way through the door.

I was still more child than woman, trying to figure out my role in the world. As a bride and a mother of two, I learned what adult life was all about, trying to discover who I was and my purpose for being. I put one foot in front of the other to find my path, learning with every step of the way. A path not chosen but thrust upon me.

My second great love, Ben, was full of fire and passion, and I leaped into the flames. Perhaps I was too vulnerable, lonely, and a little bored. The highs were the highest with the birth of two children, and the lows the lowest as the once blazing passion turned into cold ashes of disappointment and despair. I learned a lot about myself growing into my womanhood, finding my inner strength to overcome the tough times, not only to survive but thrive, realizing that a lot of the chaos I brought on myself.

I was partly to blame for the heartache that my family and I endured in my relationship with Ben. Yet, I found my courage to fight for what's right and stand by my convictions while still maintaining the belief that life would continue with my head held high and my faith in humanity intact. Finally, I realized it was okay to be happy. I believed I had every right to recover my happiness and live my life again with comfort and joy.

My last great love, Nick. My cowboy, who had a strong resemblance to a young Tom Selleck but with a deeper voice, a man who appreciated my need for independence. Nick offers a steady hand and knows when a helping hand would be accepted and appreciated. A man who doesn't crowd me or want to change me but accepts me as I am and cherishes that person. Nick restored my trust in a partner as an equal with a full, steady heat.

Nick grew up with the same morals and values of family, friends, and faith in humankind that I did. As a result, I evolved into the person I wanted to be and found happiness and fulfillment in my place in life. Nick healed my heart so that I could love again without reservation.

I don't know what the rest of my life holds for me, but I look at each new day in a big bright light of possibilities, living Nietzsche's sage wisdom, *"What doesn't kill you makes you stronger"*. I believe now that I have gained the strength of David as he faced his Goliath, striving not to become hardened by my past, but wiser. I look up in the sky, knowing grandma would be proud of the woman I have become with the strength she told me I had to overcome the turmoil that life brought my way.

My life on this earth began and will probably end in Hartsuff with my emergence as a confident, mature woman, having learned life's lessons along the way. The highs were worth the pain inflicted by the lows in my evolution. I will be forever grateful; It Started in Florence.

ACKNOWLEDGEMENTS

Special thanks to Lora Klanecky Racek, a true Nebraska cowgirl, and her horse, Gray Arrow, for allowing me to use their picture for the cover of this book.

AUTHOR'S NOTE

I hope you enjoyed this story. For more love stories that touch the heart, check out **Galway Gone** and **Coloring on the Wall** by this author, available on Amazon. Authors appreciate a reader taking the time to submit a review. All feedback is appreciated, hearing from the reader is a valuable tool for future endeavors.

Thank you.

Gabrielle Neord

www.gabrielleneord.com